Pentewan,
St. Austell,
Kernow.

Trevisa of Berkeley
A Celtic Firebrand

Acknowledgements

I wish to express my great indebtedness to the many who have helped in various ways, in the development and completion of *Trevisa of Berkeley*. My special thanks are extended to Professor David Fowler (University of Washington, Seattle), for suggesting the subject, and to Dr. Michael Seymour (Oxford) and Dr. Basil Cottle (Bristol), as well as Professor Fowler, for their guidance, wise counsel, and much patience at all stages of the project's growth, and finally to offer my most grateful thanks to my son and daughter, David and Angela Gethyn-Jones for designing the cover of this book.

TREVISA OF BERKELEY

A CELTIC FIREBRAND

by
Eric Gethyn-Jones

ALAN SUTTON
1978

Published by Alan Sutton, Dursley, Gloucestershire.
Distributed in Great Britain by EP Publishing Limited
East Ardsley, Wakefield.

First published 1978
Copyright   J.E. Gethyn-Jones 1978
Copyright In Reprint, Alan Sutton

ISBN 0 904387 20 8

Printed in Great Britain by Redwood Burn Limited
Trowbridge & Esher.
Bound by Cedric Chivers Limited, Bath.

Apologia

This essay is concerned primarily with John Trevisa, a 14th-century scholar of marked characteristics. One of these, a somewhat turbulent nature, may well have been inherited from the land of his birth, Cornwall. The other two were, (1) a dislike of the monastic and fraternal orders, and a respect for the parochial clergy, (2) a readiness to oppose with vigour and a disregard of self-interest authority, even high authority, if convinced that his course of action was correct. These latter characteristics may well have developed as a result of, or through close contact with, or a detailed knowledge of, a person possessing similar qualities, provided that the individual concerned stood out in Trevisa's estimation as a man of great mental and spiritual stature - in other words one worthy of emulation. This process need not have been deliberate, but could well have been an unconscious imitation, especially if the contact had first occurred when Trevisa was of an impressionable age.

Such a man, John de Grandisson, was Bishop of Exeter, of which diocese Cornwall then formed part, from 1327 to 1369, thus spanning almost the first thirty years of Trevisa's life. I have, in consequence, dealt briefly with the life of de Grandisson as an introduction to the main subject.

The de Grandisson family settled in the west of England during the 13th century. Their estates on the Herefordshire/Gloucestershire border included the manors of Ashperton (Hefd), Greater Dymock and Oxenhall (Glos). Ashperton usually was considered their home for at least the early years. Later Oxenhall, so John implied, was (for periods if not permanently) their place of residence.

Oxenhall is and always has been a small and insignificant manor possessing, it would seem, no imposing houses. Dymock, on the other hand, had many; the manor of Greater Dymock included the Boyce, the Castle and the Grange, while that of Little Dymock contained Gamage Hall and the moated houses of Knight's Green and Green House. The Castle and the Boyce are both very close to the Oxenhall border, indeed the former is less than a hundred yards away, and marches with the Parks Farm, a name suggestive of attachment to a large house.

Little is known of John de Grandisson's early life . I have, therefore, felt justified in using considerable licence in building up the picture of John's childhood and early adolescence, e.g., placing his formative years not at Ashperton but at Dymock Castle, which may well have been the de Grandisson home when living in that area. The incident of the peacock poaching is recorded in a less embellished form in the Gloucestershire Peace Rolls.

The life of John from the age of seventeen is largely factual, and is based upon the introduction in the three volumes of the Registers of John de Grandisson (Revd. F.C. Hingeston-Randolph), pp.24-25, *Dymock Down the Ages,* Revised Ed., (Revd. J.E. Gethyn-Jones) pp.94-96, *Dictionary of National Biography,* and the *Biographical Register of the University of Oxford to 1500,* A. B. Emden, pp.800/1.

I have, in the account of John Trevisa, taken the established records relating to him, his own statements concerning himself, and the 14th/15th-century rent roll recently found in Berkeley Castle by Professor David Fowler. This roll in all probability referred to Trevisa's family. The many considerable blanks which exist in the details of his life have been filled in in a manner which I believe to be compatible with Trevisa's character and times. There is, save in the account of his birth, a minimum of fanciful dramatization, such as will be found in the section dealing with the very early years of John de Grandisson.

There are three points that need to be made at this juncture. Firstly, this is an historical novel, striving to give the life story of a colourful cleric of the 14th-century, and to set it in a background typical of his times. This raises obvious problems. The dialogue, for example, if couched in the actual language-form of the day would have defeated the main objective of the book, viz. to make better known to the people of Berkeley, Gloucestershire, Cornwall and England as a whole, one of the most interesting yet prickly - if one is charitable this side of his character might be attributed to ebullience - figures of that period, one who made a major contribution towards the victory of English over French, and, in a measure, over Latin too, during the latter half of the 14th-century, and its final establishment as the national medium of conversation, literature and law. The average reader, had he been faced with conversational Middle English in large sections, would, with every justification, have been irritated and would have thrown the book away - this he may still do! - resulting in a continued ignorance of Trevisa and his true place in the development of a national literature. Scholars familiar with the works of the Early English Text Society may well feel offended by the absence of the 14th-century character and phrase-form - probably they would have been even more horrified at the result, had the attempt been made!

The second 'modernization' which I felt necessary was in the matter of Oxford itself. The college system, as we know it, did not exist in Trevisa's turbulent times. The newly established 'Halls' (Colleges) had not the corporate educational entity they possess today, but were much more akin to the Halls of Residence - on a minute scale of course - which form an essential part of the more modern foundations.

Those familiar with the 14th-century will, I hope, overlook the slightly anachronistic portrayal and the use of titles, such as 'Fellow', which had not then quite the same connotation that they possess today.

Thirdly, it must be pointed out that occasionally chapters overlap chronologically. This is done that certain events which have a close relationship can be narrated as a consecutive whole, and not interrupted by the intrusion of other equally factual and important incidents which, however, can stand on their own. The most obvious instance concerns the release of John Dyer. This order is dated a few weeks after the assault upon the Dean of Westbury, but for convenience sake the account is held over to the following chapter.

Italics

Italics have been used throughout in the Apologia and the footnotes, but in the main text their use has been confined to Trevisa's important translations, i.e. the *Polychronicon,* the *de Proprietatibus Rerum* and the *de Regimine Principum,* and that other major work, *Piers the Plowman,* the 'B' text of which Professor D.C. Fowler considers came from the quill of Trevisa.

Normal type has been retained for the minor works, e.g. *The Gospel of Nicodemus* and the *Dialogus,* and also all biblical translations with which Trevisa may or may not have been credited.

Chapter 1
John de Grandisson

(a) The Early Days

The daffodils had lost their pristine shimmer, and ugly brown spots could be seen on many a bloom in the dingle leading down to the brook in 'No mans land'[1]. Spring, true spring, was not yet, but its harbinger, though dying, proclaimed that the Queen of Seasons was on her way.

At such a moment William and Sybil de Grandisson's third son, John, was born at Ashperton. The new babe uttered a grunt rather than a cry as the midwife took him in her arms. 'Anwyl bach', she exclaimed, 'you will be a tough one if the Lord pleases that you grow to manhood'. Thus early the first faintest spark suggesting courage and fortitude was recognised and approved.

Some weeks later the family left for Dymock Castle, which, though recently renovated and enlarged, with the comfort of the young family much in mind, had been cold and bleak in January and February when the wind had blown consistently from the north-east, sweeping up the Leadon Vale and carrying the snow into the innermost chambers of the Castle.

As the years passed the midwife's prophecy was shown to be no idle prattle to curry favour or encourage the still young mother whose labour had not been easy: and had Myfanwy lived another fifty years she herself would have been staggered at the amplitude of fulfilment of her words - could it have been Celtic insight? Who knows?

John's early years were spent between Dymock and Ashperton where Stony Brook rises. Those rural surroundings reached out, touched and moulded the forceful yet, paradoxically, gentle child.

What a contrast there was between John and his elder brothers! For them the festive board, jocundity and martial exercises had possessed great attraction. John's interests lay elsewhere. For him the call of nature was irresistible, and in this pursuit he met and learned to love the county folk who worked his father's fields. They were to John, God's creatures and members of His great family, and not 'those serfs' of whom his brothers spoke. This feeling, though innate, was fostered in no small degree by Brother Richard, the parish priest of St. Mary's in the Leadon Vale.

Ricardus clericus de Dymock had never been able, hard though he had tried, to suppress his passion for the sporting activities of the countryside. He loved particularly the privileged pastime of falconry and his secret longing was to own and fly the swift and powerful long-winged peregrine. In his dreams he even pictured the royal gyrfalcon flying at his command. Alas! as a humble (not so humble at times, so Father Prior was heard to say) parish priest, the sparrow hawk was his permitted sporting member of the falcon family.

All his flock knew Brother Ricardus. They understood him, for he was one of themselves. He had been born in the country, and in the country his heart had remained - yes, even in those long years when as a child, a youth, a young man, he had toiled, studied and worshipped within the walls of the Abbey of St. Peter in the great city of Gloucester.

Shortly before ordination Ricardus had been sent to the Convent of St. Mary at Cormielles in Normandy. It seemed a million miles away from his native Gloucestershire, and Ricardus was homesick and sad of heart. Then came the unexpected. Brother Ricardus stood before Father Abbot wondering why this sudden summons. It was with quickening pulse he heard Father Tilo say that an unfortunate vacancy had occured at Dymock in Gloucestershire. Prior Francis of Newent Priory was asking for one who was a countryman, and, if possible, was familiar with the Dene Forest and its, at times, strange ways and customs. Brother Ricardus, so said the Abbot, had been selected because, though not a Forester, he understood not a little of the Dene Forest way of life.

Three weeks later, after a tiring journey and a rough sea trip, the new clericus de Dymock stood outside the door of the Priest's House, a small solidly built wooden structure [2], which was to be his home for many years, and he wondered what lay ahead.

Dymock was a large parish and, unfortunately for the peace and tranquillity of the district, divided in its ecclesiastical allegience. The church of St. Mary, which Ricardus served, was the spiritual home of the bulk of the population. It was a fine stone building with a squat central tower. In addition there was a small chapel at the Grange. This manor house belonged to Flaxley Abbey, by whom also the chapel was staffed. The Prior of Newent and the Abbot of Flaxley were on good terms, but not so the adherents and congregations of St. Mary's and St. John's. This feud caused the first friction between Brother Ricardus and the Prior, good Father Francis.

Will, the falconer of Sir Richard Gamage de Bois, incurred the wrath of Father Prior by calling the chaplain and lay brothers at the Grange a set of thieving foreign interlopers - his actual phrase was more picturesque than polite. Brother Ricardus agreed, privately, with Will, who had long since discovered the priest's passion for the chase, and had done all in his power to satisfy his love of good sport.

Several years later Will was again before the Ecclesiastical Court, and once more his parish priest disagreed with the harsh punishment prescribed by the Prior. Righteous wrath was kindled in Ricardus' heart, while, quite naturally, Will hated with deep-seated malevolence the judge who had dealt so hardly with him. Day by day this hatred increased, and Will became obsessed with the idea of revenge. Even Brother Ricardus could not turn the falconer from this determination, but did succeed in persuading him from the thought of personal violence. It was during these talks that the idea was born.

Father Francis had recently acquired six beautiful peafowl which filled his heart with pride and the neighbourhood at dusk with their raucous cries as they went to roost on the upper branches of the trees in the Priory Park. The plan was simple. On the feast of St. James, when Father Francis and his brethren would be fully occupied, Will and Brother Ricardus approached the park by Sandy Way, so avoiding the town. The spreading oak was not difficult even in the upper branches, and soon two birds - Ricardus had insisted that two must be the limit - were tossed down to the waiting sweating priest. The descent began. Suddenly the alarm was given - Brother Ricardus had been spied. Without a second thought Will ran, drawing, he hoped, pursuit upon himself. Silent as a ghost he slipped over the broom bank, through the wood, past the lambing barns. over the Tump and back safely to the Bois. Not so his Father Confessor. Laden with the birds, unfamiliar with the ground and not so well versed in the art of movement by night, Brother Ricardus was caught.

The following morning at a specially convened court, the parson of Dymock was charged with poaching. Father Prior was mystified; was the middle-aged priest mad or just bad? The verdict was guilty, and Brother Ricardus had time and to spare in his solitary cell to repent him of his foolishness, and Dymock had yet another parish priest.

A second influence crept into John's life during this early period, one, furthermore, which had in time Lady Sybil's approbation. The Penebrugges of Gamage Hall, though living but a mile away, had not accepted the comparative new-comers at the Castle. Lady Sybil they acknowledged was of noble English stock, but Sir William they treated with cold reserve - was he not a foreign importee [3] and a royal favourite? Sir William's brothers, Bishops of Verdun in succession (the elder retired prematurely), had, in the past, spent much time in the West and had been ostentatious in their mode of life, and this had done nothing to improve the situation. The Penebrugge children, Peter, Henry, and their sister Blanche, often, when their father was away, hawked with Will the falconer, and more than once in those early days Brother Ricardus and young John joined the party. A common love of sport made light of the coldness displayed by the older members of the families, and suspicion rapidly was replaced by respect. This feeling developed naturally into friendship, somewhat clandestine at first, but it had been consolidated well before poor Ricardus was deprived.

Lady Sybil viewed this unfolding friendship with reserve at first; later she saw in it a means whereby John, her quiet and perhaps her best-loved child, might win full recognition for her family. Blanche, she admitted, was now attractive and promised well; furthermore the girl would bring with her no inconsiderable dower. Thus the matchmaking mother reasoned, and viewed John's growing interest in Blanche with quiet satisfaction. One day, alas, John's half brother, Otho, the Bishop of Toul, saw the young couple hand in hand.

That night he took his brother on one side and in his most pompous and pontifical manner chided him for worldly thoughts. John, he said, with so serious a nature, and the backing which would be his, should turn from carnal pleasures and embrace the cloistered life. The Bishop added that a great family tradition could not easily be swept aside - a tradition which he himself and his brother had fully honoured, and which in their turn John's younger brothers, Thomas and William, had already declared their willingness one day to accept. Had he, John, forgotten their uncles, Gerard and Henry, Bishops of Verdun, and, above all, great uncle, St. Thomas, Bishop of Hereford? Would he, John, dare to break the line and flaunt his waywardness before the world? Then, and only then, dismissal came; and John, seething inwardly, left the room. That night he tossed and turned and in his anger cursed the Bishop loud and long. The prelate, on the other hand, slept well, knowing that the seeds of doubt had been truly sown.

Time passed and the still small voice which had whispered in the wood above the Bois as John listened, with dusk approaching, to the purring roll of the nightjar, and later had come with even deeper realization and had so disturbed the lad that he started violently, and the pair of otters, whose frolicking had fascinated him, froze and, in a flash, were gone: that same voice one summers's evening spoke loud and clear. This time it could not be denied or the issue postponed. God was calling him, as over 2000 years before a temple lad had started from his bed when that voice had cried 'Samuel!' several times before, upon instruction, the response had gone out 'Speak; for thy servant heareth'. Slowly the truth dawned, and his future seemed certain - but was it? That fiend of doubt returned - could he, John, sustain the loneliness that the Master promised? Was it not enough that the Church had taken Theobald and Otho, and were likely to take also Tom and Will? The cloistered life, supposedly plain, disciplined and hard, he could respect, and to it his soul might well respond; but the familiae so close at hand at Newent Priory and Flaxley Abbey did not recommend the church, nor did they show their Heavenly Father's concern for all. The friars also he kept at arms length. In theory they were God's itinerant ministers, in theory, too, their task was to reflect the Love of God to His children and to preach 'The Word' in season and out of season. The image of these local men of God was dull and tarnished. If God truly needed him then it must surely be to labour in a country parish where he understood the peoples' lives and problems, and sympathized. Would father, with bishops for brothers, not expect his son to serve with those of his own background and who talked the same language, and not amongst the serfs and cottagers? Brother John, that fat old priest, would now be at his prayers in St. Mary's. Should he not go to him if, that is, he would still be there and not reading, as often he did, to old Alice in her hovel, or leaning upon a fence discussing the harvest prospects with one of his flock? Brother John was not another Brother Ricardus in young John's eye - no one would rival in his esteem the confidant, counsellor and friend of his early days, a confidant whom vested interest and a prideful hierarchy had removed so summarily. Nevertheless to the lad Brother John, an older man than Brother Ricardus, had shown the same simple, gentle love, that understanding of the country and its people and that same disdain for the over-indulgent and self-centred occupants of the local houses that the ex-clericus de Dymock had displayed. Yes, Brother John would understand, give wise counsel and, important this, keep it.

The parish priest was in the churchyard when John arrived, and took the latter into his wooden house under the massive yew. There John poured out his very soul. First came his doubt about the call, then the argument against acceptance, and last of all, dragged as it were from the innermost recesses of the heart, his feelings for young Blanche de Penebrugge. The aged priest listened until the tale was fully told, and then, and only then, he spoke. 'I understand, my son. Nearly fifty years ago I was as you, uncertain, beset by doubts and drawn by earthly ties. The internal conflict was hard and difficult, but in the end I bent to His will, and like Holy Paul I proved God's promise "my strength is sufficient for thee!". Go home and pray for guidance and I will daily pray for you. Go, if you can, to your charming mother's family home for a rest, a holiday. There you will be free from pressure towards the priestly life, which might not be so at home with one or other of your brothers or other priestly relations frequently at hand.'

The three weeks John spent at Tregoz were soon over, but in that time a decision had been made. It was to be 'Yes' to that still small voice, but with a fervent prayer that his ministry should be amongst seculars and not within the cloistered cell and amongst a tightly closed community.

(b) *Bishop of Exeter - A Life's Work*

John from an early age studied at the Universities of Paris and Oxford. During this period there were conferred upon him ecclesiastical preferments which were but the harbinger of greater things. In 1309, when only 17 years old, he received a Prebendary of York Minster, and in the following year the Pope collated him Archdeacon of Nottingham. The first dignity de Grandisson relinquished in 1315, but retained the second until his consecration as Bishop of Exeter in 1327. John's feet were firmly planted upon the promotion ladder when (c.1322) he was appointed a chaplain to Pope John xxii at Avignon. Much of the early recognition has been attributed to influence in high places, but the great ability, integrity and, above all perhaps, the humility of young de Grandisson must have been an important factor and undoubtedly lay behind continued papal favour over many years. Pope John was no fool, and his deep attachment to de Grandisson - a mutual attachment indeed - was maintained throughout his life.

In 1317 John de Grandisson succeeded his brother Thomas, with whom he had studied at Oxford, in the Prebendary of Heydore in Lincoln Cathedral and five years later received a second Lincoln prebendary, that of Stoke. The latter he relinquished in 1323.

De Grandisson's first major assignment came in September 1326 when at the Pope's instigation he was associated with the Archbishop of Vienne, William de Laudun, in the negotiations for the Peace of Gascony. De Grandisson, while in England, held an assembly of clergy at St. Paul's and demanded without success a subsidy for the Pope. On 15th October of that same year Walter de Stapeldon, Bishop of Exeter, was murdered by a London mob. The Dean and Chapter at once elected one of their own members, James de Berkeley, to succeed. Later the king's approval was sought and obtained. The Pope at Avignon, on hearing that Stapeldon had died, made it clear that he, the Pope, reserved the right of presentation. It is thought probable that de Grandisson was the intended candidate. After lengthy negotiations the Pope accepted, with reluctance, the decision of the Chapter and of the Archbishop of Canterbury[4].

Bishop Berkeley died, however, on 24th June 1327[5]. The Pope, hearing of this unexpected vacancy, moved quickly, determined that he would not be outmanoeuvred a second time. He at once wrote to de Grandisson (10th August) saying that he intended him to be Bishop of Exeter. Two days later this appointment was confirmed, and on 18th October de Grandisson was consecrated at Avignon.

Almost at once, well before he set out for England, the Bishop-elect was confronted with a major financial crisis. The Curia, the powerful inner council of the Papacy, and often the real power behind the throne of St. Peter, declared that a considerable monetary obligation imposed and accepted by the diocese of Exeter thirty years earlier had not been paid. They blandly affirmed further that the late Bishop Berkeley had recognised the debt. De Grandisson, aware that the finances of the diocese were in an appalling state, doggedly resisted the claim, interceding with the Pope and certain cardinals. De Grandisson's case for rejection was substantial, some would maintain conclusive, but the Curia refused to allow the defendant's evidence even to be heard. After a long and bitter battle the Bishop managed to win from the scarlet tyrants a considerable reduction of the original figure.

The new prelate, when this legal wrangle had ended, left for England and arrived at

Canterbury on 5th February 1327/8. On the 17th he set out for York, where he was required to do homage to the King (Edward III) for the temporalities of the diocese, and, as one of the Lords spiritual, to attend Parliament, then in session in that city. De Grandisson, when the parliamentary sitting was over, left York (10th March) with his brother Peter. They arrived at Dymock Castle to stay with their father. John remained there until 22nd April, when he left to attend another session of Parliament, summoned on this occasion to meet at Northampton. The Bishop complained, in a letter to the Pope, of the inconvenience and expense of having to attend Parliament, where he could, so he felt, at this early stage in his episcopate make little real contribution.

De Grandisson sought and received permission from the King to leave for his diocese, and on 16th May began the first stage of his journey to Exeter, arriving at the episcopal manor of Farington on the 21st. There he held his first ordination before travelling via Winchester to Salisbury.

(c) *The Diocese of Exeter*

The Bishop-designate was thoughtful when on June 2nd he made he way almost unattended from Salisbury towards his new cure. He fully appreciated that the unjust financial burdens imposed by the Curia upon the diocese and upon himself were made more onerous by the ecclesiastical problems and the geographical and ethnological peculiarities existing in Devon, and to an even greater degree in Cornwall. These latter de Grandisson described in letters to the Pope and Cardinal friends soon after his enthronement. The diocese was, he said, a foreign land where many spoke a language understood by none except the Bretons and themselves. It was linked to England only on its eastern flank, for the rest it was surrounded by seas so tempestuous that they were barely navigable. He was living, so he declared, not merely in the ends of the earth, but 'in the very end of the ends thereof'. The Bishop stated that his manors were spoiled and bare, devoid of animals and lands uncultivated. Few rents were being paid and the buildings were in urgent need of extensive repairs. Above all apathy and occasionally open hostility to Christian teaching and way of life made the task of evangelization difficult. Here was a pen-picture that was essentially true and would have daunted most men. De Grandisson, however, was determined, with God's help, to succeed.

The new Bishop's first night in his diocese was spent in Honiton Rectory on 9th June. On the following day he was met by the Dean, sub-Dean, Treasurer and many Canons of his Cathedral and escorted to the episcopal manor of Clyst five miles from Exeter.

The enthronement at the Cathedral of Exeter took place on 22nd August and followed the English Rite without pomp or ostentatious ceremony. The day, however, was not uneventful, giving the new prelate a foretaste of the storms which lay ahead. The Proctor of the Archdeacon of Canterbury, at the cathedral door, forbade de Grandisson to enter unless he consented to be enthroned by him, thus acknowledging the right of the Archbishop to appoint to the diocese. Lord Courtenay, a cousin of the Bishop and a local official, demanded a palfrey and certain silver vessels as his enthronization dues. The Bishop, by sweeping aside these demands, which he described as 'pestiferous', showed, from the beginning, that he intended to be master in his own house and to uphold the right of a papally promoted and consecrated prelate to proceed to enthronement without additional fees, perquisities or further canonical submissions.

The Bishop during the early weeks of his episcopate undertook an inspection of the manors belonging to the diocese, and seized an early opportunity to inform his Chapter of the levy imposed upon the diocese by the Curia and to discuss methods whereby the money could be raised. He pointed out that he had, by a resolute resistance, effected a considerable reduction of the figure first peremptorily laid down. Letters were sent to all officials, e.g., Archdeacons and heads of religious houses, and it was made clear that all clergy were expected to play their part in liquidating the imposition of the Curia. The response, disappointing at first, compelled the Bishop to borrow large sums to meet the payment dates. A second episcopal letter followed in which it was made clear that the situation was urgent and that contribution was a matter of obligation. Lord Courtenay, who had been approached privately by the Bishop, wrote a scurrilous letter refusing, upon most trivial grounds, any help.

The Bishop sent a searing reply. The Prelate furthermore wrote to Lady Courtenay, thus ensuring that she was aware of the true situation. It rapidly became clear to all throughout the diocese that their Father in God was a man of complete integrity and possessing outstanding energy and strength of character; for him the path of duty must be followed whatever the cost, a path that his clergy too were expected faithfully to tread.

The Archbishop of Canterbury, soon after the enthronement, summoned de Grandisson to attend a council meeting in London. The Bishop asked to be excused on the grounds that it was inconvenient to leave his diocese at that moment and, furthermore, his house in London had been wrecked at the time of Bishop Walter's murder.

In addition to the routine affairs of the diocese, de Grandisson faced with vigour the task of continuing the programme for the rebuilding of the cathedral. The eastern part had been more or less finished, enabling the Bishop to consecrate the choir on 18th December 1328. Much money, however, was still needed for the alterations to the nave, virtually untouched since its foundation in the 12th century. The Prelate, soon after the consecration of the choir, wrote enthusiastically to the Pope that on the completion of the whole project, the cathedral 'would surpass in beauty every building of its own sort in England and in France'.

The difficulties confronting the new Bishop and the lack of co-operation from many clergy and laity was distressing, but de Grandisson in a letter to the Pope on 22nd February 1328/9 first stated that had he known fully the problems connected with the diocese, he would have suggested that a man more fitted to the many and major tasks be sent; he then courageously declared 'Nevertheless, I am striving, God approving and you commanding, to do my duty, according to my poor powers and slender attainments'. The Bishop's greatness was, indeed, parallelled by his genuine humility. It will suffice to record representative examples of problems with which de Grandisson had to wrestle.

Firstly there were a number of unsuitable heads of religious houses. One of these was Robert Bonus, Abbot of Tavistock, who had been appointed by the Pope as a result, it would seem, of faulty information. The Bishop referred to the Abbot as 'utterly irreligious and a despiser of the worship of God'.

Insubordination was a rife amongst the clergy, even those of the cathedral, while a number of officials, lay and clerical, had used the two recent long interregna and the short episcopate of James de Berkeley for personal profit. All resented the firm hand of their new prelate, who described some of the cathedral staff as unworthy of their office. These latter caused disturbances during services, jeering at readers and at ceremonial observances and dropping a variety of articles upon the heads of those below them. The Bishop bade the Dean, himself a difficult man, to take firmer control of the unruly members of his chapter.

At Whitchurch near Tavistock in November 1330 an armed band, incited by Abbot Bonus, seized the parish church and refused to allow services to be held.

In the following year, Mepeham, Archbishop of Canterbury, proposed holding a visitation at Exeter. De Grandisson, aware of the metropolitan's unjustifiable interference in diocesan affairs in the past (even entering the diocese without previous notification), disliked the prospect and obtained a Papal inhibition excluding the Archbishop from entering the diocese. The King (Edward III), too, supported de Grandisson. In June 1332, in spite of the inhibition, Mepeham arrived at Exeter intending to hold the visitation in the cathedral. The Bishop, equal to the occasion, posted his armed retainers strategically and prevented the would-be intruder from even entering the close. The Archbishop summoned a provincial council to discuss de Grandisson's stand. No action followed. The Bishop of Exeter was, indeed, a courageous man.

In 1333 de Grandisson left his diocese (a rare event) to stay with his father at Dymock Castle. Within a few days trouble broke out at Exeter Cathedral and the Bishop returned to Devon immediately. The Dean and one of the Canons were at once suspended and excommunicated. The Court of Canterbury intervened on behalf of the Dean, but the Bishop issued instructions to his Archdeacons that the directives of the Court should be ignored.

Many Rural Deans also were giving trouble. They failed frequently to fulfil their duties, appointing unfit persons as substitutes for themselves, thereby causing 'serious scandals'. The Bishop dealt firmly with these lax clerics.

In October 1333 Abbot Bonus, who previously had been handled leniently for the Pope's sake, was finally deprived because his 'enormities could be tolerated no longer'.

Yet another group of clergy caused de Grandisson a great deal of distress during the early days of his episcopate. Many clerical scions of noble houses in his diocese (perhaps this was general) tended to take great liberties, confident that their powerful family connections would give them protection from episcopal censure. They absented themselves from their parishes, became absorbed in doubtful secular pursuits and offended against the moral code. Here, too, the Bishop was impartial and firm with the offenders, one of whom he banished to the parish of St. Just-in-Penwith, near Lands End - literally to the ends of the ends of the earth!

Slowly but surely the Bishop brought law and order into his diocese and inculcated some measure of a sense of responsibility into his clergy, but ahead, totally unforeseen, lay his greatest trial of strength, strength both spiritual and physical.

There were, of course, sporadic troubles within the diocese, as when in 1340/1 a supposed notable miracle was accepted by the Dean and Chapter without thorough investigation. Great unpleasantness followed upon the exposure of this deliberate fraud. During the same period a number of infringements of 'Privileges and Liberties' occurred, and several of the major offenders were excommunicated.

The Black Death, which had come to Europe from the Far East, reached these shores early in July of 1348. This is thought by many to have been the beginning of de Grandisson's greatest hour. The plague spread rapidly from Dorset and was reported in the Diocese of Exeter before the end of the month. Its effect may be traced almost at once amongst the entries in the Bishop's register. Inductions, following deaths, resignations or exchanges, within the diocese up until July averaged 36 per year or 3 a month. Casualties among the clergy (as one would expect from the nature of their office) mounted rapidly as winter came on, and the graph of the inductions reached its peak in the following spring. The monthly totals were as follows:- 1348, June 3, July 8, August 3, September 7, October 2, November 10, December 6, 1349, January 31, February 35, March 60, April 53, May 48, June 46, July 37, August 16, September 23. These are the figures for the parochial clergy. Although the plague ceased in England in September 1349, the induction figures continued at a high level for some months before normality returned in the autumn of 1350[6].

Appalling though these figures appear, the reality becomes doubly stark when they are broken down to individual parish level. Ashburton, for instance, lost its vicar late in 1348. His successor died just before Christmas. The next Ashburton induction took place on January 1st, rapidly followed by yet another on January 11th! Monastic bodies fared equally badly, e.g., Bodmin Priory by late February had lost all except 2 of its canons. In the town itself the vicar and 1500 parishioners died. Newenham Abbey was reduced to its Abbot and 2 monks out of 23, while 88 secular employees also succumbed. Abbot Gasquet, the great authority on the medieval church in England, estimated that throughout the country 25,000 clergy, parochial, monastic and chaplains, died during the epidemic, thus reducing their number to one third or less, gaining for them the unenviable distinction of suffering the highest percentage of deaths of any individual body of people.

The Bishop was at his wits' end striving to find replacements for the parishes and heads of the religious houses. It was not possible, he wrote to the Pope to serve the vacant churches, which in many instances were lying desolate. De Grandisson then asked permission to ordain 50 illegitimate candidates and a further 100 who were under age but had attained 21 years. The request was granted. The Bishop's losses amounted, it is believed, to more than 600 parochial clergy.

During this long and trying period de Grandisson never left his diocese. A Bishop is intended to be a Father-in-God to all his diocese, and especially to his parochial clergy, interested in their well-being and in that of the parishioners under their care - does he not during an induction service describe the latter to the new incumbant as 'your responsibility and mine'? This spiritual and physical responsibility to priest and people Bishop de Grandisson upheld to the uttermost.

More than a decade later a second outbreak of the Black Death again heavily reduced the ranks of the clergy and people alike. The number of deaths was not as great as previously, for the simple reason that there were fewer to die. The effects, physical, social and economic, were far-reaching, and by the time the second great outbreak had subsided (1362), the whole pattern of life in rural England had undergone considerable change. It is calculated that between a third and a half of the population of this country died of this disease. Thus the demand for labour far exceeded the supply, and so hastened on the replacement of villenage and boon work by the system of cash wages, giving far greater freedom to the much reduced labour force. Again the Bishop displayed the same fortitude and feeling for his flock as during the previous epidemic.

Although de Grandisson is best known today as the reforming Bishop of Exeter and the one who largely systematized the liturgical colour sequence in the church, yet to the people of his day he was the giant who strode fearlessly about his daily tasks, bringing hope and comfort where death and despair threatened to take control.

De Grandisson died in July 1369, having reformed and revitalised his diocese and leaving behind an indelible mark upon the minds and lives of many of his clergy.

Chapter 2
John Trevisa, Cornwall and Devon

(a) *A Formative Period*

It was June 24th, the feast of St. John the Baptist, 1340, and a fine summer's afternoon, but Ralph Trevisa was very anxious. For days now Margaret, although a month short of her full time, was showing symptoms of labour and, obviously, was in pain. Old Bela, the village wise woman and midwife, was puzzled, saying that there was more behind it than met the eye. The aged crone's gloomy mutterings - they could hardly be termed prognostications - betrayed her helplessness, and implied that the birth would bring no joy. In despair Ralph sought out Father Peter of St. Enoder, who came at once. The parish priest disapproved of many of old Bela's practices, which he considered more closely related to witchcraft than medical lore, and at once ordered her from the bedside. Margaret, fearful and writhing in the throes of the latest spasm, reached out a sweaty hand in a silent plea for help. A moment later she blurted out 'Pray for me, Father! I swear that if the babe is a boy I will give him to God'.

Three hours later Margaret's prayer was answered, and she whispered 'Ralph, we must call him, John, after the Baptist. Go tell Father Peter'.

The good priest was delighted that all had gone well for the young couple; moreover it demonstrated to his people that prayer, christian prayer, had the edge over the mumbo-jumbory to which not a few of his parishioners still surreptitiously clung.

The following week the babe was baptized by Father Peter in the richly decorated granite font which had done duty in the parish church of St. Enoder for at least two hundred years.

Father Peter was at the Trevisa house in the following spring when Ralph's landlord, Lord Thomas Berkeley, and his bailiff arrived. His Lordship listened thoughtfully as the parish priest, pointing to the cooing babe, told the tale of the votive nature of the birth. With great deliberation Lord Berkeley, addressing both the priest and his bailiff, said 'The child, when he is old enough, must go to the Glasney College at Penryn. There he will be tutored and can go on, as others have, to Stapeldon Hall at Oxford. My brother, Sir Peter, is no longer a Canon at Glasney [1], but I will see to it that a place is found for him'. Ralph and Margaret stared at one another in amazement, for this was sponsorship indeed, and unless their child was a fool or wicked, and provided God gave him - and his Lordship too - long life, the future held great promise. Perhaps a mitre would one day sit upon that forehead, broad even in babyhood - such is parental ambition!

Later that day they discussed the turn of events and were saddened by the thought that Ralph's father, John, had not lived long enough to know that his grandson already had his tiny feet firmly placed upon the ladder leading to the priesthood. He, John the elder, had had ambitions once, both for himself and later for Ralph. An appointment as sequestrator of the revenues of Roche Church in 1328 had, however, been the height of his ecclesiastical achievement, while Ralph had favoured politics untrammelled by the burdens of the celibate life and served as M.P. for many years, representing Lostwithiel (1351, 1360 and 1362), Liskeard (1357), Bodmin (1360), Helston (1368), Truro (1369) and Launceston (1370-71).

Ralph and Margaret watched carefully as John passed into childhood. He was no fool, indeed he out-guessed and out-fought his fellows and showed a streak of stubborness - they termed it determination - which they fondly hoped augured well for the future.

Shortly after John's seventh birthday, Robert the bailiff called to let Ralph know that his Lordship, true to his word, had made all arrangements with the Dean of Glasney. John would enter the college at Michaelmas. Pride surged up in their hearts, a pride, however, that was tinged with regret, a regret which they realized was simply selfishness. They would miss their eldest and by far the brightest of their children. How grateful they felt to Father Peter, first for initially, and quite unconsciously it seemed, opening the way for John, and secondly for his tuition of the child in the rudiments of Latin, French and Mathematics as well as the basic elements of the doctrine and liturgy of the Catholic Church. Occasionally they wondered whether Father Peter's blandity on that memorable day had not covered a subtlety which would have done credit to a royal diplomat. This idea was in measure supported by the fact, which they discovered later, that the Berkeleys were not averse to encouraging with financial support promising but needy scholars.

College life for a child of seven was an awesome experience. John's fellow-students, many of whom were twice his age, looked upon the new boy with contempt and disdain, some indeed when they believed they were unobserved made his life most unpleasant - a state of affairs not uncommon in scholastic establishments even in this twentieth century. On one occasion when four eight and nine-year-olds set on John and were beating him with belts, another youngster, not much older than the victim, tore into the melee and smote the bullies hip and thigh with a processional candle. Father David scolded young William Middleworth for ruining the candle, but upheld his action. Thus began the friendship between John and William, which continued until death finally caused a temporary break in their close relationship. The fact of noble patronage, though not uncommon, at first did not help the new boy, but in time his vigour, acumen and spirit - some termed it temper - won for him the respect if not the affection of the majority.

In the August of the following year (1348) the Black Death, which had been ravaging Europe for some time, arrived in England and by Christmas had spread as far west as Bodmin.

The brethren at Glasney grew anxious as the news came in of the rapid advance of the dread disease and of its arrival in Bodmin, only thirty miles away. Stories were told, too, of the Bishop's activities in the areas of his diocese in Devon already in the toils of the Black Death. It was said that he spared not himself, and moved freely about his duties, now made so much heavier as parish priest after parish priest contracted the plague and died. On the Epiphany came the tidings that the incumbent of one of the churches appropriated to the College, had laid down his charge. The following morning the community assembled to sing a Requiem for their colleague who had died, literally saying Mass for his frightened flock. A week later Penryn suffered its first casualty, and the brethren of Glasney realized that 'Death', in his vilest and most deadly guise, was close at hand seeking whom he might devour.

This national visitation had a considerable effect upon John, who long since had settled into the routine of college life, but the impression was made through indirect rather than direct contact. This influence, inculcated no doubt by the example of the bishop and the faithful parish priests, found its expression during later life in a determination to follow the path of duty and what he believed to be God's will, however exacting and personally disagreeable might be that course.

(b) *The End of an Era*

John's curriculum at Glasney had followed normal lines. He had shown, however, a somewhat greater interest in biblical study, the classics and history than in the doctrinal, liturgical and philosophical subjects which formed so important a part of monastic education — philology and the humanities, rather than dialectics and the speculative.

Father Illtud, aware that Trevisa was rising seventeen, had discussed the latter's future with Father Prior. It had always been assumed that Oxford would be this scholar's natural stepping-stone after Glasney and before ordination, for it was well known that Thomas, Lord Berkeley, soon after Trevisa's birth, had spoken of Oxford. It was remembered even more clearly that Robert, the Baron's bailiff, had expressly mentioned the university when negotiating John's entry into Glasney in 1347.

Today, however, a fresh factor had been introduced by the newly-arrived Bishop's envoy. In view of Trevisa's growing feeling of uncertainty towards ultimate ordination, the episcopal letter was indeed an added and disturbing complication.

High Mass was over, the older students had disrobed and were making their way to the refectory when Fathur Illtud hastened up to the nearest group. It was clear from his face that something of moment was in the air and the students halted. The tone of the cleric's opening words, 'Where are Middleworth and Trevisa?', left his audience in no doubt that the matter was urgent. The silence which followed was born partly of ignorance and partly, maybe, from a feeling of comradely solidarity, a desire to shield fellow-members from authority. Were the two to be blamed for that foolish disturbance during Mass? Middleworth and Trevisa had not been involved, but had been next to those who had caused the trouble. Perhaps Father Joseph, the cantor, was out to make an example, and the more senior the victim the better, 'Now where are they?' almost shouted the agitated cleric. The students' spokesman, with reluctance, replied 'We really do not know, Father; perhaps they are helping Father Albrec with the vestments'. 'Well, find them quickly and say that Father Prior wishes to see them at once. Hurry! It is urgent.' Great was the speculation when the lads, as a group, ran back to the chapel. This was no reprimand for a chapel lark or minor offence. Trouble, real trouble, they felt awaited their colleagues. The 'Old Goat' — Father Illtud's nickname, and a most apt one they thought — was extremely flustered, and this increased their worry.

William and John were equally taken aback by the summons, and a little apprehensive as they sped towards Father Prior's room; consequently it was a relief, on entering, to be greeted with some warmth by their superior.

'I have good news for you, my sons, and may I offer you both my congratulations. Our Father-in-God, Lord de Grandisson, has selected you to enter his household for a period of specialized training. Some of the work you have done here must have impressed him, and it is believed that Thomas, Lord Berkeley, has also discussed your future with my Lord Bishop. No doubt, Trevisa, your father knows something of this, for as an M.P. these six or seven years and as a tenant of Lord Berkeley he must meet their Lordships from time to time. Perhaps Lord Berkeley or my Lord Bishop may be considering one or both of you as possible future private chaplains and wish to study you at first hand and to direct your social training.'

John bridled at the insinuation that his selection might have been the result of paternal toadying. Blushing more from rage than embarrassment he retorted 'My father has never wheedled nor whined to anyone for himself nor for any member of his family. Your suggestion, Father Prior, comes ill from a man-of-God'. 'Come, come, Master Trevisa! you must control your temper. I thought no such thing. Your father is an honourable man, and has served his county faithfully for many years. But think, my son, your father must meet Lord Berkeley and our Bishop not infrequently, and the fact that his eldest son is studying for orders must be known to their Lordships, and so it is natural that you should be considered. Rest assured, my ruffled one, my Lord Bishop has no use for favouritism. You stand or fall with him, on your own merits and on your merits alone, and yours have gained you this distinction and, may I say, this opportunity. Beware my son, and make sure that your impetuous nature and over-quick temper are kept under control, or else you, yourself and other people, could be hurt'. Prophetic words indeed. John bowed his head and begged forgiveness.

A few minutes later over their frugal fare, which should have been eaten in silence while listening to the lector, the students bombarded William and John with whispered inquiry. It was not until the meal's end that the full story could be told, and the earlier speculation happily resolved. All, however, were curious as to the reason, if any, behind the selection of two Glasney students to attend on my Lord Bishop and to receive more detailed instruction in the social graces than was customary at Glasney.

The journey from Glasney to Exeter was a wet and wearying one which took almost four full days. The arrival of the two students was unexpected, for Father Prior in his anxiety to get the lads off with all haste had omitted to send a messenger ahead with the probable date of their arrival. Temporary accommodation was, however, soon found and William and John slept soundly — what a thing it is to be young!

Father Matthew, in the absence of my Lord Bishop, interviewed the new arrivals the next morning. Both William and John found this a difficult half-hour. They were but vaguely aware of the real purpose behind their summons and of the duties and study programme they would be expected to follow. John, in particular, resented being whisked away from Glasney and the area he knew so well. He had looked forward hopefully to entering Oxford eventually, but had not expected a preliminary move. It helped a little, however, that he would be in close contact occasionally with the great Bishop for whom he had a deep veneration born of the stories he had heard of him during the days of the dreaded Black Death. This fearless man, a giant among pygmies, was to be their master, and, at times perhaps, their guide and instructor. Yes, this did make the uprooting and change of life more acceptable — maybe even a little attractive.

Father Matthew spoke of the reasons for the selection and outlined the normal routine of the household. They had been chosen, he said, because they had displayed academic ability above the average. Father Prior had reported that though inclined to wilfulness, and in the case of John had shown impetuosity and at times a temper difficult to control, they had evidenced a strength of character and adaptability which, if given the right guidance and environment, might enable them to rise above the level of the normal parish priest, and occupy positions of some importance. Father Matthew made it clear that discipline within the household was strict and that breaches of the code would lead to serious trouble. There were, he hastened to point out, considerable advantages and privileges to be gained by membership of the Bishop's family, not the least of which were (1) the use of the episcopal and diocesan libraries and (2) the association with high dignitaries of the church and state. Yes, opportunity could well knock if they applied themselves assiduously to their studies and their duties. On this note the interview ended.

(c) *The Bishop's Palace — Closing Days (1360)*

His Lordship sent for Middleworth and Trevisa. The purpose of his summons he stated at once without any preliminary pleasantries. 'My sons, you have now been with me more than a year. You have been diligent in your studies, both academic and social, and I feel the time has come for you to consider the future. Neither of you is ready for ordination, even to minor orders; indeed I am not at all convinced that your talents lie in that direction. This, however, God will reveal in due course. In the meanwhile you must continue your studies on general lines, but with a clear bias towards theology. You, Trevisa, are anxious to enter Stapledon Hall, Oxford, or Exeter College, as it is now frequently called, which was founded after my time. I have given much thought to this matter, and I have come to the conclusion that further study in a more academic atmosphere than is possible here would be beneficial. Later, in a year's time may be, you might well enter Stapledon Hall.

'You are, no doubt, aware that peace between this country and France has been restored. His Grace, the Duke of Lancaster, and the French regent signed a treaty at Bretigny near Chartres in May, and already scholars are travelling to Paris. This was to be expected and is right and proper, for however bitter might be the feelings towards England in certain sections of French life, the student community, indeed the academic world in general, is more internationally minded, and consider themselves largely above and outside quarrels which, though ostensibly national, are frequently, in reality, struggles between major families prompted oftentimes by private gain or ambition. I suggest, in view of these new conditions, that you might consider spending a year in Paris first, studying theology under the eminent Dr. Henri de Vernon. I did that, sitting under the brilliant theologian, James Fournier, before going on to Oxford to study law along with my late brother — may his soul rest in peace. Theology and the Law form an excellent preparation for any priest, or indeed any layman too, if he aspires to high office or employment in the household of some noble lord. The problem of sponsorship can be overcome provided you bind yourself for a time after the completion of your studies to enter the service of your patron or some member of his family. Go away now and think on these things, and above all pray for guidance in this matter. Your whole future depends on the decision you make. Prepare well for the future, my sons, for God may have important work for you to do. Come and see me next Wednesday after mass; by that time your minds should have been made up.'

Taken aback by the unexpected interview and the direction implied by the episcopal counsel, the young men retired rapidly, and said not a word until the students' quarters were reached. Even then their conversation was little more monosyllabic. Both felt that the burden of life had suddenly fallen upon them. Hitherto all had been, apart from the occasional brush with authority, smooth and well ordered, with 'them' taking the initiative and responsibility. Now they themselves were being called upon to assume tasks for which they felt totally inadequate.

In the quiet of the chapel they asked for strength and guidance in the decision which was being thrust upon them and for the days and years which lay ahead. Their prayers were answered more speedily than expected. They slept well that night and on the morrow the prospect seemed much more attractive than had appeared earlier.

The Bishop smiled when Middleworth, acting as spokesman, stated that they had thought and prayed a great deal about the future and that they had accepted his Lordship's advice, and were prepared to travel to Paris for preliminary studies before entering, as they hoped, Oxford.

'God has guided you, I feel sure, to this conclusion. It will be a great experience and an opportunity which comes to few. Make full use of it, my sons. Sponsors will be available. It is suggested that you leave, along with Father Matthew, fourteen days before Michaelmas. Thus you can expect to be in Paris before the feast. In the meanwhile you may return home for Lammas Day and stay there for two weeks. They will be glad of your help for part of the harvest. On your return we will have three or four weeks in which to make your final personal arrangements; in the meanwhile your entry at Paris, for which preliminary and provisional agreements have already been taken, will be confirmed.'

The weeks passed slowly — too slowly— until the Feast of Lammas dawned fair and warm. Father Matthew was, quite patently, overjoyed that Dame Fortune had smiled upon 'his lads', or, as he preferred to put it, their outstanding ability had been duly recognized and they themselves given the chance — the unexpected chance — to prove themselves. The only discordant note during those weeks of waiting came from a chaplain whose pointed remarks about favouritism — albeit always out of earshot of authority — was clearly a matter of jealousy and troubled William and John not at all.

The Festal Mass over, the pair, riding horses provided from the bishop's stables, left for Cornwall.

At Launceston the friends parted company and, having arranged to meet at the Chough Inn on August 17th for their return journey, John travelled south-westward to St. Enoder. His parents, warned some weeks earlier, were home to receive him. The two weeks passed rapidly, for John felt constrained to visit Glasney and see Father Prior and those of the staff and students who remained. Furthermore a call on the parish priest of St. Enoder and on the Berkeley agent filled yet another day. The latter call John considered both courteous and diplomatic, for His Lordship in their final interview had hinted that Lord Berkeley was interested — perhaps even financially so — in John's continued studies with a view to possible ordination.

The return journey via Launceston, where John found William waiting for him, was quiet. The hilarity of the earlier trip of fifteen days ago had been replaced by a feeling of awe and reflective nervous speculation. This was a natural reaction when one had bid one's parents farewell, and was about to embark upon an important enterprise in a foreign land where, at first, everything would be strange.

The final weeks at the Palace were full of excitement. Messengers arrived from Paris and reported that the bishop's reservations had been made and that everything was in hand. John and William were several times summoned to see the Bishop to receive instructions and be given letters of introduction and other official communications. Father Matthew fussed over clothes and general requirements and the multifarious details for the journey and for a long period of residence in a strange city. In spite of the arrangements negotiated by his Lordship, it was evident from the messengers that details were far from settled, and that a great deal would still have to be discussed and finalized after their arrival in Paris.

At last departure day arrived. After mass Middleworth and Trevisa entered the bishop's study for the formal farewell. My Lord Bishop was grave but fatherly, and after a few desultory remarks began the episcopal charge. 'You two leave today for a stay of some duration in foreign parts. Life in Paris, and in France generally, will be strange at first, and you may well, indeed in all probability will, be faced with temptations new to you, who hitherto have lived a somewhat sheltered life engendering perhaps slight naivety. You may encounter situations fraught with potential danger, spiritual as well as physical. Be on your guard. Your very journey to Paris may furnish moments of anxiety and bodily peril, for groups of disbanded soldiers even now are said to be terrorizing the countryside, seeking for loot and gratification, or else enlisted by ambitious or discontented nobility engaged in private conflict, bringing fire, sword and rapine to parts of France hitherto untouched by wars of national origin. I have warned Father Matthew that from the coast to Paris you must travel only with a large party - safety in numbers is a maxim which merits observation on the roads in France today. The difference of language should present little difficulty to you both, but have a care for local custom and convention. Respect them, for the subjects of King John can be touchy on such matters, and sometimes violent in their reaction, when these are blatantly disregarded. Guard well your letters of introduction, and may God protect and sustain you, and, later, bring you safely home. Farewell, my sons'.

The feelings of the party, to be more precise of John and William, were very mixed as they left the Palace and began the long and tedious journey to Dover. It was eight days later before they rode into the port, and, because of bad weather, a further ten before they embarked for France.

The voyage was rough and all passengers were violently ill as they lay on deck, lashed by the wind and soaked by waves which swept over the sides. It seemed to them that any moment the high seas might swamp the vessel. Mercifully the wind was almost dead astern and so the crossing was accomplished in a few hours. A chorus of 'Laus Deo' echoed along the deck as the ship, almost water-logged and with tattered sails, lurched, indeed was almost hurled, through the habour entrance, into the comparative calm waters within. Half an hour later Father Matthew and his charges set foot on French soil, and for John and William a new chapter had begun.

Chapter 3
Paris

[a] Their Eyes Were Opened

The first few weeks in France, and especially their early days in Paris, were a shattering experience for William and John. Their educational upbringing at Glasney and in the bishop's household had, naturally, surrounded them with an atmosphere of spirituality, and had established in them an acceptance of Law and Order as the norm in man's life. The blatant selfishness and patent disregard of honesty displayed in so many directions by numerous fellow-students in Paris horrified and indeed frightened the young pair, nurtured in, and fresh from, the sanctity of the cloister and the friendliness of the hearth. Thinking back upon the warnings of Bishop Grandisson they felt, as the Queen of Sheba had felt when she had actually witnessed the court of King Solomon, that the half had not been told. Gradually they began to realize that the students' attitude and behaviour was largely born of a deep desire for learning, and the grim conditions which had existed in France during the last few years. They had had to face a desperate struggle for existence, physical and academic, a soul-destroying struggle which, so they were told, had become increasingly demoralizing during the closing years of the conflict between their own country and France, when the central power had, largely, lost control, and Law and Order had virtually broken down. The feeling of horror, however, remained, but a horror now tinged with shame that England, their own country, had been at least partly responsible for those conditions which had liberated the baser elements in man's nature, even if they had not driven the students into ways of life which were either amoral or immoral.

The letters of introduction were a boon, for the name Grandisson was still held in high esteem and opened many doors which, with understandable anti-English feeling prevalent at that time, would have remained firmly shut against those 'foreigners' from England and Wales.

The tutor with whom William and John enrolled, one Master Simon de Guirec, was, if anything, pro-English, which brought them relief of mind if not of pocket!

Living conditions, which at first were, by home standards, somewhat rough, improved as the months passed. The change, indeed the marked contrast, between their life pattern in England and in Paris was such that it was fully six weeks before a reasonable mental re-adjustment could be made, and even this new standard of acceptance, which was almost a matter of guilty toleration rather than a happy acclimatization, caused twinges of nostalgia and pricks of conscience. Gradually both settled into the new academic and social way of life, and after the newness had worn off the method of debate and interlocution in the place of almost individual instruction to which they had become accustomed, made a strong appeal.

The young men realised soon after their arrival in Paris that university life there offered them certain marked academic advantages over those enjoyed previously. One of the most important was the library facilities. Bishop Grandisson's library at Chudleigh had been thrilling and had occupied them in study and pleasure. The range of books and manuscripts had been, for private ownership, considerable and authoritative. Here in Paris there was, almost, an embarrassment of literary riches. This availability of so much astonished both. One of the works which fascinated Trevisa most was the *de Proprietatibus Rerum* of Bartholomew de Glanville. The knowledge that the author was an Englishman greatly increased the pleasure. Here was a mine of information for a mind which was inquisitive and retentive. Little did Trevisa think, as he pored over the sections dealing with bees and vines on the first occasion when he read the manuscript, that in forty years time he would be translating it for the benefit of his fellow Englishmen, and especially for my Lord of Berkeley on whose estates in Cornwall, he, Trevisa, had been born.

Not infrequently, when studies permitted or tutors slept, students fore-gathered in taverns and pilgrims' hostels for relaxation and entertainment. They knew that when the wine was in the tales poured out, with, no doubt, much fanciful embellishment, travellers vying with each other in the narration of wondrous experiences. Trevisa listened with the greatest interest and with a measure of incredulity to the stories of those who had made the pilgrimage to Compostela. These drew glorious verbal pictures of the great shrine of the Apostle James, with its figured tympana depicting David, the lad, slaying the lion — some thought it was Samson — and the magnificent horseman with his cloak billowing. No one seemed sure whether it was of St. George or the Emperor Constantine. The travellers spoke with equal enthusiasm of other great churches on or near the pilgrim way, Auxerre, Vézelay, Autun, Tournus, Cluny, Moissac and Toulouse on the way south, and Angoulême, St. Savin, Poitiers and others on the return journey, if a change of route was desired. Travellers to or from Lorraine and Rhineland swore that Reims, Metz, Worms and Trier possessed abbeys and cathedrals the equal of any to be seen on the pilgrimage route to Compostela.

After several months, during which the desire to see some of these great houses of God had risen almost to fever point, Trevisa and Middleworth approached Master Guirec and enquired whether leave of absence could be obtained for a period of 3 or 4 weeks to enable them to visit a few of these monumental Christian treasure-houses. He, to their surprise, readily agreed, adding that he would accompany them, and act as guide.

A few days later the three met to formulate their plans and to decide upon the route and programme which would be followed. Their tutor pointed out that progress must be slow, for they would have to travel with the pilgrim parties; their speed would thus be controlled by the slowest member. This factor, however, would have its compensations, for it would enable them to see more of the countryside through which they would pass.

The weather was dull and cold when they set out, a factor which automatically prompted the party to move more quickly. Four days later they saw ahead the spires and towers of Auxerre, and by nightfall they were safely installed within the abbey's guest house. The following day was given over to devotions and sightseeing. It was market day, and country folk were early in town, and long before terce was over the voices of stall holders crying their wares could be heard above the babble of the crowd.

The paintings within the crypts of the Abbey of St. Germain and St. Etienne's Cathedral interested Trevisa most, especially that depicting the martyrdom of St. Stephen at St. Germain, and in the apsidal chapel where there was an unusual painting upon the ceiling. In the centre was Christ riding a white horse. At the four corners were winged figures (angels maybe?) also mounted. Could it be a representation of the Master and the Angel Host? Might it be a bringing together of Revelation chapter 10 verse 11 (Christ upon a white horse) and chapter 6, verses 2, 4, 5 and 8, where figures on horses, white, red, black and pale (green?), symbolic of domination, bloodshed, dearth and death, are recorded? The poor light and the faded paint made identification difficult. This scene puzzled both John and William.

The Abbey of Vézelay thrilled them from the moment they saw it perched high above them as they climbed the steep and windy road to its portals. The tympana within the narthex, though earlier in date, reminded them of those in the western facade of Notre Dame in Paris. It was inside, however, that interested them most. The crude carvings upon the capitals of the nave pillars were fascinating. The very crudity and the primitive savagery of the figures drove the lesson hard home — as, obviously, was the intention. The slanderer with a wild devil kicking his Adam's apple, forcing out the tongue through the lips and thus preventing the utterance of further slander, was a typical example. The miser and numerous kindred scenes compelled scrutiny and suggested to the onlooker his own guilt.

One small carved panel in the second stage of the narthex, depicting a donkey playing a small harp, reminded Trevisa of a capital in Canterbury Cathedral, whereon was carved a prancing goat strumming upon a similar instrument.

At Vézelay their tutor suddenly announced a change of plan. He felt that enough time had been 'wasted', at least that was his excuse. The visit to Cluny and Autun would have to be postponed, and their return journey to Paris begun next morning. That night John and William resolved that if a further travel period could be obtained they would try to disuade their tutor from accompanying them and again cutting short their exploration of central France. With this resolution firmly taken they, disgruntledly, went to bed. Five days later they arrived in Paris and work began in earnest.

As time went on, and they became more familiar with their surroundings they realized that Paris, too, was a veritable treasure house of antiquities and beauty. To Trevisa, in particular, it became a source of interest and pleasure. The west facade of the Cathedral of Notre Dame, with its great rose window and the wealth of enrichment of the tympana and arches of many orders enclosing the three westend entrances, enchanted him, while the murals in St. Denys, after their return from Auxerre and Vézelay, took on a new importance. It could well be said that their short trip to the south had opened their eyes to the fascination of the work of the master mason and the artist, and had planted an interest which they never lost.

The months passed quickly for John and William who, now well settled in and approving of the freer atmosphere of the university and with the excitement of the academic stimulus, found the days too short. The lectures on the normal subject of the Arts faculty, plus those 'suggested' by Bishop Grandisson, namely theology and metaphysics, and the discussions, disputes and arguments (often very acrimonious) which resulted from them, prepared the young Englishmen for the more formal and searching debates that formed an important side of student life in Paris, and in other universities for that matter. Here they began to appreciate more fully the value of an extensive library, but encountered problems even in this field. A considerable programme of reading had been suggested by Professor Jean Gerson, but the competition amongst students for the books and manuscripts readily available for their private study made the professor's target unrealistic, and capable of being achieved only by the favoured few who first obtained the coveted material.

Home-sickness had affected neither William nor John to any marked degree. This was perhaps remarkable, because both belonged to well-knit families, and had had their schooling sufficiently close to their homes for regular personal contact to be maintained, even if at times this had only been possible by letter or message. Here in Paris the situation was entirely different; they had received only one letter each from home in the first six months, and twice verbal messages from Bishop Grandisson had been delivered by travellers to Avignon. It was understandable, therefore, that whenever a lecture was based upon a book or manuscript written by a fellow countryman, or one describing England or English ways of life, they felt a surge of pride and pleasure.

After Easter a complete break from normal studies was enjoyed. Trevisa, knowing this, suggested another and perhaps more extensive pilgrimage to places of interest and repute. It was decided, following much discussion and with the advice of Master Guirec, to apply for a leave of absence of up to two months. This, it was considered, should enable them to carry through the itinerary advocated by their tutor. They would travel along well frequented routes eastward to Reims and Metz, from where they would follow the Moselle to its confluence with the Rhine at Coblenz. The passage down river to Cologne would present no problems. The return journey could with advantage be via Aachen, Liege and Reims. Thus they would visit places of great antiquity and areas of scenic beauty.

On Easter Monday, April 6th, the party rode out of Paris, and ten days later, having spent a whole day in Reims, arrived at Metz. The last two days had been of special interest to Trevisa because of the great variety of bird life seen and heard. The buzzards were even more numerous here than he remembered in Cornwall. Four, five and six could be seen, frequently together, gliding gracefully on (apparently) motionless wings and expanded tail, tilting, tacking, wheeling and soaring, using the wind and currents as they quartered the ground below, searching for the insects, beetles and small birds or mammals which formed their staple diet. Trevisa narrated to some of the party unfamiliar with this large bird how once he had taught a young buzzard to come at call to take morsels of raw flesh placed on the ground at some little distance [1].

A six-day stay had been planned for Metz, giving time both to rest after the journey of nearly 200 miles, and also to enable the cathedral and other important buildings and monuments to be visited.

The first day, naturally, was spent quietly; the only physical activity was a visit to the Cathedral for mass followed by a short tour of the crypt and choir to inspect the murals. Later in the afternoon they enjoyed a short walk by the river.

On the second day it was learnt, quite by chance, that a large river cargo boat was leaving at dawn on the fourth day for Cologne. Two nights would be spent at Trier and, possibly, two also at Coblenz, enabling cargo to be delivered and loaded. This seemed to Trevisa and Middleworth a golden opportunity to lessen the fatigue of an otherwise long trip, and would shorten the overall time if — and the if was a mammoth one — the captain would be prepared to take them and their ponies — these latter, they realized would be the main problem. They found the ship's captain (as they had been told he would be) at the Lion D'or. By the time the latter had been persuaded to carry both men and beasts the young Englishmen had parted with ten florins. The wine, which had played no little part in the final acceptance of the contract by the captain, had accounted for four of these, and also for the fact that Trevisa and Middleworth woke up the next morning in the ingle nook of the Lion D'or, and not in their beds at the Vâche Blanche. Jean Baptiste, the captain, and his mate were already astir when the young men staggered to their feet. The cold water from the well in the court yard slightly eased the thumping in the head, and, after settling the final details of the morrow's river trip, Trevisa and Middleworth walked slowly back to the Vâche Blanche, grateful that they had not been robbed during the night, and wiser men, knowing now the potency of the palatable and seemingly innocuous Moselle wine.

Their bloodshot eyes and dishevelled appearance caused caustic comment as they slunk into the hostelry and by mischance ran right into a group of their erstwhile travelling companions. Neither had even been drunk, let alone stupefied and overcome before, and both vowed that it would never happen again, that, indeed, St. Paul's advice of 'moderation in all things' would be their guiding principle. Later in the day they went to confession at the cathedral. This eased somewhat their consciences, but lightened their purses by a further florin.

The following morning they arrived before dawn at the jetty and found that their shallow draught vessel was already loaded and ready to slip downstream. The captain was, in fact, awaiting their appearance with some impatience. The problem of the ponies had taxed his ingenuity, and in the end it was decided to hobble the animals and then to build them restraining stalls with bales and other substantial goods. Thus they would not see the water or have too much freedom of movement. The voyage to Trier was uneventful and enabled Trevisa and Middleworth to rest and recover from the effects of their recent vinopotating and the very short night before embarkation.

That night they slept on board while their vessel was tied up to the quay. They were wakened early next morning by commercial activities, and after a meagre breakfast visited the town. Here they noticed a marked change in the ecclesiastical architecture. The double ended appearance (a rounded narthex at the west end as well as the apsidal east end) of the cathedral intrigued them, but the more conventional west facade of the abbey, with its great doorway having an archway of five or six orders — beautiful though the scores of figures were —failed to impress. They missed the whimsicality of the Vézelay capitals, but were struck by many of the figure carvings they studied in the cathedral, struck because of the marked similarity that they saw (or thought they saw) between them and groups of figures they had noticed in illuminated English manuscripts of ancient origin. They exercised their ponies by riding out towards Echternach, but found the roads bad and the countryside uninteresting.

The murals in the cathedral were impressive, with the crucifixion scene and the panels of arcaded saints or martyrs in the crypt, both colourful and artistic. The only criticism was that the faces of these latter figures had, they felt, no life in them.

The following morning they awoke and found that they were already underway, and by nightfall Coblenz was in sight. Here their time ashore was limited and taken up, mainly, by the exercising of the ponies. At Cologne their voyaging ended. This method of travel, although having some practical disadvantages, had saved considerable time and fatigue; perhaps, in spite of the initial monetary outlay in boat charges and wine, the financial side also had benefited.

Cologne marked the easternmost limit of their itinerary, and it was with no real regret that two days later they began to head westward, back to lectures, seminars and discussions, which, almost unconsciously, they had come to value and appreciate. They had enjoyed almost every day of their holiday — except that ghastly experience in the Lion D'or at Metz. The long glide down the Rhine valley from Coblenz to Cologne could only be described as a trip through Fairyland — the great castles perched upon the crags jutting out from the densely wooded hillsides, and the tiny village houses, often brightly painted, nestling among the water meadows of the river valley, filled them with admiration.

At Aachen they stayed for several days. The long history of the city, full of Charlemagne tradition and studded with buildings of great antiquity, positively demanded much more careful study than had been undertaken at Trier, Coblenz or Cologne. The three buildings, not all in a good condition, which attracted Trevisa's attention most were the Cathedral, the Royal Palace of Charlemagne and the Royal Chapel. The last, a two-tiered building designed, it was said, on the lines of the church of St. Vitale in Ravenna at the order of Charlemagne himself. Trevisa had heard described by Bishop Grandisson. The latter, when speaking of his early days on the Hereford-Gloucester border, had said that Robert of Lorraine, Bishop of Hereford soon after William of Normandy had conquered England, had brought over to Hereford a band of masons and artists from the Aachen area to build and decorate a somewhat similar two-tiered chapel for his own use between his palace and the cathedral which he was attempting to restore and rebuild. The local warm springs, which were held to possess medicinal properties, greatly fascinated Trevisa. Both he and Middleworth swam in the public baths and also drank of the so-termed medicated waters. The first of these experiments they enjoyed, but the latter was one that they felt did not merit repetition. They had heard of similar springs in England, but had not, as yet, seen them.

The journey from Aachen to Reims was taken leisurely. The four days spent in the latter city enabled them to see much that they, of sheer necessity, had missed on the outward trip. A whole day was now spent in the cathedral, where for centuries most kings of France had been crowned, and where St. Remi, Archbishop of Reims, in an earlier building, had baptized Clovis, the first Christian king of France in 496. The statuary both outside and in, especially on the western facade, and the magnificent coloured glass, particularly in the large rose window above the main portal, made a great impression. Trevisa, indeed, found the wealth of ancient and beautiful buildings within the city almost over-whelming, with the Basilica of St. Remi and the great Roman triumphal arch, the Porte de Mars, the finest (after the cathedral) of the ecclesiastical and secular monuments.

The young men climbed the circular stairway of the northernmost tower of the cathedral and found the view well worth the effort. They, to their annoyance, forgot to count the steps on the way down, and their novice-guide, when asked, said he did not know the number — a horrifying admission, they felt, for such a question must frequently have been asked by visitors.

Another memory of those four days and nights concerned the nightingale. Trevisa and Middleworth had, when at the Bishop's Palace in Devon, occasionally heard this songster. Here at Reims it was not a single bird, but a veritable chorus of them giving of their best in gardens, orchards and fields, in and around the city, during the daylight hours as well as at night. They attract less attention during the day because their song has phrases suggestive of the thrush and blackbird with a ripple and shiver akin to the warbler's song, but when there comes what has been called 'that marvellous crescendo on a single note which no other bird attempts', there can be no mistake[2].

The hundred miles between Reims and Paris, because of the bad weather, took them nearly five days, and when they arrived at the college they were physically tired, indeed exhausted. They felt, however, that all had been worthwhile. They felt, too, that their studies would now be resumed with greater understanding and a deeper appreciation of man and the past.

During their absence three more English-speaking students had arrived in Paris and been allotted to the Arts faculty of Harcourt College. Two, of about their own age, came from the north of England, and the third, a Welshman, from Merton Hall at Oxford, was a mature student who was beginning a second period of residence in Paris University. He had, mirabile dictu, made his way to Paris during the height of the hostilities which had led up to the battle of Poitiers, and had studied unmolested (perhaps the fact that he was a Celt had helped) until 1358 when he returned — again without interference — to Oxford. David ap Tudor, for such was his name, was reading theology at Merton, but came here for a while to study mainly the more liberal subjects. He hoped, after ordination, to obtain a chaplaincy in some noble house, preferably within the kingdom of Gwynedd, with a possibility of a lucrative preferment later. Trevisa was shocked — Middleworth less so — at the blatant way in which David spoke of his aspirations; even so the Cornishman preferred him to the two from Carlisle, whose crudity of speech and manners and aggressiveness made him wonder how they had obtained scholarships.

The summer passed, and winter soon ousted autumn. Trevisa and Middleworth felt that during these six months they had made greater advance in their studies than that which they had achieved during the previous nine. Their tutor's report confirmed this. He stated that Trevisa showed a greater aptitude towards biblical subjects — included at the request of Bishop Grandisson and really not a normal grouping in the Arts course — while Middleworth leaned more towards the humanities.

Twelfth Night in Paris was an experience, an experience moreover which was two-faced. From the religious side it resembled the keeping of this occasion in any other great city which was also an important seat of learning. A year ago, their first Twelfth Night at the university, they had been conscious of their junior status and their lack of worldly experience, and had, in consequence of this and of the episcopal warning, refused to go out even to witness the festivities and amusements in the streets and beyond the city walls. This year as rather more senior students, and feeling confident in themselves, they, with clubs under their cloaks (as a precaution) and with a torch, set out to see for themselves what their French and German fellow students had described as the merriest night of the year. They made for Notre Dame, through the city wall and came suddenly upon Pre-aux-clercs which remained a popular rendezvous for members of the university, in spite of the repeated violence of the monks of the Abbey of St. Germain, who on numerous occasions in the past had sallied forth with swords and other weapons upon the revelling students and masters, leaving casualties and even death in their wake.

The night was rowdy, and for once the students were left unmolested. The sights the young Englishmen saw shocked them. This was no youthful bacchanalia. The inebriation, they felt, was acceptable and excusable, but the lewdity and blatant lechery horrified them. One seeming instance of rape, which they attempted to prevent, they found to be no rape at all. The hysterical shrieks which had attracted their attention and prompted them to emulate the chivalrous knights of fiction were no more than the drunken cries and laughter of an overpressed consenting female. Such behaviour — it would have been slander upon the animal kingdom to have called it bestial behaviour — sickened them to such a degree that they returned at once to college.

Two days later the Master of Harcourt sent for Trevisa and Middleworth. He informed them that they were, at the request of Bishop Grandisson, to be examined for their Bachelor's degree in mid February[3]. They were then, at the Bishop's orders, to return to England and report at once to Stapledon Hall, Oxford, where fellowships had been obtained for them. This was indeed a shock, and effectively put an end to any thought of further trips to western and southern France. From now on there could be only one order of the day — 'Work!' and 'more work!'

Six weeks later, the examinations over and the degrees conferred, the long journey back to England began, and in weather that could only be described as foul. A five-days' wait at Calais, because of the stormy weather, chafed, and finally persuaded them to take passage in conditions far from ideal. The severe seasickness experienced on board, and the cold wet ride of several days to Oxford, was indeed a poor preparation for their entry upon life in an entirely strange community.

Chapter 4
Stapledon Hall 1362 - 65

(a) *Arrival — 1362*

Trevisa shivered, turned over, shivered again, and finally got up and fumbled for any article of clothing, yes, anything that might prevent the cold biting into him. He stumbled, fell and hit his head against something very hard, and swore as he had not sworn over many a day, for he was not given to so doing. Tonight, however, he was depressed, more miserable indeed than he could ever remember; yes, even in those early days at Glasney, when homesickness tore at his very heartstrings and vitals. Tonight it was different. He was still sick from the sea voyage - at least he blamed it on that, his head ached, his nose streamed and he trembled like an aspen leaf. To cap it all, his bed - if it could be called such - was thin, lumpy and fuller of lice than he would have expected, while the covering was thread-bare, and really served little useful purpose. Furthermore he was angry, with himself, with Stapledon Hall, yes, even with the one he normally hero-worshipped, Bishop Grandisson. 'Why in God's name', he almost shouted to no-one in particular, 'cannot they leave me in peace for a time? God's 'ruth! Why must I be constantly on the move? I settle down in Glasney, and before the customary time they send me to the Palace. No sooner there, with new friendships made, than it is Paris for two years at least, or so they hinted. But, Oh! No! Two years is far too long, so Oxford is suddenly to be my alma mater. Furthermore, not at the Palace, not in Paris, and again not in Oxford were the authorities aware of any reliable arrival dates - was nothing ever prepared for students? The devil take them all, officials - academic and ecclesiastical, yes, even the damned bishop who has been at the root of all three moves.' Suddenly a voice spake:-'Taisez vous my bad tempered Paris student. Bachelor of Arts you may be, and inured, no doubt, through besottery and lechery, to sleepness nights, but others wish to rest even if you do not. You are no longer in that stinking stew, but in a respectable seat of learning, where scholars are expected to behave in an adult manner, so for God's sake shut up.'

The effect was instantaneous, like a douche of cold water which suddenly brings sensibility and, if inebriated, sobriety. Trevisa had made an exhibition of himself and he knew it. That caused him to be more angry, but, this time, he held himself in check, and merely grunted 'I ask your pardon', and crawled back under the threadbare coverings.

Morning came at last, and by that time Trevisa's ill-temper had subsided somewhat. During those long sleepless hours he had honestly looked facts in the face, and had realized how favoured he had been - and was - in having firstly a patron like Lord Berkeley to sponsor him, and secondly an ecclesiastic of eminence, in the person of Bishop Grandisson, to take so individual an interest in his welfare and advancement. He was fortunate, too, he fully appreciated, in having had William Middleworth as his companion in the three moves. Furthermore, this latest change of seminary - some might term it an advancement in scholastic status - should, Deo volente, be the final one, for Oxford was the ultimate academic goal for which the earlier seats of learning had been, in Lord Grandisson's mind, only necessary stages in a carefully planned educational development. Here at Stapledon Hall, Trevisa now felt, he could put his roots firmly down.

The first few days constituted a period of exploration, of settling in - and being sorted out. He found that the educational pattern followed lines very similar to those he had experienced, and to which he had grown accustomed, in Paris. Trevisa noticed that not infrequently Stapledon Hall was being called Exeter College. This, he realized, was consequent upon its foundation charter, and, he remembered, had so been referred to, in passing, by Bishop Grandisson during one of their interviews.

One of the more mature student members of the Hall was Nicholas Sufton de Hereford, a man rather older than Middleworth or himself, but whose outlook very largely matched theirs. Nicholas was a widower. His wife, who had borne him two sons, Roger and John, had been dead for some years, and the boys were safely settled in the Cathedral School at Hereford, and it had been arranged that their Aunt Joan, their father's older sister, would act in loco matris. Nicholas, in spite of the impediment of his earlier marriage, was contemplating - rather vaguely it is true - possible ordination. This optimism was based on the fact that he had friends and relations whose influence within the diocese of Hereford was considerable. Dispensation, in view of these advantages, thus presented no great problem.

Nicholas, on discovering that Trevisa was sponsored by Lord Berkeley, courted the company of the younger man. Hereford had met his Lordship at Raglan Castle a few months earlier, soon after the latter's return from captivity. The Bluets of Raglan Castle, the Berkeleys and the de Laci family were on friendly terms. The last named had taken a great deal of interest in Nicholas; indeed their patronage had been vital in Hereford's acceptance by Stapledon Hall, and instrumental in his chance meeting with Lord Berkeley.

Trevisa learnt much from Hereford about the Severn-side family, their military and naval enterprise and achievement and the splendour of their estate and mode of life. Thus soon the pair became a trio, with a long lasting friendship being forged which was to have a profound influence upon all three, and bring benefit — or so some thought, though others disagreed - to the whole country, and particularly to the future well-being of the church.

Work began in earnest for Will and John on the Monday following their arrival. The lectures and disputations were of a very formal nature, but frequently lacked lucidity and interest, indeed the former were often more speculative than informative - or so Trevisa thought. Middleworth agreed. The more ambitious students, those with a clear objective, considered that not infrequently the discussions between themselves were amongst the most profitable periods or sides of their studies. Trevisa was profoundly thankful for the experience gained in Paris; where the English School was conducted on a somewhat freer and more personal basis, and was, consequently, less worrying to those commencing their studies at a university.

(b) *A Grandisson letter, and a trip to Berkeley*

Soon after their arrival in Oxford a letter came from Lord John Grandisson, Bishop of Exeter, addressed jointly to Middleworth and Trevisa. Its contents were varied. First there were congratulations to both of them on their work in Paris, and the attainment of a bachelor's degree. His Lordship wished them well at Stapledon Hall, and gave advice on many aspects of life at the university, which they would find, he said, differed considerably from that experienced by them in France. The final section of the letter, addressed to Trevisa only, dealt with recent events in Berkeley in the Severn Vale.

'You will have heard, no doubt, that your patron, Lord Thomas Berkeley, has died full of years, and that his son, Sir Maurice, has succeeded to the Lordship of Berkeley. Lord Maurice, you will have heard tell, was badly wounded and taken prisoner during the battle of Poitiers. A ransom, amounting to £1080, was paid recently for his Lordship's release, and he is now living in his castle close by the Severn shore. He is, as a result of the severe wounds he received in battle, and perhaps of personal privation during captivity, not in good health. You owe a great deal to the late Lord Thomas and the present Lord Maurice, although you may feel, in view of the latter's long years of enforced stay in France, that he has had but a small place or part in your patronage, and that, in consequence, you owe him little. Let me remind you, however, that he is your patron, and has been so since his noble father died during your period of study in Paris. I counsel you to obtain an exeat from your Provost for the purpose of meeting your patron. My letter will be your justification and authority for making this request. You should then proceed, with all reasonable dispatch, to Berkeley, and there offer to his Lordship, firstly your sympathy on the death of his noble father, and congratulations on his own safe return from captivity. Secondly you should express your deepest gratitude for his continuation of the patronage you have long enjoyed of the Berkeley family. Finally you should pledge your fealty to his Lordship and assure him of your faithful service to himself and his family at all times.

'This journey will cost money, for you will need to hire a horse and will incur other expenses. You should receive from the bearer of this letter three nobles to enable you to undertake the expedition and also a letter addressed to my Lord of Berkeley and sealed with my personal seal. That letter, you will, yourself, deliver into his Lordship's own hand and none other. I trust that the horsemanship you displayed when in my household has not deserted you. May God's Blessing and protection be with you now and always. Joannes Exon.'

The following morning Trevisa sought out the Provost. The latter on reading the letter said:— 'Well Trevisa, my Lord Bishop clearly takes great interest in you and your future. You and Middleworth, when studying in his household, must have made a favourable impression. You are indeed fortunate. You, Trevisa, have my permission to go to Berkeley, but for your own sake let the period of absence be as short as possible, or your studies may suffer. Come and see me when you have made all arrangements and are ready to leave.'

In spite of the co-operation of the Stapledon authorities, and the help of William, it was gone noon two days later before Trevisa passed through the city gates. Further time was lost at Eynsham ferry, and it was nearly six o'clock before he drew rein at the King's Head in Burford. The following night Trevisa spent in Cirencester, where he noticed with interest signs of earlier, and clearly, luxurious habitation. Mine host of the Fleece was proud of his town's dead but distinguished past, and delighted to have an attentive listener. 'Certes, Master,' he said, 'Zirun werr a vamous place in long-gone days. They do say that afore the Romans did come the natives had a king's palace yere, and that his kingdom reached to Caerglow on the Severn - the town us now calls Glaster. The Romans easily conquered they, for 'un were a peaceful people, and built great buildings, housen, temples and the like. The Saxons, they do say, destroyed all that. Later thic town were built atop of the ruins, for stone there werr a plenty for our housen.'

Trevisa inquired of Berkeley, but mine host confessed that he had never been there. 'I've heard tell,' he said 'that there be a massy great castle, where a holy king, named Edward, I trow, werr shut up for months. In the end he werr voully murdered by a red hot iron thrust up his arse into his guts. And all acause his cruel wife wanted to marry her lover - the perishin' 'arlot. I've heard tell that there be a wondrous church and many other holy buildings for monks and nuns. There be a port too, not a massy great un like Bristow, but where small ships can come. That be all I knows, Master. Oh! Thank ye zir! Your lordship be kind. I'le call ye early, for it be a tidy step ye take tomorrow. Good night me Lord! And thank ye!'

It was mid afternoon before Trevisa first saw the grim rose-grey pile of Berkeley Castle, surrounded by oak and elm, standing upon the edge of a modest plateau and flanked to the south and west by a green expanse where meadow and marshland mingled, and where, in the further distance, the swift-running Severn shimmered in the rays of the declining sun.

An hour later he rode over the causeway which crossed the boggy stream and water meadows at the eastern entrance to the town of Berkeley, and separated the castle from the cluster of buildings and fishponds which later he came to know as Longbridge Priory or Hospital.

Trevisa was nervous as he rode slowly up the slope towards the castle. For the first time since his entry to Glasney he was meeting - quite alone - a new domestic situation into which he would have to fit, a community whose interests, unlike those at Exeter, Paris and Oxford, would not be primarily academic - and all this without the companionship of Will. At the top of the rise he drew rein. The castle's dry moat lay on his left and marched with the graveyard wall along much of the southern side of the church. The main approach to the castle, it was clear, lay to the south west. This raised a problem. Should he dismount and walk his horse through the burial-ground, or should he return to the causeway and take the road into the town, from which, undoubtedly, there would be a direct route to the castle?

While considering the alternatives he suddenly saw the answer to an earlier unspoken question which had formed in his mind as he had neared the causeway. The church had been visible through the trees, and to the north, at some distance but still, it seemed, within the churchyard, stood a tall square tower. It clearly was not attached to the church. Could it be yet another example of the separate towers described by Nicholas Hereford as towers of defence for villagers in times of terror and incursion? Nicholas had said there were nigh on a score between the river Severn at Westbury and Shrewsbury. So here was yet another church, for a community, no doubt. Were all local villages and small towns in the area so well served by Mother Church? If so, he thought, no wonder the old saying 'As sure as God is in Gloucestershire.'

Slowly he turned - lest by walking his horse through the churchyard he should give offence on his very first visit - rode down the slope to the road, and made his way through the town to the castle.

At the entrance to the inner courtyard Trevisa waited fully twenty minutes after a page had gone to acquaint Lord Berkeley of the young student's arrival. The delay increased the degree of apprehension, and the return of the lad with a summons to attend immediately upon his Lordship did nothing to lessen that feeling.

The heavy door creaked and closed behind him, and to Trevisa the suspended portcullis hung for a moment overhead like the sword of Damocles, and was a grim reminder of the changes, dangers and chances of this very mortal life. He entered the keep door, and, after mounting two stairways and passing along sundry passages, was ushered into the State Room - or so it seemed. Seated upon a high backed chair of considerable proportions was a man of medium height, gaunt and obviously far from well. He, silently, beckoned Trevisa forward, and, having acknowledged the latter's obeisance and accepted the proffered missive, he motioned him to a nearby chair. Lord Berkeley then broke the episcopal seal on the letter, and read and re-read the contents before speaking a word. The task completed, he raised his head and, looking hard at Trevisa, said, 'So you were the babe whose birth caused such a stir on our Cornish estates, and of whose future so many prognostications were made? My late father spoke on several occasions of his steward's report, and of his own meeting with you when you hung still upon your mother's breasts. My Lord Bishop writes that you have pleased him well by your industry and diligence at the University of Paris and that you are now at Oxford preparing for possible ordination, and, later, personal service with our family. I am glad at last to have met you, and I welcome you to Berkeley. I understand from his Lordship's letter that your present visit may well be very short. I hope, however, that - in view of the great distance to your home - you will look upon Berkeley Castle as a second home to which you can come and be welcome as occasion arises.'

'Thank you, my Lord, for so warm a reception and, indeed, for all that your Lordship and my Lord, your noble father, have done for me over many years. I pray that I will bring no discredit upon the ancient and honourable name of Berkeley, and that in the days and years ahead I may be enabled to pay back in faithful service some small measure of the incalculable debt I owe. Please accept my heartfelt thanks.'

'Well, Trevisa, you will be tired. Henry here will arrange for your meal and also accommodation. Sleep well. I will see you again in the morning. We can then discuss certain matters, including your return to Oxford.'

Four days of generous hospitality followed, during which Trevisa toured the town and manor, and found yet another house of a foreign order in Berkeley itself, at the junction of Stock Lane and the Salt Street [1].

Trevisa was cheerful as he rode up the Cotswold escarpment on his way back to Oxford, but in a strange paradoxical way was apprehensive. He had liked Berkeley town and its friendly people, and above all he had been greatly impressed by my Lord Berkeley. The latter was, however, a sick and tired man. Should he die suddenly - and this could well happen - or should grave misfortune fall upon the Berkeley family where would he, Trevisa, find another patron? This thought bothered him, but long before Oxford's forest of towers and spires had come into view anxiety had passed, for experience, personal and observed, had shown that Isaiah's assurance 'In returning and rest shall ye be saved; in quietness and in confidence shall be your strength:' was well founded.

The summer months passed comparatively peacefully, although in late July there was talk of another possible visitation of the Black Death. Fortunately in this instance rumour was indeed a lying jade.

Trevisa and his more immediate college companions, Will and Nicholas, soon settled into the academic routine, with the trivium (grammar, rhetoric and dialectics) forming the foundation of their studies. The quadrivium including arithmetic and music - which were considered the most important items in this group, especially for those destined for the Church or hoping for employment in the houses of the nobility, was scarcely touched upon, but were reserved for future study.

(c) *An Idea is Born*

The news in 1362 that the Lord Chancellor, at the recent opening of Parliament, had made the inaugural speech in English travelled fast, causing considerable comment, especially at the universities and amongst religious communities. Most of the older members of the University of Oxford were astonished, and many even horrified by the break with tradition.

The evening after the report of the speech had reached Stapledon Hall, Hereford, Middleworth and Trevisa discussed this unexpected innovation. The first, turning to Trevisa, asked 'Well John, what are your feelings on this startling change of policy?' Trevisa thought for several seconds, and then replied 'I was incredulous, as, I suppose, was almost everyone, when I first heard the news. I believe, upon reflection however, that it was a natural and most welcome step. In many walks of life, except, perhaps, within Mother Church, Latin is no longer the medium of even official communication, as once it was; while French, formerly taught in most scholastic establishments, is rapidly being dropped from the curriculum, and is, in consequence, little understood by the ordinary person. Personally I believe that this action of the Chancellor was an excellent move, and will be, I hope, the forerunner of other and even more important acceptance of English in official circles. I only wish - a forlorn hope no doubt - that our fathers in God would allow mass to be said in English and the Scriptures to be translated and read openly and freely in our native tongue. The licence issued to lay folk to hold and use such turnings are negligible in number, and even those books are recalled by the bishops when the licencee dies. Perhaps this latest innovation may encourage greater understanding of peoples' needs and an increased measure of tolerance, even liberality.'

Middleworth laughed and said, mockingly, John! John! You are a strange person, a non-authoritarian, at times almost to a revolutionary degree, and yet on occasion a kindly starry-eyed idealist. Don't let the friars, or bishops for that matter, hear you talking thus. Mark you, I think you may well be right, but the time is not ripe, or indeed opportune, to preach openly so strange a new thesis. Let the Lord Chancellor make further official speeches in English, and let other members of the ruling bodies in Church and State follow suit, and then you can begin to lead a crusade for the general introduction of the English Bible for the English people. For the moment have a care, and do not speak out impetuously, whatever your inner feelings may be, for if you do, you may well suffer for it, and for that matter, so might Nicholas and myself as your known companions, for the Bishops' net is wide and of a fine mesh, landing fishes both great and small.'

Hereford at once rounded on Middleworth, saying, 'You are playing for safety,

Master Will, a policy of which, frequently, I disapprove. Many of us in Hereford, Salop and Worcestershire have openly encouraged the replacement of French with English, both in official and private business. Much goes on, too, in our village churches that might not meet with episcopal approbation - if the matters were reported, which, of course, we hope will not happen. We might consider embarking on some work of erudition while here at Oxford, although I doubt its acceptance, because of our humble status. We might, as an alternative, select one or two major works, currently popular, whether they be historical or philosophical, and turn them into English for their own more general use, enjoyment and educational profit. There would be, I should think, no general adverse reaction to this; indeed most folk would probably welcome the scheme. The hierarchy and those hellhounds, the lecherous and greedy mendicants, might well oppose the idea, lest an extension to the turning of biblical works should develop, and thus a grievous inroad be made into preserves long looked upon as their own, with, in the case of the friars no doubt, a considerable diminution of their, often, illgotten income.

'Well, friends, it is late and, as an inquirer of the watchman saith, "What of the night?" The latter replied "The morning cometh and also the night ... come ..." and mass will be upon us ere we know. Let us retire, for no useful purpose will be served by exhausting ourselves with discussion and speculation at this stage. We all have much study - the main purpose, after all, of our presence here - ahead. Let us, for a year at least, concentrate on that objective. Goodnight, John. Goodnight, Will.'

Hereford's advice was accepted and followed, and for some weeks the normal academic routine alone occupied the minds and filled the days of the trio. Suddenly an unexpected and chance remark to a Regent Master at the Schools once more unsettled Trevisa, and to a lesser degree Hereford and Middleworth. A student, obviously with some feeling, said:- 'Master, my Lord Bishop of Lincoln says that to read the Scriptures in English can be dangerous, and in some cases sinful; yet the Abbot of St. Peter's in Gloucester doth encourage much turning in his scriptorium, and, it is said, allows the less learned and lay brethren to read God's Holy Word in their native tongue. This double voice, a twofold standard, accepted if not laid down by dignitaries of Mother Church, much puzzles some of us. Holy Paul said "I had rather speak five words with my understanding, that by my voice I might teach others also, than ten thousand words in an unknown tongue." Doth not this declaration support the reading and hearing of the Scriptures in English here in England?' This simple statement, and the final appeal for guidance, were, obviously, made as a result of deep feeling, and demanded from the tutor some clear -and authoritative - explanation. The latter, patently overcome with emotion, placed his right hand upon his head, but said not a word. The atmosphere was pregnant, tense, indeed overpoweringly so; even the normally more noisy students were stilled, as though petrified, anxiously awaiting authoritative guidance on a policy concerning which there had been heated debate within the university, especially between the more radical and vocal students and the friars.

Suddenly a tall robust figure rose from a bench at the back of the hall and spoke:- 'Certes, John, no point is served by hesitancy and havering. Have the courage of your scholastic convictions, my friend. I, as a school-master, say that the questioner is right when quoting St. Paul; more, much more, can be learned by hearing or reading a few verses which can be understood than listening to unintelligible jargon or repeating, jackdaw fashion, words and phrases which to the unlearned have little or no meaning. Forget for a moment the haughty Bishops with their erudition and long traditions, ignore the God-damned friars with their vested interests and their undoubted influence in many households, and instead speak your mind and shame the devil.' The speaker at once sat down. Silence reigned, a silence full of expectancy; then the Master, obviously full of pent up emotion picked up his things and left the Hall, followed by a growing torrent of jeers and abuse.

(d) 1363-64

During 1363 three events occurred the imprints of which were indelibly stamped, indeed seared, upon the mind and memory of Trevisa. Some critics maintained that the second of these experiences also exercised a profound, even a baneful, influence upon the lives and characters of many others, including Hereford and Middleworth.

Early in February rumours began to circulate that a Master John Wyclif, a scholar of distinction, vicar of Fillingham, Lincolnshire, and, of greater interest to some folk, one who enjoyed the patronage and personal protection of the illustrious, if occasionally difficult, John of Gaunt, would shortly be returning to the university. This Wyclif had studied at Merton and later had been elected Master of Balliol, a post he had vacated as recently as 1361. Wyclif, during those years at the university, had acquired a considerable reputation in the Schools. His intellectual ability and incisive and at times ruthless oratory had been variously admired and feared. He had openly shown his dislike of formalism, cant, ostentation and indolence and many other traits which, he held, were oft displayed by friars and not a few members of the ecclesiastical hierarchy, both in this country and across the channel. Weeks passed, and the talk of this fire-brand's possible return died down.

Many students, including Hereford, Middleworth and Trevisa, complained that, during the Lent and Summer terms they had been grossly overworked. Their studies, seminars, lectures and disputations had so occupied their waking hours that almost no purely pleasureful pursuits had been possible, and even necessary physical exercise - essential for health's sake - or indeed anything that had no direct bearing upon their academic curriculum was forbidden. The long vacation, in consequence, came as a welcome and much needed break. Thus it was, with cheerful hearts that the majority of students left for their homes or those of relatives and friends.

Nicholas Hereford, spurred on by the thought of reunion with his sons, whom he had not seen for many months, was the first to leave Stapledon Hall, vowing that he would reach Mordiford in two days. The ease with which he obtained a mount, despite the heavy seasonal pressures, amazed many and irritated not a few.

Nicholas, before his departure, had promised John that if, during the vacation, conditions permitted he would ride to Chepstow and cross to Berkeley port by ferry and convey to my Lord of Berkeley John's respectful salutations, and would inform his Lordship that John would present his personal greetings and obligations during his return journey to Oxford.

John and Will found the hiring of horses, because of the heavy vacational demand, difficult, and they learnt that the ease with which Nicholas had obtained his mount resulted from the fact that the main stable's farrier had a brother in Hereford who knew well Nicholas and his family. A personal connection can, at times, be of great help. When the two finally set out they, thanks to the dry and warm weather, made excellent progress, and by early afternoon on the fifth day had reached the Chough Inn at Launceston. There they, at once, unsaddled, fed and watered their horses. Both, theoretically, might have pressed on and reached their respective homes before midnight, in Will's case well before. Over a mug of ale and a meal of cold mutton and bread and cheese they discussed the advisability of continuing or remaining at the Chough for the night. Mine host, eavesdropping and overhearing their conversation, came up to them and said, 'Pardon me Masters, but I erd ye a tarking. Don ye be voolish and ride on today. They beasts bent vit for another twenty or thirty mile or more. Let un rest ore night. You Master [to Will], youm small and your road be shorter, perhaps no arm might come to ye. But you zor [to John] thy road be long and uncomely. It be parsed vour oclock and more, and Bodmin Moor be yander. Yer bay must rest a while, two hours for sure, so itle be dark afore ye see Bodin town. And zer, ave ye erd tell of the moor ore nights? Happen the orse go lame? Waril ye do? The pixes be sprac under the moon, an ul lead ye, may hap, into a bog, as many a beast and rider er gone. And there be rabbin varmints in them high tors. They do come down ore nights on lone riders, and they be never seen no more. An zer, do ye no Dozy Pool where King Arthur's sword werr cast? On moonlit nights, they do say, the battle, long and bloody, be fought again. The noise, I erd tell, chills the soul and drives out the vits. Look at auld John yander. Ee werr like usen until one night ee werr caught near Dozy. The next day a shepherd found un wanderin, and ee were draft, like ee be now. No, zers, rest awhile and leave early a morrow.' Trevisa thanked him for the advice, and, after further thought, they decided that the local's opinion was sound, and that common sense, from the point of view of their horses and themselves, and reasonable discretion, dictated a night's rest and a day-light crossing of Bodmin Moor.

The following morning, before the sun had risen, mine host woke them with a mug of mulled mead, and an hour later they bade each other God's speed, and, with obsequious gramercies from mine host sounding in their ears, they set out on their several ways.

Trevisa, as he approached the trackway leading to Dozmary Pool, had a strong urge to visit this historic stretch of water of which he had oft heard but never seen. He had made good time since leaving Launceston and the day promised fair, so he turned left handed and headed for this misnamed upland lake.

He noticed, after covering half a mile, wisps of sea-mist billowing up from the valley to the south and drifting towards the lake, which he could see in a fold of the ground, perhaps a mile away. Trevisa had covered three quarters of that distance when the mist suddenly thickened, and within seconds, or so it seemed, it became so dense that even the shimmer of the wind-rippled water two hundred yards away was blotted out. Movement now was, virtually, impossible, for to have attempted a retracing of one's steps along the but roughly defined track would have been, with the moor's evil reputation for bogs, foolish in the extreme. Trevisa was not unduly perturbed and after a few moments, to rest his horse, he dismounted and sat on a granite boulder and, loosing the bit but retaining the rein, allowed the horse to crop the short grass.

A snipe, uttering his harsh scarpping cry, flew, unseen, right overhead. Almost at once the danger call of the curlew sounded close at hand, and the raucous croaking of a heron echoed through the mist, and then, like a thunder clap, the air was rent by a cacophany of moorland bird alarms, to be followed, within seconds, by the beating of wings on water and the sharp whispering of pinions as the whole eneden population lifted from the waters of the lake. Countryman though he was, and knowing each call and sound, Trevisa was conscious of a chilly feeling creeping up his spine. The horse, too, became restive, stopped cropping and came close to the man. Ten minutes later, as rapidly as it had appeared, the mist cleared, and the sun shone once more.

Trevisa mounted and rode quickly back along the track to the road, musing, and deciding that the local stories of battle noises on moonlit nights were an understandable interpretation, by an uneducated and superstitious people, who by mischance, had undergone at night an experience which he, although knowing the true origins of the sounds, had found unnerving even in the day time. Four hours later, which included a short stop at Bodmin, Trevisa saw the familiar white-washed stone walls of Trevessa Farm and its outbuildings perched upon the rise above the roadway to Truro.

Trevisa's homecoming was an experience for which he was not fully prepared. He knew, of course, that his eldest sister, Cordelia, had caught the plague two years earlier, but had recovered. He had heard, too, that his mother had been ill. The sight he saw on entering the courtyard, however, deprived him, momentarily, of speech. Could this contorted figure, barely recognisable as an intelligent human being, really be his favourite and once beautiful and vivacious sister? Was this walking skeleton, with eyes deep sunken, indeed his jolly and greatly loved mother?

Too late was his recovery, for the startled and stark horror present on his face had been observed. That involuntary reaction, momentary though it was, had betrayed him, and the burning regret of that lapse haunted him, as did his mother's sad greeting, for years.

'Yes, John, my darling, you may well start, but did you not know of our condition? We two, Cordelia and I, have suffered much, and we pray daily that God in His mercy will soon end our affliction and lighten the burden and sorrow of the family. Come inside son, you will not be as conscious of our hideous and repulsive appearance in the house, and we have hot mead and mulled ale to quench your thirst. Father is away, but will be back in a day or two.'

Trevisa rushed forward and, stifling his feeling of revulsion, affectionately kissed both; but as he did so he sensed that they felt that this show of endearment was not spontaneous, but rather a disciplined act of filial duty — pietas pushed to its limits.

'Thank you, John, but you need not have punished yourself so, for we would have fully understood. Come in and meet Richard and Rachel. They have grown so much that you will scarcely know them. Judith is staying with Aunt Margaret, and Thomas has gone into Truro.'

The appalling events at Trevessa caused John drastically to revise his plans. Originally he had intended to spend several days visiting old friends, and making duty calls on the parish priest, the college at Glasney and the Berkeley agent. He conceived now that it was his sacred duty to spend almost his entire holiday at home to ease some little of the pressures which were present, and, if possible, to erase or at least partly to cloud over the cruel memory in the minds of his mother and sister of his reaction to their ghastly physical condition. That first night Trevisa spent largely struggling to pray, asking forgiveness for the harm done by him to his loved ones, and pleading that they might be helped and strengthened to bear the bitter and heavy burden of suffering, both physical and mental. For the first time in his life he openly questioned, in his own mind, the love and kindness of God towards his children. How could He allow good people, innocent people, to suffer so, and still expect to be called the God of Love? The psalmist had said .. 'I have been young, and now I am old: and yet saw I never the righteous forsaken ...', while the Master, himself, had promised to be with his servants to the end of time, and, according to Holy Paul, had given the assurance that God's strength, sufficient to meet every occasion, would be granted to all who truly served Him. In face of the tragic sufferings of his mother and Cordelia the promise seemed vain and cruel mockery — the vilest and most blatant sinner could, justifiably, jeer and laugh. He thought of Job, but it brought him no solace, nor did it make him any less bitter towards the Godhead. For several days John scarcely left the house, save in the evening when he accompanied the sufferers on their nightly perambulation in the garden. He talked incessantly, telling them of life in Paris and Oxford, emphasizing the funny incidents and exaggerating, perhaps, his own and William's stupidity, in an endeavour to raise a ghost of a smile or even the resemblance of a laugh. Each night when he strove to pray and when he reviewed the events of the day, it all seemed so forced, so foolish, and at times he thought even unkind. Suddenly on the fifth day, when telling of his ineptitude during the early days in Paris, his reward came when Cordelia uttered what, obviously, was an attempt at a laugh and said 'John! John!! You loon struck lad! But then, you always were simple and too trusting.' Trevisa laughed heartily, too, for here was the first real sign of a break in the calamitous and seemingly impenetrable barrier which so suddenly had sprung up between his loved ones and himself. As the day wore on so the tension and reserve lessened, the interchange of conversation and behaviour became more natural, and within two days relations were back to the normal homely ones that he remembered of old.

Then it was that Trevisa felt at liberty to fulfil his extra familia obligations by visiting those persons and bodies who had made so easy his educational progress to Paris and Oxford. These duty calls — and he derived much pleasure from them — were of necessity shorter than had been intended. This was, however, fully understood by all.

Time passed too quickly, and Trevisa, on the feast of St. Bartholomew, realized that if he was to have time to call on the Lord Bishop of Exeter and on my Lord Berkeley he would have to leave within two or three days.

This final period John devoted entirely to his family, and by the day of departure had dawned he felt that his holiday, brief though in reality it had been, had, after that disasterous beginning, accomplished a little in the way of mental rehabilitation in Cordelia's case and perhaps a more genuine acceptance of life's buffetings by his mother. John, however, found himself increasingly bitter that two persons who had striven sincerely to fulfil their christian duties and obligations should be made to suffer the physical and mental degradations with which his mother and sister had been smitten.

Trevisa's visit to the episcopal residence at Chudleigh was brief, for the Bishop was on the point of leaving for Honiton to conduct an ordination retreat. His Lordship did, however, delay his start so that he might question John closely on conditions in Paris, and the somewhat radical ideas which he had heard were creeping into Oxford life; not that he himself was against change, if such brought a better understanding of life and a clearer appreciation of the need of sound learning and balanced judgement.

It was raining, and had been for some hours, when Trevisa cantered up the long causeway to Berkeley Castle. He was tired, wet through and ill at ease. He had for some miles been attempting to analyse the cause of this feeling, but had found no answer — perhaps it was a premonition, he hoped not, or maybe it was merely a weary body causing mental depression?

His unexpected arrival, unexpected because, so he found later, Hereford had been prevented from paying the visit to Berkeley, presented no real problems. The steward found Trevisa a change of raiment and led him to the high table where Lord Berkeley was conferring with his principal tenants and neighbours, Sir Nicholas Berkeley of Beverston, Sir Thomas Bradston of Bradston and Sir John Poyntz.

'Come sit you down Master Trevisa; you have, I think, met these noble gentlemen before. We have been discussing the increasing labour difficulties on our estates, and have come to the conclusion that a great measure of decentralization of husbandry may be called for. This would at least lessen our own worries over finding men to work on our farms. The small tenant farmer would then work his own fields, helped no doubt by his family to a far greater degree than at the moment. I believe that as long as the reeve made frequent inspections of each farm and holding the land would not suffer and we would be rid of many, and time absorbing, problems. What say you, Master Trevisa?'

'My Lord, I know little of these high matters, but your Cornish agent's mind seems to be considering a similar policy; but then, my Lord, you must be fully aware of this.' 'No I was not. I had, it is true, given my agent written permission to make any arrangements he deemed necessary. He is an extremely good man and will, I know, do his best. Let us, for a moment, put these problems, important though they are, on one side and see to your needs, for you must be tired, and for sure you will not wish to be wearied by the ever-increasing agricultural difficulties. Have they fed you yet, and also allotted you a place wherein to sleep? The staff, because of the shortness of notice, may grumble and say that there is no room to spare. This, of course, is rubbish, for there is really plenty of room.' 'My Lord, your chamberlain has been most kind, and everything has been settled.'

'Good! Well, tell us something of Oxford affairs, and particularly of your own doings. I hear that there have been some troubles relating to points of religious convictions and teachings, and that the friars appear to be at the very centre of the controversies. I fully appreciate that many of these men are good and sincere members of the university, but they certainly tend to stir up trouble at almost every step. They also display a narrow-mindedness which seems to render them incapable (and maybe unwilling) of even discussing in a quiet and impartial manner the beliefs and doctrines cherished by others - but then we all have our weak spots, haven't we?'

An hour later Trevisa, tired out, mentally as well as physically, retired to bed.

The following day, after a further interview with Lord Berkeley and fortified with substantial refreshment, Trevisa set out for Oxford, and, in spite of the heavy going - made so by the rain - he rode into the hiring stables by the evening of the next day. There he handed over his mount, to which he had become greatly attached, and returned to Stapledon Hall where he found Will and Nicholas, who had arrived two days earlier, discussing the latest rumour concerning the possible return of Master John Wyclif.

There was an air of expectancy in the Hall, and speculation was rife, but not everyone in the university contemplated Wyclif's possible return with equanimity, let alone enthusiasm. Then, quietly and, strangely, unheralded, the ex-Master of Balliol took up residence, as a commensalis, at Queen's.

His comparative affluence - he was in receipt of the income of the rectory of Fillingham in Lincolnshire and of a prebend at Westbury-on-Trym in Gloucestershire - precluded him from holding a fellowship. He had not yet received his doctorate, and consequently attended, of obligation, lectures and disputations. He was, nevertheless, because of his erudition and accomplishments, a figure of distinction at the university, and many sought his company.

Hereford one day attended a lecture whereat Wyclif took an active part in the discussions which followed. On the former's recommendation both Middleworth and Trevisa were present when Wyclif was next known to be amongst those expected to 'oppose'. That evening the three friends discussed their respective impressions of the new member of Queen's Hall, and it was Hereford who began the conversation:-

'Well, what did you think of Master Wyclif when you heard him this morning?'

Middleworth was the first to speak:- 'I was most impressed. He is, of course, a man of great ability, but then we all knew that. In addition, however, he struck me as one possessing character and personality to a remarkable degree. His delivery was good and his method of presentation concise and clear. I was interested to observe the reactions of certain friars present, and I had the impression that they and Master Wyclif were not in full accord. Did you notice, however, that small group of parochial clergy who arrived rather late? How intently they listened, especially when he suggested the need to have the Scriptures translated into the vernacular for more general use. I was captivated by the man and felt, and still feel, that if ever the opportunity occurred I would count myself privileged to work or study with or under him.'

Trevisa then spoke:- 'I agree with most that Will has said. He is a great man and one who makes a marked impression upon his audience, though easily that impression could be hostile. I was not, however, as fascinated by him as clearly was Will. I would need to know Master Wyclif a great deal better before I would be prepared to give a definite opinion of him - in spite of his apparent enthusiasm for colloquialism in the Scriptures. What do you feel, now that you have heard him three times and have had the opportunity to talk personally with him?'

Hereford replied:- 'I have tried, while you two have been talking, to analyse my own thoughts and impressions. I, like you, John, consider him somewhat enigmatic, but even so his forceful nature appealed to me, and I also would be happy to be more closely associated with him, but with, perhaps, more reservation than Will obviously feels.'

Thus began a relationship which affected all three to varying degrees, and brought one to imprisonment and almost to the stake.

(ε) *Avignon (1363/4)*

The Council of Stapledon Hall, both individually and collectively, were exercised that Papal confirmation of certain bequests and appropriations, long overdue, had not been received from Avignon. Queen's Hall, too, were perturbed. The fate of the lucrative rectory of Sparsholt, near Winchester, still hung in the balance. They felt that unless the legalistic requirements of the Curia were quickly settled other interested parties, by means of powerful secular influences, might well succeed in taking over this prize. It was rumoured that the Abbey of Abingdon in particular was interested in its acquisition - and it was well known that they were prepared to go to considerable lengths to achieve so attractive an estate. There was, in addition, the matter of the long-awaited licence for the building of their chapel. Both communities met their problems by similar democratic methods.

The Queen's Hall body decided, after much debate, to send a college representative to see the legal agents of the Curia and to press for an early settlement of both the rectorial appropriation and the chapel licence. It was agreed by Queen's that their delegate would wait until both matters had been finally negotiated, even though this might entail a considerable stay in Avignon. The Provost, Henry Whitfield, by general agreement was appointed to undertake this mission, and authorized to engage a protective servant to accompany him.

At Stapledon Hall, too, the feeling at first was that it would be best if the Provost himself could represent their case to the Curia, but they were fully aware of the domestic difficulties involved. Before a final decision had been made they heard that the Provost of Queen's was going in person. The latter was an ex-member of Stapledon Hall, and, they thought, might be persuaded to handle their case at the Avignon Court. The majority in council felt, however, that even if this arrangement could be made, a member of Hall - a junior member, remembering the possibility of considerable delays - should accompany the Provost of Queen's as an observer, and with an eye to the future. The need for carrying through similar negotiations on behalf of Stapledon Hall might well arise in the not very distant future, for further appropriations had been promised, though it might be some time before these materialized. The Provost suggested that either Will or John be nominated. 'Fellow members of Stapledon, the choice of one to represent our Hall at Avignon is limited by several factors, while some amongst us have qualifications which would be of advantage on such a delegation. Firstly, some of us have important commitments here in Oxford or in this country and really cannot be spared. Secondly we have to face facts which are not always pleasant. The journey to Avignon may in winter time take four weeks or even more, while the sporadic troubles in Bergundy and Poitou could cause even greater delays. Thirdly there is the uncertainty of the time which will have to be spent waiting for the decision of the papal court. Our delegate could, if fortune smiles, be back by February, but a delay until July or August is not impossible if the courts are exceptionally busy or the lawyers pernickety and difficult. These considerations must surely rule out most senior members of Hall. We are fortunate, however, in that we have amongst us two, Master Middleworth and Master Trevisa, whose university commitments would not forbid them taking up the necessary role. Furthermore both have studied at Paris and have travelled extensively in France. Their experience therefore could be of great advantage to our representative. I therefore, as your Provost, propose that one of these two be nominated, indeed if necessary detailed, for this work. What think you?'

There was no dissentient voice, and so the Provost called forward Middleworth and Trevisa and said 'You, gentlemen, have heard the argument, and the decision that one of you two shall go on our behalf to Avignon, as an observer and trainee-negotiator, with an eye to the future.'

Both expressed their preparedness to go, but it was clear to the Provost that Middleworth had done so from a sense of duty, whereas Trevisa accepted with enthusiasm. The latter, naturally, was thus chosen. Provost Whitfield, when the Avignon journey was being informally discussed at convocation, was approached by the Provost of Stapledon Hall and asked whether he, as an ex fellow of Stapledon, would be prepared to undertake similar business on behalf of that body [2]. They, Stapledon Hall, would send a junior member of Hall as an observer and trainee, adding that their nominee, John Trevisa, had spent more than a year in France and was fluent in cultural French, and had a working knowledge of several dialects spoken in the central and northern provinces; accomplishments which would be of advantage to a party whose journeying might occupy several weeks, particularly in winter. Stapledon agreed to pay Provost Whitfield £3 for his supervisory work.

Provost Whitfield consented and, a week later, with Byrland as guard and servant they began their long journey. In London Whitfield exchanged the college grant of £23 into florins at a rate of 3/1¼d. [3]. Trevisa too, did similar business with the merchant bankers.

The channel crossing, in spite of the lateness of the season, was smooth and uneventful, and their journey from Calais, via Boulogne, to Crecy was equally easy and pleasant. Five miles out from Crecy news reached them that some mercenaries hired, it was said, by the Duke of Orleans, were blocking the road ahead and demanding a heavy toll from travellers. The whole party including Whitfield, Byrland and Trevisa decided to return to Crecy and wait a while for this threat to purse and limb to remove itself. Two weeks later they reached Paris, where Trevisa visited Master Guirec, and met also several of his former collegians. The weather turned for the worse south of Paris and considerable diversions because of floods were necessary. Between Nivers and Forges their party narrowly missed a confrontation with a miscellaneous band of unemployed soldiery. These delays were frightening as well as frustrating and drained their financial resources to an alarming degree, and it was seven weeks after leaving London that Whitfield and his companions rode into Avignon [4].

There, having been well advised before they left England, they lodged at the English College, [5] where the charges were considerably less than at the common Inns, although the customary feast for their fellow inmates - the socii, given soon after their arrival, caused further financial concern.

Queen's being a northern foundation, Whitfield had been advised to consult three lawyers on the Curia's legal staff, Appleby, Albrick and Humberford, [6] who came from Cumberland and Westmoreland. The expected preferential treatment was hardly forthcoming. Delay after delay, both in the matter of interviews and court hearings, convinced both Whitfield and Trevisa that though their legal advisors and counsels might be their fellow countrymen their primary concern was their own personal enrichment and that of the Curia.

Trevisa was horrified, and one day after a more than usual frustrating interview with Master Humberford questioned Whitfield:- 'Provost, these lawyers are clerks, supposedly men of God, are placed here to care for the finances and affairs of the Curia it is true, but, surely also to help those who come with petitions and pleas? To my mind they are little better than Jews, money grubs and traders who conduct their business in a way that is hardly honest and with little or no attempt at christian charity. The cardinals, bishops and other members of the Curia must see what is going on, must know that the image of Mother Church being created by members of their office is hardly one which conforms to the Master's dictum to love thy neighbour as one's self. Indeed the whole court life stinks. The jostling for position and favours, the blatant greed and dishonesty, the kept women of some members of the heirarchy, all this and much else adds up to a total or almost total renunciation of Christ and His teaching. Frankly, Provost, this following upon the family matters of which you know are undermining my faith both in God and my fellows, and I am beginning to wonder whether I can consequently go forward for ordination.' 'John! John! You must not let the malpractice of a small number of God's servants disturb you so, for there are black sheep in many flocks, and even among the ranks of the episcopate. Think of our own Bishop of Exeter, the godly Grandisson. Consider the hundreds of humble parish priests living obscure - as the world judges - lives amongst their people. Remember the men of erudition and devotion at the university. These are Christ's true disciples, and outnumber, I believe, the Judases of His ministry. The weather seems set fair for a few days, so why don't you ride off for a short rest and forget the frustrations of Avignon. It will do you good, and there is nothing you or I can do here but wait on circumstance. Go tomorrow and come back in a week's time. I can promise you nothing momentous will have happened.'

Trevisa accepted this kindly offer. Aix with its hot springs fascinated Trevisa more than those he had seen at Aachen, and the colourful harbingers of spring beautifying the countryside brought to him a peace and tranquility of mind that he had not known for many months. Every season had its attractions, but to John this reawakening of nature, this annual resurrection, the symbol and earnest of man's immortality, was the queen of all seasons, and God's greatest demonstration and reminder of His love for mankind.

On his return to Avignon Trevisa found, to his amazement, that the negotiations had suddenly speeded up and had almost been completed. In consequence the plans for their return journey to England were well in hand.

The journey, because of the longer days and better weather, from Avignon to Calais took only 18 days,[7] as against seven weeks during the outward trip. Five days later, after an absence of more than six months, they saw once again the towers and spires of Oxford.

(f) *Stapledon Hall - The Wanderer Returns*

Trevisa, on his return to Stapledon, found that both Hereford and Middleworth had formed a close attachment to, if not a friendship with, Wyclif; and were, obviously, much influenced by him. This, remembering the deep impression made upon them, particularly Middleworth, when they first met him, was understandable. Almost half a year had passed, during which they had manipulated, as far as was possible, lectures and similar obligations so that contact and association with Wyclif might be maintained. They called upon the great scholar in his rooms at Queen's and clearly, in spite of differences in age and background, a mutual bond had been, or was being, forged. Trevisa, in consequence of all this, at first found it difficult to pick up the relationship with Hereford and Middleworth which had existed before leaving for Avignon. Fortunately old feelings soon began to re-assert themselves and by mid-May their friendship was once more back on a sound and thoughtful base.

Trevisa, occupied mainly in re-accustoming himself to the daily routine of university life, had little time at first to ponder upon the events in France. He did, it is true, recount to Hereford and Middleworth his experiences, and spoke somewhat of his observations and of the unfavourable impression made upon him by the atmosphere at the Papal Court. It was not, however, until months later that he realized how deep an impression the journey to Avignon had made.

(g) *Autumn 1364 to mid-1365*

The late autumn of 1364 began for Trevisa, Hereford and Middleworth a time of tension and heart-searching. The most exact and immediate of the difficulties affecting the three was the death of Middleworth's patron in November. The Provost made it clear that unless an alternative sponsor could be obtained within a reasonable period he, Middleworth, would be required to leave Stapledon. Trevisa's problems, and to some extent Hereford's dilemma, were of a personal nature, and in measure self-inflicted. The tragedies at Trevessa had shaken the former's faith in God; indeed, at times, he doubted His very existence. In addition there was the general outlook and attitude of the higher echelons of the Church and the extreme venality and worldliness of so many of the clergy, particularly the established leaders. He had been deeply distressed by what he had observed, and more so by the realization that this horrifying state of affairs was not confined to Oxford or England, but was patently present, and may be at its worst, in Papal circles. These blatant examples of worldliness amongst those supposedly representing the more able and emultatory sections of the christian community suggested that to a considerable extent 'The Church' was rotten, and false to its reputed founder. All this weighed heavily upon Trevisa's mind, and in some measure Hereford, too, had been shaken and offended. The effect upon the younger man, however, was intense depression and a sharp conflict of conscience. How could he, now a doubter, be a fervent and faithful advocate of a church whose modes of life, as represented by so many of its principal leaders, sickened him? Middleworth counselled continuation, pointing out that the examples which had so distressed them all represented but a tiny fraction of the whole body of the church, and that many of the clergy in the parishes were faithful in the ministry of the word and sacraments, and upheld to the best of their ability the standards expected of ordained followers of Christ.

Involvement in college affairs developed, and this, added to the increased pressure of their studies, tended to thrust their troubles, doubts and mental conflicts into the background, and, for a time, even Will's loss of patronage and the difficulties over a replacement seemed unreal - the spirit of laissez faire (a very human failing) can be a pernicious and dangerous disease, which in extreme cases may paralyse the will to fight or to uphold a principle.

Christmas and its twelve days came and went, and by mid-February, the trio realized that the moment of decision was at hand. The life of study at Stapledon, leisurely in very truth in spite of the progressive demands of Hall and Schools, had gained a hold, a considerable one, upon them, and in their hearts all three knew that they would resent bitterly the renunciation of that which they had come so much to value. They appreciated also that in the final issue, at least with Hereford and Trevisa, it was a moral battle between selfishness and duty. They were enamoured of the university atmosphere, and hated the thought of leaving it and abandoning the prospect of ordination. The idea of taking minor orders only, and engaging oneself to some noble household in a purely civil capacity, which had been suggested during their deliberations, Trevisa considered fundamentally dishonest. Potentially there were real advantages in such a step, for the 'benefits of clergy' conferred clear privileges, and offered vital protection if one became involved in many types of offences or strove over-keenly to advance one's position by methods which were not strictly legal. Enter civil employ, yes, indeed this would be almost the only course open if they did not go forward to the priesthood, but to do so by way of minor orders principally for the potential advantages these gave ought not to be their policy.

Trevisa prayed and pondered deeply on his own personal problem, painfully aware that it was a decision which involved others beside himself. He had a duty to those who had sponsored him over many years to fulfil their expectations, but could he, beset by doubts, with honesty of mind and purpose go forward to ordination? He, in his innermost being, wanted to believe, as he had done for the first twenty years of his life, but that comforting spiritual certainty, that quiet drifting over the sea of life leaving everything - up to a point - in God's hands, was no longer possible. The earlier feeling of hostility had evaporated, but the doubts remained. He could not with sincerity and conviction preach the gospel of a deity whom he did not really know, and with whom he had completely lost touch; and, finally, the label 'clergy' repelled.

The case with Nicholas was very differeint. He still believed implicitly in a good God who cared. His problem was the celibate life, which was implied, but not always practised, by those in deacon's and priest's orders. Was he, a widower, truly called to such a future? This was Hereford's dilemma.

Trevisa, after much heart-searching, realized that for him there was no choice. He would have to tell the Provost, and then go and make his peace with Lord Berkeley - a somewhat daunting prospect!

The interview with the Provost was brief. The latter expressed surprise that Trevisa, after his long, careful and kindly guidance by a succession of christian tutors, and with the personal spiritual backing and sponsorship of my Lord Bishop of Exeter, should, as he put it, 'so lightly and wantonly spurn the sacred calling to which, obviously, you have been destined since childhood.' He concluded, 'I am ashamed and humiliated that one of our familia should betray the Master and disregard the wishes of those who have enabled you to achieve this highly desirable position in the academic world. Go, if go you must, but once you have left, never again darken these doors.' With that he turned his back on Trevisa, thus peremptorily and effectively dismissing him.

Hereford, hearing of Trevisa's decision, and knowing that Middleworth had failed to obtain another sponsor, felt that he too should leave Stapledon at mid summer. Life at the Hall without Will and John appeared to lose much of its attraction, even though his association with Wyclif was slowly blossoming into a vague form of friendship. The die was cast, but with Hereford and Middleworth there was in the back of their minds a nebulous but unexpressed thought, hardly to be accounted a hope, that fate, which had frowned on them of late, might perform a volte face, thus enabling them to return at some time to their alma mater.

A week before their departure date Middleworth received a request to go at once to see Master Wyclif. The latter, as Middleworth entered the room, rose and greeted him :- 'I am glad you came quickly for the matter is of some urgency. You are the only one of your triumvirate who is, literally, being forced out of Stapledon Hall, and that through dire misfortune. I have been sorry for you, more sorry indeed than I have been for your friends who, after all, have in a sense, voluntarily decided to leave Oxford. You retain your desire to continue your studies and perhaps seek ordination. I have observed you carefully over the last few months and I believe you and I can work closely together. His Grace, Archbishop Islip, has appointed me Warden of Canterbury Hall when it is re-constituted, before Christmas may be. His Grace, at my suggestion, has agreed to grant you a secular fellowship. In the meanwhile Merton College will, for your present support, admit you as a fellow. May I receive your answer by tomorrow please, so that the details can be finally settled? No! No! Think well over the offer before you decide. If your answer is yes, your colleages must hear of it first from you. Farewell. Please no thanks, for the moment at least.'

Trevisa and Hereford were delighted with the news. Later that evening Middleworth suggested that they should reverse their decision and remain at Oxford. Both believed however that, attractive though the idea was, they must get right away to, as Hereford put it, sort themselves out.

Chapter 5
Berkeley 1365 - 69

(a) *His Lordship's Secretary*

The homecoming of Maurice, Lord Berkeley, in 1361 had been an occasion of joy and merriment amongst the tenantry, a joy that was tinged, however, with sorrow that their Lord was but a shadow of his former self. The wounds which he had sustained at Poitiers and the long years in captivity had sapped his strength and shattered his hitherto vigorous body. His Lordship, compelled physically now to forsake campaigning and martial exercise, turned to the more peaceful and less arduous genteel pastimes of entertainment and the chase. In addition two other occupational interests helped to mitigate the frustration caused by the restrictions on his physical activities.

His Lordship kept a vessel, the 'Berkeley Castle', which, with peace prevailing, traded with France and Spain. The chief exports carried were corn and wool from the Cotswolds. Wine was the principal return cargo mainly for the Castle cellars, although on one occasion at least two tuns of wine were set aside for the captain and and crew! [1]

Lord Berkeley, during his enforced stay in France, had interested himself (as far as conditions allowed) in vine husbandry. On his return home he soon began implementing a scheme conceived during the days of captivity. After careful thought his Lordship selected a suitable site and developed a vinery [2] with his merchant ship providing means of contact with the French growers and an easy method of transportation of the stock required.

Hugh Bradstock, Lord Berkeley's steward, found life hard with the heavy additional domestic and social burdens thrust upon him by the changed routine now developing. As the months passed it became increasingly clear that Hugh would require help in some departments of his manifold duties. Fortunately at that moment in time, in the Year of Grace 1365, fate favoured the steward.

John Trevisa had fought with his conscience for a long period. The goal of ordination, which had been held up before him since his school days at Glasney, and which had seemed so attractive and yet so natural, now no longer appealed. After much prayer and thought Trevisa journeyed to Berkeley to talk with his Lordship and to explain why the scheme out-lined by Lord Berkeley's noble father long ago and tacitly accepted during these many years of sponsorship by father and son was not coming to final fruition.

Lord Berkeley was quiet as John, with great deference, yet with dignity, poured out his very soul. The young man spoke openly of his doubts and dealt fully with his feeling of remorse that the kindness extended to him for nearly twenty years was not being repaid in the way in which his Lordship had every right to expect. He begged forgiveness for thus failing his sponsor; furthermore, with diffidence, he enquired whether he might serve his Lordship in some capacity in a position where the learning he, John, had acquired might be of advantage.

For some moments the nobleman made no reply, but pondered over the obvious mental anguish of Trevisa and the evident mental and spiritual conflict that must have taken place. At last he spoke:-

'I blame you not, Trevisa. This change of heart has come about through honest doubts engendered clearly by the cruel afflictions suffered by your family and by your critical observations during your stay at Avignon. Perhaps you need more time to re-adjust yourself, and, please God, to re-establish your relations with Him. Your vocation once seemed so strong that I cannot believe that you will not find your way back. These harrowing experiences may be God's way of testing you. Why not stay at Berkeley for at least a year and see whether there comes a change of heart? You may find that the priesthood is, indeed, God's plan for you. There is much to do here in Berkeley for which you are fully qualified. You can be my secretary and also assist good Master Bradstock, my steward; he needs help now that I cannot play as active a part as I could wish. I believe you need more time to think and pray for guidance before the future is made clear. Go, think it over. Henry there will arrange your sleeping quarters. We will talk further tomorrow. Good night.'

Before he retired that night John arrived at a decision. He would accept his Lordship's offer, strange though the life would be after the academic atmosphere to which he had been long accustomed. He did not really relish the suggested position, but felt that he owed it to his benefactors, past and present, to give them service, however humble, in lieu of the chaplaincy which it had been mutually understood would follow ordination. That night John slept well, better indeed, than for many weeks - perhaps there was truth in the Arab proverb brought back by the Crusaders, 'At the Inn of Decision men sleep well.'

John found life at Berkeley both full and strange. As secretary he became heavily involved in arranging and supervising much of the entertainment then in vogue in the big houses, music, dancing and the visits of the conjurers, minstrels, mummers and a host of those whose profession it was to create merriment and induce mirth. When the season, weather and his Lordship's whims decreed the house-party might, even at short notice, follow hounds and chase the noble buck through dark Micklewood or over the Hill to Almondsbury. The steward also required the new secretary at frequent intervals. Thus with these many and often exacting duties John was busier than he had ever been, and his books, his few precious books, which for years had been his solace and joy, lay neglected, and his self-imposed study programme wrecked. All this was frustrating and uncongenial, but John's conscience drove him on, for was he not rendering thanks, as well as service, to his patron?

There were, however, periods when these duties were largely laid aside. Lord and Lady Berkeley from time to time visited friends and relations, and it was customary for John to travel with them. His duties then were light. No Berkeley steward was there to call upon his time, and as a guest's retainer there was for him little responsibility for normal routine and entertainment - this rested upon other shoulders, The Lord be Praised! Scribing and attendance upon his master were largely nominal and gave John leisure for personal pursuits. The annual visit — progression might be the better word - to Raglan, Hereford, Wigmore and Malvern, whence they made a return direct to Berkeley, staying for the night at the Berkeley manor of Upton St. Leonard if his Lordship was fatigued, was the highlight of the season and planned with military precision. Lord Berkeley and the principal members of his party embarked on the Castle barge at the Salthouse and picked up the trows at the town wharf half a mile down the Avon. The convoy sailed down the Severn and up the Wye to Chepstow port, from where it was a pleasant day's ride to Raglan Castle where Sir John Bluet and Lady Katherine, his wife, kept open house, and where Elizabeth [3] captivated many hearts [4].

At Raglan the emphasis was upon the chase, although at night Taliesin, the family bard and an important person in a Welsh household - 'Y Bardd Teulu' was his title - took control. On the western side of the Severn the gentlemen of a houseparty patronized these musical gatherings much more than in the Berkeley Vale or Cotswold Plain. John loved those evenings for they reminded him of similar gatherings in his native Cornwall, where the Welsh harp and penillion singing had close counterparts.

It was, however, at Hereford than John felt most at ease. The de Laci family, with whom the Berkeleys' stayed, were more cultured than many of their neighbours and the conversations in the evenings were upon a higher plane. Furthermore his Oxford associate, Nicholas Hereford [5], who came from Mordiford, 3 miles south of Hereford, was a friend of the local family, and, naturally, they often met. Nicholas was ten years older than John, and even after leaving Oxford had maintained an interest in the consolidation of the English tongue for common use, including the legal and ecclesiastical worlds. To him Norman-French as a means of communication between Englishmen was abhorrent, and one of his quarrels with the Church was the insistance upon reading the Bible in the Vulgate or Latin text. That, he rightly pointed out, deprived most Englishmen of the privilege of reading the Scriptures and understanding their message.

One night Nicholas and John discussed this matter, and Nicholas reminded the latter that the saintly Bede and the Great Alfred, feeling strongly that their people should be allowed to read God's Word for themselves, had undertaken personally the task of translating certain books of the Bible into English. The Curia, and through them the bishops of this country, had frowned upon the policy, for which a revival of interest had, as both knew, already begun to manifest itself at the great University of Oxford.

They occasionally discussed Master John Wyclif, reminding themselves that while at Oxford they had listened with considerable interest to debates in which the latter had taken part. Hitherto John, reared in a community atmosphere, had tended, in spite of his independent nature, to be orthodox in doctrine. In other directions he did not always conform. He had long considered that the right to read the Scriptures in English belonged to all, and favoured, too, the translation of other works so that their contents might be readily accessible even to people of limited scholarship.

In Nicholas, John found more than a kindred spirit but less than a mentor. Both missed the challenging atmosphere of Stapledon and the Schools, and so the bond of mutual interests drew them even closer together. Hereford was an educated man and an old friend, experienced in the world and having ecclesiastical family connections within the diocese of Hereford, who possessed a good brain but was somewhat lethargic in enterprise and lacking in the fixity of purpose needed to achieve greatness. Nevertheless, and perhaps understandably, because he now missed the intellectual stimulus of Oxford, John turned to Nicholas, giving respect to the older man, and in a way, unconsciously maybe, accepting his guidance in the new life upon which he, John, had but lately embarked.

Towards the end of the Berkeleys' stay at Hereford John, with his Lordship's leave, accompanied Nicholas to Ludlow. There they met a William Langland, a chantry priest of local birth. Langland, like Trevisa, had enjoyed noble patronage and had been trained for the priesthood in Great Malvern Priory. Alas for high hopes! The patronage died with the eclipse of the Despencer fortunes, and with the added disadvantage of illegitimacy advancement within the Church became a very remote possibility. Langland himself finally (and effectively) had killed any hope of future promotion by marrying – a handicap that only the death of his wife would nullify, and then only by a dispensation.

John thought of William Middleworth, his Glasney colleague, whose loss of patronage had, for a time, threatened to prevent that able student from completing the anticipated progress, via Oxford at least, to a chaplaincy in some noble house or an incumbency in the secular church. Mercifully, Master Wyclif had come to Will's aid, and now the latter was firmly established at Merton, Laus Deo! William was not likely to commit the arch folly, as Langland had, of taking unto himself a wife, and so might expect that further patronage and promotion would come his way.

On his return John found his party's plans changed. Lord Berkeley was fatigued and had decided to forego his Malvern visit and to set out for Berkeley, if the weather was good, early the very next morning. He would travel by short stages, resting at Dymock Grange on the first night and at his own manor of Upton St. Leonard on the second. John was disappointed. The holiday had been a welcome change of routine and he had enjoyed the company of men of similar tastes, and especially that of his old friend Nicholas.

The sun was shining as Lord Berkeley and his small party left Hereford at 7 a.m. The remainder of the retinue, including the ladies and children, were making a later start, having decided to travel back to Raglan before returning to Berkeley. A messenger had already ridden ahead to warn Sir John and Lady Bluet that the alternative plan, discussed earlier, was being followed and that the party hoped to be at Raglan by nightfall.

John enjoyed the leisurely ride to Dymock where the Wynniatts[6] and the lay brothers had prepared accommodation for the invalid. That evening, when his master had settled in, John walked down the half mile to the church and to see also the ruins of the one-time Roman town[7] with the stones of which, it was said, the Church, Grange and many other local houses had been built.

In the late autumn of 1365 Robert de Roskaryk, the steward of the Berkeley Cornubian estates, travelled up to see his Lordship and to report on the year's workings. He brought with him, in addition to the manorial accounts, a long letter from Trevisa's father, Ralph. This was read and re-read many times, a fact that did not escape the notice of Lord Berkeley, who wondered whether a request for leave of absence might be made by his Cornish secretary for the purpose of visiting his parents. It was not, however, until the following spring that the wish could be granted, enabling Trevisa to make the long journey to St. Enoder. Margaret Trevisa, even more crippled now, and with a perpetual cough, twittered (if excited but almost unintelligable babblings can be likened to bird noises) when the news arrived that her favourite child was coming home, even if only for a few days. In the strength of those two weeks of rest and refreshment — spirit-wise, not physical — John felt fitter than he had been for months, for life in Berkeley had become increasingly exacting.

(b) *Sporting Activities*

Bred in the tradition of the large rural estates Maurice, Lord Berkeley, from childhood had been devoted to all forms of country sport. Hawking ranked high in his Lordship's estimation. At the tender age of five he had been given a merlin, and had, under tuition, flown this, the smallest of the native hawks, at blackbirds, fieldfares and sundry other members of the feathered fraternity. Merlin, for thus he named him after King Arthur's magician and counsellor, slept in his room, and on more than one occasion came with Maurice into the Great Hall, despite the protests of his nurse, but with the indulgent approval of Lord Berkeley, his father. The tiny predator appeared never to sleep, but to have his bright beady eye perpetually traversing the whole room as though on the watch for a tasty thrush or a juicy blackbird. On one occasion a sparrow flew in through a window of the Great Hall just as Maurice and Merlin, unhooded, entered through the main door. In a flash Merlin, insecurely jesselled, pursued the intruder. The sparrow, never a respecter of persons, degrees or dignities, had ignored the Salt and flown on to the High Table. Then, seeing his arch enemy approaching with the speed and accuracy of an arrow became too petrified for flight, and instead fluttered almost drunkenly deeper into the forest of glasses, horns, mazers and other vessels arranged and waiting for my Lord Berkeley to make his choice. Merlin's first and direct attack foundered against a flagon of ale behind which the sparrow had at the last second taken refuge. Merlin, furious that his victim had tricked him so, hurt and incensed by his crash, was indifferent to Lady Berkeley's screams as the liquid cascaded over her dress, and rose, stooped, swooped and darted hither and thither seeking his prey and wreaking havoc, devastation and consternation at the High Table, and causing considerable sly amusement below the Salt. For several seconds these aerial attacks continued until the hawk, slow to recover from an abortive thrust that had been checked violently by a heavy sconce, was grabbed by Father Mark, the domestic chaplain. Poor Merlin, somewhat bedraggled and with pinions slightly singed, was banished for ever to the mews, while Maurice was hustled from the Hall before his father, whose temper, at times, was over sharp, could lay his hands on him, Later Maurice became more ambitious, and flying Merlin at snipe in the castle meadows, or at other small birds did not satisfy. The larger members of the hawk family from the mews were taken out, strictly under the supervision of Henry Nelmes, the falconer. Partridge, pigeon, dove, quail and the smaller species of duck were the usual quarry, although the pheasants, newly established by Lord Berkeley more for visual pleasure than sporting enjoyment, were sometimes sought. These noble birds were really too heavy, and their preference for running rather than flying made them the very bane of the falconer's life. Maurice chose rather to hunt the wily pheasant with his long bow, for this presented a twofold challenge, first the successful stalk — and how quick of hearing and cunning they were, especially the colourful cock — and secondly the skill to hit a target that was both small and constantly on the move, except during those occasions when the cock proudly displayed himself on some tummock or grassy bank. Hawking and archery and the coursing of the hare and rabbit all held the affection of Lord Maurice, but it was to the mounted chase, however, that he became most firmly attached, and it was to him a most bitter blow when he returned from captivity to find that his war wounds had deprived him of full participation in what he termed the King of Sports.

Trevisa found Lord Berkeley's passion for sporting activities a source of considerable interest and pleasure. At times, however, his own involvement in the preparation and supervision, resulting from his administrative responsibilities with the steward, was both heavy and frustrating. My Lord's huntsman, Will Trotman, was on occasion compelled to act as Field Master because of Lord Berkeley's physical limitations. This task he, as a castle servant, found well-nigh impossible, especially so when certain of the ladies decided to participate in the chase. Aspiring Dianas, although adding a pleasing dash of colour, caused many problems, particularly those ladies who were convinced that they were fully the equal of the Goddess in venery accomplishments. The basic difficulty was their almost total — and blatant — disregard of the normal and necessary disciplines of the chase. On the days of female participation to hope that silence would be maintained, when buck were being driven through a line of bowmen secreted behind trees or bushes, was both unrealistic and vain. The ladies' inability to keep still for any length of time was almost equally irritating, spoiling many a shot and occasionally ruining the whole drive. The most tragic result of this indiscipline witnessed by Trevisa happened near Aust. Hounds were running a fine stag on a semicircular line which was taking them gradually nearer to the steep cliffs above the ferry. A young horsewoman, possessing greater equestrian skill than common sense, or venery appreciation, and perhaps, wishing to be to the fore at the kill, cut across the arc of the line and burst from a thicket near the cliff's edge as the quarry, with hounds closing in, made a final spurt to gain possible safety by means of the brook which, half a mile through the cover and down the slope beyond, flowed into the Severn. The wretched hunted creature, faced suddenly with this foolish female, whose streaming hair and flying garments gave her a ghastly appearance, hesitated, and perhaps smelling the river, now his last hope, to his left, turned, thereby allowing his canine pursuers to draw almost level, and bounded over the cliff's edge for the water below. The tide was out, and his brave leap carried him far out over the rock face, but not far enough. Seven of the leading hounds, confident and convinced that their moment of triumph was at hand, marked the cliff's edge too late and died with their intended victim, Trevisa, who was well up with hounds and saw the whole sorry episode, felt that the young woman fully deserved the verbal flaying administered by His Lordship later that day.

On another occasion, when the hunt was lighthearted and the field somewhat mixed and scattered over much of Michaelwood, Trevisa, tired, rather bored and dry, dismounted by the Damery brook to quench his thirst. The glade was quiet, the sun shone and a fallen tree lay upon a mossy bank. How inviting was the scene. He had no responsibility that day, so why should he not rest awhile? The temptation was irresistible, and within minutes Trevisa was sound asleep.

Later, how much later he neither knew or cared, he became vaguely conscious that he was not alone. Slowly Trevisa opened his eyes, and, staring owlishly at the figure standing over him, recognized Mistress Ann, daughter of Henry Saniger whose brother, Elias, lived at Wanswell Court. Collecting his sleep-dulled wits, Trevisa sprang to his feet and bowed.

Trevisa had, for some months past, suspected that Mistress Ann frequently sought his company, as for example when coming away from mass or at social gatherings. John, feeling acutely his lowly position as secretary to his Lordship, had been studiously correct on these occasions, and had avoided carefully being drawn away from the general assembly; although he had admitted to himself that such a tete-a-tete might not be without its attractions, for physically Ann was certainly a comely young woman. Had she been of more humble origin a tumble or two might have been considered.

Before John could collect his wits and phrase a polite greeting Ann spoke:- 'Well, Master John, you are most discourteous. Firstly, you slumber in the presence of a lady, and, having been wakened, you are tardy with your salutation. I decree that you must pay a forfeit for your misbehaviour. You will kiss me twice; once for being caught asleep, and once for failing to coin a gracious greeting. Come now, Master Trevisa, pay your debt like the gentleman you surely are.' With that she flung her arms around his neck, drew him to her, pressing her mature young body against him.

Trevisa, taken thus completely off his guard, responded with alacrity, forgetful of the fact that at any moment, for all that he knew, members of the field might suddenly appear. Ann's breath, less fetid than that of some of the demi-mondes of Paris, and the proximity and pressure of her body, took him by surprise, and decorum and discretion were cast on one side. Ardour was matched with a sudden release of pent-up, and hitherto unsuspected, passion, which in its turn was welcomed with an eager abandon.

An hour later, as his mount bore him back to the castle, Trevisa thought over this sudden and unexpected assault, and his complete, willing, and indeed enthusiastic capitulation. Ex-candidate for Holy Orders though he was, he felt no real shame, only surprise and elation. Never had he envisaged such an experience in relation to himself, neither had he anticipated a feeling so powerful and fundamental. Was this the true love of which the romantic poets, especially those of France, had written? He reflected, with anticipation, on Ann's words as they had parted:- 'Darling John, we are made for each other. We must contrive to meet again soon. Farewell my love.' *'Homme propose, mais Dieu dispose'*.

The next day Henry Saniger and his daughter were riding near the Ness when Ann's mount trod on a hare at rest in its form. The scream of the maimed creature — and no animal cry is more human-like — startled the horse, which, with ears flattened, bolted. Ann strove to gain control, and for a moment, so it seemed to her father, she was succeeding, when, to his horror, he saw the horse stumble, pitch right over and for a moment remain motionless. Seconds later, and before Henry could reach the spot, the animal struggled to get to its feet, but fell back and lay still. When her father arrived he found Ann, battered by the flailing hooves and crushed, dead beneath her dying mount.

The news numbed Trevisa. His own loss was as nothing when compared with the fact that because of him a christian soul had died unshriven and in mortal sin. For Ann there had been no time for the saving grace, comfort and consolation of confession. No opportunity had been afforded to his loved one, but still his companion in peccavidity, to attempt any amends for their stolen hour. The thought and prospect filled him with abject horror and deep contrition. He alone remained. Upon him rested the frightening responsibility of attempting a reconciliation, both personal and vicarious, with man's maker. It was many weeks, a period of inexpressible misery, before Trevisa had formulated a scheme of self-imposed penance which satisfied, and that only partially, his heavy demands. His own confession, fully made with Father David, the human intermediary, brought much in the way of penance but no easement of heart, mind or soul. Week after agonizing week Trevisa, by prayer, almost fierce in its intensity, and meditation, sought solace for his soul, but only as a secondary consideration. His prime concern was the mitigation of Ann's purgatorial pains, for which he felt, and in a measure, was responsible. 'God', whether He was a God of Love or an indifferent omnipotent tyrant, would, so the Church taught, demand that Ann should suffer the fires of hell for that hour of ecstacy in Michaelwood - and all because she had been taken so cruelly without chance of shriving. He, Trevisa, the equally guilty party, had been spared to make full confession, an exercise which had eased his burden of mind and heart not at all, but had left him with a mental torture comparable, he felt, with that of the damned, amongst whose ranks he conceived he must now be numbered — and that in spite of Father David's words.

Trevisa, in despair, finally begged leave of absence to visit Will, for whose wisdom and balanced judgement he had a profound regard.

The result was, in general, negative. The advice to continue in prayer and meditation seemed futile, for this he had long been doing fervently, but without personal benefit. One fresh suggestion, however, emerged. Will, on the second day of John's visit, with great diffidence said — 'John, you once were bent upon a clerical career, and then doubts assailed you. I hate to refer to the afflictions of your sister and mother, but it appears that your experience at home, two or three years back, further undermined your fundamental christian beliefs, and resulted finally and after much conflict of conscience, as I well remember, in your leaving Stapledon Hall for Berkeley, saying that you could not preach a gospel in which you felt little confidence. I wonder, just wonder, whether you were and are being tried, as once was Job, so that you would be compelled to face up to yourself? Both you and he lost in tragic circumstance dearly loved ones; and for Ann's unhappy death you, I believe completely without justification, hold yourself morally responsible. Is God stripping you of your dearest earthly attachments so that you can serve Him with greater freedom and devotion? This is a possibility you know. Perhaps ahead lie important tasks as a parish priest, or even as a turner, for which work you are singularly well fitted.   Pray thoughtfully and long for guidance, and it will come.'

Trevisa, on his return to Berkeley, followed Will's advice for a long period, but with no marked improvement. One evening in August Trevisa felt more than usually dejected and his prayers even more formal and futile. In despair he rose from his knees and went and sat on a bench against the wall of the north aisle. Could Will be right? Might God, indeed, be calling him back to a life of service which he had rejected? Could these personal sorrows and losses be a method of compulsion, forcing him to review again those fundamentals which he, in the days of peaceful conformity, had accepted without question, but which, at almost the first touch of the lash, he had so suddenly abandoned?

Job had been even more cruelly treated, being deprived of his entire family, his friends and his health, but he had never fully turned his back on God; indeed in his dejection he had seen himself as never before, and, finally, had found his way back to an acceptance of God and His over-riding love of man. Trevisa, at this point, went and knelt at the Altar of St. Maurice at the east end of the aisle.

Time suddenly ceased to have relevance, and in some strange way he felt in a state of etherealization. A robed figure, taper in hand, emerged from the turret stairs at the west end and walked down the aisle. Trevisa, as the figure approached him, heard himself saying, 'Who are you father? I have never seen you here-to-fore.' 'My son, I am brother Bernard[8] who served in the great abbey of Berkeley in the days when good King Edward sat upon the throne of this land[9]. What tumultuous times those were, even in saintly Edward's reign! Satan bothered us much in those days, and especially when the notorious witch of Berkeley was entombed. Fear of Lucifer drove the entire chori clericorum, then chanting the psalms round the body and somehow off their guard, from the building[10]. The church, later was exorcised by my Lord Wulfstan, our Bishop, and we had peace. Today I bear a message for you. Master William's words are those of the Master Himself, and you will disregard them at your peril! Return, my son, before it is too late. You are subborn and headstrong, yet like the oat crop on over-rich soil you bow too easily before the wind of adversity. There is much for you to do. Use the gifts God has given you for His Glory and for the benefit of his family. Thus, and thus only, will come peace of mind, my son.' With that the figure vanished, and Trevisa was alone.

Had this been a dream, a figment of his distraught mind, or was it a reality? So much depended upon the answer. Trevisa kept his counsel until later in the year when Nicholas and William came to Berkeley. During their discussions on their respective and, perhaps, conjointed futures, Trevisa told them of this incident. Both colleagues believed the visitation to have been a reality, a deliberate divine manifestation, and counselled acceptance of what they termed 'Divine conditions of reconciliation'.

Trevisa, for Ann's sake and almost hers alone, but with, at first reluctance and considerable apprehension, accepted the prospect of total ecclesiastical discipline.

Trevisa's second winter in Berkeley began early, and its severity after St. Nicholas-tide clearly taxed the weakened condition of Lord Berkeley. He, as well as those around him, began to feel that his earthly pilgrimage might soon close.

It came, consequently, as no surprise to Lord Berkeley's secretary to be summoned into his Lordship's bedroom to receive instructions for the drawing up, along with Hugh Bradstock, the steward, Sir Nicholas Berkeley and Sir Richard Acton, preliminary details for the betrothal of Thomas, Lord Berkeley's eldest son, to Margaret, daughter of Gerrard Warren, Lord de Lisle of Wengrave in Buckinghamshire.

The negotiations were protracted and the financial details keenly disputed by both parties. Trevisa's meagre aquaintance with the law of inheritance and its peculiar and precise phraseology worried him, and he was relieved when a legal scribe from St. Augustine's Abbey arrived for the closing formalities. The final contract was signed, sealed and witnessed at Berkeley on Wednesday next after the feast of the Holy Trinity 1367.[11] The principal items of the settlement were (1) a payment (over a period) of eleven hundred marks by Lord de Lisle to Lord Berkeley, (2) the future bride and groom were (because of the former's tender years — she was but seven) to remain with their respective fathers for four years.

During the later summer months Lord Berkeley's health deteriorated rapidly. It therefore was decided after frank and full discussion to bring forward the religious ceremony thus lessening somewhat the extent of Royal wardship should, as now was anticipated, Lord Berkeley not live to see his eldest son's coming of age. The die having been cast, both at Berkeley and Wengrave the tempo of life suddenly changed, and all was bustle and excitement. The terms of the contract were once more carefully scrutinized, lists of those to accompany Thomas Berkeley were drawn up and their liveries designed and contracted out — even Lord Berkeley, although he knew he could not undertake the journey, had made for himself a 'sute of ... cloth of gold'[12].

Trevisa was amazed by the multifarious and multitudinous details involved, and the magnitude of the work necessary to organise and fit out the meiny which would accompany the fourteen-year-old bridegroom, and, last but not least, the extent and depth of the legal and ecclesiastical requirements. However, by dint of hard work, careful planning and lavish expenditure — and the secretary felt that this last, from the Berkeleys' point of view, was a very sound financial investment — the target dates were achieved.

On 5th November Lord Berkeley and the bridegroom, from the bedroom above the portcullis, watched the assembly of the parties in the outer and inner courtyards. The three accompanying household knights, Sir Nicholas Berkeley, Sir Richard Acton and Sir John Tracy entered the room and reported that the company, more than three hundred strong, was ready to move off. Lord Berkeley gave them thanks and while drinking the stirrup cup gave them, and Master Trevisa, their final instructions and committed his son Thomas to their care, warning them also that there must not be any, even apparently trivial, last minute alterations in the marriage settlement.

Thomas and the knights led the esquires from the inner courtyard and took their place at the head of the main body. A trumpet sounded and a mighty cheer arose from the column, the retainers lining the ramparts and the hundreds of townfolk and tenantry who had crowded outside the castle walls to see the colourful cavalcade and to wish happiness and God's Blessing upon the Berkeley heir and their future Lord.

The day of the wedding began in mist, but by ten o'clock the sun had broken through. This greatly cheered everyone, and especially those — and they were not a few — whose belief in the ancient adages was firmer than their christian convictions. 'Blessed is the Bride upon whom the sun doth shine' was to them an article of faith as deeply ingrained as the Credo or the Ava Maria.

A vast assembly converged from many directions upon Wengrave where the Berkeley and de Lisle retainers lined the route to the church and occupied vantage points within the building itself. A short while before mid-day Thomas Berkeley and the principal members of his meiny arrived to take up their station.

Master David Milkesham, Vicar of Berkeley, and Master John Trevisa had ridden to Wengrave with the esquires, but on the wedding day, because Master David was taking a minor part in the service and Master John, as my Lord Berkeley's secretary, had certain official duties to perform, they made their way independently to the church.

Trevisa, and to a lesser extent Master David, were astonished at the kaleidoscopic appearance of the scene as they passed along the path leading to the porch. There the Berkeley meiny — some within, others without — awaited the arrival of the child-bride. The knights, Sir Nicholas Berkeley, Sir Richard Acton and Sir John Tracy, 'were suted in their liveries of fine cloth of ray furred with miniver, And the esquires in their liveries of courser ray and less costly furre: And the young bridegroom himself was in scarlet and satin and a silver girdle'[13] It was indeed a fine sight.

After the ceremony Wengrave House witnessed a banquet which exceeded any similar occasion that could be remembered, and the riotous entertainments, too, with minstrels, mummers, tumblers and dancing bears, were on an unprecedented scale.

Before, however, the heady wines had taken full control, and my Lord of Misrule, tinsel-bedecked and jester-like, and his crude courtiers could place their stamp upon the junketings, the bride was whisked away by her nurse and tire-woman. Two hours later Trevisa and the vicar escorted a reluctant, protesting and slightly inebriate groom to his chamber and there, in turn, mounted guard upon their charge. Lord Berkely's orders had been precise and firm, and Thomas, rebellious at first, finally accepted the limitation upon his freedom. Two hours after midnight Sir Richard Acton, as an appreciation of their entertainment, handed the minstrels forty shillings [14] — a gesture that was well received. He then retired to bed, thankful that the day — and evening — had gone so well.

Two days later the bride and groom, having met but once more, and that for an official farewell, parted to live on their respective estates until the parents and advisers should decree that the marriage could be consummated without taxing the health or physique of the couple, or endangering the well-being of the next generation.

The home coming was an anticlimax. Thomas and his meny were tired, and they had no bride proudly to parade. In addition they found their Lord in a serious condition. A temporary recovery followed, but with the advent of May Day it was clear that the end was at hand. On 8th June Lord Berkeley died, and Thomas, now 15 years old, succeeded.

The funeral service for Lord Berkeley took place in St. Augustine's Abbey in Bristol. With its black crape and plumes and the doleful dirges of the familia it was an impressive though sombre occasion.

Neither Trevisa nor Master David had part or place in the service, and both felt that Lord Maurice should have been laid to rest in Berkeley Church where Lord Thomas III, his father, had been buried, only seven years before, and not at the abbey in the tomb of a mother whom he could scarce remember [15].

With the death of Lord Berkeley, John's position changed. The new Baron was but 15 years of age, and although now a married man, at least legally, had not the need nor the desire to retain a secretary as well as a chaplain. John was employed more and more in the dull routine of estate management under the steward, and less and less upon tasks where his mental ability or his social training could come into full play. Henry Bird looked on at John's change of status with pity, and suggested, after a while, that he, the chaplain, should speak to his master and his Lordship's uncle and ask whether Lord Berkeley would revive the sponsorship for John at Oxford and, in view of William's connections with the Berkeley Cornish estates, whether his Lordship might consider helping William Middleworth in a similar manner should, in the future, this become necessary [16]. If the chaplain's suggestions received a favourable response, then a return to the university for Trevisa could reasonably be expected.

The young Lord and his advisers received their chaplain's request calmly, and finally, in view of John's faithful service over four years, often in a more menial position than perhaps was justified, agreed to renew the sponsorship if a place could be found. With considerably greater reluctance, and only because of the long association of John and William through most of their academic career, was agreement reached that the latter too, should be helped if the need arose.

With the priesthood now a clear objective, Queen's Hall, with its distinctly religious character [17], was the obvious choice for the new entry.

Negotiations were opened by the Abbot of St. Augustine's, Bristol, who suggested, when he interviewed John and William, that dispensation might be obtained for Nicholas too, to proceed to orders, and that a Herefordshire sponsor might be found.

Months passed before these negotiations were successful. They concerned matters of great delicacy. Firstly Queen's Hall was founded, theoretically at least, for students from the North of England [18] and furthermore its fellows were expressly required to take orders. The latter regulation was acceptable as they were resolved, with God's help, to seek ordination, but all were West-of-England by birth and connection. Secondly the marriage of Nicholas, although this had ended with Emma's death, was, indeed, a formidable hurdle. Fortunately the Abbot had friends in high places, and the King, although aged and less agile mentally than he had been, was persuaded, in view of the distinguished military sevice rendered to him by the late Lords Thomas and Maurice Berkeley in France and Scotland [19], to lend his support to these petitions.

It was the spring of 1369 before all the arrangements had been completed, and May was in before Nicholas, John and William took up residence at Queens's and began to re-establish the close relationship which had existed in their time together at Stapledon Hall [20].

Chapter 6
Queen's Hall

(a) *On to Priesthood*

Trevisa, now a regent master, found himself occupied with lengthy compulsory periods of teaching and discussion in the Schools: all this was in addition to his ordination preparation. His return to Oxford, in spite of these heavy commitments, brought him great joy. He, Hereford and Middleworth were together at Queen's. This would allow the close relationship which, earlier, had been established at Stapledon Hall to be revived and strengthened. It might, indeed, enable some of the grandiose projects discussed during those earlier days to be brought to fruition. What castles in the air they had built - such is the enthusiasm and self assurance of youth.

Trevisa's happiness was increased by the fact that Middleworth's misfortune, at being involved in Master Wyclif's expulsion from Canterbury Hall, was now (partly through the patronage and influence of my Lord Berkeley) being set right. Indeed Middleworth's fellowship truly meant as much to Trevisa as did his own. The biblical scholarship of Hereford would count for a great deal if ever the ephemeral dreams of Stapledon days, of an English Bible for the English people, should begin to be a practical proposition.

Lastly there was the contentedness of mind, which comes only when a nagging doubt of uncertainty has been resolved, when the die has been cast or a definite course of action finally and irrevocably accepted. This decision to proceed to ordination was made all the more natural by the knowledge that his friends and colleagues were intent upon the same objective.

One doubt, and that, it appeared to Trevisa, of little importance, had at times entered his mind. Stapledon Hall was a West of England foundation, established for men from the diocese of Exeter, or, if vacancies allowed, other western dioceses such as Hereford and Worcester. There at Stapledon Hall they had been, ethnologically, amongst their kith and kin. At Queen's they were in a measure - if foundation statutes counted for anything - entering a strange world, the world of the dour, determined and hard north. The northern folk, it was said, were clannish, more united indeed than the normal southern community. Trevisa felt, however, that with the two other known southern fellows, Richard Thorp whom he had met occasionally at the Sanigers of Wanswell in Berkeley - a family he greatly respected - and Henry Whitfield, almost a contemporary of theirs at Stapledon in the early days, they would be able to hold their own, should occasion demand. Was this arrogance or an inability to assess the importance of foundation terms of reference?

Trevisa, although almost thirty years of age and an ex-member of two universities, because maybe of his hitherto somewhat sheltered life, had still much to learn of the power of intrigue and cruelty bred of jealousy, and especially when masquerading under the guise of religion.

Trevisa, and, to a lesser degree, Hereford, from their first day at Queen's reacted unfavourably towards their fellow freshman, Thomas Carlisle. The latter was a vigorous northerner previously employed by the hall in the collection of its rents, dues and debts in Cumberland and Westmorland [2]. Their feelings towards Carlisle suffered further deterioration when they learned from the authorities that the latter was to be admitted to the office of acolyte in November [3], whereas they were being deferred until March [4]. Carlisle, they recognised, had had considerable administrative experience and, clearly, was possessed of real ability. They believed, however, that his academic background and scholastic achievement did not merit this precedence. It was, however, his rugged bluntness and aggressive manner, so often associated with those nurtured in the bleak hill country south of the Scottish border, which jarred most. There was no element of class snobbery in their rejection, rather an aesthetic revulsion. The lack of politeness and polish grated upon southerners whose formative years had been spent in surroundings where those qualities were held in some esteem, even if not always demonstrated. The somewhat phlegmatic Middleworth was more tolerant than his colleagues - his years at Canterbury Hall, and his involvement in the Wyclif troubles, had compelled him to develop, metaphorically, a protective outer skin which enabled him more easily to ignore jibes and loud crudities. This tolerance Middleworth preached to his ex-Stapledon friends. The advice, more was the pity, fell on deaf ears. Carlisle, for his part, left Trevisa and Hereford in no doubt of his feelings towards them.

In this lack of cordiality lay the seeds of future friction which developed into mutual distrust, and finally into open conflict. The situation was exacerbated later when the Provost, Henry Whitfield, once of Stapledon Hall, began, it was alleged, to show favours towards southerners, both those already in residence and those applying for membership, in a manner contrary to the foundation statutes.

Those first few months at Queen's constituted a period of considerable educational and physical activity. Advancement to the priesthood could only follow, normally, an intensive course of theological and philosophical discussion and study, both at the hall and in the schools. So absorbed was Trevisa in these studies and so occupied in his rapid progress through the minor orders - he was made acolyte on 3 March 1370, subdeacon on 29 March 1370, deacon May 1370 and finally priesthood on 8 June 1370 - that he failed to consider carefully enough the details of a proposition made to him during the busy weeks between his subdiaconate and being made a full deacon. This misfortune hung like a spiked collar around his neck for the remainder of his academic life.

A chaplain, Gilbert of Grimsby, had been appointed Treasurer of Queen's Hall in October 1369. The chaplain, obviously, lacked training in these matters, maybe even adequate instruction in his duties. Perhaps, too, he was by nature dilatory or unbusinesslike? The result, in any case, was disastrous to Trevisa. At the end of seven months Gilbert was heavily in debt to the Hall and resigned, although the term of his appointment had not expired. The authorities thereupon presented Trevisa with the office - debt and all! The latter, probably because of his heavy commitments and deep involvement in ordination obligations, failed to detect the subtleties - even if it was not downright deception - of debt responsibilities until it was too late. His protests, and those made on his behalf by Hereford, were of no avail. The northern element had passed the burden to a southerner, a piece of sharp practice that pleased them well. His duties as treasurer - an office for which, frankly, he realized he was unsuited, and in which he had no interest - also took up valuable time, time that he wished, with his priesting approaching rapidly, to devote to the study of the Scripture, the history of the Christian Church and the writings of the early fathers. The debt Trevisa stoutly, at first, refused to acknowledge, but in the years that lay ahead he reluctantly and with bad grace accepted the responsibility, and entries in the hall accounts over the next twenty three years show that he made some effort to discharge it and, finally, succeeded [5].

Trevisa, as priesthood became imminent, felt two regrets, the second amounting to a deep sorrow. Firstly he would have liked to have been ordained in what he termed 'his' cathedral, i.e., Exeter. His title, however, being Queen's Hall, and the distance to Devon so great, this desire, he recognised, was unrealizable. The death, a year previously, of his early mentor, indeed his idol, the great Bishop John Grandisson, was by far the more poignant cause of sadness. What a thrill it would have been if he, Trevisa, could have knelt before the fearless yet kindly Bishop of Exeter Cathedral to receive the laying on of hands for the office of a priest. My Lord Bishop of London, though eminent, was, in Trevisa's estimation, a man of but moderate stature when placed alongside the one who, in the cause of right and justice, had, on different occasions, withstood alone his archbishop, the King's lieutenant, and almost the entire vested interests of the Church and State within his own diocese; a man who had strode courageously through his cure during those long months when the Black Death stalked through the land heavily depleting the ranks of his clergy and their flocks; a man who had ignored Papal orders so that he, Grandisson, could ordain additional priests, and so bring much-needed spiritual comfort and consolation to his people. There was a man whose counsellor was God, from whom, too, came the strength, physical and moral, to fulfill his high office during four decades of almost unparallelled difficulty and danger.

The journey to London for priesting was uneventful, and it was a surprise to the three members of Queen's to find themselves, amongst seven others for priests' orders, being accommodated in the Bishop's Palace for the ordination retreat. This was an honour they had not expected. Five of these were Oxford men and all known to the Queen's contingent. The remainder of the candidates, mainly for the office of deacon or subdeacon, were in outside lodgings. Three of those being made deacon were from the diocese of Exeter and, like themselves, had studied earlier at Glasney.

The retreat, lasting ten days, was, so felt Hereford, the oldest of the Queen's party, a test of physical endurance, as much as a final preparation for the various offices to which candidates were being presented. Trevisa and Middleworth agreed, but complained more of the platitudinous nature of many of the addresses, and their abysmally low academic standard. All three held that the friars (for whom they held no brief, indeed whom they cordially disliked) at their Oxford pre-ordination course gave their candidates meat worthy of the occasion, whereas they were being fed with a literary and theological diet of milk such as Holy Paul gave, so he wrote, to the people of Corinth. It was, indeed, they considered, an insult to candidates of their maturity and scholarship. The quality of some of the lectures was so sub-standard that Trevisa for a moment even wondered whether this might have been done of deliberate policy to teach candidates humility and the abjuration of intellectual arrogance. John Tracey, of Carlton in the Diocese of Lincoln, on the fourth day was so incensed that he protested to the Bishop himself. The resultant reprimand was stern and lengthy; the substance of it could succinctly be precised by saying that a deacon of some thirty days standing was in no position to criticise senior clerics of proven ability and considerable reputation in the Church. Slowly, too slowly for

Trevisa, who had grave difficulty in repressing his irritation, Sunday June the 8th approached.

The day dawned fair with the promise of heat. The latter condition candidates and staff alike feared, for the length of the service, the victular abstinence and the combined weight of garb and the accoutrements of ecclesiastical ceremonial imposed considerable strain upon all those taking part. Was it a sum of these factors which was the cause of an unforgettable experience for Trevisa at the climax of the service? As he knelt before the Bishop and felt the laying on of hands, Trevisa was conscious of two voices speaking. The louder droned in Latin, 'Receive the Holy Ghost for the office and work of a Priest in the Church of God, now committed unto thee by the imposition of our hands. Whose sins thou dost forgive, they are forgiven; and whose sins thou dost retain they are retained. And be thou a faithful dispenser of the Word of God and of his Holy Sacraments; In the name of the Father, and of the Son, and of the Holy Ghost. Amen.' At the same time, through that pattern of words, a voice, crisp and clear, whispered in his ear, 'God Bless You, my son!' Fanciful Celtic imagination? Self-deception? Maybe, but to Trevisa a living reality, and an assurance of Life Eternal.

(b) *Post Ordination*

After priesting, and while still preparing for parochial life, Trevisa felt that he could embark upon his long-suppressed ambition to help popularize the English tongue in literature, by translating some of the more serious and important works from the current Latin long used in manuscript and book productions. The recent proclamations of legal and national matters in English [6] heartened Trevisa. This could be the thin edge of the wedge splitting slightly the support hitherto given towards the use of Latin or Norman French for other than the spoken word.

Could not members of Queen's undertake the translation of some of these Latin text books, or ones of special merit, for the benefit of the layman, and thus drive the wedge deeper into the current prejudice and, maybe, even popularize the English tongue? This subject the group of southerners discussed repeatedly, but important and more mundane matters seemed to be forced upon them, and a decision on this possible enterprise was postponed. Trevisa realized that his domestic duties as treasurer, irksome though at times these could be, had their compensatory side. How pleasant it was to ride out to some of the quiet country villages, where Queen's had interests, and to exhibit or examine parochial muniments in the parish church or to collect Queen's Hall dues or rents! Expenses were paid eventually, so the financial outlay to himself and his companion - or companions - of the journey was small. The physical costs at times were considerable, for the hired mounts were often restless, bony and hard of mouth. How glad Trevisa was of the long days he had spent in the saddle at Berkeley. Of his companions on these Oxford expeditions only Hereford and Middleworth, both experienced horsemen, really enjoyed themselves or appreciated these country rides, and especially so in winter. Trevisa found that the most interesting and pleasureful of these parochial visits was that to Newbold [7]. Here the vicar, Master Richard De Le Bere, was a sincere and faithful yet jovial parish priest. In addition he was a considerable scholar and sympathetic to the policy of the promotion of the English language in every phase of life. He kept a good table, and, obviously, did business with a vintner who had important connections in Burgundy and the Rhineland. Yes, Father De La Bere was a connoisseur in matters of food and wine, and one could be certain of a satisfying day, intellectually and gastronomically, in his company.

Trevisa approached Doctor Wyclif on the subject of English translations, receiving some moral support but no promise of active assistance. Master Wyclif said he was so occupied with philosophical dissertations that he could not undertake - certainly in the early stages - any actual translation. He might, however, he declared, be able, if they so wished to supervise their work within a term or two. He pointed out, by way of encouragement perhaps, that they were well placed for such an undertaking in that the amount of material, books and manuscripts, in the libraries of colleges, halls and religious communities was considerable.

(c] *A Moment of Perplexity*

Trevisa was uncertain. Hesitancy or irresolution was something to which he was unaccustomed. The great biblical project was drawing to a close. His own major commitments, the Gospels of St. Matthew and St. John, the Epistles to the Romans and St. John and the Book of Revelation had been completed, while several apocryphal works were well in hand.

Nicholas was labouring hard with the Old Testament, while William had already finished the Gospel of St. Luke, the Acts and several of the Epistles.

Doctor Wyclif had examined most of the completed books and, in general, had given them his approval. Yes, the end was clearly in sight. It had been a mammoth task that he, Trevisa, Hereford and Middleworth had begun full five years ago. Looking back, John had to admit that had it not been for the persistent goading of Wyclif the translation of the Bible into English - the whole Bible - would not have reached its present advanced stage. The approaching completion of this project brought a sense of achievement, and relief too. There was still the same burning zeal for this missionary enterprise of bringing the Scriptures to the people in their own language - and many of the untranslated non-canonical works also were both edifying and instructive. Trevisa felt, however, that with the main objective, the Canon, accomplished - or nearly so, he needed a change of subject matter. This was understandable. But what should be the alternative?

Should it be the translation of some secular work such as Bede's *Historia Ecclesiastica Gentis Anglorum*, or the *De Regimine Principum* of Aegidius Romanus? Should he not, on the other hand, work through that satirical poem *Piers the Plowman* [8], so new and so popular with the masses? The author was a man of strong feelings, one who revolted against corruption in high places, and not least amongst church dignitaries, a humble cleric whose very vocation made him fully aware of the extremes of ostentatious affluence and abject poverty which marched cheek by jowl in village, town and city - a state of affairs which the monasteries and the hierarchy of the Church at large accepted without much protest, which, indeed, their way of life, their privileged way of life, supported.

John, so fully in accord with the didactic core of that work, felt that the subject required expansion and heavy underlining, and needed, too, to be given a new look, with greater and clearer emphasis upon the indispensability of honesty, integrity and humility in the Christian life. Trevisa believed that the whole poem should be recast and expressed on a higher plane, so that it would be seen clearly to be an attack upon selfishness, greed, pride and the misuse of God's gifts by mankind in general, but especially by the favoured minority of whom the friars were not the least offenders.

Trevisa, however, had for years, indeed since the distant days in Bishop Grandisson's Palace when he had first been introduced to Higden's *Polychronicon*,[9] ambitiously longed to be able to give that work, and others like it, to his own people in their own tongue. He did not at first recognise in his uncertainty a struggle of conscience, duty towards his fellow beings versus a personal ambition disguised somewhat with a halo labelled 'benefit to mankind'.

Discussion with his colleagues was fruitless. Wyclif, himself already an interested party, a scholar of international repute, a dignitary of the Church and backed by powerful patrons, could not see the *Piers the Plowman* problem as the younger man saw it. Hereford, too, had a more privileged background, with relations occupying high places in the Church, and in consequence, reacted rather differently to the crying social problems of the day. He was, so Trevisa feared, beginning to show signs of personal ambition. William Middleworth, alone, seemed to have an appreciable understanding of John's quandary; but he, too, appeared to look upon it as an intellectual rather than a moral issue.

After much prayer, accompanied by real agony of spirit, the decision was made. The revision of the poem in a form more intellectually acceptable to scholars and men of influence in Church and State must come first. Trevisa consoled himself with the thought that the translation of Higden's *Polychronicon* would only be deferred for a time. This die having been cast, came next the problem of obtaining access to a reliable manuscript of the poem.

The deciding factor in the mental struggle had been the political and in a measure the sociological changes which had taken place since *Piers the Plowman* had first appeared, short though the intervening time had been. The feelings of the common people, Trevisa knew, had altered considerably. Five years ago they had grumbled at the Church and State, whom they accused of grinding them down, but armed rebellion was something that had been almost unthinkable. Today in the Year of Grace 1377 the fires of revolt were beginning to smoulder, and could well burst into flame in the not very distant future. Trevisa likened the national feeling of tension to that which, in a different context, appertained in Queen's Hall. Some years ago, in spite of initial reluctance of the northern members of the Hall to accept the new southern fellows who had been elected in 1369 and in 1374, there had been little open demonstration of hard feeling. This opposition had increased, and bitterness and militancy of spirit had been finding expression more frequently of late. This reached its climax with the change of Provost in that same year. The removal of Henry Whitfield from the office of Provost came suddenly. He had realized for some time that malign forces were at work, and that his deprivation was a possibility. The sense of grievance, when the blow finally fell, was made even greater - and shared by the group of southern fellows - when it was learned that Thomas Carlisle had been elected in his stead. Rumour, and some less responsible members of Hall, suggested that Carlisle's elevation might well have resulted from the considerable influence which, it was hinted, his attractive young sister, Elizabeth, exercised over his Grace, the Archbishop of York. Trevisa and Middleworth discounted this scurrilous gossip, and felt that the preferment of a northerner was an attempt to implement the terms of the original foundation charter, and, at the same time, to undermine the growing influence of the southern faction. The selection of Carlisle, they considered, could be looked upon as a reward for his financial acumen shown during his 'taxgathering' days, rather than a recognition of academic distinction or scholastic attainment.

(d) *Expulsion*

As the weeks passed and the preparation for the *Piers the Plowman* project began to take shape the domestic situation within Queen's Hall worsened. The northern faction, supported as they were by the Archbishop and the King, grew more arrogant, making life for the southern fellows uncomfortable, and even intolerable. Wyclif, himself a northerner, Hereford, Middleworth and Trevisa discussed the situation and concluded that events seemed to be moving inexorably towards a final crisis. In consequence it was decided that they would for their part, as far as possible, keep out of the controversy and redouble their efforts to complete the work, now mainly revisionary, on their biblical translations so that if normal facilities should be withdrawn, and one or more of their quartet expelled, the task, being in so advanced a state, could still be completed without too much difficulty. It soon became clear, however, that a purge had been decided upon: the northern group were determined to reduce the numerical strength of the southerners, and the latter, by their opposition to the new provost, had furnished the former with the opportunity they needed. It was obvious, too, that the victims would, if possible, be drawn from the group of scholars working on the biblical translations. The hand and seal of vested interests and episcopal spite were patent when the charges were heard.

The verdict, expulsion for six fellows [10], split the ranks of the biblical translators. Hereford, Trevisa, Lydford, Whitfield and the other two were given a week in which to leave. Middleworth received, so it appeared, a suspended sentence, while Wyclif, a commensalis and not a fellow, was not mentioned in spite of his close association with several of the southerners. Perhaps his northern origins saved him? Hereford and Trevisa realized that reading and borrowing facilities would, with their expulsion, be withdrawn at least by Queen's. This would render further work on *Piers the Plowman* virtually impossible, because that manuscript was on loan to Queen's Hall and not to Trevisa himself. Hereford, too, with the library facilities withheld, could see that the remaining work on the apocryphal books could well soon come to a standstill. Two whole days were spent by those under sentence in discussion of these personal problems, and slowly a plan, a desperate plan, evolved.

The southern group outnumbered the northerners and felt that they rather than their rivals represented the Hall. The Provostship of a northerner had been imposed upon them from above and only maintained by archiepiscopal and royal support. They, the majority, in spite of the constitutions of the Hall, looked upon themselves as the victims of jealousy and greed. They would, therefore, if necessary, move out and set up their own establishment within the university, trusting that Wyclif's influence would obtain for them official recognition. The next three days were spent in seeking accommodation and formulating their final plans and constitution. The first objective was soon achieved. Two adjoining houses in St. Ebb's Street, vacant and in reasonable condition, were leased for six months. Two men-servants, a cook and chambermaid, were secured and at once given the task of preparing the places for immediate occupation.

At this point troubles began to mount. Wyclif refused to negotiate with the Council of Regent Masters on their behalf, considering that to do so would increase the antagonism of the clerical hierarchy towards him, and might well, through seeming to flaunt the King's command, prejudice the patronage of the Duke of Lancaster and others of high degree. It is just, however, to point out that the well-being of the biblical translation project and not personal safety was the major factor in his decision.

Trevisa and Hereford then met privately certain members of the Council. Their reception gave the conspirators - one might almost call them rebels - some ground for hope. They were told, unofficially, that though the Council could not condone, let alone support, such conduct and would not for the moment extend recognition to a virtually schismatic community, it would make no attempt to suppress it or even to interfere with its everyday working. This immediate neutral attitude, almost a 'hands off' policy, and possible recognition within a year or two, was really more than had been expected. It gave them heart, and made them feel that at least a short period of comparative quiet was a real possibility. Should this materialize, and if certain manuscripts should be borrowed or access to them be granted, then an appreciable section of the biblical project still outstanding might be completed. The availability of these manuscripts was, indeed, the major problem, and one for which no clear solution could be seen. Trevisa, as they left Wyclif's quarters to retire to bed, beckoned Hereford and Thorpe to follow him. Inside his room the Cornishman outlined a possible, but drastic, plan which he had conceived during the fruitless meeting, but which, for personal reasons, he had not wished to divulge to the whole party.

Slowly but succinctly the scheme was unfolded. On Martinmas, two days away, the University Council would be assembling in the Schools. Carlisle, as Provost of Queen's, appointed by the Archbishop, would most certainly be attending, as, in all probability, would his entire staff. The Hall, in consequence, would be almost empty, save for a few servants, for much of the day. The six under sentence of expulsion would not be expected, indeed allowed, to attend, and so their absence would cause no comment. 'Let us,' suggested Trevisa, 'announce tomorrow that we will finally be leaving Hall on Martinmas or the day after. Our goods and chattels can soon be packed and moved to St. Ebb's - two hours will suffice if speed is desirable. Why not, in fact, transfer some non-essentials tomorrow and so ease the final operation? Thus on Martinmas by the time the usurping Provost and his sycophants and toadies have left for the Schools all, or almost all, of our baggage will be in our new accommodation.'

'I suggest, Nicholas, that directly everything of ours has been conveyed to St. Ebb's Street, we return to Hall, ostensibly to check up and see that nothing of our property has been left behind. This, however, will have been carefully seen to earlier. On our arrival we will proceed at once to the library and 'borrow' for our use those books and manuscripts which we deem essential for our work. We might even go one step further and, if possible, obtain the Hall seal, charter and other insignia, claiming thereby to be the true corporate collegiate establishment of Queen's under our rightful Provost, Henry Whitfield? I, for one, have never accepted Carlisle as a genuine superior. You two also feel strongly on this matter. I am sure we can count on the active support of our numerous southern and Welsh colleagues at both Exeter and Merton, even if we adopt the more aggressive and ambitious scheme. Balliol, with its Scottish and northern elements, will, no doubt, side with Carlisle and his crawlers. Our united strength, however, would be expected to discourage open violence from fear of physical retaliation. Eventually, of course, the Archbishop or the King or both, will be drawn in and we will be compelled to return everything. I trust, however, that by that time our main task, the biblical translations, will have been completed, or very nearly so. I must take also the *Polychronicon* manuscript, for my remaining biblical commitments have almost been completed. I will, I fear, have to abandon the *Piers the Plowman* rewrite for the moment. That, Nicholas and Richard, is what I propose — what think you?'

Silence followed, a pregnant, startled silence which stifled, momentarily, comment and reply. Nicholas, eventually, spoke first. 'John! This is truly a bold plan on the grand scale, and such a one that only you could have conceived - so simple, yet so daringly devastating. This, obviously, was why you were not your usual vocal self during our earlier discussions. I thought it most strange, but attributed it to your great sorrow that your several translations might have to be abandoned. I see now how wrong was my assessment. You are like my native river Wye, most dangerous when running silently along.'

Thorpe nodded agreement, but said nothing.

'Tomorrow early,' continued Trevisa, 'we must discuss the plans more fully with our lawful Provost, Whitfield, and with Lydford and Frank. In the meanwhile sleep well, for we have hard but delicate and perhaps dangerous work ahead.'

At noon the six assembled in Hereford's room - by far the largest. Trevisa again went step by step through the details of his proposals. From time to time Whitfield scowled and shook his head - clearly he was not in full accord. He spoke first, 'My friends and colleagues, this is nothing less than revolution, and contrary to every conception of law, order and discipline. We must not, we cannot, commit theft, nor can we depose the duly appointed Hall authorities. Trevisa, your fiery Celtic temperament has taken control and your normally shrewd and sagacious judgement has been warped and clouded by a desire for revenge for what we all believe to be victimisation. We must not do this thing. If, however, you persist in the attempt I will be no party to it. I will leave tomorrow for my archdeaconry.'

Trevisa, grim-visaged, sprang to his feet, but before he could speak, Hereford thrust him back and said, 'Provost! Your words do you no credit, and slander an honourable man. The blame for our expulsion, if blame there be to apportion, lies at your door. You it was who persistently and flagrantly broke the constitutions and precipitated this unhappy state, wrecking both our careers and the opportunity of giving to our people in their native tongue the complete works of Holy Writ. You, with your archdeaconry, and also your canonry of Exeter, suffer least of all. Shame on you for your petulant outburst. Go! We want no craven, no chicken-livered companion, with us in our struggle for survival and our rights! But before you go we must have your solemn word, as you will answer to Our Lord, that no word of this will be divulged, now or in the days ahead, and if you break that word, as God is my witness, you will suffer for it. What is your answer, Provost?' Whitfield blustered, but agreed.

Lydford next spoke, 'What does the learned Doctor, who himself is so concerned with these translations, think of this audacious plan? And Middleworth, too, what are his comments?'

Thorpe, the senior fellow present rose, and, quietly, pointed out that this enterprise was the concern of the six people present in the room. They, and only they, were being expelled. Doctor Wyclif was a commensalis, a Hall guest of honour indeed. William Middleworth had long been his close colleague and confidant - had he not followed his mentor to Queen's? 'Middleworth is a fellow as we were, but though a southerner has not been actually expelled. Perhaps his recently acquired royal patronage lies behind this leniency. We feel that we must not involve those of our friends, who have not lost favour, in our scheme even to the extent of discussions. The possession of our secret might constitute an awkward and uncomfortable bedfellow for the learned Doctor and our old friend William Middleworth, and create a sharp conflict of conscience - should they, or should they not, divulge the details to the authorities, and so wreck our whole campaign? This risk, for their sakes and ours, we dare not take. Well comrades, are we resolved? If so, I suggest we go about our lawful and unlawful tasks.'

By nightfall all members of Hall were aware that the six would leave by Martinmas at latest. Furthermore much of their impedimenta had already been deposited at their new accommodation.

Martinmas dawned cold but dry. This the rebels realized was a factor much in their favour, for it would lessen considerably the risk of damage to the books, manuscripts and other valuables - were they fortunate enough to obtain them.

The final clearing of their rooms was begun early, and by the time the Council had gone into session the last of their goods and chattles, except for a few old garments, had been transported to St. Ebb's. This completed, the conspirators returned to Queen's and assembled in the library, which, to their relief, was empty. Lydford and Thorpe fetched the old garments and baskets for transportation, while Frank, Hereford and Trevisa, working rapidly from their list, gathered as many of the required works as they could find. These included:-

Unum librum Catholican
Unum bibliam
Moralia beati Gregorii super Joob
Concordanc
Crisostomum super Matheum
Augustinum de civitate Dei
Doctorem de Lira in parte super proverbia Salmonis
Liram super salterium
Librum super Genesim a diversis tractatoribus
Tabulam philosophie et theologie

To Trevisa's dismay Higden's *Polychronicon* was not in its customary place. Frank, however, remembered Carlisle discussing certain passages from it the previous day, and they concluded that the manuscript might well be in his rooms. Now came the problem of how to obtain the keys giving access to the chests where the charter, seal and other valuables were kept. The Provost's room posed a similar problem. The rehearsed plan was quickly put into operation. Frank and Lydford, each carrying a small bottle of ale, engaged the janitor in conversation and gradually lured him out of his lodge. The waiting Hereford and Trevisa quickly slipped through the door and selected the necessary keys. How grateful the latter was now for the earlier term of office as treasurer of Queen's, thus giving him the needful knowledge for the identification of the keys and the location of the respective chests. It was a relief, also, to see Carlisle's room key upon the desk. Ten minutes later Hereford, Thorpe and Trevisa passed through the lodge gates and the charter, seal, treasure-chest keys and that of Carlisle's room and other valuables, as well as the *Polychronicon* (what a relief to Trevisa it had been to find this in Carlisle's room!), — all loosely wrapped in the old garments — were on their way across the city. Lydford, as the trio passed, received the code word of success and, after a decent interval, followed them. Frank remained until the ale had been consumed and, bidding the janitor farewell, made his way up the High.

(e) St. Ebb's

Four friends from Stapledon Hall and three from Merton joined the newly established six that evening, partly to welcome them into their fresh lodgings, and partly to reinforce their numbers, should the Queen's authorities react with speed and violence. Before seven o'clock shouting was heard in the street and heavy blows shook the stout oaken door. Hereford opened the grill and saw a crowd of ten or twelve — led by Carlisle himself — waving clubs and bows. Only one sword, and that worn by the Provost, could be seen.

The besieged were relieved, for the forces against them could well have been twice that number. Thorpe, through the grill, then addressed Carlisle:- 'Why come you here with sticks, staves and bows? Have you not done enough harm? You have caused our fellowships to be taken away, distinctions and privileges that were legally bestowed, and expelled us from your community. Our future, and our life's work for the cause of Christ, may suffer by this cruel and unjust deprivation'.

Before this appeal had ended Carlisle stormed to the front and roared:- 'Thieves! Vagabonds! You shall pay for this I promise you.' Thorpe replied:- 'Silence my friend! Your blusterings and threats fall on deaf ears, for we fear you not. We strive to serve God through these translations, so hinder us not, lest thou find thyself opposing God's will, and suffer for it.' The grill closed with a snap as the first arrow hit the metal frame and shattered. The door was again attacked with clubs and several arrows came through the windows. The assault, it seemed, had begun in earnest. Suddenly the attackers withdrew fifty yards and there conferred. This move worried those within, who wondered what devilry was being planned. Trevisa, almost in soliloquy, said:- 'They are up to something. Can it be that they will try to find a large post or log to use as a battering ram? Our counter to that, my friends, must be boiling water from the window directly over the doorway. This ruse will need to be executed with accuracy and speed if we are to avoid the shafts from any archer whom they place strategically to cover the approach and employment of a battering ram party.'

A quarter of an hour later the attackers made a concerted assault upon the door with clubs and shoulders, but the stout planks held firm. Stones and hot water — it had not come to the boil — hurled from above scattered the enemy, who retired to a safe distance from whence they kept up a torrent of abuse. An hour or more passed, but the clamour showed no sign of abating, and the besieged wondered whether Carlisle was remaining in the hope, or expectation, may be, of reinforcements, which might enable them once more to rush the door — perhaps this time with a battering ram — and force an entrance. After half an hour Alexander, a fellow of Merton, proposed that, as there appeared to be no opponents at the rear of the buildings, he should slip out, along St. Ebb's and make for Merton by way of the river meadows, and gather a band of southerners and sympathizers — he thought he might recruit eight to ten. With these he would then lead an assault upon the attackers rear, at which moment the besieged would sally forth. Thus, in theory, caught between two forces, the enemy might well be put to flight. All this presupposed that Carlisle and his men had not mounted a successful attack before the relieving force had been mustered and brought to the start line.

Minutes passed — minutes that seemed laggardly and interminable — a time of waiting which tried the nerves of all within. Suddenly there was a babel of voices from the eastern end of St. Aldates Street. The besiegers turned, as one man, to see what this noise represented, and realized at once that whoever those approaching might be, their intentions, obviously, were hostile. As Carlisle's party closed ranks to repel the attackers, the besieged, led by Hereford and Trevisa, sallied forth from their 'fortress' and with staves (they had no other offensive weapons) whirling entered the arena. The affray was short lived. Surprise and weight of numbers proved too much for the Queen's contingent. Seven managed to break through the Merton ranks leaving the remaining six (including Carlisle) virtually prisoners of war. These were taken within, where the casualties were attended to and the unconscious man — felled by a swinging stave — revived.

The essentials completed, Trevisa turned to Carlisle and said:- 'Provost, this whole ugly affair is not of our making. For some time you have deliberately made life, for a number of us, well nigh unbearable. Finally you contrived the expulsion of six of us, despite the fact that several, under the direction of Doctor Wyclif, were fully engaged in the translation of the Bible into our native tongue, thereby we hoped, extending Christ's Kingdom here on earth. You and your masters, including my Lord of York and his Grace, the Archbishop, have forbidden us to continue this work. We believed that God has called us to this important task. May I remind you of the reply given by Holy Peter and the Beloved Disciple to Annas, Caiaphas and other members of the Council when they forbade them to speak or teach in the name of Jesus? Peter and John answered them thus — "whether it be right in the sight of God to harken unto you more than unto God, judge ye". Think, too, of the warning given by Gamaliel to the Jewish rulers who had arrested the apostles a second time. That fine doctor of the law said:- "Refrain from these men, and let them alone: for if this counsel or this work be of men, it will come to nought: But if it be of God, ye cannot overthrow it; lest haply ye be found even to fight against God." '

'You may go now, but beware that you seek not to avenge yourselves for this day's work, nor strive to harm our community. I sware by Almighty God that if you do so you yourself will suffer for it.'

The exiles continued their self-appointed task the following day while the servants removed as far as possible the scars of conflict. Finance, however, was the most urgent problem discussed at their council meeting held on the third evening in their new quarters. Rent for six months had been secured, wages for the servants, too, were in hand for a month or more, and food and drink enough for several weeks were stored within. Wages and victuals would, no doubt, present a problem after a month or two, and although, through the good offices of kind friends, this period might be extended, to Lent or Easter or even Michaelmas, the situation could well become embarrassing. Trevisa finally suggested that he should ride to Berkeley and seek his patron's financial support for the completion of the biblical project. He pointed out that Carlisle could not be expected to sit down quietly under the recent indignities. He might well fight shy of direct violence, but would undoubtedly be, even now, seeking powerful political and ecclesiastical backing — and his case could be made to appear damning — to put down their scholastically schismatic body and to haul their members before an Archbishop's Court on several quite heinous charges. Finance, Trevisa pointed out, was but one aspect of their need; the other, and perhaps — in the final issue — the more vital, was support, vigorous and vocal, in high places, over and above that which they might well receive from Doctor Wyclif's patron, the noble Duke of Lancaster. Lord Berkeley, for all his lack of years — he was still less than thirty years of age, had many and powerful friends who were not confined to the ranks of the laity. Time, Trevisa pointed out, was vital, and was not on their side. He would ride at dawn and return within the week, if his master was in residence at either Berkeley or one of his neighbouring houses. Trevisa suggested, furthermore, that one other of their number should at once approach his patron, and that after both had returned to Oxford the remaining members might also strive to obtain the moral, physical and financial support which he now felt they would need desperately in the weeks and months ahead. This policy, then, was accepted.

Soon after dawn Trevisa left the city behind him. He did not force the pace, walking the bay up hill and at regular intervals. The 'Bull' at Burford produced a reasonable cold meal and a tankard of mulled ale at 10.30. The ostler rubbed down and fed Berkeley Star a light meal, and by 11.30 rider and mount were heading for Cirencester, where again they rested and ate. It was dark before Trevisa saw the lights of Tetbury, and nearly fifty miles had been covered since dawn — a heavy day for man and beast. The hospitality of the Community of St. Nicholas was lavish, and a tired and rather saddle-sore Trevisa slept well. The following morning the remaining eighteen miles to Berkeley were covered before mid-day although the road down the Cotswold escarpment into Dursley — if road it could be called — was slippery with the wet chalk, and necessitated extreme caution and some deviation.

The sentry above the gate greeted the priest with surprise, and it was some seconds before he grasped that the message for his Lordship was urgent — but then Will Nelmes was always markedly slow in the uptake, though loyal and trustworthy.

That evening the youthful nobleman, but recently returned from the wars, listened carefully to the cleric's tale, told with a frankness characteristic of the man. Trevisa admitted freely the illegality of several of their actions, but claimed that the official charges against himself and his colleagues were ostensible only — had not these very conditions existed ever since the election of Hereford, Middleworth and himself nearly ten years ago? It was also true that another southerner had been elected in '75, but hardly a voice had been raised against the policy on either occasion. The real reason for the late outburst was, no doubt, the unease felt by a few members of the hierarchy — a feeling fanned by the friars — that the Bible should be an ecclesiastical preserve, and that it should be withheld, a hidden book, from the common man whose Latin was negligible, or non-existent. A second reason, so said Trevisa, and one that confirmed the hostility of the bishops and friars alike, was that one of the principals of the biblical translation campaign was Doctor Wyclif, whose teachings had, of late, come in for sharp criticism from entrenched authority, who saw, no doubt, in the project further evidence of Wyclif's heretical beliefs, and confirmation of his open undermining of ecclesiastical status and privilege.

My Lord Berkeley listened intently, but said not a word until the cleric had done. After a few moments of silence out shot the questions:- 'Is it really desirable or lawful to translate the Scriptures, so that anyone with but little learning can read therefrom? Is it not better that the Word of God should remain in a tongue understood only by the erudite who may thus be able to interpret fully and correctly the meaning of each paragraph and phrase to those of us who have not had your schooling?'

'My Lord, there is nothing sacrosanct about any language.[11] It is merely the medium for social intercourse, for logic, for instruction and the dissemination of all knowledge. One nation doth frequently translate works of erudition and interest of another tongue into their own for the use, enjoyment and enlightenment of its people. Have not Aristotle's books, and the works of other authors, been translated from Greek into Latin, and into French also? There is nothing unethical in translating these and other books into English. Holy Writ has been subjected to the same treatment with, again, no protests. Did not the seventy translate the Hebrew Scriptures into Greek for the use of the Jews of the Diaspora and their Gentile proselytes? Later were not those same Greek Scriptures translated into Latin for the Western Church whose tongue it largely was? It cannot be unlawful to give Holy Writ to our people in a language they understand. Think back, my Lord, to Holy Bede. Seven centuries ago he gave Englishmen the Gospel of St. John in the language of the day, and our great scholar-King, Alfred, turned much of the important legal code and of the psalter out of Latin into English. He caused other works to be given in like manner to his people. All this and much else happened without protest, indeed with evident approbation. The faith, doctrine and history of Mother Church must still be taught, and why not through the medium of the Scriptures themselves? And be it remembered that those same Scriptures are today not read in their original tongue, but in a translated version. At no time in the past was it judged unwise or sinful to give Englishmen Holy Writ in their own language. The opposition, my Lord, today is roused largely by the preaching brethren, the fat friars, who so often interpret the Scriptures as pleaseth them, and from which they derive no mean advantage. I myself have heard them misquote and mistranslate. To me it hath seemed at times that those mistakes were intentional, for many of those men - friars and others - are learned priests. Maybe they saw therein some advantage or financial gain. They tend to grow fat and lazy through their blasphemous fraud.' His Lordship rose to his feet:- 'You, yourself, have heard this cruel deception being perpetrated?' 'Yes, my Lord', replied the cleric, 'and not only once. I recall two occasions, one in France and another in England. Once near Oxford I challenged a statement by a friar; whereupon I was branded an heretic - and at once he sought to incite the crowd against me. These friars, often are an evil and corrupt community, and in the making clear of God's Word they see the ruination of much of their financial gain. My Lord, I implore you to support Doctor Wyclif's project, in which I, too, am playing, and have for some years, off and on, played my part. I served faithfully your noble father before my ordination, when he befriended me; and I sware, as the Holy Family and Blessed Peter and Paul are my witnesses, I would not deceive you in any matter, and will always remain your loyal servant.'

Trevisa sat down, and my Lord of Berkeley spoke slowly - 'This, Master Trevisa, is a matter of some moment and needs much thought. If I agree to your request, at once I line myself up against Mother Church, in the person of the Archbishop, and that is no light affair. Furthermore the friars have their feet under the table in many great houses, and possess the ears of half the nobility of England. I will talk with you tomorrow after mass. In the meanwhile take a horse and ride over to Wanswell and bid Master Elias Saniger dine with me at four o'clock. The Sanigers will be pleased to see you and to have news of their friend, Richard Thorpe, your companion in misfortune. I will send a horseman to Bradston also and request Sir Henry's attendance, too, at dinner. You may be with us, if you wish, but depart when the table has been cleared. I must leave you and think.'

The following morning at mass Trevisa sensed that his mission had met with some success. Confirmation of this came directly he met his Lordship in the withdrawing room. His patron's words were brief and to the point. 'I discussed your request with Sir Henry Bradston and Master Elias Saniger, and we agreed that biblical translation is desirable. We will communicate with certain people and solicit their support should, as you feel possible, influential personages be persuaded to attempt strong action against you. I counsel you, Master Trevisa, do not become involved in the weird doctrines put forth occasionally by Doctor Wyclif and certain of his friends. Be circumspect, and pay no heed if invited to support their cause. The learned Wyclif may have the patronage of my Lord Duke of Lancaster, but in all probability will be proscribed for his denial of certain doctrines held by Mother Church. To attack transubstantiation is to attack the very words of the Master Himself, when He said in the Upper Room, "This is my body, this is my blood" - or so it seems to me and to many others. Translation is one thing, heresy is a very different matter. While on the subject of turning Latin books into English, have you considered the possibilities of translating important non-biblical works - historical ones for example - into our tongue? This might be considered when the present project has been completed. Finally, I am sending Jenkins back with you to Oxford. He is a fine horseman and a good servant. You may find him useful. In addition, should an emergency arise he could bring me word within a few hours. I ride to Gloucester this afternoon so will bid you farewell now, and may God support and protect you.'

Trevisa found all well and quiet on his return to Oxford. Hereford, continuing his labours, had been assisted for two days by Middleworth, and Wyclif had joined them one evening to discuss progress. Lydford returned three days later, whereupon Hereford and Frank set out to seek further support and backing, in case of necessity. The response of the patrons was somewhat disappointing. Hereford and Trevisa alone achieved any marked success. In addition to Lord Berkeley, Bradston and Saniger, two of the de Bohun family and Sir John Oldcastle applauded their stand, promising aid, both financial and personal. The qualified support of the de Bohun family was unexpected but most welcome. Young Henry, son of John of Gaunt, also offered advice, and promised, if really necessary, physical backing. All had declared their willingness to seek support for the acceptance of the principle of 'An English Bible for the English People'. The Grandisson family, and in particular Sir Peter, although — as Nicholas put it — 'riddled with episcopal tradition', were guardedly approving. It seemed that the West, more than the South West, gave support to the open Bible.

Chapter 7
A Return to Berkeley

(a) *An Ill-Timed Arrival*

To Trevisa there was no obvious alternative to Berkeley for himself when the final departure from Oxford was imposed upon the rebels, indeed he desired none other. His patron already knew of the expulsion from Queen's and the setting up of the rival establishment. He had, indeed, expressed the opinion that 'Authority', especially after the expropriation of the seal, silver and books - he had refrained from terming it theft, would ultimately be compelled to take firm action, rusticating if not imprisoning the malcontents. No doubt Lord Berkeley was already prepared for his return.

The arrival at the Castle was ill-timed, for my Lord of Berkeley was entertaining Henry Blebury, Abbot of St. Augustine's, who at dinner had been holding forth upon the evils of a party of militant hooligans, 'no doubt tainted with these new-fangled doctrines repugnant to Mother Church', who had caused considerable trouble at Oxford. It appeared that the Abbot had only heard one name mentioned, a someone called Thorpe, reputed to have come originally from Bristol.

Trevisa, on entering the great Hall, was soon noticed by his patron, who beckoned him to come above the salt. Reluctantly, having heard snatches of the coversation, Trevisa moved forward to the High Table, where he was placed nearly opposite the high dignitary, to whom he was introduced as Lord Berkeley's future domestic chaplain.

The Abbot, hearing that Trevisa had recently been at Oxford, asked for the latest news of the trouble at Queen's, and of his own feelings concerning the dispute. The priest, choosing his words carefully, spoke slowly and said, 'Well, Father, the dispute has been resolved. Some members of the group have returned, so I believe, to residence, while a few have dispersed to other establishments. The Provost of Queen's appears satisfied with the outcome.' Lord Berkeley quickly turned the coversation into other channels.

The next morning, when mass had ended, the Abbot took his host on one side, saying, 'My Lord, may I have a word in your ear?'

'I am at your service Father, let us go to the outer courtyard, the sun is out and the gentle walk will be beneficial to us both. Well, we are alone now. Can I be of service to you, Father Abbot?'

'No! No! My Lord! My object is not mendicity, but to sound a note of warning. Last night at table you suggested that Master Trevisa might one day become your domestic chaplain. I counsel you, my Lord, to consider carefully, very carefully, the wisdom of such a move. Trevisa's replies to my questions last evening were, at times, evasive. I discussed the matter with my chaplain, Father Michael, and he seemed to feel that Master Trevisa knew more than he revealed. Father Michael could not be certain, but he thought that he had heard such a name connected with the trouble at Queen's. Trevisa may be an able man, indeed a considerable scholar, but I suspect that he has been associating at Oxford with men whose doctrinal beliefs would, at times, seem to be unorthodox, to say the least. Furthermore, his own conduct has not always been acceptable to the authorities, or so it is reported. I doubt whether my Lord Bishop would sanction such an appointment if your Lordship applied to him. I certainly could not, after my chaplain's comments - and what he did not say, conscientiously support your request for such a licence, should my Lord Bishop consult me on the matter.'

'Father Abbot, you are, I conceive, concerned for my moral and spiritual welfare, and for this kind thought I am deeply grateful. Are you not, however, a little hard on this priest, a man who was born and bred on my Cornish estates? Trevisa was educated at Glasney, and later, entered the establishment of Lord John Grandisson, who more than fifty years ago succeeded my relation [1] as Bishop of Exeter. In both instances his reports were glowing, and his orthodoxy unquestioned. Furthermore from Paris and Stapledon Hall no detrimental comments were received.'

'Well, my Lord, I can appreciate your feelings and your wish - and duty also - to defend one who has had the benefit of Berkeley patronage for most of his life. Do not, however, in your kindness, perhaps mistaken kindness, damage your own image and reputation in the eyes of your peers or of Mother Church.'

'Thank you Father Abbot, I will ponder well upon your words.'

Soon after the departure of the Abbot and his train Lord Berkeley sent for Trevisa and demanded an account of the latest developments at Oxford. On hearing the whole story his Lordship laughed and said, 'Well, what is Queen's loss, is my gain. You can now be licenced to me at once as my chaplain. In view of Father Abbot's feelings on the matter of the recent expulsion of 'certain rude and vicious madmen' from Queen's, it would be foolish in the extreme to approach my Lord Bishop requesting approval for your appointment, for Father Abbot will, I judge, move quickly in this matter. He may well warn the Bishop of the dangers of introducing a possible fiery heretic and iconoclast - newly expelled from Oxford - into his diocese. We must act with speed coupled with caution, for Father Abbot, in his present mood, will not shrink from attempting to influence, to his advantage, the choice of my chaplain. I will have no illiterate or thieving mass-priest, nor Father Abbot's toady, as my father confessor who would reveal my secret thoughts to the highest bidder.

'There is another matter which may guide - and help - us in this problem. I intend shortly to visit France, furthermore I could well be employed in warlike expeditions into Scotland. Lady Margaret, my wife, now of full age, has expressed the wish to accompany me on some of these travels, certainly to France. She has asked whether it would be possible to attend mass daily on the peaceful expeditions. Perhaps his Holiness, Pope Urban, for a consideration - a handsome consideration of course - would issue a two-fold licence, firstly for the use of a portable altar-stone (and this request is not infrequently granted), and secondly giving me leave to appoint a suitable and learned chaplain to celebrate thereon. Thus we may circumvent any possible action by Father Abbot. Later if these petitions are granted, I will make further application to the Pope for the privilege of naming a successor to Master David as vicar of Berkeley. Master David, of Melkesham, was thrust upon my grandfather, and though in some respects a good parish priest, is one who has never fully studied the wishes and welfare of my family. He fails to appreciate the needs and feelings of those above the status of a cottager or tavern-keeper. You, Sir

Priest, have shown, when here earlier in lay employ, that with your country background and innate love of rural sports and pastimes, you have an understanding of the lives and problems of most strata of country folk, and your enterprise in translation reveals your desire for their betterment. Scholar you may be, but a human one, and it is such we need in place of the good Master David. I must leave now. We will meet again tomorrow to formulate our plans. In the meanwhile ponder over the method of approaching his Holiness.'

Later that day the priest retired to the keep chapel to pray and think. The idea of settling down as a domestic chaplain even to the youthful Lord Berkeley, much though he, Trevisa, admired his ability and, indeed, what he termed his radical but realistic outlook on life, did not attract him.

The urge to present the English people with important works of history, general knowledge and the Bible itself, was still uppermost in his mind, and he felt that this was intended by God to be one of the major items in his life's mission. Would he here in the west, so far from Oxford, have sufficient time and facility, and above all sympathy, to continue that which to him appeared so important a task?

Then there was the suggestion that when Father David ceased to be vicar of Berkeley, either by departure or death - and he had been parish priest for twenty-nine years, he, Trevisa, should succeed to the cure. Lord Berkeley had made it plain that he wished his chaplain also to be vicar, a combination of offices which, on paper, appeared natural, but which, in Trevisa's mind, could be difficult, and might create agonies of conscience, and a conflict of duties which could well be insoluble.

He could not abandon his work, this mission, when his total contribution to turning had been but a limited amount of biblical translation. The putting on one side of *Piers the Plowman,* too, was a troubling thought. No, he must talk sensibly - and frankly - to my Lord of Berkeley, who might grant him leave at times to continue this life's ambition - even if only in a modified form, provided, of course, that a return to Oxford was permitted. If not, he might even be compelled to consider that upstart establishment in the fenland, though Heaven grant that such a course would not be necessary! The distance alone was daunting, while the facilities, it was said, left much to be desired. The air, he had been told, was unhealthy, and the natives, at times, barely civilised.

(b) *The Die is Cast*

The following morning Trevisa had opportunity to see His Lordship alone. Knowing the possibility of interruption the priest came quickly to the point:- 'My Lord, I have given much thought to your assumption that I should become officially your domestic chaplain. I am deeply, indeed very deeply, conscious of the many kindnesses bestowed upon me - and my family too - by your Lordship and my Lords your father and grandfather. I have had the honour of serving the late Lord Berkeley as personal secretary for a considerable time, and during that period came to love, and look upon, Berkeley as my real home. However, I have also, within me, a vital urge, as your Lordship is aware, to see English people with a literature written in their own language. My Lord, you are a well informed person, and have an understanding of the modern trends.   No longer is French understood as once it was, even scholars are now giving instruction in English instead of the former language, and lately some official documents were issued, for maybe the first time, in the native tongue. Latin is no longer widely understood. The result is that our people are being deprived of the means of self instruction and amusement, because so much is still available only in languages with which they no longer are familiar. It was this thought and realization which drove our small group at Queen's to translate - somewhat hurriedly and imperfectly I fear - the Scriptures. I have some skill, which God has given me, in this turning, and I feel, and believe, that I have a duty not to give up this work completely. I would appreciate, and would feel highly honoured to be your domestic chaplain, but I would like the opportunity to continue in some measure translating works of importance into English for our people. Would you, my Lord, envisage this as a possibility, or would the duties as chaplain preclude such exercise?'

'Sir Priest, I have known you since I was but a child, and have always understood that your scholarship was considerable. Consequently let me make two points. First, I realize that you could hardly be expected to settle down to a rude and rustic life deprived of all intellectual contacts and occupations. Such a life would, for you, be little removed from incarceration, to which was added mental torture. The second point, and one you should have recalled, is that I, too, have sat at Doctor Wyclif's feet [2], and like you and him, have a leaning towards popularising the vernacular. I fully appreciate the change of policy and emphasis in our schools in the matter of French and English. Last year I went to Cornwall and talked with a relation of Richard Pencriche and men of similar tastes. I am aware that increasingly English must become the language of trade and literature, as well as of social intercourse; indeed the Church and the legal system must ultimately come to terms with this new-found feeling of separateness, of Englishness, the desire of our people to be a nation apart, no longer tied to the lands of France, Normandy, Aquitaine, Poitou or Guyenne, by family links whereof the blood has run thin, and continued largely because of the ambitions of warlike and grasping men. No, Father, I should not expect you to give up completely your important work; indeed I would wish you to continue what you already have begun. Neither the abbeys of Bristol, Gloucester, Hereford nor Malmesbury - all within comparatively easy distance of Berkeley - are devoid of scholarship, and all have libraries of considerable importance. These places you might visit with some degree of regularity. If the Provost of Queen's relents, and you become once more persona grata to the Council at Oxford, I see no problem in your returning for specified periods for study, to forward the project so near your heart. Does this satisfy you? I need you as my father confessor, my guide and my counsellor. I am young, and in some degree inexperienced, and ahead, and not so far ahead maybe, could be problems of great complexity, and even dangers affecting the whole of this country. What is your answer?'

'My Lord, you are most generous, and your understanding astonishing. I rejoice that Your Lordship feels as I do, and so with these assurances, I most gratefully accept the office of chaplain, subject to official ratification by his Holiness.'

(c)*Papal leave and a diplomatic acceptance*

Trevisa found the next few months a period of tension and anxiety, for the negotiations with the Vatican and with Queen's were protracted. The Papal office, by tradition and practice, moved ponderously, appearing to be unconscious of, some maintained indifferent to, the need for haste in most petitions and supplications. Of course an honorarium - one must not suggest the word bribe! - to certain officials could, and often did, expedite matters. Both Lord Berkeley and Trevisa were fully aware of these practices - as indeed were most people of position, and appropriate action had been taken. Nevertheless it was late in October before the Papal permissions, dated 7th July 1378, arrived [3].

Lord Berkeley lost no time. Within a few days copies of these important documents were sent to the Bishop, notifying his Lordship that Lord Berkeley was making formal request that a portable altar, duly consecrated, might be dispatched to Berkeley Castle, at the episcopal convenience of course. Lord Berkeley also informed the Ordinary that he would be most grateful if his Lordship would licence Master John Trevisa as domestic chaplain. Lord Berkeley thought it likely that the Bishop would not be pleased by this request, for by this time the Abbot of St. Augustine's would, undoubtedly, have given his Lordship a full and colourful account of Trevisa's arrival in Berkeley and the suspicion expressed by Father Michael, Abbot Blebury's chaplain. The Abbot might well have suggested that Trevisa was an undesirable cleric. Lord Berkeley felt reasonably certain, however, that my Lord Bishop, whatever his personal feelings, would not refuse to recognise and honour the Papal mandate.

Lord Berkeley, at the same time, despatched a further formal request to the Papal office that he might be granted the patronage of the vicarage of Berkeley at the next voidance. His Lordship assured the members of the Curia that he had no complaint against Master David of Melkesham, the present incumbent, who had been a conscientious minister of the Word and sacraments for more than thirty years. His Lordship, indeed, expressed surprise that the vicar had not received preferment after such a long and faithful service. The former added that it was in the expectation of some such promotion for the vicar that he was making this petition.

Lord Henry Wakefield, the Bishop of Worcester, woke with a splitting headache. He reflected with irritation that he had had his doubts concerning the cask of malmsey, newly broached, when he had taken but a glass two nights ago. Last night, admittedly, he had thoughtlessly consumed rather more than had been good for him. The fault for this, however, lay not with himself but in the circumstance of the evening. That boring envoy of the Archbishop would not go to bed - the wretched fellow! How he loved the sound of his own voice!

The Bishop rang his bell, summoning his domestic chaplain, and prepared to rise; the latter effort, however, brought considerable discomfort. Later in the morning Lord Berkeley's letter was placed in the episcopal hand, a somewhat shaky one withal, and remained there unopened for several minutes. Finally the seal was broken and the contents carefully considered, after which the chaplain was sent to locate the Archdeacon.

The Archdeacon read Lord Berkeley's letter and, after a pause, said:- 'My Lord, this, is indeed, unfortunate; though, mark you, my Lord, I am not sure that I fully agree with all that the Abbot of St. Augustine's wrote and insinuated. That Trevisa was involved in the troubles in Queen's there is no possible doubt, but it seems equally clear - your Lordship will recall that you ordered me to make enquiries - that there was considerable provocation. The new Provost is a rude, harsh and, I found, an unpleasant man. Furthermore I understand that he himself did not come out from the troubles with a shining and unbesmirched reputation. I have it on substantial authority that he received a verbal reprimand and has been ordered to restore the fellowships to those expelled, should they make representation. If they wish, however, to return as commensales - and this to my mind is a more likely request, for most, if not all, concerned now hold preferments, the financial emoluments of which might well exclude them from receiving a fellowship, they must be accepted. I smell the hand of his Grace of Lancaster behind these directives. Finally my Lord Berkeley is not one to be thwarted lightly. He is held in high esteem in court and military circles, and his voice is not ignored in substantial ecclesiastical spheres. It would, my Lord, I believe, be unwise to cross him, and at the same time disregard the Holy Father's instructions, especially when the issue, which looms so large in the mind of Father Abbot, is, in reality, the comparatively insignificant appointment of a domestic chaplain. It is better that his Lordship should be under an obligation to you - however slight - than that his ire should be roused.'

'I agree, and will comply with both requests. I will also arrange that the licencing shall take place at Berkeley, in the parish church. I will, furthermore, carry out this duty personally. While at the castle (and of necessity my Lord Berkeley will be compelled to invite one to stay) I will investigate the possibility of having this Trevisa appointed to one of the numerous chantries at Berkeley. If this can be achie ved we would have a better opportunity of keeping an eye on, and hold upon, this not so young firebrand.   What say you?'

'A very sound plan, my Lord, and also if I may say so, a most subtle move.'

(d) *Achievement and Future Strategy*

Lord Thomas was surprised to receive his Lordship's reply almost by return. He was even more astonished at the friendly tone of the epistle.

'Trevisa, you are indeed singled out for preferential treatment. You will receive the licence from the Bishop himself, and not at the hands of his Archdeacon or the Rural Dean. I congratulate you, but, at the same time, we must be on our guard. I feel that his Lordship's visit portends more than a friendly gesture. Maybe he wishes to see both you and me, and to warn us of dangers in certain practices or people. Time, however, will tell, and at least our main objective is being achieved. I wonder whether his reply will be as benign if and when I am able to inform him that the Holy Father has granted my request to exercise the right of patronage at Berkeley's next voidance?'

'That, my Lord, may well be a horse of a different colour, and let us not build too high hopes upon the outcome of your latest petition to the Curia.'

There was upheaval at the Castle when the size of the Bishop's entourage was known - and grumbles too from those whose accommodation would be affected or whose chores would be greatly increased. The look-out on the keep gave ample notice of the episcopal train's arrival. The considerable column was sighted crossing the heath and could be heard well before its head reached the causeway bridging the watermeadows below Canonbury.

That evening my Lord Bishop requested that Trevisa should be interviewed by himself, but in the presence of Lord Berkeley and the Archdeacon. Lord Berkeley agreed; and, when the meal had ended, instructed his steward to remove all retainers from the Hall - Lord Berkeley, himself, gave the ladies 'leave to retire'. There remained at the high table only Lord Berkeley, the Bishop, the Archdeacon and Trevisa.

Lord Berkeley then spoke:- 'My Lord Bishop, I am most appreciative of the singular honour bestowed upon us by your visit to Berkeley Castle, and I am grateful for your Lordship's personal interest in the licencing of my chaplain. Master Trevisa is, I know, equally conscious of your kindness. It is, no doubt, concerning tomorrow's ceremony your Lordship wishes to speak.'

'Thank you, my Lord. Yes, I had thought to speak of these matters, but I understand that my Archdeacon has already explained the procedure both to Master David Melkesham, your vicar, and also Master Trevisa. Isn't that so Trevisa?' 'Yes, my Lord, he has given us full instructions.'

'Good. We can in consequence come at once to the real purpose of this meeting. My Lord, let us not beat about the bush; and Trevisa, please understand that what I shall say, indeed must be as your Ordinary make abundantly clear, is intended for your future good, and is not in the nature of an official reprimand. You, Master Trevisa, were concerned, somewhat heavily involved, it is said, in the late troubles at Queen's Hall at Oxford. Certain facts and suspicions were reported to me, but, because those fellows, whom rumour said were behind the troubles, all came from the west, I had previously caused my Archdeacon to make careful, but discreet, inquiries into the whole affair. I reached the conclusion that though the expelled fellows offended greviously against law and order, and behaved disgracefully towards authority, and flaunted even the Archiepiscopal and Royal instructions, yet they had been considerably provoked. This, mark you, Master Trevisa, is no justification for their actions and their defiance of the highest authority in the land. I have considered all this most carefully, and I believe that you, Trevisa, may well have been unduly influenced by a person, or persons, whose doctrinal utterances have, of late, become suspect, and whose views on canonical obedience leave much to be desired. If I licence you tomorrow, I will expect that you will abjure these heretical views with which, no doubt, you became familiar at Oxford, and that you will in future accept all lawful authority and injunction. That, my Lord Berkeley, is all I wished to say to your chaplain, but I felt that your Lordship should be present when I gave my charge. Your Lordship will, I know, fully support me now and in the future.'

'My Lord Bishop, I fully appreciate all that you have done and said, and I am sure Master Trevisa is most grateful for the interest and pains your Lordship has taken in the investigation of the Queen's troubles and their causes, and also for your Lordship's understanding and patronage.'

Two days later the Lord Bishop lodged at St. Peter's Abbey in Gloucester, and Trevisa had already begun life as the official chaplain to Lord Berkeley and his establishment.

Chapter 8
Polychronicon

(a) *The Preparation*

Months passed and spring had given way to summer before an answer came from Queen's.

It ran somewhat thus:- 'The Provost and Council have received the application of Master John Trevisa, supported by Lord Thomas, Lord of Berkeley, to be allowed, at some future date, not specified, to take up residence in Queen's Hall for the purposes of study and research. The request has been carefully considered and, bearing in mind the restitution in full of college properties feloniously taken in the recent past, the Council give tentative permission in general principle. The final details of date and standing will need to be discussed when Master Trevisa is able to be more precise, and preferably when the latter can be present to answer possible questions. The appointment of Master Trevisa as chaplain to Lord Berkeley, involving, no doubt, certain financial considerations, may make Lord Berkeley's chaplain ineligible for a fellowship; in which case there would appear to be little or no objection to Master Trevisa's entering Queen's as a commensalis. This alternative status might indeed give him greater freedom of time and choice of subject, thereby enabling him to order his research programme and study timetable in a manner better suited to his personal wishes and needs.'

This was a relief, but the ease of mind was tempered by the knowledge that a return to Oxford was a pleasure that would probably have to be deferred indefinitely, perhaps for several years. A chaplain, so soon after licencing, could scarcely expect to be granted leave to study, thus abandoning his recently acquired cure. The expedition being mounted in support of the Duke of Brittany was a further complication. Lord Berkeley had been invited to bring a contingent, and appeared to have every intention of going; but was he, the chaplain, to be included in the Berkeley party? The problems of supplies and transport, of necessity, limited the number of non-combatants that could be taken on a distant campaign. A casual remark of his Lordship, 'It is fortunate, Sir Priest, that my requests to his Holiness have been granted, and that the portable altar has already been consecrated and delivered by my Lord Bishop', however, seemed indicative.

Trevisa enjoyed his new status, and he felt that his already considerable knowledge of Berkeley and its people, much of it gleaned while he was secretary to his Lordship's father in the 1360's, gave him a distinct advantage. The uncertainty about the expedition and himself worried Trevisa, and then suddenly, and unexpectedly, Lord Berkeley, at high table, turned to his chaplain and said:- 'How are your preparations going, Sir Priest? You realize, I hope, that I will expect you to celebrate mass for me, and also for the retinue? You must, in addition, be prepared to help with the sick and wounded, and to comfort the dying, though, please God, these will be few. You will fully appreciate all that I have been saying.'

'Thank you, my Lord, for clarifying my position. I had assumed, after thinking about the licencing, that your Lordship would require me to act during the expedition along exactly the same lines as here in the castle; in other words in a twofold capacity, first as your domestic chaplain, and then as chaplain to the Berkeley contingent.'

'Yes, with, be it remembered, the emphasis on the domestic side.'

'My Lady Margaret will, of course, not be coming?'

'Certes, NO!'

'Is it your Lordship's wish that Master David, the vicar, shall act as chaplain to the castle during our absence, or would the chantry priest of St. Maurice be a better choice? The latter would appear to have a clearer appreciation of the needs of the nobility and of their way of life. If I may be so bold, I would commend the latter, Father Thomas. The mensa, vessels and vestments will, I hope, be carried on a baggage waggon and not on a pack-horse?'

'Steady and slowly, Trevisa! Your questions tumble one after another. Firstly, your deputy while you serve me in Brittany. Father David has a large cure, and is a busy man. He would scarcely welcome the additional work which a temporary attachment to the castle would involve. Father Thomas, on the other hand, could well afford the time. Furthermore, Lady Margaret has confidence in him; so Father Thomas it must be. I leave you to work out the details with Thomas, and you can then report to me. Secondly your priestly luggage. This, and your own personal things, will be loaded on my waggon train, and you, yourself, will ride with my immediate meiny.'

(b) *Brittany and Return*

The pace of preparation gained momentum and rumours increased in number and variety of subject. Consequently when it was announced that the crossing would be made to Calais and not by the more direct, though longer, sea route to Brittany many laughed and discounted it. Later, when it became clear that this was indeed fact, experienced campaigners recalled that last year's expedition had been aborted by shipwreck on a large scale.[1] Many were relieved by this change of plan which thereby reduced the sea voyage so greatly. They were prepared to endure the greatly increased march to avoid what some called the fearsome perils of the deep.

The march on French soil proved much longer than anticipated, for their leader, Thomas, Earl of Buckingham, took them some 200 miles south before turning northwest for Brittany. Many of the experienced common soldiery, and some also amongst the nobility, felt that so long a march, much of it through technically enemy territory, and the parade round the outskirts of Paris, was foolish, in that it risked the loss of fighting personnel and, equally important, gave the opposition in Brittany more time to prepare.

To Trevisa these changes of plan were very acceptable. Having suffered violent discomfort on the short Calais crossing in the past he had been somewhat dolorous about the voyage from Southampton. Furthermore the ride south and round Paris he looked upon with pleasure, and the route north-west to Brittany was largely through a new and exciting countryside. As time passed Trevisa and many of the more thoughtful nobility became depressed by the vacillation of leadership and the protracted and - apparently - useless siege. This military manoeuvre, by its waste of time, virtually wrecked the whole expedition. Indeed, it seemed as though Buckingham and his men had incurred divine disfavour. King Charles of France died, and Charles, the Dauphin, ascended the throne. The Duke of Brittany made his peace with the new king, and the English forces, consequently, were no longer required; they had, in fact, become an embarrassment to the Duke. The English government, too, were embarrassed, but financially, by the sterility of the campaign and the heavy monetary drain. The cost of this abortive attempt to re-establish the prestige and position of the Crown and their one time ally, the Duke, was said to exceed a hundred thousand pounds.

Berkeley in the spring! How pleasant it seemed to Trevisa as their weary and depleted party rode in one May morning. The prospect, however, was a sobering one. The widow of John the Smith would have to be seen, and so would Betsy Nelmes and Alice Trotman, as well as the families whose menfolk had been crippled and maimed. Lady Elizabeth, the widowed mother of Lord Thomas, had already been informed of the death of her third eldest son, Sir John. Nevertheless she, too, would have to be visited. [2] These pastoral visitations, the first of this nature since licensing, daunted him. What could he say to those wretched women which might comfort them, now that the man of the house, the bread winner, had been killed or crippled? It was a grim task, and 'war' had lost any glamour it may once have had for him.

(c) *A Growing Urgency to Return to Queen's*

Lord Berkeley, summoned to attend Parliament on 21st July 1381, invited his chaplain to accompany him. The offer was readily accepted. The description of the splendour and antiquities of this ancient institution had always interested - captivated would hardly have been too strong a word - Trevisa; and now that there had been considerable agitation that some of the opening speeches should be made in English his desire to witness these time-honoured procedures had increased. The mood of this venerable body seemed to be changing, suggesting that an even greater interest and measure of support for the wider use of the native tongue might be expected in the coming years. Trevisa felt elated. His was not quite the lone voice crying in the wilderness. He had, he now realized for the first time, others in many walks of life who were equally anxious to throw off the shackles of foreign domination, represented by Latin and Norman-French, and to establish English as the language of an independent and sovereign people who were the equal of any of the civilised nations of the world. This thought gave him great comfort, and hardened his determination to begin his own contribution towards this great movement in the not very distant future.

October produced weather comparable with that enjoyed in May and June. Many were the remarks that the winter would be much helped by St. Luke's 'little summer'. Trevisa, with the prospect of a dry, fair period, approached his patron:-

'My Lord, the feast of the kindly doctor is over and we will have no major church festival before All Saints. May I have leave to ride to Oxford and begin negotiations with Queen's about the possible return to commence work on the Higden's *Polychronicon* or some other major text which will meet with your Lordship's approval? Master Middleworth and Master Hereford are, I believe, in residence at the moment and will, no doubt, support my application.'

'Why, yes. The present time will be most suitable from my point of view, and if the fine spell holds it will be an enjoyable ride and a pleasant stay. Do you require a further letter of recommendation?'

'Thank you, my Lord. A letter outlining the purpose of my proposed return to Queen's would, indeed, be most helpful, and support from one of your Lordship's standing would considerably enhance the chances of a favourable outcome to the negotiations.'

'Very well, you shall have it tomorrow.'

'Thank you, my Lord.'

The Oxford visit was a success in every way. Firstly there was the reunion with Middleworth and Hereford. This, in itself, was exhilarating, and the prospect of rejoining them in Hall, even if only for limited periods, was attractive. Then there was the real purpose of the visit, the seeking of opportunity to commence, single-handed, to open up a wide world of interesting literature for his fellow Englishmen and, at the same time, fulfilling his Lordship's ambition to be recognized as a patron of learning. This objective was brought appreciably nearer during that week of warm October weather. The Provost surprised Trevisa by his friendly manner. The latter pondered over the cause of this change of attitude as he, later, recalled and reflected upon that central and vital interview:-

'Well, Trevisa, it is good to see you once again.' - an opening remark which astonished Lord Berkeley's chaplain - 'I understand you wish to discuss the possibility of returning to Queen's. I would like to hear fully what you have in mind.'

'Thank you, Provost. My request is simple, but I fear a trifle vague. I wish to resume residence at Queen's to work not as a full-time student or researcher, but on a somewhat more independent basis. My chaplaincy to my Lord of Berkeley is not a sinecure, but a responsible and pleasant appointment. This in itself would preclude the normal university status and way of life. The purpose of my requested periods of temporary residence at Queen's is to make a translation of Higden's *Polychronicon* for my Lord Berkeley. This somewhat ambitious project will have to be fitted in with my normal clerical duties. At the moment there is little hope of time to spare for a worthwhile period of study at Queen's, but it is conceivable that the situation could change materially - and speedily too. The Lady Katherine Berkeley, the relict of my Lord's grandfather, Lord Thomas, is considering the establishment of another chantry in Berkeley Church. Should this happen the chaplain may well be asked to accept part-time responsibility for the Castle. That, I believe, to be the meaning behind Lord Berkeley's statement that "in the foreseeable future conditions may well develop which would enable my chaplain to take up residence in Queen's for periods of up to five or eight weeks should this be deemed necessary." Your suggestion, Provost, that commensalis status might suit my requirements seems sagacious. This would leave me freer and more independent, enabling me to devote most of my energies to the project - at least to the *Polychronicon* and subjects germane. That, briefly, is the story behind my request.'

'Well, Trevisa, that is more or less how I envisaged the situation, and it was the general basis upon which your request was discussed in Council and our decision taken. I have considered carefully certain secondary reasons put forward on your behalf, and I feel that your plea - subject to satisfactory financial and other arrangements - will be granted when you are able to present a formal application giving appropriate and specific details. That, I feel, is as far as we can go at this moment. I am glad that you have put the past behind and now wish to return to Queen's. Farewell, and my felicitations to your eminent patron, Lord Berkeley.'

'Thank you, Provost, for seeing me personally, and for your courteous reception. Farewell.'

Trevisa, reflecting later upon the interview, wondered at the affability of the Provost, and delighted at the near certainty of being able to take up, in what he hoped would be the not too distant future, residence at Queen's and work on the *Polychronicon* - if that was indeed the final choice of my Lord of Berkeley.

(d) *Thomas, The Magnificent*

During 1382 two important events occured, the first national, the second essentially domestic and destined to bring about great changes in the life and custom of the Berkeleys.

King Richard in January married Anne of Bohemia. This brought great happiness to the young couple, who were genuinely in love, while the nation hoped, and many felt, that her stabilizing and strengthening influence would help her husband in the precarious life of sovereignty that he had inherited. The principal factions striving for power within the realm, the youthful, 'King's' party, and the older, grim political campaigners, looked on and tried to assess the differences which this obvious love match was going to have upon the King and their own positions.

Lady Berkeley's father died on 28th June, and the baronies of Lisle and Tyes comprising twenty-four manors were inherited by Lady Margaret and doubled the already considerable Berkeley estate [3].

Almost at once the lavishness of the Berkeley way of life increased. As the years passed the increased spendour of the household and entertainment, the rapid expansion of recreational facilities and, as a result of these changes no doubt, a widening of social influence, all became apparent.

Countryman though Trevisa was, he felt, at times, that these recreational displays seemed to savour of ostentatious opulence. He realized, however, that all this was not a deliberate, and so prideful, display but a spontaneous expression of joie de vivre.

Lord Berkeley was, indeed, dedicated to sporting activities. This was fully demonstrated by the extensive stables which he maintained both at Berkeley and Wotton [4], and the number and differing breeds of hounds which his Lordship kept for hunting various species of the local fauna, ranging in size from the hare to the noble red deer. Hawking, cock fighting and similar rural activities were also highly favoured.

His patron, having increased the size of several of the parks upon the estate, to improve the amenities of the chase, also built an extensive boat house near the castle bridge at the bottom of High Street. There was kept his Lordship's sumptuously appointed pleasure barge for use upon the Berkeley Avon and the open reaches of the Severn. Near the boat house was the quay for the use of the trading vessels which served the castle and borough.

Furthermore Lord Thomas reared large numbers of pheasants. These, however, were looked upon as ornamental additions to the parks and gardens, and not as objects of sport [5] - in this respect he differed in outlook from that displayed by his father.

Lord Berkeley, as a result of these changes in his pattern of life, acquired in some quarters the title of Lord Thomas, the Magnificent. This description hurt Trevisa, who felt that his patron did not deserve a designation which, though given generally in admiration, had also more than an element of denigration.

The pressure of events over the last six months had almost driven Lord Berkeley's petition to the Pope, for leave to exercise the privilege of patronage for the parish of Berkeley at the next voidance, from his and Trevisa's mind. Consequently it came almost as a shock when, on the feast of Lammas, a messenger arrived bearing with him, from the Papal agents in the City of Westminster, the sought-after bull.

Lord Berkeley at once sent for his chaplain, and on the arrival of the latter said:- 'You suggested, when we discussed my petition to the Holy Father for the next turn for the patronage here in Berkeley, that the chances of success might be slim - in comparison with the petition for a portable altar and the right to appoint my own chaplain it would be, I believe you stated, "a horse of a different colour". Well, Sir Priest, that pie-bald, black, red or grey charger has cantered into the courtyard of Berkeley Castle, and is now safely stabled. What say you, my friend?'

'The Papal permission has actually arrive, my Lord? Certes! Your Lordship must have written most persuasively, and you merit congratulation on these three consecutive successes in little more than as many years. After so great a silence I, myself, had felt that the original frail hopes had faded considerably, and that the final prospect was somewhat bleak. How will my Lord Bishop swallow this latest draught? Certainly the Abbot of St. Augustine's will not like it. Lord Henry of Worcester, I feel, will accept the situation arguing, as he must have done over the chaplaincy, that the appointment of a single incumbent, as with a chaplain, is of too little significance to precipitate a major verbal or even legal confrontation. The fact that there is at the moment no vacancy, and that Father David, though far from well, gives no indication of wishing to resign, nor does it seem that the advancement for which he once looked will materialize. You, my Lord, will, I presume, notify my Lord Bishop in the near future and so give him opportunity and, above all, time to reconcile himself to your Lordship's latest achievement?'

'Hasten slowly, my friend! The ink is scarce dry on the papal parchment, and Master David is far from dead. No, Sir Priest, we shall see, and I will select my opportunity with care, for I do not wish to upset, let alone antagonize, our Father-in-God.'

(e) *St. Andrew's Chantry. 1382-1384*

The Lady Katherine, when well on in years, consulted with her late husband's grandson, Thomas IV, Lord Berkeley, who was most indulgent towards his step-grandmother, on the possibility of endowing a new chantry, dedicated to Blessed Andrew, in Berkeley Church. Agreement on broad principles was quickly reached between his Lordship and Lady Katherine, and it was anticipated that the royal assent, episcopal sanction and other formalities would be obtained within a year at latest.

Trevisa, on hearing of these proposals, approached Lord Berkeley and asked leave to return to Oxford for the purpose of study and to work upon further translations. The chaplain pointed out that with an additional chantry priest available, the chaplaincy needs of the castle could be fully satisfied. Most 'mass-priests', Trevisa emphasised, because of the lightness of their obligations, were anxious to obtain further duties. He added, with perhaps a trace of courtly flattery, 'I am sure your Lordship, with your deep concern for the advancement of knowledge, would favour the translation into English of Dom Ranulf Higden's *Polychronicon,* a project which, you will recall, we have frequently discussed. That is the task, a most formidable one, which as your Lordship knows, I have in mind. I would, of course, endeavour to continue the record of events in this country up to this present time. I have had a strong sentimental attachment towards this work since my school days when our Father-in-God, Lord John Grandisson, took William Middleworth, a fellow scholar with me, you will remember, at Glasney, and myself into his household for a period as part of our training. The *Polychronicon* was in the Bishop's library [6] and it was his Lordship's practice to hear the students read and translate this and similar works. Lord Grandisson considered it desirable that our language should be re-established as a medium for presenting the Bible as well as secular literature to the people.

It was then, I believe, for the first time, that the idea was conceived of playing a humble part in this enterprise by translating, if I ever had the ability, knowledge and sponsorship, some of the more important works from the Latin and French into English'.

Lord Berkeley recognized that this was a reasonable request. Further discussions took place between them, and it was finally decided that Trevisa should return to Oxford for periods of unspecified length of time during the next two or three years, beginning in the autumn of the following year, thus giving more than sufficient time for the establishment of the new chantry, and to finalize the earlier tentative arrangements with Queen's. Trevisa was delighted with this decision, being confident that the translation of the *Polychronicon,* gigantic though the task might be, could be completed, at latest, by the summer of 1386.

(f) *An Early Grammar School*

The Lady Katherine was indeed loved and respected by all who knew her. Her reputation, even when a mere child, had been pleasing to her parents, Sir John and Lady Clyvedon, although they occasionally felt that her conduct exceeded the limits of decorum and gentility. Indeed the sympathy of their daughter for domestics and the menial - especially the young - at times worried them and made them wonder whether she had been contaminated by the poisonous harangues of evil agitators who claimed that all men were equal. The doggerel couplet:-

> '*When Adam delved and Eve span*
> *Who was then the gentleman?*'

was arousing stupid thoughts in many minds. How preposterous was this idea! God had created man for various stations, and it was blasphemous to suggest that there should be equality of opportunity. Later, as the young wife of Sir Peter le Veel of Charfield, Lady Katherine had showed similar sympathy with those in humble station.

This attractive lady, widowed tragically early, captivated the middle-aged Thomas, Lord of Berkeley, whose wife, Margaret Mortimer, had died in 1337. In 1347 Lord Thomas and Lady Katherine were married - like had attracted like. Her Ladyship certainly found in Lord Thomas a partner who was in greater sympathy with her social work than had been her parents and her former spouse. The Berkeleys, perhaps because of their clerical connections and inclinations, had a deeper appreciation of something more fundamental than 'noblesse oblige'. Had not members of the family in the past been patrons of learning and public benefactors? Lord Thomas had himself given support in 1328 to a poor but able scholar named William Stinchcombe [7], and had continued this grant until the need passed. He had told her, too, that he had promised sponsorship to a young lad on his Cornish estates, but it was some time before he confessed to the strange circumstances of that contract which, upon full reflection, he admitted savoured more, much more, of sentiment and superstition than of common sense.

During her second period of widowhood her Ladyship, then living at Wotton, had shown that she was no wild revolutionary who in her enthusiam to help those of inferior degree despised her peers. Indeed she possessed a social conscience, pietas and uxorial respect to a remarkable degree [8]. The foundation of the chantries in the churches of Wotton and Berkeley where masses and prayers for members of the family might be said daily was but one example of her inner feelings.

It was while the final details of the foundation of St. Andrew's Chantry at Berkeley were being formulated that Lady Katherine began to realize how serious were the affairs relating to the Grammar School at Wotton. Repeated requests and questions were met by evasive answers, and grave disquietude was aroused in her Ladyship's mind. Suddenly the end came. The master absconded. The school closed and a pile of debts only remained. It became clear, during the subsequent investigation, that for some years the financial affairs had been mishandled. Many people were involved, including some of distinction, and although one or two could see that disaster was imminent, they hesitated to speak out for fear of offending powerful forces, and they hoped too that their worst fears might be unfounded. Others remained silent lest they should be caught up in the scandal when the final crash came. Some blamed the aged master who, to curry favour, had played into the hands of certain parties, who did not hold with educating the poor lest they might rise above their proper station.

Her Ladyship's main concern was that the school might be re-founded as soon as possible to give, once more, local boys of talent the opportunities to achieve their potential, whatever their social background. She sent her faithful James Trotman to Berkeley with a letter for Lord Thomas, her late husband's grandson, whom she had always looked upon as her grandson too, although his father was the son of Lady Margaret, her husband's first wife. Lord Thomas felt a genuine filial affection for Lady Katherine, and had always treated her with the greatest consideration, as could be seen by the readiness with which he had granted leave for the alienation of numerous properties for the founding of the chantries.

Lady Katherine requested his Lordship to allow his chaplain, Master John Trevisa, to ride to Wotton for discussion on the problems involved with the re-establishing of the Grammar School. She realized that this wise and able scholar might be at Oxford working on his translation of the *Polychronicon* for Lord Berkeley. Should this, unfortunately, be so, would his Lordship allow a letter to be sent to Queen's Hall asking the Berkeley chaplain to spare two days at Wotton to discuss, as a matter of urgency, the scholastic position and to advise Lady Katherine.

Four days later Trevisa read and re-read Lady Katherine's letter, noting that she was prepared to make available generous endowments for the school. Her request for him to make suggestions as to a suitable warden, and even concerning the curriculum, indicated to him that Lord Berkeley had seen Lady Katherine and had both approved, in principle, her plans and had offered advice as to their implementation. Trevisa, after consideration, decided to talk the whole matter over with Master Thomas Cornwall [9] and Master Richard Pencriche, whose knowledge of the changing methods of education was considerable. Furthermore they both strongly favoured the more general use of the English language in schools. What a pity John, the father of Thomas, was no longer alive so that his wise counsel might guide their deliberations.

Pencriche and Cornwall readily agreed to examine with Trevisa the many problems posed by the Wotton school scandal. They met Trevisa three days later at Queen's, and it was decided, in view of Lady Katherine's emphatic assurances of adequate endowments for a re-foundation, to defer for the moment discussion on the financial issues, and to concentrate on the task of selecting for Lady Katherine's consideration several suitable candidates for the post of warden. The final choice must be an erudite and able teacher - many learned scholars, as the three well knew, lacked the faculty of imparting their knowledge in such a way that it was easy of assimilation by the young. They felt too, that he must be one who would be in sympathy with Lord Berkeley's and Lady Katherine's known patronage of English.

They decided, after several hours of discussion, to adjourn until the following morning, and during the interval to draw up a list of possible candidates for the wardenship, and suggestions as to the constitutional requirements.

They met again in Trevisa's room and within an hour had reduced the names to three. This short list was made up of two members of the university, Master Reginald Povey, a fellow of Stapledon Hall, and Master John Sergeant of Stone of Merton, while Master Robert Cronham of the parish of Brimsfield was the sole survivor of the purely parochial clergy.

Trevisa favoured Povey. Here was one, so he argued, who had had considerable experience in the academic world and had proved his worth. Furthermore he was a countryman, and had served in rural parishes including, for a short time it was true, Dumbleton, in Gloucestershire. Trevisa knew him and his ability in teaching, and believed that Povey would be prepared to accept the position which, because of the scandal, could well be a task of some difficulty. Cornwall and Pencriche, however, considered that Master John Sergeant should be preferred - but would he accept? His academic standing as a regent master, his strong and forceful character and his intimate knowledge of the Berkeley Vale and the Cotswold Edge made him, they pointed out, the obvious choice. Trevisa still resisted, arguing that whereas Sergeant was an excellent lecturer with older and more mature members at the university, his forthrightness and somewhat quick temper made him a less suitable instructor for the young. He was reluctant to add that he distrusted Sergeant, whom he feared was slightly tainted with the known family propensity towards favouritism, and, some maintained, deceit. In the end, however, Trevisa accepted the judgement of his colleages, feeling that perhaps his own discernment had been clouded by his dislike of Sergeant's uncle who had founded the chantry in Stone Chapel and was constantly complaining - quite needlessly Trevisa considered - that Master David de Melkesham, the vicar of Berkeley, was devoting too much time to St.Mary's and that parochially and sacerdotally the hamlet of Stone was being starved. Sergeant senior was indeed, at times, a difficult gentleman who might even turn dangerous.

Master Cronham, all three recognized, was an academic of ability, and the fact of royal patronage, even though this was of a general nature, would give him considerable standing when dealing with local persons and bodies. His knowledge of the Cotswold Edge after nearly three years at Brimsfield would also be an advantage. His real weakness lay in a somewhat quiet nature. It was decided in the final analysis that this last quality, pleasant and, in most instances, desirable, would be a handicap in a situation which had been brought into being and exacerbated by conflicting influences, some of which were powerful and far from being benign.

Master Pencriche accompanied Trevisa to Wotton. Lady Katherine accepted their suggestion that Master Sergeant would make a suitable warden. She told them that Master Sergeant's uncle, John Sergeant of Stone, having heard a rumour that her Ladyship was concerned about the closure of the Grammar School, and was interested in its possible re-establishment, had craved an audience with Lady Katherine and had begged leave to put forward for her Ladyship's consideration as a possible warden the name of his nephew. This action had irritated Lady Katherine. Later, hearing the recommendation of Pencriche and Trevisa, she reversed her earlier decision and agreed, subject to the approval of Lord Berkeley as Lord of Wotton as well as of Berkeley, to appoint Master Sergeant.

Lord Berkeley's affectionate consideration for Lady Katherine was amply demonstrated by his arrival on the following morning, to consider the appointment of warden, the terms of the foundation charter for the school - for new foundation it must be in view of the recent events, and the alienation of the certain lands in the manors of Wotton and Cam, which would provide the necessary endowments to secure the future of the school.

These important discussions occupied only two hours, and the following day Trevisa and Pencriche set out for Oxford, bearing with them Lady Katherine's invitation to Master Sergeant, an invitation which he accepted with alacrity. Within a week Master David, the vicar of Berkeley, had drawn up a draft of the proposed consitutions, which when it had been copied, was forwarded to the King's officer and to the Bishop for their approval and licence. The processes for institution and alienation had been set in motion, but it would be many months before the final negotiations would be completed.

The institution, after many delays, finally took place on 3rd August 1387 [10], but by that time Trevisa had left Queen's and was heavily involved with Berkeley affairs. He felt too, that Wotton Grammar School was not really his close concern, and that Berkeley obligations must take precedence. More than once, however, that nagging still small voice had questioned this decision, asking 'Is it possible that "personality" is the real reason for your refusal to attend?'

(g) 1385. The Emergence of Purvey

Doctor John Wyclif died on 31 December 1384. The news of his passing travelled fast, bringing widely differing reactions. The hierarchy rejoiced that death had stilled the voice of one who had bitterly denounced them, and who, in spite of papal excommunication and episcopal censure, had miraculously retained his freedom. The hierarchy was bewildered, however, that the radical followers of the great doctor were not as dejected as might have been expected. This vocal minority, in point of fact, had outstripped the master in some directions, and at times had resented his restraining hand. Many, however, mourned that the greatest intellectual of the day had been taken from them, and felt that the world of scholarship was incomparably the poorer.

The death of Doctor Wyclif came as a shock both to Lord Berkeley and his chaplain. The former had long looked upon him as an enlightened reformer, and reflected with pride that once he had, in a scholastic sense, sat at his feet. To Trevisa the death was one that should have produced stronger reaction and deeper sense of loss, or so he judged, but, strange to relate, the chaplain did not experience any really personal feeling of deprivation and sorrow, something which surprised him, and produced symptoms of a mild guilt complex. Trevisa, in sheer self-defence, analysed this outlook and came to the conclusion that it was the result of a combination of several factors. Firstly he, Trevisa, was not, and never had been, fully in sympathy with some of the tenets maintained and promulgated by Wyclif and his associates. Secondly he had never had the intimate relationship with the great doctor that Nicholas Hereford, John Purvey and, in a measure, William Middleworth had sought and enjoyed. The one strong link between the master and himself had been the biblical project and the desire to make an English Bible available to all Englishmen who could read. That task had, by and large, been completed, and so the bond with the greatest scholar of the day, at best somewhat loose and tenuous, had been broken. The result was a feeling of surprise, tinged with regret, that a stout advocate for a greater measure of democratization had left the stage, never to return.

Trevisa and Lord Berkeley were sorrowful, but reflected that their former mentor in biblical translation had been fortunate in coming under the protective wing of my Lord John of Gaunt. This patronage had, undoubtedly, saved him from prison at least, and possibly the stake itself. Master Wyclif had escaped while his able pupil, Nicholas Hereford, had twice been arrested and placed in confinement.

As the days passed Trevisa speculated on the future of John Purvey. Would he return to Oxford or transfer to one of the new colleges at Cambridge or, perhaps, enter lay employment?

The passing of his master so soon after retirement to Lutterworth was to Purvey a grievous blow, both personally and from the viewpoint of biblical translation, especially now that Wyclif had accepted for general use the principle of smoother interpretation, an idiomatic rather than a literal rendering of the Jerome text. Purvey had never been able to accept the ruling that a verbatim translation was less dangerous, less liable to heretical error [11]., than the more intelligible method. Purvey knew well that Middleworth, Thorpe, and Trevisa were of like opinion and Wyclif himself had long adopted this practice in his own personal writing. Of Hereford he could not tell, for the latter was still in custody, and when last they had worked together at Oxford the stilted word for word rendering was considered by most scholars - including Doctor Wyclif - the only permissible one for works which would have a general as against a private circulation. Had not Rolle translated thus, and was not his work fully accepted? Of course the common practice of glossing, followed in much biblical translation, made the verbatim method essential, but then those translations were being produced for study rather than popular use, and it was the latter objective for which he, Purvey, and Trevisa had always striven.

Suddenly the scholar, hitherto overwhelmed by the academic deprivation, awoke to the practicalities and problems of his physical future, for Lutterworth Rectory could no longer be his home. He thought first of his former colleagues, and then of possible places of residence and occupation, and finally debated with himself the chances of obtaining patronage which would enable him to pursue an academic career at a university. Both Middleworth and Trevisa were temporarily at Oxford continuing their respective studies, and Thorpe was, he believed, in or near Bristol. The latter town seemed to Purvey the obvious place in which, for a time at least, to settle. Trevisa was chaplain at Berkeley less than twenty miles north of Bristol, and Middleworth to the south of that town. Thus the latter place might well become the rendezvous for the four members of the sextet still at large.

He felt, however, now that Doctor Wyclif had died, that he must redouble his efforts to complete the revision of the English Bible, possibly with a little help from one or more of his former colleagues. But first he must go to Oxford.

Three weeks after his master's funeral [12], Purvey left Lutterworth for the last time, taking with him to Oxford several books and manuscripts that Wyclif had borrowed, and hoping that they might be re-issued to him or to Middleworth or Trevisa. His surplus belongings, which amounted really to very little, were left in the care of the squire, in the hope that one day he, Purvey, might reclaim them.

It was near noon three days later when Purvey, having travelled for much of the way in the company of a party of pilgrims bound for Canterbury, dismounted at Queen's Hall. He was disappointed that neither Trevisa nor Middleworth was in Hall, and that the former, having gone over to Dorchester Abbey to consult a manuscript, might not be back for several days. He found to his amazement, however, Provost Carlisle much more friendly than he had expected, or remembered. He was almost effusive in his offers of hospitality.

Later that evening, Middleworth returned and was surprised, and delighted, to discover that Purvey had arrived. He at once sought him out and expressed his genuine sorrow that their great mentor had passed from their midst, a passing which he fully appreciated represented a far more personal loss to Purvey because of the latter's close association with Wyclif in the intimacy of Lutterworth. That evening they discussed the future which for both of them was somewhat uncertain. Their respective plans, if the tentative and rather nebulous ideas floating round in their minds could be termed plans, were decidedly fluid.

The following two days were spent examining portions of the revised translation of the Bible which Wyclif and Purvey had been engaged upon when the former had died. The next morning Trevisa received news of Purvey's arrival at Queen's and soon after noon set out for Oxford.

That evening, while Middleworth was visiting Merton, Trevisa and Purvey retired to the former's room and reviewed progress on the biblical translation project. The

Cornishman was impressed by the amount achieved and the vast difference in smoothness and intelligibility which the new and rather radical method made possible. Later Trevisa, when Purvey had unburdened himself and talked vaguely of the future now that Lutterworth could no longer be his firm base, asked 'Why do you not come to the west? My Lord of Berkeley has many friends and powerful relations, such as my Lord of Warwick, and no doubt a chaplaincy could be arranged if such a post would be acceptable to you. Did William tell you that he is hoping for some sort of preferment in the west within a year or two? It is possible that my patron himself would welcome you at Berkeley, as a disciple of our late colleague and mentor - though, mark you, his Lordship never held with Master Wyclif's lollardy, no! Not even when he studied under him some years ago.' Soon afterwards Purvey, pleading tiredness, retired. That night however, sleep deserted him, and he pondered over the suggestions put forward by Trevisa. Berkeley, Bristol or Bath, hitherto only vague names, had now an attractive ring about them, and the prospect of re-establishing some kind of literary association with certain of the former Queen's community - Trevisa, Middleworth, Thorpe and if he ever came safely out of custody, Nicholas Hereford perhaps - appeared attractive. It was four o'clock before he fell into a fitful slumber.

Purvey's arrival in Bristol in 1385, and his obvious intention to settle in that city, caused consternation in certain quarters. The Abbot of St. Augustine's and, later, Bishop Henry Wakefield of Worcester, were perturbed - and did not hide their feelings. In spite of this official displeasure, Master John Purvey gained a considerable foothold and influence in several Guilds within the city, especially the Weavers.[13] Hereford, having regained his freedom and returned safely to England,[14] appeared in Bristol, and his heretical teachings aroused further concern. The hierarchical antagonism towards the ex-members of Queen's worried Lord Berkeley. His chaplain was, of course, an old friend and colleague of William Middleworth, Nicholas Hereford, Richard Thorpe and John Aston, and to a lesser degree of John Purvey himself. Lord Berkeley was indeed perturbed by all these comings and goings. He realized that Trevisa could not be expected to cut himself off completely from his erstwhile companions. Nevertheless the obvious hostility of the Abbot to 'change', and his dislike of Trevisa, made plain some years back, coupled with the friendship between the Abbot and Bishop Wakefield, boded ill. Lord Berkeley felt that the frequent meeting of certain of that small group could be considered dangerous, and he warned his chaplain of the possible consequences of his journeys to Bristol to visit Purvey and perhaps other men who were suspected of, or even charged with, herecy. He reminded him of the adage that birds of a feather frequently flock together', and that there was some truth in the saying that those who played with fire might easily get burnt.

Trevisa was astonished to observe the rapid rise in the numbers of people who gathered themselves around Purvey. It surprised him for, good man though Purvey might be, he was promulgating doctrines which differed fundamentally from those of the Established Church. Groups of people (sympathizers or disciples might be the better designation) began to flock to Bristol and, going back, set up their own cells. This led, so Trevisa gleaned later, to Purvey being invited to preach, mostly in the open air and house groups — did not Holy Paul do these things? — in numerous parishes throughout the dioceses of Worcester and Hereford[15].

One day late in the year Purvey confessed that he had been in touch on doctrinal issues with former Queen's colleagues who had been very much of one mind with Wyclif, and who, because of harassment and personal persecution by the so called 'Mother Church', were bitterly exposing her worldliness and corruption. He said, amongst other things:-

'I have heard recently from Nicholas Hereford and also John Aston. The former is, as you know, now safely back in England, and says that he will visit Bristol again, when opportunity occurs. I had considered going to work in London, but I have settled in so well here, and I am finding so many who feel as I do on important issues, that I may easily make this city my main centre. You told me at Queen's that I would like the west, and find people friendly. You, my friend, did not over-state the case, and I am most grateful to you for the initial suggestion and your subsequent kindness. Those few days last month at Berkeley, for example, were both relaxing and pleasant. I passed through your area a short while ago to preach at Wheatenhurst — John Aston had suggested my name. It was a moving experience, for the building was packed with people of all ages, including some most unexpected persons. I was not able to call when returning because of shortness of time. Next week I go to a place — I have forgotten the name — between Tewkesbury and Worcester. If the weather holds I will enjoy this so-say missionary journey. If ever you are in need of help — you tell me that the vicar is a sick and aging man and you have to take over parochial responsibilities at times — I would be delighted to help. I promise, if invited to preach, not to warn people against making their confession, nor will I recommend the doctrines of my late mentor and of Nicholas!'

'Thank you, John. I would like to invite you openly, but at the moment unless very hard pressed, I dare not, for obvious reasons. If the need was desperate I would ask for your help, but would expect you to refrain from any form of biased exhortation or sermonizing — at which you are, I know, a most able exponent! And one piece of advice, my friend, there are many here in the west, as well as in Oxford or London, to whom Wyclif and his later doctrines are anathema. Vested interests, especially those ecclesiastical, are powerful hereabouts.'

'Thank you for the word of warning, I will take heed. Oh! Have you heard of the reprimand received by the abbot of St. Augustines?'

'No. Tell me.'

'You will remember Archbishop Courteney some time ago held a series of metropolitical visitations here in the west. Well, in Bristol he inspected St. Augustine's, and was displeased with the dress of the canons. What he said to them at the time is not known, but the official letter of censure was copied and smuggled out. I cannot show it you, but it went something like this :- "At our recent visitation it was found that the canons, by the uncleanliness and greasiness of their leather boots, habits and vestments of the altar, were a scandal to beholders!" All that in spite of episcopal favour! What a magnificent subject for a condemnatory sermon! Can you not hear our late leader, God grant him rest!, verbally flaying the canons of St. Augustine's, denouncing them for their betrayal of the priestly office, and accusing them of sloth, and probably of gluttony, fornication and various other deadly sins! I have thought of composing such an address, but as yet have come to no decision.'

'How humiliating for the proud abbot! Perhaps it may do him good. I must leave now. Call in for the night when you ride back from the Worcester engagement, if you can spare the time. I will not be returning to Queen's to continue work on the *Polychronicon,* until after the Epiphany. Farewell!'

'God Bless you, and my humble obedience to his Lordship.'

Trevisa was tired. It was true that Master David had recovered from his latest bout of illness and was once more on duty. That duty from St. Nicholastide to Epiphany had not been of the lightest and he, Trevisa, had had to cope with considerable parochial work. The imminent return to Queen's was a cheering thought. The stay could well be an extended one, for the danger of a French invasion was much in people's minds and undoubtedly Lord Berkeley, again this year, would soon be spending much time raising and arming soldiery in different parts of the country to repel possible attack[16]. There was, however, talk of a campaign in Scotland and of Lord Berkeley's being involved. Well, if that expedition *did* materialize it could not be before the late spring, and so there would be a period of several months — or so he hoped — during which he could concentrate very largely on the *Polychronicon.* Perhaps he might even finish the actual translation by that time? A week later he was at Oxford and the worries of Berkeley were thrown off, or even forgotten for a while.

(h) *Expedition to Scotland*

'I feel, Trevisa, that this expedition will be one of considerable movement — the rendezvous is at Newcastle-upon-Tyne, a journey of three hundred miles and more, during which you will have little opportunity to exercise any worth-while ministry. From then on we will be constantly on the march. This is to be a full levy, which means that the might of England will be present — a vast host — and the Scots would be unwise to give pitched battle. They will, I believe, concentrate on skirmishing and hit and run attack, mainly on the laggards and isolated units.

I feel that to accompany our contingent of fifty-five men[17] would be largely a waste of your time. You would occupy yourself much more profitably by staying back here and dividing your time between Berkeley and Oxford. You were saying some time ago that the *Polychronicon* translation was not progressing as you had wished and had expected. This break might give you just the opportunity needed to complete, or at least to benefit that project considerably. Furthermore Scotland — leastwise the areas through which we will largely be campaigning — is a wild and barbarous country, even though it has a rugged charm and beauty. No, Trevisa, you will be well advised to remain here where, after all, the more important part of your cure lies.'

'Thank you, my Lord. You are probably right. I well remember our campaign in Brittany. On that expedition it was — except for the static periods of siege — largely a question of riding day after day, and being able to see or talk with the one or two immediate companions on the march. I felt then — mark you I enjoyed the sights and scenery — that the work for which I was ordained was being neglected. The Scottish campaign, as you envisage it, is likely to be even more frustrating for a priest. So, with your permission, I will ride with you to Gloucester, Worcester or Winchcombe, depending on the decided route, and will celebrate mass for the contingent. I will then return to Berkeley, where I will spend much of my time. I will, however, put in several weeks work on the *Polychronicon*, mainly at Oxford, of course. Again, thank you, my Lord.' With that Trevisa left the hall. Half an hour later, mounted on his ageing Berkeley Star, he rode over to Halmore to visit the sick and to arrange for the wedding of John Copiner and Isobel Fuller, a young couple who had, he suspected, anticipated the nuptial knot.

Trevisa, as he rode back that afternoon, reflected on future possibilities. Father David was certainly failing, and his present illness had aged him considerably. It seemed to Trevisa that retirement, at least, could not be delayed more than two or three years at most. Yes, he, Trevisa, enjoyed these short periods when he acted in loco vicaris, but in a measure he feared the time when, as incumbent and chaplain to my Lord, there would be a dual responsibility and occasionally, perhaps, a conflict of interests and obligation. Well, that lay in the future, and there was much sense in the scriptural enjoinder 'sufficient unto the day is the evil thereof'.

(i) *A Royal Visit and The Chapel Inscriptions*

The prospect of a royal visit pleased Lord Berkeley and Lady Margaret, and at once John Neale, the new steward, and other domestic officials were briefed, and preparations began. In their turn tenants and the lesser gentry were given their instructions, and the lists of victuals and accommodation expected of them were despatched.

Trevisa was warned that whatever stage had been reached in his translation, the project would temporarily have to be laid aside. The thought of such a summons did not displease the chaplain, who felt that staleness was affecting his work and that a short break might well be benefical to himself and his task. Trevisa mulled over the idea for a day or two and found that he had become completely unsettled, and that, in consequence, his *Polychronicon* translation was suffering. Finally he saw the Provost and craved leave to return to Berkeley at once, and not to await the direct order from his patron. The following day he set out for Berkeley.

During his leisurely ride Trevisa had time to think and to plan for the royal visit. He, as chaplain, would be expected to make some contribution to the preparations in progress at the castle. The chapels, clearly, were his sphere. The old one, St. John's in the keep, had really become his own semi-private domain, and so could be largely forgotten — or at least take the second place to the newer 'family' chapel of St. Mary. What could he, Trevisa, do there? Could he decorate or smarten up the chapel? At first, apart from new rugs and kneelers for Lord and Lady Berkeley and for the more important members of the royal party, there seemed little that could be done in the short time available. Suddenly inspiration, or so he deemed it, came to his aid. The roof timbers of the chapel were smooth of face and were painted white — so treated to help protect them from damp and worm, at least this had been stated by the master mason of that day. Could not these beams be embellished and given a new look, thus brightening up the whole place? The question was, how could this be accomplished? Before Berkeley was reached a decision had been made — subject to Lord Berkeley's approval and the availability of a competent artist or sign-writer.

Lord Berkeley motioned his chaplain to be seated, and then said:- 'Well Trevisa, what is this idea of chapel decoration which has caused you to ride helter-skelter to

Berkeley days, indeed weeks, before your presence was vitally necessary? Mark you, I am delighted to have you here once again, but I hope that your scheme will not involve too much time and labour for our staff.'

'My Lord, the plan is simple and will occupy but one man, albeit an able man. I have in mind to decorate the roof timbers with texts or passages taken from Holy Writ. Black letters on the white would show up well. To aid variation some initial letters might be picked out in red, and maybe, simple foliage enrichments introduced occasionally. That, briefly, is my suggestion. The King, after my involvement in the disturbances at Queen's, and with the more recent troubles concerning my associates Master Hereford and Master Purvey, might not approve of these texts in English, so I would advocate that they be from the Latin version, with passages also in the "polite" Norman-French so beloved not long since at Court. If speed is essential the writings could be selected from the book of the Revelation of the beloved disciple of which I have a copy in the latter translation. The Latin verses will, of course, present no problem.'

Lord Berkeley appeared lost in reverie. This brooding, if such it was, augured ill for the proposal, so thought Trevisa. Suddenly the silence was broken:-

'Sir Priest, yours is indeed a splendid idea, and one, moreover, which would, no doubt, meet with royal appreciation. Time, or rather lack of it, is the only stumbling block. See the steward at once, and if a skilful man can be found — and spared from the essential works — then you may begin right away. I must leave at once, so it is over to you to press forward with the work, if the labour can be found and you can furnish the necessary biblical material.'

'Thank you, my Lord. I will do my best.'

Three weeks later Lord Berkeley inspected the Revelation passages painted upon the beams [18], and turning to his chaplain said:- 'Trevisa, I congratulate you on your idea, and the artist, too, on his handiwork. It is an impressive enrichment, and has added much to the character and atmosphere of the chapel. I see what you mean about further work to complete the scheme, and I agree. Like you, however, I feel that all that can be effected before the visit, indeed all that needs to be done at the moment, has been accomplished, and that any further remaining decoration deemed necessary can be undertaken at a later date. Thank you, my friend and confessor; I am most grateful.'

Excitement mounted as the visit of the king drew near. Few folk in Berkeley, saving the Lord and his Lady, had seen the son of the Black Prince and grandson of the great Edward, although several old retainers in the distant past had served under royalty represented by those military giants either in France or Scotland. One or two others had caught a distant glimpse of the boy-king, Richard, when Parliament had met at Gloucester late in 1378. The ladies in particualar twittered like starlings on a tree at the prospect of seeing the Sovereign at close quarters, perhaps of even meeting him face to face. Their menfolk, on the other hand, spent much time attempting to restrict in some measure the desire of their wives to spend such vast sums of money on personal adornment that they might outshine their nearest rivals, and perhaps, even impress the King himself.

The townspeople and many of the villagers from Bradston, Newport and Wick lined the route as the royal cavalcade rode down from the heath to the Longbridge and through the town, while others from Ham, Stone and Bevington crossed the Avon brook at the Salt House and crowded round the entrance to the castle drive.

The visit itself was a disappointment locally, for neither King Richard, nor Anne, his Queen, appeared much in public during their stay in Berkeley, except on two occasions when they hunted the deer in Michaelwood and at Hill. It is true that they strolled on the castle walls and in the garden, and once the King looked round the parish church. Artistic though the King was, the latter visit was prompted more by curiosity after reading Archdeacon Mapp's crude but colourful story — probably containing no grain of truth — of the debauchery which, supposedly, had caused the closure of the ancient Abbey of Berkeley. Trevisa felt that this recluse mentality of the King was both wrong and foolish. Richard was in need of support and popularity in these rather uncertain days, and the more he could build up the image of the gracious and people-loving monarch the better for himself, and indeed for the realm at large. In his contact with those within the castle walls and especially when in a small party, whether they were those of his own retinue or Berkeley retainers, he was courteous, though, at times, somewhat reserved, a failing, if such it could be called, for which his lack of years might be blamed.

(j) *Completion*

Yule-tide in the year of Our Lord 1386 was a season of great joy to Trevisa. He was indeed experiencing a greater happiness than he had known for many years. The holiday octave was at the same time a period of considerable social activity, which denied him time that he would have liked devoted to the *Polychronicon*. Earlier in the year he had hoped to have completed the translation by the feast of Christmas, thus enabling him to present the finished work to his Lordship on the latter's natal day, the eve of Epiphany. The fates, however, had frowned. The problems over book seven had ruined his planned programme, which had been further upset by the difficulties in obtaining parchment. It really was scandalous that adequate stocks of this vital commodity were not held by St. Peter's Abbey with its well established scriptorium. Reflecting, Trevisa wondered whether the trouble over Purvey had made the librarian reluctant to help one who, so rumour ran, with, he was compelled to admit, considerable truth, had been rebuked for association with the reactionary followers of the late Canon Wyclif. In spite of repeated frustrations Trevisa was cheerful, and with justification. The mammoth project — and when it had first been contemplated more than ten years earlier its extent had not been fully appreciated — was slowly reaching completion.

Trevisa, after Epiphany, once more began the task of checking his translation with the borrowed text. It was March before a start could be made on writing out the fair copy. This work, simple enough for it was merely transcribing his own hand, Trevisa had thought to complete in two or three weeks. Alas! Other duties and obligations, social as well as parochial and priestly, impinged upon his time and so caused further delay. Slowly but surely, however, the work went on, and on Quasimodo, 14th April, Trevisa realized that at last, at long last, the end was in sight.

During the night of Wednesday/Thursday, 17th/18th April, sleep almost deserted Lord Berkeley's chaplain. The fair copy had been completed and carefully checked. All that remained was the composition of the colophon and the titling of the cover. Trevisa had, after compline, made several attempts to draft the former, but inspiration seemed to have deserted him, and in the end he laid the parchment on one side, feeling that after a night's rest his mind would be fresh and clearer, and that words would flow more easily. Alas! Restorative slumber eluded him, and he turned and tossed, enjoying peace neither of body nor mind. He got up and drank almost a jug of wine, but sleep still stood afar off. Trevisa, an hour later, rose a second time and in desperation seized his quill and once more made an assault upon the colophon. Two membranes were used and rejected before the priest threw down his pen and dejectedly flung himself on the bed. His mind, now fully activated, but deeply frustrated, continued to deny him sleep. As dawn began to break over the Cotswold escarpment and filtered through the window slits sleep came, fitful at first, then deep and sonorous. At seven o'clock a servant entered the chaplain's room and, after much shaking, roused the sleeping cleric, who, at first, found difficulty in assimilating the message that Lord Berkeley wished to see his chaplain at noon.

The latter, still in somewhat of a daze, washed and dressed, and at once, quill in hand, sat down at the table. Grim of purpose, he plied his pen, determined now to abjure — for the time being at least — high-sounding phrase and apt alliteration. The colophon should be brief, extremely so, setting down the essential facts of date and place of completion, and the name and style of the recipient of this magnum opus. Within minutes, and with no more than one rough trial copy, he wrote

'God be thonked of al his nedes this translacioun is I-ended on a thorsday the eyghtethe day of Aueryle, the yere of oure lord a thousand thre hundred foure score and sevene, the tenthe yere of kyng Richard the second after the conquest of Engeland, the yere of my lordes age sire Thomas of Berkeley that made me made this translacioun fyve and thrytty. Deo gracias.'[19]

The titling, too, was quickly done, with, perhaps, a little greater care of hand and with exuberant flourishes which, however, hardly qualified for the term illumination. Trevisa sat back and viewed critically the title page, and turned again to the colophon. Yes, he was satisfied; and, being so, he rose and went down to the kitchen to seek something substantial to assuage the hunger which had suddenly overtaken him.

It was a contented Trevisa who entered the Great Hall as the sun reached its meridian, contented because he was well fed, and because the parcel beneath his arm represented a great personal achievement in translation, and also an important contribution to the campaign for the production of serious works of interest and education for English people in their own tongue.

Lord Berkeley was seated at the high table, deep in conversation with a stranger, as Trevisa passed under the gallery. The chaplain paused, uncertain whether his presence was now required; indeed he felt that his arrival, in spite of the exactness of the hour, might be ill-timed. These doubts were, however, soon despelled when Lord Berkeley looked up and beckoned Trevisa forward.

'Lord Dudley, this is my worthy chaplain and confessor, Master John Trevisa, a man upon whom I lean, and before whom you may speak freely.'

'Sir Priest, you are indeed honoured; never, I think, have I heard a chaplain thus introduced to one to whom he is not known.'

Trevisa recoiled before this fulsome greeting, and at once, metaphorically, put up his guard, but replied civilly:- 'My Lord Berkeley, I feel, exaggerates his dependence upon me, and you, my Lord, have read into the first part more, much more, than was intended. My patron is one who stands firmly on his own feet, and needs little guidance in matters civil, political or estate-wise. In things of the Spirit we have, it is true, at times deep discussion, but that, I conceive, is not more than normal.'

'Trevisa, Lord Dudley is here on urgent national business which he and I must discuss carefully, and of which you and I will talk, and ponder deeply maybe, later.

You and I will, I fear, have to defer the examination of your translation of the *Polychronicon*, which I see you have with you, until tomorrow. This is a pity, and, to me a great disappointment; but state matters must take pride of place over a personal pleasure which, after all, is only being postponed.'

Trevisa accepted these words as a dismissal, and, with a courteous farewell to his patron and the visitor, turned and left the room. Lord Berkeley had invited, yes, almost ordered the translation, and now that it was complete he could not spare even five minutes to examine it. Trevisa was deflated, and indeed resentful, and quoted to himself:-

'Put not your trust in princes, nor in any child of man!'

Two days later Lord Berkeley sent for his chaplain, and, when the doors had been closed, said:- 'You will recall that on Thursday Lord Dudley was present when you brought in your translation of the *Polychronicon*. He came on a highly delicate and confidential matter, but one which I told him plainly I would need to discuss fully with you. He was reluctant, at first, to accept this condition, but finally agreed.

You and I have often of late speculated on the outcome of the King's minority — supposed rather than actual — and the decision of a group of noblemen who wish to control the affairs of state, either directly or through an acquiescent sovereign. Let me remind you that less than a year ago they dismissed de La Pole from the Chancellorship, and appointed a small committee to reform the royal household. Later came the realization that their ultimate aim was oligarchical rule. The King, it is said, chafes, and many feel that, sooner or later, a major clash between himself and this body of ambitious and aggressive subjects is inevitable.

On Thursday our guest came to sound out my position, demanding, after preliminary inquiries to which my replies were non-committal, where I would stand should an armed conflict develop. I was, I continued, on good terms — or so I hoped and believed — with my King, but had close friends, such as Lord Henry of Bolingbroke, amongst the dissident nobility. My decision concerning taking sides in any conflict, even if it should be imminent, could not be taken in advance, but would have to be made in the light of future events. This did not satisfy our friend, who went away disgruntled.'

'Well, my Lord, your reply was excellent, and, so I would judge, perfectly truthful. I fear, such is the pressure of the noble lords, that King Richard must challenge them, otherwise he becomes a mere puppet, a position he will not willingly accept. I cannot see Richard gaining on easy victory, a bloodless one I mean, unless he can sow seeds of dissension amongst the opposition — and this he may well do. You, my Lord, must tread warily. This is not, at the moment, your quarrel, and may never be. It is the concern, really, only of the ambitious branches of the Royal and Ducal houses. Do not become involved, if you can avoid it.'

'Thank you, John, my friend and confessor. I will heed your sagacious advice, and "procrastinatus" shall be my motto.'

(k) 1387. *An Episcopal Reprimand* [*re Purvey*].

Trevisa was surprised and somewhat nonplussed when a messenger from St. Peter's Abbey, Gloucester, arrived bearing a summons couched in language which could only be described as peremptory, bidding him present himself at the Abbey to meet the Lord Bishop of Worcester and answer accusations of misdemeanour. These charges were not specified, but the cleric, after much thought, felt that any indictments must have some connection either with the chapel alterations in the castle, or else his relationship with Master John Purvey. Both subjects, if maliciously misrepresented, could be built into a story liable to engender episcopal wrath. The priest's conscience, however, was clear, and he felt that he could, with the support of his patron, refute any charges brought against him on these counts. Trevisa felt relieved that Lord Berkeley was at home. The chaplain was confident that, after discussion with his Lordship, a reasonable defence against either possible charge could be formulated.

My Lord Berkeley was sympathetic but confident, and suggested to Trevisa that he was taking an unnecessarily gloomy view of the letter, despite its cold and authoritative phraseology. He pointed out that the epistle, clearly, had been written by one of the episcopal notaries, perhaps the junior archdeacon himself, a man who lost no opportunity of exercising his delegated power to terrorise or humiliate his fellow clerics — a most unpleasant character, indeed, was the Archdeacon. Lord Berkeley promised, however, that he would, if the charge or charges were of a serious nature, come forward at once in his chaplain's defence.

This assurance gave Trevisa confidence. His Lordship's voice, he knew, carried considerable weight in high places, and he felt that the Bishop might hesitate to clash violently with his patron over a matter so trivial as the disciplining of a castle chaplain. The result of these thoughts was that Trevisa slept soundly that night, and set out for the Abbey soon after dawn with a light heart.

Trevisa, on his arrival with half an hour to spare, was greeted brusquely, and the impression was immediately conveyed that he, Trevisa, was out of episcopal favour, and that the interview was likely to be in the nature of a trial — but what was the charge?

The Bishop came straight to the point:— 'Master Trevisa, it has come to my notice that Master John Purvey, one time amanuensis to Doctor Wyclif, has been to Berkeley on several occasions of late, and that he has celebrated mass both at the castle and in the parish church. Furthermore, it is said that he had been known to preach at St. Mary's and, out of doors, has addressed more than one assembly. Is this true? I cannot believe that you have been so stupid and ill-advised as to have connived even at these evils. I hope that the reports which I have received are no more than idle gossip.'

'My Lord Bishop, basically there is some truth behind the accounts that have reached your Lordship's ears. I invited Master Purvey to stay with me at Berkeley Castle, and he did celebrate mass twice during that visit, once at the parish church and once in St. John's Chapel in the castle keep. Purvey is a priest, and his orders, to the best of my knowledge, have never been called in question. He celebrated fully vested and used the prescribed form and words, and none other. The reason, my Lord, why I invited Master Purvey to stay at Berkeley was a very practical one. Your

Lordship, is aware no doubt, that Lord Berkeley is desirous of possessing certain books of reference in the common tongue. One of these is the *Polychronicon,* that learned world history by Ranulf Higden. For some years I have been engaged upon the translation of this work for my patron, and by last February the task had almost been completed. Your Lordship will know that Master Purvey has the reputation of being a scholar of considerable ability and standing. I was anxious that my Lord Berkeley should possess a translation of the *Polychronicon* that combined accuracy with facility. Consequently I approached Purvey, whom I knew to be in Bristol, and requested him to inspect, and, if needs be, to correct my manuscript. This he willingly agreed to do. During Purvey's brief stay at Berkeley, Master David, the vicar, fell ill suddenly, as Your Lordship knows, and at short notice alternative arrangements had to be made. The brethren at Longbridge, because of illness, were unable to assist. Master Purvey, seeing the problem, offered to help. This offer I, acting in loco vicaris, gratefully accepted. I, as the resident, naturally made the journey to Stone and Hill, while Purvey took the mass both in the castle and parish church. The report which your Lordship received that Master Purvey preached in church and addressed an assembly out of doors, though literally true, is, indeed little more than a travesty of that same truth. At the High Mass in St. Mary's he spoke for two or three minutes on the gospel, reminding the congregation of the need for constant vigilance against temptation, and stressed the power of prayer. My Lord Berkeley was present — at my suggestion — and reported that there was no trace of heresy in a single utterance. This he is prepared to swear upon oath. Finally, to term 'an address' the short conversation which Master Purvey, on returning from the Church, had with some members of the castle garrison, on the subject of their families, their duties and life generally in Berkeley is the grossest misuse of the word 'address', and a malicious fabrication. I had just returned from Hill, and was present for the whole of the time in question. My Lord, there are men, even some in high position, who delight in spreading defamation and libel (often by innuendo), and others whose exaggerations, unintentional maybe, are almost a way of life. In addition, Master Purvey's association with Doctor Wyclif some years ago has damned him in the eyes of many, whose hounding and harrying of him is uncharitable and, indeed, unchristian.'

'Master Trevisa! Master Trevisa! You presume too much upon your position as chaplain to my Lord Berkeley, and go too far in your criticism of your betters; have a care! I accept that you consider Master Purvey to be innocent of heresy and ecclesiastical subversion, and I am prepared to believe that the motives behind your actions were, in your eyes, pure. I, as your Bishop, warn you, however, to be on your guard. Master Purvey, is, indeed, an able scholar, possessing a good brain and a glib and facile tongue. You say you find him useful in your work for my Lord of Berkeley. Maybe so, but to associate with him too closely could be to imperil your immortal soul. He may be far cleverer and more dangerous than you think. I counsel you to break off this association, lest you become contaminated and risk serious embroilment with the officials of the archbishop. Please convey my respect to your patron on your return to Berkeley.'

It came, therefore, as no surprise to Lord Berkeley's chaplain, when, some weeks later, the Bishop of Worcester issued a mandate inhibiting, amongst others, Master John Purvey from preaching within the diocese. Trevisa noted that the names of Master Nicholas Hereford, John Aston and John Parker were also included in that same list [20].

Early in 1388 an outbreak of a spotted fever spread rapidly along the Severn Valley. Its origin, rumour declared, was a sailor who had returned to Frampton after a voyage to Spain. Within three weeks cases were known from Elmore to Hill. Father David, vicar of Berkeley, though far from well, spent long hours in the saddle visiting the sick in the outlying hamlets of Halmore, Wick, Clapton and Stone. The town of Berkeley had, so far, miraculously escaped the disease. One afternoon when returning from Halmore, where he had been administering the last rites to old Alice Taylor, his horse stumbled when crossing the brook near Wanswell Court. Father David slipped forward and fell head first into the water. By the time he reached home he was numb with cold and the next morning severe spasms of rigor developed and, to the horror of the community, he lapsed into a coma and died that night.

Trevisa, at the express request of Lord Berkeley, immediately took charge of the parish, and his Lordship sent a message to the Lord Bishop telling him of the vicar's death, and explaining that with Palm Sunday and Holy Week so near at hand he had instructed Master Trevisa, his chaplain and, by reason of the papal mandate, vicar designate, to assume unofficial charge of the parish until such time as the Bishop felt able to institute Master Trevisa, or send a locum to take temporary charge if the interregnum would be of long duration. Lord Berkeley pointed out the urgency of the situation in the Severn Valley, due largely to the fever epidemic, and added that it was rumoured that Master Richard Wynchcombe, rector of Slimbridge, had been taken with the fever and was desperately ill.

To Lord Berkeley's surprise the Archdeacon of Gloucester arrived five days later. The Bishop, deeply involved with important parliamentary affairs, but appreciating the need for prompt action, deputed the Archdeacon to act on his behalf by inducting and installing Master Trevisa, and to investigate the situation at Slimbridge. Furthermore he had been instructed to do an unofficial visitation and report back with all speed.

Trevisa, during the service of institution the following morning, requested the official instruments. The Archdeacon, slightly hesitant, replied:— 'Master Trevisa, you fail to appreciate fully the present pressure and stress upon our Father-in-God, Lord Henry. His political duties are not light, while the administration of a diocese as large as Worcester imposes a heavy burden. In addition there is this crisis in the Severn Vale. My Lord Bishop felt that it was necessary, especially in view of your patron's message, to act quickly, too quickly indeed for the legal papers to be drawn up and prepared for today. These will be completed and sent to you when the entry has been made in the Episcopal register [21]. In the meanwhile there are many witnesses today to your institution, more than sufficient to establish the validity of your cure here in Berkeley. Never fear, my son, there is no malice nor malignity behind this omission, which is the direct result of the urgency of the situation and the time involved in normal documentation.'

'Thank you, Mr. Archdeacon, I now fully understand.'

Later the Archdeacon left for Slimbridge where he found the rector conscious, just, but very weak.

Chapter 9
Changes of Fortune

(a) *Projected Return to Germany and Oxford*

Lord Berkeley, as patron of the newly translated *Polychronicon* and basking in a not inconsiderable beam of reflected glory, listened carefully to his chaplain's suggestion that the time was fully ripe for a further attempt to bring works of major importance to the English people in their own language. The interest shown in John's translation of the *Polychronicon* was evidence enough of the demand for such serious works of reference.

The project outlined by Trevisa was the translation of the *De Proprietatibus Rerum* of Bartholomew Anglicus, with also a tentative suggestion that a more flowing translation of at least some of the biblical books - especially those of the New Testament — was urgently required. Both these tasks, congenial enough to John, might well necessitate a great deal of travelling, even to France and Germany and possibly to Rome itself, to examine manuscripts of the *De Proprietatibus Rerum* and others germane to the main subject. John was also anxious, should he be in Lorraine, to revisit Aachen. He had been greatly impressed by the culture and friendliness of the people in that city when there a few years earlier[1]. Later, the chaplain pointed out, some time at Oxford would also be needed to discuss his translation with other scholars, and to decide upon the policies for the final phase of the campaign to help his people the better to read and understand God's Holy Word.

His Lordship cross-questioned his chaplain on the time and cost factors in which he, as sponsor, would be closely involved. Lord Berkeley had been perturbed when he understood that 'a full year and perhaps more' would be needed for the overseas stage of the research, and that at a later date a further period of 'at least six months' in Oxford might be necessary. He ended the interview by saying that he would need time to think carefully over the many problems which the plan would create.

Two days later Lord Berkeley sent for John and announced that he had decided to give the project his blessing and, more important still, his financial backing. They then discussed the many arrangements that would be necessary to be made. His Lordship insisted that a temporary chaplain, of whom he would have to approve, should be engaged and made responsible too for the parochial duties. St. Augustine's Abbey, Bristol, might well assist in this matter, indeed they would, no doubt, be delighted to have a hand in Berkeley affairs. Residence, in his Lordship's view, did not present any difficulty. The priest could take over Trevisa's room at the castle or he could live at the Chantry Cottage where there was adequate accommodation for the normal chantry priest and a locum tenens. Lord Berkeley insisted that the details of the scheme, and especially the overseas section, should be drawn up clearly and, furthermore, that it should receive the King's approval. He felt, he said, that with the friendly relationship existing between his liege lord and himself this would not be difficult to obtain.

The weeks passed quickly with the bustle of the many preparations which had to be made. His Lordship was somewhat choosey over the temporary chaplain, and it was not until three candidates had been rejected that one was finally found who satisfied Lord Berkeley.

Before the arrangements had been completed news reached Berkeley that a further crisis had arisen between the King and his Council. Confirmation followed within a few days. The King, it was suggested, wished to sweep the whole constitution on one side and rule, through his favourites may be, without consultation with Parliament or his Council. The establishment of an absolute monarchy at this moment in time would create, so it appeared to Trevisa, a serious potential danger and could well be but a prelude to despotism, a situation which, remembering the present crisis, could quickly erupt into civil war.

Lord Berkeley and his chaplain discussed these events and, in view of them, decided that it would be wiser to postpone the latter's visit to France and Germany until the present troubles had been resolved. They felt, however, Oxford being only two or three days ride away, that the proposed return to Queen's Hall could be undertaken.

Ten days later Trevisa set out from Berkeley and spent the night at Tetbury, where he stayed with Father Andrew, the parish priest and an able scholar. Far into the night they discussed the proposed translation of *De Proprietatibus Rerum*, and both agreed that it was a pity that Father William Middleworth, with his profound scholarship, had not found it possible to join with Trevisa in this project. Trevisa, despite retiring so late to bed, was early away in the morning and by nightfall had reached Queen's.

The following two days were spent in settling in, making arrangements for the use of the manuscript of the *De Proprietatibus Rerum*, recently bequeathed to Queen's, at the request of Master John Trevisa, by Simon Bredon[2], and above all in visiting his friends at Queen's, Merton and Exeter. Trevisa discovered that the recent political manoeuvrings, almost unconsciously, insinuated themselves into most conversations and had made a deep impression even in the higher academic circles. This fact increased his own concern, and it was perhaps not surprising that he experienced great difficulty in concentrating upon the allotted task. For three weeks he persevered, but found his thoughts constantly turning to the national events and their probable profound effect upon the peace of mind of his patron. Trevisa himself, although he would have been reluctant to admit it, was extremely exercised over the recent actions of the King; as anxious, indeed, as he had been earlier over the Council's policy of governing the country with little or no reference to the Sovereign. Both courses of action were wrong, and it seemed to bode ill for all. Rumours were numerous and conflicting. Finally he laid aside the manuscript of the *De Proprietatibus Rerum* and turned first to Holy Writ for guidance, but found that even the Master's directive to 'Render unto Caesar the things that are Caesar's, and to God the things that are God's' and the apostolic leader's injunction to 'Honour all men, love the brotherhood, fear God, honour the king', did not quite satisfy him in the peculiar circumstances then prevailing.

How should the opposing parties act? How far could each go without (a) offending God, (b) bringing chaos to the country? Above all with whom should he, and Lord Berkeley too, side if open conflict resulted?

Finally Trevisa turned again to the *De Regimine Principum* of Aegidius Romanus.

Here at least he would find a dialogue of some length, and depth too, which had considerable bearing upon the conduct of rulers, and outlined also the responsibilities of subjects. A copy of the *De Regimine Principum*, undated and without a colophon, was, he knew, in the library at Merton. Permission, through the good offices of the librarian, a Fellow and an old acquaintance, was soon obtained to have access to it.

On the very first folio Trevisa found the heart of the vexed subject outlined. How relevant was the advice given! 'He that desires to make his principate perpetual in himself and in his children and successors shall study with great busyness that his governance be kindly. Never man is made kindly rector, that is to say governor, if he desireth to be prince by passion, that is by suffering or by will. But if he is a keeper of right he shall ordain to command no thing without reason and law ..... And Christian religion desireth to keep and save rightful rules of the reign by wit and law and not by self will[3].'

Trevisa read on with avidity, and the further he read the more relevant it seemed to the conditions existing or which he feared might exist, if the King or Council gained complete control. By the time the last folio had been read and assimilated the resolve had been made that the *De Proprietatibus Rerum* project must be postponed, and that the *De Regimine Principum* should take its place in the priority of translation. Here was a book all men should read, for it was a guide to conduct generally, and one which all rulers should be encouraged to study.

Mid-December came and still the task was far from finished. Such was his desire to complete his work that his return to Berkeley for the great festival of Christmas, instead of being a period of joy and pleasure-making, seemed almost a time of frustration and delay. Even the Christmas dinner, with the triumphal entry of the boar's head resplendent with an apple in its jaws and with the trappings of rosemary and bay and the swan which followed with its wings and tail spread out and its bill all gilded, did not stir Trevisa as of yore, nor did it, even momentarily, banish the project from his mind.

The twelve days of Christmas over, Trevisa set out, after the Epiphany High Mass for Oxford. Before Dursley had been reached a heavy snow storm set in and it was not until late on January 10th that he drew rein at Queen's.

Before the end of the month rumours began to circulate that the existing political calm was but the lull before the storm. It was said that the noble council members believed the King had played them false. Their interview at the Tower with King Richard, when they had sternly rebuked him for the breach of his coronation oath and for plotting against them, appeared now to have made no lasting impression upon his majesty. Their reminder, too, that the heir to the throne, Thomas, Duke of Gloucester was of full age, and 'by ancient statute and recent precedent'[4] could, by the peoples' will, be elected King, had done no more than arouse the royal ire. The council members, Trevisa believed, were not now prepared to accept this situation without reaction. This, if and when it came, could be considerable. Trevisa, after much thought and when the rumours had become even more alarming, decided to return to Berkeley before serious trouble, the repercussion of which might even reach the Severn Vale, broke out. He had finished nearly half of the *De Regimine Principum* and would, Deo volente, return in the not too distant future to complete its translation.

(b) *Recall to Berkeley*

Trevisa, on the next morning as though to confirm his reluctant resolve to return in the near future to Berkeley, received a long delayed message from Father Joseph, the chantry priest acting as his locum at Stone. This stated that Father Joseph was worried over the attitude of many Stone people, including the churchwardens. Few were co-operative or friendly, and some — mainly the officials — were openly hostile. The purport of the letter, obviously, was that Father Trevisa should return as soon as possible, when he, as vicar, might be able to get to the heart of the matter and so prevent a grievous situation from worsening.

Trevisa was shocked and unable to account for the, apparent, sudden deterioration of relationships at Stone. The folk had been, or seemed to have been, so natural and friendly at Christmastide.

The following day he went to Merton and completed the section of the manuscript on which he was engaged and made tentative arrangements for further work at some future date. He then paid his battels and prepared for an early start the next morning.

Dawn, bright with a touch of February frost, found Trevisa crossing the ferry at Eynesham, and late in the afternoon he called on Father Andrew at Tetbury. Trevisa's intention had been to feed and rest his mount for two or three hours and then to ride on to Berkeley in the hope of arriving at the castle before midnight. Father Andrew, however, deterrred him from this foolish plan. The deciding factor was that his host appeared to have some knowledge of the affairs of Stone, and Trevisa felt that it would be prudent to be as fully conversant as possible with the difficulties which lay ahead. and to discuss with a fellow priest, and one of great experience, methods of dealing with the known and the problematical.

Father Andrew's manservant had a cousin in Stone who had spoken of several visits to the hamlet by the Dean of Westbury both before and after Christmas. The cousin had reported that rumours were circulating that certain of the church officials had been persuaded to lodge a complaint of parochial neglect, not against the locum tenens but Trevisa as vicar and the one ultimately responsible for the cure of souls within the parish. Father Andrew pointed out, however, that these stories had been circulating for several weeks and that neither he nor his manservant had any idea of the present situation.

Trevisa, on his arrival in Berkeley the next morning, was astonished and horrified to hear from Father Joseph that the Bishop's consistory court — to which the locum had not been bidden — had already considered the accusations of the Stone officials, and that he, Trevisa, had been summoned to answer a charge of dereliction of duty. It seemed to Trevisa, from all reports, that he had been already judged, indeed pre-judged, in absentia, and his guilt and sentence already determined. Lord Berkeley, however, felt that the charge, when the people of Stone had been put on oath and faced the chaplain, and when Father Joseph had given his testimony, could not be substantiated.

Trevisa was perturbed. The imminence of the court — less than a week away — necessitated rapid decisions and prompt actions. The delay to Father Joseph's message was indeed making things difficult. The first move, obviously, was to see the people at Stone who had lodged the complaint, and this would have to be done at once.

Trevisa became increasingly irritated that afternoon as he went from one Stone official to another — one, John Sergeant, was away, but the others were at home or sufficiently near to be traced and seen. All were evasive and clearly nervous. Each blamed the other for the initial move and said that the church arrangements were not really adequate, and that not having a resident chaplain they had felt neglected. When questioned about specific examples they were vague, saying that the complaints had really come from the congregation rather than from the officials. It became more and more apparent that there was an outside organizer behind the trouble, and the conviction grew that Father Andrew and his manservant were correct in their assumption that the visits of Dean of Westbury were not unconnected with the affair. What worried Trevisa most, however, was the statement made by one of the officials that they would not be present at the court. They had been told that having made affidavits at the earlier hearing their presence would not be necessary and that a proctor would represent them. This, Trevisa realized, was an ingenious method of preventing them being cross-examined under oath at the trial by himself or his representative. He felt that he would have to obtain without delay powers of subpoena. He returned at once to the Castle and saw Lord Berkeley, and within the hour a messenger was riding hard for Gloucester where he would spend the night at St. Peter's Abbey and leave for Worcester early the next morning. It was hoped that the Archdeacon — if the Bishop was not present — would agree to the granting of powers of subpoena. The reply could not be expected before the fourth day, giving only forty-eight hours to serve the summons on the Stone officials and ensure their presence at the trial.

Alas! on the morning of the fourth day the lather-flecked rider drew rein in the courtyard and it was clear at a glance that the mission had not been successful. The answer, a verbal one, from the Archdeacon was brief and lacking in any cordiality:- 'Please tell Master Trevisa that it is far too late for his request to be considered'. Trevisa was surprised at the terseness of the reply and that it was oral. There was now nothing to be done but to rely upon his own statements (or those of his proctor if he himself was not allowed to speak), and those of Father Joseph. It remained to be seen how sympathetic the President might be, and how prepared to listen to argument.

The courtroom was crowded when Trevisa and his proctor, Richard Glym, appointed by the Court, arrived. John Wendon, the Stone officials' proctor, and a few parishioners were present, but of the officials themselves there was no sign. Trevisa felt that the scales were indeed heavily weighed against him.

The President, obviously anxious to start, called for prayers well before the time set to begin. He then outlined the purpose of the case before the court. 'We are here', he said, 'to establish whether or not Father Trevisa, vicar of Berkeley, in whom the care of the church and village of Stone has been vested, has been negligent of his duties in that corner of God's vineyard. The clerk will now read the evidence given by the officials of Stone Church at the earlier inquiry. Master Richard Glym, proctor for the vicar of Berkeley, will then be asked to answer the charges, after which I will speak. Finally, judgement will be pronounced.'

The Clerk stood up, bowed to the President, and, with a smirk upon his face which made it clear that he relished his task, recited in a simpering voice:-

'Master John Trevisa, perpetual Vicar of Berkeley, was found guilty at the consistory of Worcester of depriving the parishioners of Stone of services of Holy

Communion and other parish rights. He was sentenced to find a fit chaplain to reside in Stone and thus restore to the parish all its rights and privileges recently withheld. All this will be at the charge of the Vicar of Berkeley.[5]' He then read the evidence given by the Stone officials so that the new panel 'might judge for yourselves whether or not the condemnation was just.'

Trevisa, as the question and answers were reported, became more and more convinced that the whole affair had been carefully planned and that the real objective was, not the restoration of the amenities of which the people of Stone were supposed to have been deprived without any consultations, but his own censure. The opening question to each of the four officials had been simple and clear. It was equally obvious that the reply 'Yes' had been expected. It went thus :- 'When Father Trevisa returned to Oxford you were most unhappy were you not, with the arrangements made for the celebration of mass and the general maintenance of Stone Church and the care of the souls of the parishioners?' The second question was framed thus:- 'Did you approach Father Trevisa and complain?' To which the answer, 'We tried to, but he was always in a hurry, and so we were not given any real opportunity to make a formal protest,' had been given. The third, and its reply, had also the air of 'preparation' behind it: - 'Why did you not speak to the locum?' 'He was clearly doing what he was told, and furthermore he too was usually dashing away to say mass at his chantry Altar in Berkeley Church or off to visit some sick person — usually in Berkeley, Alkington, Halmore or Ham. We rarely saw him in Stone.'

Master Glym then rose and on Trevisa's behalf denied all charges, stating clearly that there had been full consultation, and that the arrangements had been accepted with apparent pleasure. He was surprised, he said, at the charge of offhandedness and lack of sympathy by the vicar. All this was completely out of character in the case of the defendent. He expressed sorrow that the petitioners — or as he preferred to call them the complainants — were not present to be questioned on certain points. Finally he asked leave to call Father Joseph to testify. The request was not granted, on the grounds that the locum did not enter into the case, which was in essence between the vicar of Berkeley and the people of Stone. Expostulation merely brought a Presidential reprimand; whereupon Master Glym sat down.

All this appeared to Trevisa as a well thought out and stage-managed trial with himself as the villain of the piece upon whom inevitably retribution would fall. It came therefore as a surprise when the President turned to him and said:- 'Master Trevisa, what have you to say to these charges?'

'Mr. President,' replied the accused, 'I am astonished beyond measure, and horrified too, on several counts. Firstly that my application for a subpoena to be served on the officials of Stone was not granted. Why was I not permitted to meet the accusants face to face? This would have been but common justice. It appears to me that someone was afraid of allowing me to question them.'

'Trevisa! You overstep the mark! You appear to be accusing the court of our Father-in-God, Henry, Bishop of Worcester, of evil practice. Another remark such as that and I will arraign you for gross contempt. Continue with your evidence, but mind your words.'

'My second point is that I made, as Master Glym has already stated, the arrangements for the care of Stone in my absence with the complete agreement of the officials there — Mr. Sergeant stated that they were fully acceptable. During the

Christmas period the people of Stone had ample opportunity to approach me and express any dissatisfaction. They, however, said nothing of this, and indeed seemed cheerful enough. I have checked with Father Joseph, and he has assured me that he has fully carried out the duties as laid down. That, Mr. President, is all I have to say, for I completely deny all charges.'

The President immediately stood up and addressed the Jury :- 'Members of the Jury, you have heard the evidence of the Stone officials and the denial of the accused. You must bear in mind that almost half a score of men — and women too — from Stone, persons who are obviously intelligent and honourable or they would not be holding office in that parish, have made these protests — we have the affidavits of four. They have stated categorically that from the beginning they were dissatisfied with the plans made by the vicar. You must recall that there was not one dissentient amongst their number. Father Trevisa is an able scholar who has spent many years at the Universities of Paris and Oxford. He might indeed be better suited to the academic rather than parochial life. He denies the charges and seeks to assure you that all was well when he left for his Alma Mater, that in fact the people of Stone were well satisfied with his arrangements. Could it be that, academic that he is, he failed to see the signs of dissatisfaction? Was he so imbued with the thoughts of returning to the seat of learning that his head was in the clouds? Was he, may be, so mindful of the attractions of university life that he became indifferent to the welfare of the parish of Stone? Members of the Jury you will consider your verdict.'

The Jury, with barely a token consultation amongst themselves, said that their verdict was unanimous. This was brief and to the point:- 'We find the accused guilty on all charges, and we approve the sentence passed on him by the Consistory Court of Worcester, that the vicar of Berkeley, shall, at his own cost, find and cause to reside in Stone a fit chaplain to minister to all parishioners there the sacraments and sacramentals and other parish rights as well in life as in death.' [6]

The President rose, thanked the Jury, pronounced the formal sentence and closed the court, thereby effectively silencing any possible protest or request for a re-trial.

(c) *Episcopal Censure* 1389

John smarted under the Episcopal reprimand knowing full well that the complaint had been a manufactured one which had hoodwinked the Bishop. The Dean of Westbury had disliked him from their first meeting when Trevisa had criticized the lector in the refectory. This had been a foolish and unnecessary remark, but John generally spoke his mind, and in any case the young novice, a scion of a noble house it was evident, obviously thought well of himself and read with pronounced affectation. He needed to be put in his place. It was only after the meal had ended that John learned that the lector was a nephew of the Dean.

The officials of the Stone Chapelry, messrs. Sergeant, Guliane, Hikedon and Chapman, had, before John left for his trip to Oxford and London, been perfectly satisfied with the proposed service arrangements for the period of absence. Stephen Hikedon had, indeed, described them as generous, and had declared that the Chantry priest from Berkeley was fully acceptable.

The Dean, soon after John's departure, had visited Stone and called on a number of people, and from that moment the situation had changed. At the Bishop's enquiry the officials swore on oath that they and their predecessors had not been happy over the scheme proposed. They also vehemently denied the insinuation of the defence that the Dean's visit to Stone lay behind the suggested change of heart and the subsequent complaint to the Bishop.

John was furious, and later at Berkeley discussed the whole affair with John Poleyne, one of Thomas Berkeley's esquires, and others of the tenantry. They agreed that the Dean, known to be of a vindictive nature, had been the architect of the trouble. The friendship between the Dean and the presiding judge at the Inquiry also had weighed heavily against Trevisa in as far as powers of subpoena had been disallowed, and so vital evidence for the defence had been, virtually, suppressed. Both cleric and tenant swore that it was high time that Robert, the Dean, should be taught a lesson; he had arrogantly interfered in the affairs of several parishes within the vale for nearly two years — far too long?

(d) *Retribution and Repercussions*

The next day John Poleyne suggested that an armed demonstration should enter Westbury College and demand an apology from the Dean, and also that restitution in coin should be made by him for fines which recently had been levied on certain local churches at, it was believed, the Dean's insistence.

Trevisa, still furious at the unfairness of his condemnation and indignant that a fellow priest should have so blatantly perverted the course of justice, and aware also of the scandalous way in which this eminent churchman had bullied a number of the lesser and more timid parish and chantry priests, agreed in broad outline with the scheme. Trevisa felt, too, that the Dean had stirred up trouble for him not only because of his foolish criticism of the nephew but as much perhaps because he, Trevisa, had brooked no interference from the college in matters relating to Berkeley Church and its chantries and chapelries. In this latter controversy he had received support from my Lord Berkeley and also from the Abbot of St. Augustine's.

Trevisa, before the punitive expedition set out, informed his patron. The latter's reactions were, 'I shall officially know nothing of this affair. By all means teach that corpulent popinjay a salutary and even painful lesson, but for goodness sake be careful not to kill or even maim him. That would be a little difficult to laugh off.'

The party, nearly fifty in all, was made up of a dozen fully equipped men-at-arms, several archers from the forest of Dean and nearly a score of other retainers armed with an assortment of weapons which included halberds, swords, spears and even clubs. In addition there were Trevisa, John Poleyne and the sons of several local gentry who were anxious to take part in this raid just for the hell of it. All were mounted so that the whole enterprise could be accomplished during the hours of darkness and the return to Berkeley well before dawn ensured.

The raiders rode through Rockhampton, avoided Thornbury and arrived outside the college well before midnight.[7] The sleepy janitor stared open-eyed at what seemed to him a vast horde of silent soldiery led by men of obvious position. Overawed and still befuddled by sleep and the ale earlier consumed, he obeyed the order to open the gate. With the enjoinder to keep silent, and encouraged thereto by a sword-point at his back, the janitor led the assault party to the Dean's sleeping-quarters. Such college retainers as were disturbed were speedily herded together under guard in the courtyard.

The Dean, awakened to find his room full of armed men, at first sat up and blustered. A dagger held lightly across his throat rapidly changed his manner. In terror his eyes searched for a friendly face amongst the crowd. Suddenly sighting Trevisa he shrieked 'For the love of God and by the prayers of Peter and Paul call off these murderers'. John Poleyne with a gloved hand smote him lightly across the cheek and said, 'You hypocrite! You who have treated with scant mercy many within your power, and being a priest have perjured your immortal soul, and perverted justice, do you now whine for mercy? Come now! Confess your sins and make restitution (Where it can be so) before you die. You unjustly dealt with the chantry priest at Aust and robbed him of two marks, so make good that theft, with interest too! Here are quill and ink and parchment, admit your guilt of perjury before the Bishop's court — What was the bribe you offered the judge that day, and what pressure did you impose upon those people of Stone which made them put their souls in jeopardy by lying in their teeth? Look not for mercy from your victim here. Master Trevisa, as a true man of God, might forgive you for himself, but as custodian of the well-being of others he bids you give back, in kind and character, what you so wrongly stole away. And as your death-bed confessor he commands you, at the peril of your soul, to do all this and more so that you may hope for mercy from the Judge of all mankind. So now Mr. Dean, get down upon your knees and cleanse your black heart before you die!'

With that the terrified cleric was dragged from his bed and half stumbling, half carried, was brought out into the street. There he promised that full financial restitution would be made, and as far as in him lay, all grievances put right. In the turmoil, the pen, ink and parchment had been left behind in the bedroom, and so a verbal recantation of his perjurous statements in the Bishop's Court were accepted — upon an assurance of a personal confession to the judge (who, Trevisa felt certain, already knew the truth and connived at the miscarriage of justice) and a promise that the findings would be reversed.

Bearing in mind Lord Berkeley's caution, the victim, to his relief and surprise, was then allowed to make his way ignominiously back through the gates, across the courtyard in full view of his guarded retainers, and on into his quarters. These latter stared open-eyed at their master, their normally stern master, in mud-spattered nightshirt and bare-footed, running past like a hunted felon. More than one felt that a little humbling and ridicule was most opportune and would do their hard and arrogant Dean and master no harm.

The punitive party released the remaining prisoners, mounted their horses and made their way home confident that they had been instrumental in rectifying numerous wrongs and that their actions would win the approbation of God and man.

The Dean spent the following morning after mass in deep meditation, not on things spiritual, as might have been expected of a churchman of high degree, but on mundane matters. Should he report the whole affair to the Bishop? Well not the whole of course, but the assault only, omitting, naturally, the reason for the attack and humiliation. What backing would last night's thugs have if the matter was forced out into the open? Dare he NOT make some protest? What would the brethren, and retainers too, feel and think if he lay down under this public insult? He knew he must take action, but what? He would need time to decide, and his plans would have to be laid with subtlety and great care. At that moment the angelus rang and the Dean knelt in prayer.

The Dean found it most difficult to decide upon a course of action. He had to safeguard his own good name, and yet ensure that retribution and severe official censure should descend upon Trevisa. A clear charge of assault upon his own person must be established, and it must be demonstrated beyond all reasonable doubt that Trevisa was acting in personal revenge, that it was his spite at being found out, and his fury that his lack of faithfulness in his parochial ministry had been laid bare

This was the gist of the letter, nay the report, on the further misdemeanours which, several weeks later, the Bishop of Worcester perused in his study. There was something not quite 'right' in the letter, indeed something incomprehensible in the whole affair. He had felt a little of this when he had read the report after the Trevisa trial. Now with this latest incident the conviction was growing that there was much more behind the presented facts, if only it could be discovered. Trevisa was known to have been one who had little respect for authority and more than once had taken part in open rebellion, but always there had been a cause, a reason, mistaken maybe, but one in which he believed implicitly. Furthermore, never before had there been any suggestion of dereliction of duty, nor any record of personal violence. This matter required investigation, thorough investigation. The following day the senior Archdeacon and the Abbot of St. Peter's Abbey, Gloucester, were summoned to see his Lordship on the Eve of the Transfiguration or the day following.

On the seventh of August the Bishop, the Archdeacon and the Abbot met at Hartlebury Castle. They studied carefully the report of the trial and also the complaint lodged by the Dean of Westbury. All agreed that on the face of the evidence presented by the prosecution, Trevisa had been negligent and irresponsible, but noted that Trevisa had vehemently denied this, and had stated on oath that all arrangements had been accepted willingly by the people of Stone. The clerics reflected that Lord Berkeley and his noble father, had always spoke highly of Trevisa both as a man and a priest. The two pictures did not match. After much discussion it was decided that the Bishop should approach my Lord Berkeley for permission to hold an inquiry, headed by the Archdeacon and the Abbot, in Berkeley Castle. To this Trevisa, the chantry priests of Berkeley and Stone and the principal lay representatives from Stone would be summoned by episcopal writ, countersigned, if agreement could be reached, by Lord Berkeley, who would, naturally, preside at the Court, as it would be held in the Castle.

The Great Hall seethed with excitement when my Lord Berkeley and the Bishop's representatives entered the chamber and took their seats at the High Table. The Noble Lord opened the proceedings by stating that the Court had been summoned to inquire deeply into certain matters which affected the honour of several local persons. He reminded those summoned that their witness was upon oath and that if later it transpired that any had lied, he or she would come before his manor court and would be dealt with in a manner approved by himself and from which sentence there would be no appeal, save only to his Majesty or to his Lords in Council.

The Archdeacon then rose. 'My Lord Berkeley and my Lord Abbot, I beg leave to outline the reason for this inquiry. It is well known that in February last Master John Trevisa was charged with negligence in spiritual matters and was found guilty, which guilt and sentence were confirmed at a subsequent Court.

On 25th May last this same Master John Trevisa, it is alleged, accompanied a riotous mob which invaded the holy precincts of Westbury College, disarmed many retainers and savagely assulted the Dean. Hitherto the priest so charged has always been diligent in his duties and normally respectful to his superiors. My Lord Bishop has charged me and my Lord Abbot to seek an explanation for conduct which is so out of character. My Lord Berkeley graciously allowed this inquiry to be held here and has kindly agreed to preside. I now call upon Master Trevisa to step forward and state his case.'

Trevisa at once rose and made his way down the Hall. 'My Lords and those assembled here, I plead not guilty to the first charge, and provocation and greatly extenuating circumstances in the latter. May I repeat what was said at the Bishop's Court, that before my departure for Oxford in October last, I made all necessary arrangements for the Sacraments and services at Stone Chapel — arrangements which were declared acceptable to the elected representatives of that church. Later, well after my departure, the Dean of Westbury visited some of the church officials. From then the attitude of the parish of Stone changed. It is my contention that the Dean quite deliberately bribed or compelled the Stone officials to give false evidence, evidence which resulted in my condemnation. The reasons behind this persecution I believe are two-fold. In the first place, I, unknowingly, criticised his nephew — the young man merited it, but perhaps my remarks were imprudent. Secondly, it is well-known in this district that the Dean has bullied and ridden roughshod over several parish and chantry priests. I, with the loyal backing of my patron, Lord Berkeley, am one of the few who have been able to withstand him. For this the Dean dislikes me.

'When the sentence had been passed upon me — the vile condemnation of an innocent man which was prompted by spite — several persons, of whom I was one, decided that the tyranny of the Dean must be ended-once and for all. Consequently a party was formed to force a confession from the Dean and to extract from him a promise that the wrongs committed by him should, as far as possible, be put right. This we did. The Dean made full confession that he had put pressure upon the Stone officials, which caused them to bring the charge and give false evidence. Furthermore, he promised to make full restitution to the priests whom he had robbed and oppressed. One of these, Father James of Aust, from whom the Dean wrongfully withheld two marks, is here today to give evidence. Furthermore there are present in this Hall several who heard the said Dean's full confession and are prepared to testify thereto. As God is my witness, I sware that this my testimony is true in all respects.' With that the vicar of Berkeley returned to his place and sat down.

A buzz of conversation broke out and it was some seconds before the Archdeacon could make himself heard. 'Let Father James come forward and make his statement, and will those who were present at Westbury, when, it is said, the Dean in a confession admitted perjury, thus preventing justice being administered, be ready to give their evidence.

The Aust Chaplain, obviously overcome by the occasion, stammered and stuttered but finally made it clear that Trevisa's statement about the two marks was true, and that the Dean's actions were unbecoming and dishonest.

John Poleyne and seven others — several of them of good family — swore that they had heard the Dean state that he had persuaded the Stone officials to bring the charge against Master Trevisa and to give false evidence.

My Lord Berkeley called back the last seven witnesses, and cross-examined them as to whether they were fully certain that their evidence was correct in all respects. Finally he said 'Are you prepared to swear upon Holy Writ that the Dean admitted perjury?' This they did.

The Archdeacon then summoned John Sergeant of Stone to come forward and give evidence. 'What say you', asked the cleric, 'to these statements sworn on oath, that you and others from Stone conspired with the Dean of Westbury, to obtain the condemnation of the vicar of Berkeley? Before you reply ponder well, and reflect that the Judge of all mankind stands here with us, waiting to hear you speak.'

The witness, white-faced and trembling, hesitated then blurted out 'My Lords forgive me! I lied, I lied. The Dean said that Master Trevisa was a selfish and lazy priest and needed to be punished for many misdeeds, which cleverly he had covered up. I ask forgiveness for these lies.'

One by one the other Stone officials said much the same, and when the last had sat down the Archdeacon, the Abbot and my Lord Berkeley retired to consider the evidence and to decide upon their course of action. In the chapel of St. Mary the Virgin they remained for nearly an hour.

The Archdeacon, on the re-opening of the Court, bade the Stone officials stand and pronounced sentence upon them. 'You men of Stone have offended grievously against God and man, and have caused an unjust sentence to be imposed upon a man of God, and brought discredit upon him and the Ministry. That you were duped by one who was your superior is clear, and this my Lords and I have taken into consideration. We have now decreed that on the next four Sundays at the hour of noon you, each and all, come sickness, wind or weather, will go in procession round Stone Church clad in your shift, and bearing a wax candle of 1 lb weight in your hand. You will proclaim loudly and as long as the candle lasts that you have committed gross perjury. On the two Sundays following you will do the same at Berkeley. This is your purgation. If you fail to fulfil our orders my Lord Berkeley will have you imprisoned for as long as it pleases him. You will each pay a fine of half a mark to the manor court within three months. You may now go.'

The Archdeacon then addressed the members of the raiding party and the parish priest.

'You, gentlemen, are not guiltless. You may say you were provoked, and so you were, but that does not give you leave to take justice into your own hands and storm Westbury College, terrify its inmates and brutally handle a man of God, even though you believed that he had done things unbecoming to his high office. You will, each of you, say three extra Pater Nosters for the next week and contribute a quarter mark to the manor court to be used for the poor. You too may go.'

Lord Berkeley then rose and declared the Court closed.

That evening the Archdeacon and the Abbot discussed their report for the Bishop and especially the recommendations concerning the Dean of Westbury. To them it seemed there were two possible courses open to the Bishop, now that the perfidy of the Dean had been established. He could be removed from office. This would involve courts of inquiry and could, if appeals were made to the Archbishop or even to his Holiness, drag on for months, indeed years. The alternative was to ignore the whole affair as far as the Dean was concerned. The latter would, no doubt, soon hear of the Berkeley inquiry and findings, but would, with no reply to his letter, be kept in suspense as to the Bishop's intentions with regard to him. This latter course the Abbot felt would be the better. The Dean had suffered great humiliation already, and the lack of obvious episcopal support would be sufficient further punishment and might prevent trouble in the future. If however incidents did occur at a later date, then the Dean must resign or be found a place elsewhere. The Archdeacon agreed and the Bishop, later, accepted the recommendation.

Months passed and although the local clergy were not subjected to the same gross interference, yet no attempts were made to redress the wrongs inflicted or to repay the debts.

Finally John Poleyne and Master Trevisa sought an official interview with Lord Berkeley. John Poleyne pressed for a second visitation with, this time maybe, episcopal knowledge, but, naturally, without his Lordship's overt support.

Lord Berkeley approached the Bishop. The latter disliked intensely the whole idea, but the prospect of possibly long and costly litigation for the Dean's removal — and there was no guarantee that the higher courts would take the desired course, especially as the offender was closely allied to powerful families — worried his Lordship. In the end, with great reluctance and with a firm injunction that the person of the offender should not be harmed, his Lordship gave consent for one more unofficial attempt to force the Dean to conform.

The raid, for it was nothing else, planned with the greatest secrecy, was carried out three weeks later when the moon was full'[8] and followed closely the pattern of the earlier affray. The cold February air, however, made the Dean's midnight nightshirted frolics bodily almost unbearable. This perhaps accounted for his less rigorous resistance both mental and physical. Finally, an assurance was wrung from him that his earlier promises would soon be implemented. The leaders of the expedition felt certain, however, that the acceptance of the terms was made purely on the score of expediency. Consequently they removed coin and goods to the value of forty pounds as surety for their fulfilment.

The Dean, the very next morning, feeling that a second approach to the Bishop would be fruitless, appealed direct to the King and left for London to arrange for a relation to present his letter. The document read thus:-

'To our very dread lord the King and to his very wise Council complains Robert Dean of the Collegiate Church of Westbury in the County of Gloucester of John Poleyne, squire of Thomas Berkeley of Berkeley, knight, of this that the said John with a great number of men armed and arrayed with habergeons, swords, bucklers, daggers, sticks, bows and arrows riotously assembled in manner of war against the peace of our said lord the King, the Statute of Northampton and other statutes and ordinances in such cases provided, came to Westbury aforesaid the morrow of the feast of Holy Trinity the eleventh year of our said lord the King [May 25, 1388] by night and besieged him there and broke open the doors and entered by force into his chamber and took the said Dean lying in his bed and dragged him out of his house into the street tearing his clothes and there assaulted, beat, wounded, and maltreated him so that he was in despair of his life and then imprisoned him and threatened to kill him so that for fear of death he promised to make a fine with him and to give all his goods to suffer him to have his life.

'And then the said John Trevysa, John Breton, Richard Curteys and John Smyth of Westbury of whom he complains in the same manner followed by a great number of men riotously assembled armed and arrayed in warlike fashion in manner of an insurrection the Monday 12th February, the 12th year of our said lord the King [1389] came to Westbury aforesaid and there broke into and forcibly entered the house of the said Dean and his doors, against the peace and the aforesaid statutes in order to kill him, and assaulted, beat, wounded and maltreated his servants and took and carried away his goods and chattels to the value of 40 pounds and committed other great oppressions to his cost and damage in contempt of our lord the King to the oppression, terror and bad example of the whole country and to the damage of the said suppliant to the amount of £100 for which he prays that a remedy may be ordained by our lord the King and his said Council for God as a work of charity, because the said suppliant cannot have justice nor recover against them by the common law because the said John Poleyne is so great a maintainer of quarrels and so much encouraged by the great lords [seigneurie] in the aforesaid country [pais].' 9

The King, when the letter was finally presented, was furious that a high official of the Church had been subjected to such indignations, and that the earlier appeal to the Bishop of Worcester had proved fruitless. A letter was despatched to Lord Berkeley demanding that he should take immediate action and have the offenders severely punished. A full report that this had been carried out would then be rendered.

Lord Berkeley, on receiving this letter, conferred with the Bishop, whose scriveners wrote out a detailed account of the background to the dispute and a full report of the proceedings of both the Bishop's Court and that held in Berkeley Castle. Armed with this document, Lord Berkeley petitioned for and obtained an audience with the King.

His Lordship emphasized that the apparent lack of action by the Bishop after the first raid had been prompted by mercy and consideration for the Dean and his relatives. The Dean, obviously, had not repented and consequently it would be better that he should be forced to resign and transfer to another house. Would His Majesty give his consent that this should be effected without delay and thus avoid a major scandal? Thus attack was met by counter-attack.

Further long discussions followed in which the Bishop of Norwich — the only prelate then present at Court — joined. The King finally agreed to notify the Dean that he was handing over the complaint to the Bishop of Worcester.

The Bishop of Norwich suggested that Master John Trevisa should be recompensed for the pain and anguish of the previous persecution by a canonry at Westbury, when one fell vacant. This proposal was also given the royal approval. Consequently it was a relieved Lord Berkeley who on the morrow rode westward.

A few days later news reached Berkeley that his Lordship's mother, the Lady Elizabeth, had died. At once Lord Berkeley and his chaplain set out for London. The funeral took place in the Church of St. Botulphes[10]. The occasion was quiet and the ceremonial of the simplest; even so Trevisa was thankful that, though he had a part to play, the organization was in other hands.

Chapter 10
Problems and Tragedy

(a) *John Dyer*

John Dyer, the chaplain of Berkeley Chantry [1], was a worried man. The chaplain of Stone Chantry, Thomas Norton, had warned him to cross the river, for John Sergeant of Stone, a trouble-maker if ever there was one, had sent to the Lord Bishop complaining that Dyer was an associate of evil men who were constantly breaking the King's peace. In addition there was John's marriage to Agnes Nelme, long accepted locally — and approved of, too, by many, who held that a priest should be allowed to marry as other men, for how else could he understand fully his peoples' problems? This offence also had been officially brought to the Bishop's notice, by Sergeant's friend the Archdeacon of Gloucester, of course. The episcopal reation had been swift — too swift for John. The Sheriff of Gloucester, acting he said on the Bishop's orders, rode to Berkeley, arrested the chaplain, proclaimed Agnes a harlot, and imprisoned the former in Gloucester gaol.

Trevisa, on hearing of the Sheriff's sudden seizure of Dyer and realizing that it was yet another instance of Sergeant's animosity towards Berkeley in general and its clergy in particular, at once sought out Lord Berkeley upon his return from Michaelwood Chase. His Lordship was tired and angry, for sport had been bad, even worse his favourite hound, indeed the pack leader, intent upon the tiring stag, had by accident roused a slumbering boar which spring from its lair and launched himself at the passing hound. Brave, faithful Caesar, deeply scored from shoulder to hind-quarter, died within minutes, and the stag, given this breather, had escaped. His Lordship, nevertheless, agreed to discuss the matter with his private chaplain when dinner had ended.

Lord Berkeley listened to the tale of woe, paused a moment and then said:—
'Well, what can the chaplain expect? He has broken God's law in marrying, and must take the consequences. No doubt, too, there would be some truth in the other charges also.'

'My Lord, you are tired, and so not as charitable as is your wont, furthermore it has slipped your memory that we considered Dyer's marriage some time ago, and that we concluded that he was within his right. With Your Lordship's leave I will point out the basic arguments relating to the controversy.

'Firstly celibacy of the clergy is not forbidden by divine decree. It is purely a man-made law having no scriptural authority. The prophets of old, including Moses, the great law giver, felt free to marry. One at least of the Master's inner band — we would term them bishops today, Peter, was a married man, while Blessed Paul said that it was better for a man to marry than to burn. An edict proclaimed by a bishop, even St. Peter's successor, the Pope in Rome, nor yet a canon formulated by a General Council, if it has not the weight of Holy Writ behind it, cannot be held to be above debate. Dyer's attitude is "What was allowable to Holy Peter must be permitted to me, if my conscience is clear, as clear it is". You will recall, too, that my Lord Bishop Wakefield, when Dyer's marriage was raised in friendly conversation tacitly accepted the situation by saying "Dyer is a good man, and God, clearly, has blessed his ministry in Berkeley. The marriage has not been brought officially to my notice, and I do not want to know about it". His Lordship feels, maybe, as I do, that this is a matter for the individual conscience, but he dare not make an episcopal ruling along those lines when many uphold the infallibility of the Holy Father's decrees.'

Lord Berkeley yawned and said, 'Very well, John, I will discuss this further tomorrow, and we will do our best, you and I, to get Dyer our of prison.'

Before noon on the following day a messenger rode across the drawbridge bearing a letter to my Lord Bishop. Its contents were placatory yet firm.

The Lord Lieutenant begged his Lordship to reconsider the action of 1st March, Holy David's day. The Sheriff, on his Lordship's orders it was said, had entered the Berkeley Hundred, Berkeley itself, and even the very church of the Holy Mother, and there, without reference to the parish priest or to Lord Berkeley, had arrested and forcibly dragged off to prison a chaplain, one John Dyer, of a Berkeley Chantry founded by the late Lord Thomas Berkeley. The Lord Bishop had, no doubt, acted in good faith, believing that Lord Berkeley was fully aware of the situation and approved. The latter then stated that (1) no one in Berkeley had been previously informed of the intended arrest, (2) the actions of the Sheriff's men in the church was, by their violation of the law of Sanctuary, gross sacrilege which merited severe episcopal censure, (3) Lord Berkeley declared most emphatically that there was no evidence for connecting Dyer with any subversive or unruly elements in the area, and that the charge was trumped up and born of malice and chagrin, constituting another example of Sergeant's slanderous busybodying, with which he, Lord Berkeley, would now deal, (4) His Lordship reminded the Lord Bishop that the second matter, the marriage of Dyer, had been known — and accepted — over many years, and had the approbation of the people of Berkeley who witnessed to Dyer's exemplary way of life. It should be remembered, too, that the marriage of God's ministers had full scriptural backing from Moses down to Holy Paul. His Lordship continued that most people were aware that even today celibacy of the clergy was by no means universally practised. The Prior of Hereford, the Abbot of Flaxley, six of his monks and more than fifty clergy in the neighbouring diocese of Hereford openly enjoyed the connubial state, [2] with some paying regularly and cheerfully, the 'cradle crown' [3] and were still permitted to administer the Word and Sacraments. (5) Lastly, Lord Berkeley begged my Lord Bishop to issue forthwith an order to the Sheriff to hand over the person of John Dyer to Lord Berkeley's 'mainprizes', John Trevisa and Henry Hedlam.[4]

Three days later the Bishop read Lord Berkeley's letter and frowned. It was indeed a delicate situation which had arisen. That sacrilege had been committed was now self-evident, and, with Lord Berkeley backing, if the charge was pressed, matters could be unpleasant. Again with the accusation of evil association the ground had suddenly become bog-like and quaky, for his Lordship's word would be preferred to that of John Sergeant of Stone.

The marriage of John Dyer was indisputable, and was a heinous offence by canon law, yet even here there were problems. Lord Berkeley was right; there were instances of alliances between priest and woman, and had been for centuries. Had not Giraldus Cambrensis complained of its prevalence in his day? My Lord Bishop of Hereford was having considerable trouble in this direction, due no doubt to the proximity of Welsh and Dean Forest influences.

These unions, morganatic, concubinage or declaratory, call them what one wished, were often exemplary in character, and the resultant children, such as John Cornwall, the Oxford scholar, were occasionally ordained — after dispensation of course. Many of these so termed marriages were accepted by parishioners and ignored by certain Bishops. Bishop Wakefield, however, had secretly long wanted to make a salutory example in his diocese, and here was a clear case; but, solid though the facts were, it would be defended and fought vigorously, thereby bringing the whole controversy of celibacy into open debate, with Lord Berkeley sponsoring Dyer, and no doubt, bringing up the arguments of lack of scriptural backing, validation of long custom and episcopal connivance in many instances. Few bishops would welcome publicity on this subject, for it would, doubtless, result in a new outbreak of these illicit unions. Master Trevisa, unquestionably, was behind this strong protest, and had, perhaps obtained the Hereford figures from his old associate, the one-time lollard, Master Nicholas Hereford, recently released from prison. Trevisa was supplying the arrows for Lord Berkeley to loose. That priest was as clever as a cartload of Moroccan monkeys and entirely ruthless if occasion demanded. Rarely did he make a false move, and his defence of Dyer would rally public support. It would be better to flay Dyer orally and to impose a nominal fine and penance. To do much more, under the circumstances, could conceivably bring about dire trouble. No, the best plan, one based on expediency, was no doubt the correct one.

Later that day my Lord Bishop called his Archdeacon and bade him ride to Gloucester, and there admonish Dyer and fine him three pence. He would also censure the Sheriff for the sacrilege, but particularly for being so foolish in the carrying out of his duties — actions which had made it far more difficult for his Lordship and were among the main reasons why the charges against Dyer would be so different to press home.

The following day Lord Berkeley's messenger left with a letter to his Lordship stating that my Lord Bishop, after examining the case fully, had sent his Archdeacon to admonish Dyer and impose a nominal fine, so that Dyer would be released to the mainprizes, John Trevisa and Henry Hedlam, at his Lordship's convenience. The Bishop added that the Archdeacon would also severely censure the Sheriff.

On the first of April John Trevisa and Henry Hedlam received custody of John Dyer in Gloucester gaol and the chaplain of the Berkeley chantry returned safely to his cure.

(b) *The Churchyard (1390) and, later, a Fair.*

Some months later Lord Berkeley sent for his chaplain and said:— 'Canon, I wish to discuss with you a matter on which I have spent much thought. You know that my noble father fought in France and brought back with him ideas which he developed here in Berkeley. The vinery on Pedington bank is but one example, while the smaller one at Wanswell must not be forgotten.

Another and more far reaching innovation he mentioned to me once or twice, namely further alterations to the castle, and particularly methods of strengthening its defences. These vague thoughts, he said, were directly engendered by the castle patterns which he had seen at the wars and during captivity. Because of his ill-health after his return he felt unable, physically, to undertake all that he would have liked. I have pondered long over his, to me, vague plans. Recently, on my return to England, I passed Bodiam Castle and saw there in that new creation some little of what my father had talked. We cannot imitate that building for we have here a structure and lay of ground that cannot be adapted to that model, built ab novo. We can, however, and should, do something to improve our defences, for the times are worrying, and civil war, which God forbid, could well break out if the King continues in his present way of life. You will say "but how can I, a man of God and of peace, advise you on military matters?" Sir Priest, you can and must, for the plan I have in mind involves the churchyard. You are my bedeman, but I recognise that you, as vicar, have, beyond the castle walls, a duty to your greater flock, part of whose churchyard I need to enable me to carry through my scheme of defence. You must also be the link and intermediary between the Abbot of St. Augustine's and myself in this matter. I trust that you and he, and your parishioners also, will not follow Naboth and refuse your 'vineyard' when I make my offer! Furthermore I do not wish to antagonize Mother Church, as did my ancestor full two hundred years ago — and suffered for it!'

'My Lord, this is a matter which, as you clearly understand, must be handled with the utmost care, for its repercussions could well be considerable and unfortunate. Your illustrious ancestor desired, you may recall, the same objective, and because his approach was impetuous and arrogant he was reprimanded, fined, and, more distressing still, lost for ever the friendship and trust of the Abbot and Brethren of St. Augustine's. [5] This latter possibility, my Lord, must be avoided at almost any costs. Mother Church is a powerful friend, but can be, on occasion, an implacable persecutor of gross offenders, amongst the ranks of whom you must never be accounted. Be patient, my Lord. Let me ponder over this delicate matter and take private counsel with my Lord Abbot and others, before your Lordship makes the formal request. I will also sound the wardens on this matter, but they, knowing your generosity to the parish church, indeed to God's Kingdom in general, will not be unsympathetic. John Nelme, of Alkington, Richard Attwood of Hinton and John Tyler of Ham, will, for sure, fall in with your wishes. I have some reservation about Henry Saniger, the Mayor of the Borough. He feels his responsibilities heavy upon his shoulders to protect the community, its interests and amenities. He could, and would if ruffled or slighted, appeal to the Knights of the Shire, to the Bishop, indeed even to the Archbishop himself for aid against what he might term your Lordship's sacrilegious intentions. Win him over and you will have an able ally. Why not see him yourself? That gracious gesture might convert him lock, stock and barrel.'

Lord Berkeley took his chaplain's advice and saw Henry Saniger. His Lordship made it clear to the Mayor that he was seeking his help in forwarding his plans, pointing out that a strongly defended and defensible castle was a real deterrent to a would be aggressor. The town of Berkeley would, no doubt, be somewhat safer when it was known that the rather vulnerable north-western approaches to the castle had, militarily, been vastly improved. It was pointed out, quite truthfully, that the times were, potentially, dangerous and that civil war, which was no respecter of persons, could well break out at any moment.

The Mayor, taken aback that his Lordship had called to consult him, and not to issue an order or make a demand, was at first suspicious and rather dour in his replies. Soon, however, his attitude mellowed — perhaps the visit and demeanour of his caller boosted his ego — and he became both genial and vocal. Yes, he saw the need, the urgent need, of defence development for the sakes of all. He would, he promised, use all his influence upon his fellow wardens and the aldermen of the town to persuade them, if such was necessary, that his Lordship's plans were for the common good, and must be carried through with all haste. The proposed payment to Mother Church had no direct influence upon the Mayor's attitude, except in so far as it convinced him that this was no seignorial seizure but an action motivated by consideration for the whole community. The assurance of reverent reburial in consecrated ground for the bodies of parishioners carried great weight.

The Mayor, as Lord Berkeley was preparing to leave, put in a sly question, 'My Lord, when these necessary works have been completed, and the castle made secure from sudden attack, and the town less attractive for attempts at plunder, might a licence to hold a market and fair be applied for and granted? The possible danger to the castle from a packed market town, with foes disguised as countryfolk mingling with the crowds, has in the past been given as a reason for the refusal of previous request.' [6]

His Lordship stiffened, but, remembering his chaplain's advice that a soft answer will often accomplish more than a rough tongue, merely said 'Well that is a possibility which we can consider when the time is ripe.'

Such was the mayoral energy that within a few days Henry Saniger and other wardens and church officials met his Lordship, bearing with them the news that no objection would be raised to the appropriating of a section of the churchyard, provided that the reburials, as agreed, would be reverently carried out, and a slight yearly remuneration made to the Church. They, at the same time, made a formal application for a fair.

After lengthy discussion My Lord agreed to recompense 'with a yearly rent of 6s. 8d. to the parishioners for amends, out of three tenements in Berkeley, and for the buying and maintaining of a little sans bell, whereby the garden that was formerly in that place was destroyed;' [7]

The Abbot of St. Augustine's, softened no doubt by a suitable sum of money, also agreed, and so this matter was resolved.

True to his word Lord Berkeley considered carefully the question of a fair, and when all defensive works had been completed, obtained a grant in 1394 for a fair to be held on the vigil and on the day of the Invention of Holy Cross, called Holy Rood Day (May 2nd and 3rd), each year. [8]

(c) *Abroad Again*

The troubles and frustrations of 1388/9 were over. These, it must be admitted, had been made even worse by the somewhat vigorous retaliatory actions against the Dean, although there was a measure of truth in the euphuistical claim that these operations were in the nature of salutary lessons administered upon a bully for the protection of the weak. That at least was the view point emphasized by Master

Trevisa and by John Poleyne, and no doubt others in Berkeley Vale agreed.

Trevisa, with these worries behind him, recommenced the preparations for his journey to France and Germany. He, after much discussion with William Middleworth, had determined to embark upon the translation of at least two further works from the Latin. The first and shorter was to be the *Gospel of Nicodemus*. This fragmentary biblical manuscript had fired his imagination in the distant Devon days, when he and William had formed part of Bishop Grandisson's household. There he had read and reread this uncanonical gospel and it had left upon his mind a deep impression. The long and detailed account of Our Lord's trial had aroused his interest, and the vigorous defence by Nicodemus, made in the face of the determination of the Jewish hierarchy to procure the death sentence, was still a source of inspiration to the middle-aged priest, and on more than one occasion in the past it had encouraged him to resist staunchly entrenched authority when the cause was patently just. The hostile interrogation of Annas and Caiaphas by Pilate, Trevisa felt, was more in keeping with this just, though rugged and at times ruthless, Roman Governor.

The coming forward of certain people who had been healed by the Master, e.g., 1. Veronica, the lady suffering from an issue of blood for twelve years, 2. the man born blind, 3. a leper; to give evidence in Christ's favour, too, was what might have been expected. In many other ways this gospel, so thought Trevisa, was more revealing, more 'human', and in some respects more inspiring than the four canonical gospels of the New Testament.

The urge to continue the translation of the *De Regimine Principum* of Aegidius Romanus was, of course, increased by the continued strained relationship between the King and many of his nobles, some of whom declared — not always openly! — that Richard was not the embodiment of kingship, and that in the interests of the country, which may well have meant their interests, it would be better that a stronger and more vigorous leader, from their own number of course, should be at the helm.

The vicar of Berkeley, remembering the trouble resulting from his last period of absence while working at Oxford on the translation of both the *De Proprietatibus Rerum* and the *De Regimine Principum,* laid his plans carefully and ensured that should difficulties occur when he was abroad, or should complaints come in after his returning, no blame could be attached to him. To this end he consulted his patron who, true to the earlier agreement, readily gave his blessing. The second step was to obtain Royal approval for leaving the realm for so long a period. This would necessitate the nomination of one or more locum tenentes for Berkeley parish and its castle. Trevisa approached two colleagues from Queen's.

The one was William Faryington, a canon of Chichester and prebendary of Marden and but recently appointed rector of Astbury in Cheshire, [9] and the other was Robert Hodersale, a Doctor of Theology and rector of Northchurch, Hertfordshire since July. [10] These both agreed to care for the cure of Berkeley and the chaplaincy of the castle. This they were able to do because their own parochial responsibilities were largely fulfilled by curates, thus allowing the nominal rectors to continue residing at Queen's or to take up other appointments.

Trevisa was confident that with such distinguished scholars as locum tenentes the Royal approval would be forthcoming. Thus it was no surprise to the vicar when the following document:—

'Master John Trevisa, vicar of the church of Berkeley and canon of the Collegiate

Church of Westbury (who by the King's leave is about to depart to the parts beyond the sea, has the King's letters of general attorney) under the names of Master Robert de Hodersale, clerk, and Master William de Faryngton, clerk. Witness the King at Westminster the 5th day of November [1390]. [While] Robert [sic] de Faryngton clerk received attorney as far as the rent of the aforesaid John in England [is concerned]'. [11]
finally reached Berkeley Castle on 22nd day of December. A month later the Berkeley vicar handed over his cure and his chaplaincy and set out on his travels.

(d) *The Death of Lady Margaret*

Trevisa arrived back in Berkeley on 15th March 1392, later than had first envisaged. This delay had been built up gradually and was due to several factors, two of which, however, were primarily responsible. Travel had been more difficult, especially during the winter months, than had been expected. Secondly, more copies of the *De Proprietatibus Rerum* and a greater wealth of biblical manuscript had been available than had been expected. These had constituted an embarrassment of riches.

The Town of Berkeley had altered little since John had left it fifteen months earlier. There was, however, an air of the deepest gloom hanging like a pall over the whole countryside, for the beloved Lady Margaret was ill — dangerously ill. For months she had ailed and now had taken to her bed. Physicians came and went, but the alternating attacks of fever and shaking fits increased. There was, it was generally agreed, no hope of recovery. Father Dunstan had prayed daily with her Ladyship and the Abbot of St. Augustine's, Bristol, had administered the Viaticum. The result was, indeed, in God's hands.

John was shocked when two days later at Wotton he knelt by Lady Margaret's bedside. Her flesh had wasted away and the eyes had sunken deep into the head. The chaplain could see full well that rumour was in this instance no lying jade and that the earthly pilgrimage of her Ladyship was drawing rapidly to a close. The end came on March 20th. [12] Lady Margaret was barely thirty years of age when the last enemy of man snatched her away from her husband and Elizabeth their tiny daughter.

The funeral, on Lady Day, was a spectacle such as had not been seen at Wotton in living memory. The weather was fine, as it had been for ten days and more, and the tenantry and friends from the Vale and Cotswolds filled the large church to overflowing, such was the esteem in which Thomas, Lord Berkeley, and the Lady Margaret were held by all and sundry.

Within a few weeks, however, gossips, in spite of the obvious grief of his Lordship, were beginning to speculate upon whom Lord Berkeley would now marry; for it was assumed that a vigorous man of thirty-eight, without a male heir to succeed to the considerable estates, would most certainly remarry so that the name of Berkeley should continue. These ladies were doomed to disappointment.

Lord Berkeley, directly the funeral was over, returned to his castle in the vale and for a time saw no one outside his own family and staff. In May, obviously after much thought, he approached the King and craved permission to travel abroad for a year, perhaps a little longer, so that fresh sights and new faces might help to ease the bitter blow which fate had dealt him. King Richard willingly agreed to the request.

His Lordship, when the royal assent had been received, sent for John and told him of his plans to travel to France and perhaps to Italy. The actual itinerary was, of course, vague as yet, but would soon begin to take shape. Lord Berkeley then spoke of John's future. 'You have now completed the first part of the project which we discussed and agreed upon two years ago. The second half, your time at Oxford, still has to be undertaken. Have you given the matter of the continuation of the task much thought? You may well feel that it is essential to return to Oxford in the near future so that there shall be as short a break as possible in your studies and research. If this is so, then the period of my absence abroad would appear most convenient. Should you need more time at Oxford than the six months originally suggested, I will, naturally be responsible for the additional rents and college dues. I have spoken to Father Dunstan and he will be prepared, subject to leave of absence being granted by his Abbot, and this he thought would willingly be given, to act as locum tenens for up to another year if necessary. I will, however, be frank with you and say that if speed is not vital and you could defer going to Oxford until after my return I would be grateful. I have, of course, made all arrangements for the Lady Elizabeth's care and well-being during my absence, and I am confident that all will go well. With regard to the future, I am, as you know, in the process of arranging a covenant with my Lord Thomas Beauchamp, Earl of Warwick, for the betrothal of Lady Elizabeth to his son Richard. [13] This contract I would like to see settled before I leave for foreign parts in a few weeks time — this, however, may not be possible. When these negotiations have been successfully completed I shall feel confident that Lady Elizabeth's more distant future will be assured — as assured, that is, as any father has a right to expect. After all Elizabeth is a considerable heiress in her own right, and an alliance with the Beauchamps, especially to the heir, will establish her as a lady of the first rank in the Kingdom — or nearly so. All this is very comforting. I would, however, feel happier were you to act as her chaplain, confessor and tutor and so be at hand for general supervision, thus ensuring that my wishes at all times are being carried out.'

John, who, in deference to his Lordship's sorrow, had refrained from mentioning Oxford, was surprised that the details of the earlier arrangements had been remembered. He was amazed, too, that bowed down by his bereavement and burdened with the plans for his foreign travel, Lord Berkeley should spare time to consider his chaplain's wishes and even to make tentative arrangements with the promise of considerable support. Unhesitatingly Trevisa replied 'My Lord, I shall be honoured to serve the Lady Elizabeth and to watch over your Lordship's interests. A deferment of a year or so in my return to Oxford will be of advantage. I might well, in the meanwhile, even persuade William Middleworth to return with me so that we can again work together on some biblical translation.' John saw these events as an opportunity to repay in a small way the long and generous patronage accorded him by the Berkeley family. He was especially grateful for his Lordship's support during the inquiry following the incident involving the Dean of Westbury, which, but for his Lordship's prompt action, might well have attracted to the chaplain a royal reprimand, possibly even imprisonment. Lord Berkeley in silence shook the chaplain by the hand and retired.

That evening, when reviewing the day's events, the cleric thought of the proposed marriage negotiations, and he was not entirely happy — common practice though these dynastic alliances were. 'Perhaps', he said to himself, 'I am becoming sentimental in my old age!' Still he could not but feel that these young folk were being treated as mere pawns to be moved impersonally by the scheming senior members of two ancient families for the creation of large estates and the establishment of more influential power blocks. This particular match was, he felt, more male in concept than the Earl and Lord Berkeley were prepared to admit. If Lady Margaret had not died this proposed marriage might not have had so swift an acceptance in principle.

Lord Berkeley was walking on air; to him this opportunity to advance his family's fortunes and status constituted one of those glorious opportunities which rarely appear, and must be quickly grasped. It was indeed the tide of fortune — good fortune — to be taken at the flood. Although he could not know it, not being possessed of foresight, slowness in the completion of the contracts might well have ruined the whole enterprise and changed the destiny of the Berkeley family. All this, however, was still within the womb of the future.

(e) *Guardianship — Casus Belli*

The departure of Lord Berkeley ushered in one of the most irritating and frustrating episodes in Trevisa's experience, or so in later years he was wont to declare. He had been deputed by his patron to act as tutor, chaplain and confessor to Lady Elizabeth, and he conceived that he was — in a very real way — guardian of the child, great lady though she might be, and, embryonically even greater.

The canon found, however, that others in the castle household held equally strong convictions which, moreover, did not accord with his. Sceptics amongst the poets had often warned, 'beware of the ladies', and how right they were! Trevisa's only serious clash was with the nursery staff, headed by a matron of ample proportions, despotic nature and a searing tongue, who objected to the canon's daily visitations and his assumption of guardianship. This fearsome lady one day, following a visit by Trevisa during which acrimonious words had been exchanged, turned to her sycophants and stormed:— 'How can any man take over-all charge of a little girl of under seven who has lost her mother and is now deserted by her father? The father of a large family from the common people might struggle through; but a priest, what hope has he? Why! he would not be able to do her hair or comfort when she cries herself to sleep, as no doubt she does — doesn't she? All this is womens' work, so let the priest stick to his prayers and masses — and leave confessions out too, for what could a small child have to confess?

This and much more the matron threw at the canon's head. Expostulations were laughed at and useless, and Trevisa felt that he was being made to look a fool by the nursery harridan and her toadies. In spite of this, Trevisa, true to his promise to Lord Berkeley, continued to visit Lady Elizabeth almost every day, and insisted on regular hours for her instruction in the christian faith and in the arts, but even these concessions had only been won after bitter battles and the threat of presenting a damning dossier to Lord Berkeley upon his return. The weeks and months passed slowly and Trevisa's self-control was tested to its limit. Every day the canon prayed for strength to maintain what he believed to be his duty to his patron, and to hold himself in check when dealing with the cursed army of prideful and pestilent women of the nursery.

The climax came when old Maggie, the matron, whose brother lived on the Berkeley estate at Portbury, proposed that the whole nursery should move to the Berkeley house in that parish for an indefinite period.

Trevisa pointed out that a short holiday for Lady Elizabeth would be acceptable, and would not conflict with the obligations imposed upon him by Lord Berkeley. The sour-faced matron turned and shouted 'The time and length of this visit is entirely in my hands and I will not be dictated to by any man, least of all a priest who is, after all, only half a man.'

The cleric paused, then shaking with rage said:— 'I have given a solemn undertaking to my Lord to maintain a watchful eye upon the Lady Elizabeth's general welfare, as well as caring for the religious and schooling side. This charge I cannot, and will not, abrogate.'

'You may be vicar of Berkeley and chaplain to the castle, master priest, but you will not order me about on this matter. My word and my wishes are final.'

'Madam, I must have an assurance from you that your visit will be only for a limited stay, and, as you are so truculent, you will now sware this on God's Holy Writ, for clearly I cannot trust any lesser oath.'

'Be damned to you, you interfering old toad! I'll do no such thing, and that is my last word.'

'Madam, your unreasonable and pig-headed insistences to thwart my Lord's wishes would lead me to think that you may have thoughts, or plans maybe, for participating in some of those riotous and bibulous orgies at Portbury for which your brother is notorious. It is my sacred duty to protect an innocent child from the possibility (however slight) of moral, yea even physical, contamination.'

'You bloody priest! How dare you say such things!'

The canon rode that afternoon to Beverstone and spoke to Sir John Berkeley, to whom he explained the situation and said that he intended assembling the castle household and publicly threatening madam Maggie with excommuncation, and thereby forbidding the staff to accept her orders.

Sir John thought a while before speaking. 'Are you not making a mountain out of a mole-hill canon? I should have thought that with your persuasive tongue, of which I have heard tell, you would have had little difficulty in making her see sense.'

'Sir John, I have tried, and tried hard, but with no success. But before I take the final step, and conscience compels me to maintain my pledge to my Lord Berkeley, I deemed it right that you should be acquainted with my intentions.'

'Well canon, I cannot interfere with your conscience, but I will come down with you, and together we will have one final talk with this troublesome lady.'

At first the matron held her ground, reiterating that the timing and duration of the Portbury visit was a matter for her, and her alone, to decide. Her arrogance and dictatorial attitude angered Sir John, who finally turned on her and said:— 'My good woman, remember that you are a paid servant. I am Lord Berkeley's deputy during his absence, and you will take orders from me whether you like it or not. You, naturally, do not wish people to tell you how to run the nursery which has been put in your charge. Others, however, have charges of at least equal importance. These persons have every right to your co-operation. The Reverend Canon, here, has, as I myself was told by Lord Berkeley, been ordered to keep a careful and watchful eye upon the Lady Elizabeth and also to supervise her schooling and religious instruction. The canon is a reasonable person and will not interfere in the nursery, but the instructions given by Lord Berkeley were explicit and must not be questioned. Canon Trevisa must be consulted on the date of the visit to Portbury and will decide, I said decide, on its duration. In all matters which come within his province you will give him instant and cheerful obedience. Do you understand? If you cannot accept my terms, then I know of one, a close relation, who would willingly come and take your place until Lord Berkeley returns. Now madam, what is your decision — one word only, please, "yes" or "no"!!

'My Lord, you are very hard, but I must accept. But God help that priest if he interferes.'

'Silence Woman! One more word, and you will leave within the hour. And let me not hear of any further difficulties created by you. Be gone to your nursery, and learn to behave yourself.'

'Canon, she is clearly an extremely difficult woman. I will talk the whole problem over with my wife, and if there should be any more trouble from her in any department of the household — I will speak to the bailiff about it — she must go. There will be no problem over an excellent replacement, and when Lord Berkeley returns I will discuss the matter with him, and suggest that the matron is replaced. A woman like that — however excellent her testimonials may have been — is not a fit person to have charge of the Lady Elizabeth in her early formative years.'

Armed neutrality was maintained between the matron and the cleric until Lord Berkeley returned. It was, as Trevisa said later, when the matron had departed, the most unpleasant period during his many years in Berkeley.

1392/3 (f) *The funeral of the Earl of Suffolk*

Later in the year Thomas Howard, Earl of Suffolk, died suddenly. The family requested, because of their close local ties, that the funeral might take place at Stone and that Master Yardley, the late Earl's domestic chaplain, might assist.[14] News of the arrangements travelled fast, and it soon became clear that the funeral would be a large and representative one. Canon Trevisa, sensing that this service was being considered an important occasion, and knowing his fellow clerics, anticipated trouble, for prestige — more fancied than real he held — would be considered to be at stake. It was possible that the Archdeacon, with his customary pomposity, would metaphorically storm in and attempt to take control, and that Master Yardley would interpret 'might assist' as meaning the taking of the major portion of the service, including, may be, the actual interment. The Rural Dean, too, might arrive with offers of relief, and, if the Archdeacon should be engaged elsewhere, expect to be consulted and given a leading role. It could well be a difficult situation.

The events turned out much as had been feared, save that the Archdeacon sent an apology — and a deputy! The latter, mercifully was the Rural Dean, thus two only could possibly be held as having any arguable right to take a part.

The apportionment of the service produced heated discussion. The Rural Dean, by virtue of his office and also as representing the Archdeacon, demanded the right of the interment. The canon refused, and the Rural Dean blustered and threatened.

The former, however, was adamant, stating emphatically that as vicar of the parish he had every intention of exercising his right. Master Yardley was, frankly, ridiculous, attempting to achieve his objective, the taking of the interment, by a sentimental approach, striving to play upon Trevisa's better nature, but all to no avail. The vicar was too wily a bird to fall for that bait, and far too indifferent to the feelings of a ridiculous and effeminate chaplain, to give up his privilege. Sir John Berkeley, representing his more eminent relation, supported Trevisa, feeling that the position and standing of both Lord Berkeley and himself, would be reflected in the outcome of the argument. With this backing Trevisa issued an ultimatum: either the visiting clerics would accept the allocated sections or not take any part. Both, fearing the repercussions of exclusion from active participation in the service, accepted.

The Rural Dean, a verbose man and in his own estimation an eloquent orator (this was not the general opinion) was allowed to give the panegyric, and Master Yardley received the readings. One of these, however, in view of the large gathering, Trevisa insisted should be read in English and suggested St. John 14 1-13. This latter, the Canon felt, would be an eminently suitable passage to form the foundation upon which the Rural Dean could build up his eulogistic appreciation of the Earl.

The funeral, in spite of the shortness of notice, drew a large congregation. This was, perhaps, understandable, indeed, inevitable, by reason of the Suffolk estates in Malmesbury and Thornbury and their alliance with so many local families. The church and churchyard were full to overflowing for the service, and afterwards for several hours the green nearby was reminiscent of a fairground scene, save for the lack of stalls; while the Berkeley Vale hostelry across the way was drunk dry before the last grumbling local lurched through the door and staggered home.

Chapter 11
The De Proprietatibus Rerum

(a) *Berkeley Fair*

Directly the grant had been received the preparations for the fair were increased, and its affects were felt by almost all members of the community. The Borough Council, shop keepers, and free tenants, as well as the Estate, realized that here was an opportunity not so much for junketing, as for financial gain, and also for improving the standard of life.

Here into their midst would come — or so they hoped! — the chapmen and traders who would bring in kinds of food not grown locally, luxuries as well as necessities. The cheapjacks would be there with their pots and pans, their bright and attractive materials, and even garments. If Berkeley was lucky there might even come merchants from overseas with a wonderful variety of goods such as exotic silks, linens and cloths, spices, jewels and a hundred and one desirable commodities designed to draw the eye and loosen the purse strings. It was, indeed, an exciting prospect.

To the more far-seeing there appeared the possibility of an additional advantage. The outside salesman would be bringing in goods from far afield. Could not these same merchants and itinerants — as well visitors from the neighbouring towns and villages — be tempted to purchase the local surplus goods and commodities? Many looked upon 'Tam O'Avon' as slow of wit, but at the 'Bush' one night in early April he said to mine host:— 'John, I be o'mind to make a mite at thic yer vair. Elvers by runnin late, an'll still be a comin' up river in early May when thic tides be 'igh. I'll sell un cooked, and I'll sell un live to the foppes an they junketers; and then, maybe, I'll buy me a new jackut.' One or two looked at Tam, and wondered from whence had sprung this spark of shrewd business acumen.

Contact was made early on with the Welsh cattle traders as they passed through Chepstow, Monmouth, Ross, Newnham, Newent and Dymock, [1] and also with market authorities in centres such as Gloucester, Bristol, Bath and the Forest of Dean. The establishment of the Berkeley Fair was proclaimed — for a monetary consideration of course — at fairs up and down the west country, so that the hoped-for merchants, peddlers and traders of all kinds might be encouraged to set up their booths, and a great variety of entertainers might be attracted.

The weather in early May was fine and warm, and crowds poured into Berkeley from near and far. The town had never in living memory, no, not even when King Richard and his Queen had paid their visit, known such a concourse of people. Lord Berkeley, to whom the booth dues were to be paid, set up a tolbooth for the purpose of settling all disputes — and these latter were not infrequent at fairs as well as markets. His steward was detailed to keep a sharp eye on events, and to work in close conjunction with the captain of the castle guard. The latter had been ordered to have fifty men, armed with staves and clubs, patrolling the town, with a further twenty-five men-at-arms and twenty archers on standby duty within the castle, but ready at a moment's notice to ride, should real trouble arise. His Lordship was anxious that there should be no serious disturbance or clashes at this initial fair — hence the considerable show of strength.

Business was brisk, and the cheapjacks and their fellow vendors found a ready sale for their wares, but they discovered that the locals were not as naive as they had expected. The performing bears, jugglers and entertainers generally had enthusiastic and relatively generous audiences, but at nightfall only the vendors of food and liquor were still at their stalls.

Trevisa spent much of the day walking quietly through Canonbury, the Market Square, Salter and High Streets — the areas where the majority of the booths had been erected. He talked with parishioners and strangers alike, and listened with amused interest to the haggling over prices which seemed to take place at almost very booth and stall. He had not realized the extent of his parishioners' innate shrewdness. As the hours passed, and he noticed the effect of excitement and of the unaccustomed liquor upon young and old, he began to worry. His worst premonitions seemed, almost inexorably, to be heading for their feared finale. His anxiety was mostly for the young and inexperienced. A sudden increase in the number of baptisms around the feast of the Purification — it was almost blasphemous that this should mark the natural season — could, and probably would, result from the alcoholically induced uninhibited activities of the next few hours. He had straitly warned his people at mass last Sunday, but he saw quite clearly, as he made his way down Stock Lane, Jumper's Lane and up High Street in the early evening, that his words, like those of the Ava Marias sung by all but a few days before, had been forgotten by the groups of young folk making their way to the castle meadows or the Severn shore. Where the boys and girls were Berkeley born and bred it really mattered little; for in many cases it would, in all probability, mean only an anticipating of events by a comparatively short period — a few months or a year or two maybe. Where strangers were in the party — particularly if they were boys — the results could be more unfortunate. He tried to console himself, however, with the thought that the infusion of new blood could, on occasion, improve the breed. In High Street he turned up St. Michael's Lane, with its high cross,[2] to the church and asked forgiveness, in anticipation, for the members of his flock who might not be in their present — and that comparative — state of Grace by day-break. Similar intentions were made at mass the next morning.

Lord Berkeley, the Mayor and many of the leading citizens breathed a sigh of relief when their fair had ended. It had been an experiment, and as such it had been markedly successful. No rioting and no serious troubles had occurred, and local traders, tenants and buyers had been, generally, pleased. The lave and drag-net fishermen in particular had reaped a rich harvest, both for Lord Berkeley and themselves. All, including the Steward and Captain of the Guard, had learnt a great deal. The teething troubles had been few and of minor importance; consequently Castle and Town felt that they need lose little sleep over future fairs, provided guards were vigilant yet sympathetic. Mothers alone — if the parish priest be excluded — were fearful; but then, for them, daughters are almost always an anxiety until the nuptial knot has been tied.

Later that summer Trevisa began negotiations which would enable him to return to Queen's. Lord Berkeley had of late been pressing him to resume work on *De Proprietatibus Rerum*. The canon viewed the proposed residence at Oxford with mixed feelings, a state of mind that he had never previously experienced.

(b) *Queen's Once More*

Trevisa, on his return to Oxford, discovered during his first interview with Master Carlisle, the Provost of Queen's, that the newly acquired canonry of Westbury had given him considerable standing both in the Hall and at the University.

The Provost's opening remarks set the pattern for many greetings and comments which came Trevisa's way during the early days of his return:—

'Welcome back, Canon', were the Provost's opening words, 'We were delighted to hear that this long overdue honour had come your way. The Chancellor of the University and the heads of Halls and Colleges have, for years, been complaining bitterly that an undue proportion of the non-residential, as well as the full residentiary, stalls in our Cathedrals and Collegiate Churches are being filled by foreigners employed by the Court or Curia, and that genuine scholars, academics and intellectuals are being neglected in these allocations. [3] It is true that Queen's has been more fortunate than some during the last two decades, for others besides your good self, for example Masters Whitfield, Hereford and Wyclif, have gained recognition. We must not, however, pride ourselves too much, for some of these honours were conferred upon our alumni either while they were commensales or after they had ceased to be in residence. We are indeed pleased that you will be amongst us again, even though your residence may be but temporary and intermittent. I hope that your erudite colleague and close friend, Master Middleworth, who, as you know, has also come into very temporary residence again, will one day also receive a prebend.'

Trevisa was taken aback and slightly embarrassed by such effusiveness and, having thanked the Provost for his welcome and declared his own pleasure at returning, retired to his rooms.

Later that week Trevisa and Middleworth met to discuss their respective plans.

Trevisa, as the weeks passed, found that the preaching of the late Master Wyclif against the Papacy and entrenched clericalism had taken a firm root in the university, and its spirit had become quite militant since his, Trevisa's, last period of residence. Many of his fellow senior members of Hall looked indifferently on, while others — there are always, or almost always, rebels and trouble-makers in any large community — and certain of the nobility too, were more active in their secularistic leanings, the latter, it could well be, hoping to benefit personally should any confiscation of church property take place.

The fact that the King was in Ireland, endeavouring to re-establish the personal position of the sovereign, did not help matters; indeed it encouraged the newly-termed Lollards in their policies and the more openly to express their feelings. The Canon thanked God that his patron, despite his early training under the great scholar and his real regard for Purvey, had fought shy of involvement in the policies and practices, and he, Trevisa, was profoundly grateful that though Lollardism had become a running sore in Bristol, and had established cells fairly widely in the west, it had had no impact whatsoever in his large parish. Even so he felt that with this possible additional hazard facing his people he would need to consider the advisability of shortening his periods of residence at Queen's to ensure that all was well within his cure. If these suspect doctrines and anti-clericalisms should be infiltrated into the Berkeley Vale then he must be on the spot, or easily available, thus enabling him to deal with this cancer in its early stages. Trevisa discussed these changes with Middleworth, who was equally appalled by the militancy of the new generation of Lollards at the university.

'Yes, John, I fully agree. Many of those declared disciples of our one-time mentor now go far beyond his teaching, and would, if they had their way, do much damage to Mother Church. Mark you, I subscribe, to a great extent, to the thesis, in a measure that of Wyclif, that the Papacy, that is the Curia, should not be allowed to bleed our church and country in the manner, and to the extent, we see around us.'

'Certes! Will, that is the injustice which, at times, almost drives me into the rebel camp. Our Church is being exploited for the benefit of foreigners, and an alien power that is largely losing, indeed one is often temped to say has already lost sight of, its spiritual commission and has become carnally minded and motivated. Christ's Church is one, but sections of that body should not unduly dominate another, nor parasitically or vampire-like drain it of its life's blood.'

'John! John! You allow your Celtic temperament to run away with you. The situation may be unpleasant, indeed it is, but it is not as bad as to justify talk of parasites and vampires. Let us drop the subject and begin to consider our respective projects which, after all, are the purpose and reason for our presence here in Queen's. How is the translation of the *De Proprietatibus Rerum* progressing? I suppose that you are still checking your earlier work on it, and have scarcely begun to break new ground?'

'Yes, and what has amazed me is the inept way in which I handled those previous sections of translation. It is clear that even five years ago I had not rid myself of the stilted verbatim method. Furthermore it is patently clear that either I was extremely careless in my work previously, or else that today I am a better scholar than I was those few years ago — and I am sure that I am not! Enough of egoistical prattle and pomposity. What of your work and future?'

'Well, there is little, really, to tell. I labour on, and from time to time wonder whether the long and oft-promised royal interest will ever become manifest. I do not, however, worry now, as once I did, when the patronage problems bore heavily upon me, that recognition is not forthcoming. Indeed I sometimes wonder whether this lack may be a divine method of maintaining me in a state of humility which my natural disposition does not easily accept. It is late, John. I will away. Good night!'

(c) *Conscience Causes a Change of Course.*

Trevisa, acutely conscious of his newly acquired cure, became increasingly troubled in conscience by the obvious length of time that would be necessary to translate and comment upon passages in the text of the *De Proprietatibus Rerum*; for the latter was, truly, a magnum opus. Trevisa, following his normal custom when uncertain or deeply concerned on any matter of major importance, sought out Middleworth so that his, Trevisa's, worries on the arrangements made for Berkeley's spiritual coverage during his periods of residence at Queen's, necessary to complete the latest project, might be examined by an impartial observer.

'William, my old friend and counsellor, once more I turn to you for advice. In the past when I returned to Oxford from Berkeley I was leaving a minor responsibility, that is, my chaplaincy to my Lord Berkeley, and clearly with his Lordship's approval, indeed almost at his behest, that I might produce for him certain works of translation, as well you know. Today the situation is vastly different. I am still, it is true, chaplain to Lord Berkeley and his castle with its familia. Today, however, I am, at the same time, vicar of a large rural parish. I know full well that his Lordship desires me to continue my work for him here at Oxford, but conscience of late has begun to trouble me. Am I really justified in absenting myself, the installed shepherd of souls in Berkeley, from my people for long periods? I know full well that an efficient locum has been found and that he is living in the parish; so seemingly satisfactory coverage has been arranged. In spite of all this, am I justified, really justified, in fulfilling this programme, or am I being recorded in the Lamb's Book of Life as an unfaithful steward?'

'John, you are a man of many parts and, at the same time, you have several distinct sides to your character. Your present troubled mind is caused by what you believe to be a basic conflict between two of the latter. You are ever determined, often ruthless almost to the point of cruelty, in pursuing what you believe to be a duty, or maybe the suppression of tyranny or evil in almost any form. At other times you can be gentle, considerate and self-effacing to the very point of foolishness. These two forces domiciled within you are unconsciously at variance. You are a scholar with gifts as a translator, at the same time you're a visionary, a man with a mission, the object of which is to bring works of interest and erudition to the people of this country in a language understood by them. Finally you are at heart a lover of people — perhaps that accounts partly for your visionary objectives. While you were merely — I use this word deliberately — chaplain to Lord Berkeley you were free to exercise that mission to the full, because your patron was also eager that these translations should be undertaken, and it mattered not whether his motives were acquisitive or altruistic. The moment, however, you accepted the cure of Berkeley, complications and mental conflict developed. You, as I have said, love your people, the aged and the young, and you wish to serve them — and, my friend, you do, both in person and by able proxy. At the same time your patron and your own innate sense of mission brings you here to Queen's for the better fulfilment of what you secretly (perhaps subconsciously might be the more accurate word) feel to be your life's work and purpose. These two aims, parochial and academic, are compatible, but only so if you are realistic and tightly control yourself. At the moment, and for months past, you have not done this. Instead you have striven at high pressure to pursue both tasks with all your natural vigour. You obtained an excellent locum for Berkeley to enable you to satisfy your patron's wishes and what you believe within your heart to be your primary vocation. Having done all that, having satisfied your parishioners and the ecclesiastical authorities on all issues, you are driven by your sense, a mistaken sense I believe, of duty to your Berkeley folk to race down to your parish at frequent intervals to be with 'your people' and to check that all is well. These trips are physically and mentally exhausting. While here at Oxford you work almost all the hours that God gives to enable that 'other duty' to be honoured to the full. John, my friend, this cannot go on, or if it does you will soon break down, and neither of these life's works will benefit — do not the Scriptures say a live dog is better than a dead lion? The ideal solution would be for you to follow Blessed Paul who said "this one thing I do", and to have but a single objective and mission, parochial or academic. But for you, my friend, with your nature, make-up and sense of duty, a decision such as this would break your heart and render you ineffective, or so I feel. What then is the solution, if there is one which will adequately meet your heavy demands?

It seems to me that, in spite of the excellent locum, you, to satisfy your conscience, will have to spend more time in Berkeley. I do not, necessarily, mean physically playing an active part in parochial affairs, but merely being there, on the spot, just in case old Mrs. Trotman wishes to make her confession and will only do so to the vicar, or to be at hand should a major parochial tragedy occur. You are not practical enough, John, not hard enough I would like to say, to allow you to work on quietly here without worrying about your flock in a distant field, even though the hireling is a good and faithful priest. Does that mean that I am advocating an outright abrogation of that other life's mission? No! Not, my friend, if you and I can find favour in the eyes of certain members of Queen's. My suggestion is that you approach the Provost and beg permission to be allowed to take the manuscript upon which you are working down to Berkeley for periods of up to, perhaps, a month. It was largely through your influence that it originally came to Queen's and not Merton. Furthermore you have been working on it intermittently for a long time, while others appear to pay little attention to it. You have, therefore, good grounds for asking, and ample justification for expecting, generous consideration and treatment. If this privilege is granted you could spend alternate months at Berkeley and Oxford. This should ease your over delicate conscience and still enable you to make good progress in your translation. Mark you, John, you would have to exercise great personal discipline, firstly by not interferring with the locum's work in the parish, and secondly by a whole hearted devotion, even when in Berkeley, to the academic work in hand. I fear, John, that this has been almost a homily or a sermon, but in defence I can justly plead that you asked for my advice!'

'I am most grateful, old friend, for that advice, homily or sermon, call it what you will. I listened carefully, and you have, I believe, found the best solution — provided that the Hall authorities will agree. It certainly is a far better plan than that which I followed when working on a part of the *Polychronicon* some years ago. Do you remember the many hours I spent transcribing part of the text at Queen's and later took those transcribed sections down to Berkeley where I translated and annotated them? That was a more time absorbing method and, with its two stage development, one which gave greater opportunity for errors to creep in. Well, Will, I have kept you up far too late discussing my troubles. Let us now put them on one side and retire. Good night, my friend. Good night, and may God bless us, and may our plans come to fruition.

Five days later after three sessions of deep discussion, which at times verged upon the acrimonious, the Provost and fellows of Queen's agreed in principle to the proposition that Trevisa might take on loan the manuscript of the *De Proprietatibus Rerum* for limited periods and work upon it at Berkeley. There were, however, certain important provisoes. It was laid down that someone, and of necessity this meant Lord Berkeley, should pledge themselves to a bond of fifty marks which would become forfeit should the manuscript be damaged or lost, and that two pence should be paid for every week, or part thereof, that the manuscript should be absent from Queen's. Those conditions and other of lesser significance, Trevisa, on the day following, bore with him to Berkeley for the consideration of his patron. To say that Trevisa was disappointed with the proposed terms would be an understatement. He was furious, feeling as he expressed himself to Middleworth, that 'the Hall has let me down. I it was, who was instrumental in the acquisition of the manuscript for Queen's — did not many of Bredon's books go to Merton? This gift was made to Queen's specifically that I might work upon it. I believe I could have persuaded Simon Bredon to give it to me personally on the understanding that later, when my task had been completed, the original would be handed over to the Queen's library. This I did not do, believing that the manuscript should be available for general consultation in a library, rather than reposing in the possession of an individual. Having made this personal sacrifice I would have thought the terms could, indeed should, have been more generous. Once again we see the truth of the scriptural warning "put not your faith in princes, nor in any child of man!" No, my friend, I am disgusted, but, of necessity, must accept their conditions, or at least attempt to persuade my Lord of Berkeley to agree to them.'

Trevisa felt frustrated when, on arrival at the castle, he learned that Lord Berkeley was away at Portbury, at least he had gone there some ten days ago saying that his return would depend upon local circumstances, and that he might, indeed, find it necessary to see his brother, Lord James, at Raglan. He anticipated, however, being back, in any event, within a month, probably well within that time. Trevisa, at first, considered riding immediately to Portbury, but upon reflection decided that this might well be a waste of time. If his Lordship had had to cross over to Raglan he would, no doubt, have left Portbury before Trevisa arrived. On the other hand, if Lord Berkeley was returning direct to Berkeley, it would seem possible, indeed from what he had said, probable, that he would be arriving within a very few days. Furthermore there was no certainty about his return route. The canon, therefore, decided to remain in Berkeley and await his patron, occupying himself, in the meanwhile, by visiting friends as well as a few of the seriously sick, and also checking some of the membranes of his translation, adding personal comments if and where necessary.

His first call was at Wanswell Court, but his luck was out, for the serving maid said that the Sanigers were staying with the Thorpes in Bristol and might not be back for several weeks.

Brother Michael at Bradston College was engaged on floor repairs in the porch of the chapel; a heavy job this, and clearly a break was more than welcome, urgent though the task was! Trevisa learnt from the chaplain that old Betsy Nelmes, aunt of Henry Saniger, the ex mayor of Berkeley, was desperately ill, and that the family believed that it was, as they put it, 'a bad and sure job'. He rode in to the Marlepool Farm, on his return journey, and to his astonishment found the old lady propped up in bed and able to speak. The family had been equally surprised when 'Gran' had, some hours since, suddenly regained consciousness and demanded a horn of ale, and even more amazed when she sunk the contents (admittedly the horn was only half full) at a single draught — such, occasionally, is the vitality of the very old!

True to his word Lord Berkeley returned within the third week and was taken aback to find his chaplain at the castle. That evening Trevisa narrated in detail the reasons for his unexpected appearance at Berkeley, and awaited with some apprehension his patron's reaction. This was immediate and enthusiastic — far, far more than he had expected, or even hoped.

'John, my old friend and confessor, this is indeed an unexpected pleasure and an excellent idea, and I welcome it whole heartedly. Of course I will pay the dues demanded, and, if damage or loss results from the arrangements, I will pledge myself to reimburse the Queen's authorities. I want you to translate this latest work nearly as much as you do, but your enforced absence in Oxford deprives me of a counsellor upon whom I have long learnt to lean heavily. This scheme, suggested by Master Middleworth, which you have just outlined, and which the Hall appear to have accepted, will enable you to continue your work. It will mean, however, that you will be at hand for much longer periods to give advice should need arise - and in the present strained atmosphere the matter could be both serious and urgent. Yes, my friend, you can ride back to Oxford as soon as you wish, for the sooner you do so the quicker will be your return to Berkeley. I fully endorse what Master Middleworth emphasized, that while here working on the translation you must — metaphorically — not be here parochially. I, and I alone, will be privileged to call upon your time, and only then if the cause is urgent.'

(d) *Student Riots*

One of the periodic student clashes was building up at the time of Trevisa's return to Oxford. It smouldered for a few days undetected by the authorities, but finally burst into flame.

Trouble began in an unexpected quarter. A clash occurred at the Mitre. Two Welsh students from Merton became involved with northerners from Queen's Hall. The jibe, 'Taffy was a Welshman, Taffy was a thief,' was answered by the insult of 'Border bastard! Was you father a Scotsman?' In the ensuing brawl the two were overpowered and badly beaten up. Trevisa heard of this the following morning and warned the Provost of possible repercussions. Two days later it began. Merton members negotiated with fellow students from Wales and the south and waylaid northerners in a carefully planned series of ambushes all over the town. The master-mind, it was said, was Gwilliam ap Gethin, a red-head from Neath and a nephew of Gethin Goch, [4] Owen Glendwr's successful captain. Casualties mounted, and Queen's was in an uproar. Trevisa and the Provost saw the southerners of Queen's and Merton and threatened them with dire punishment if they persisted in their scandalous behaviour.The students truculently turned on the Provost and the Canon, and reminded them that they themselves had played leading roles in somewhat similar factional activities less than twenty years earlier. Trevisa stormed and threatened, pointing out that in their day there had been little physical hurt inflicted, and even less material damage, and, although certain college authorities had been temporarily deprived of some administrative baubles, very little real harm had resulted. He further pointed out, as supporting evidence, that he and the Provost — who had been Provost during the troubles — were on the best of terms; this was said with a slight twinge of conscience.

Provosts, Proctors and other officials leaned heavily on the students,and almost as suddenly as it had begun the trouble ceased.

(e) *Further Troubles*

The return of King Richard from Ireland at, it was said, the express wish of the

Episcopal bench, certainly strengthened the position of the monarchy, and was, in a way, a personal triumph for Richard.

Some thoughtful persons, standing as it were on the perimeter of the tournament field and having little or no involvement in power politics, while feeling maybe that it was good for the country that the sovereign should not be absent for long periods from the centre of government, might well wonder whether the reasons behind this sudden return would inflate his ego to such an extent that he might once more develop despotic tendencies, and again act in a manner which would endanger the precious but precarious Pax Britannica.

Oxford buzzed with excitement and speculation, and many were the informal discussion heard in college, hall and hostel. Trevisa, once more back at Queen's after a month in Berkeley, was of those who felt slightly apprehensive. One night at the Lamb and Flag a member of the small group drinking their ale or mead — he was a fellow of Oriel — turned to Trevisa and asked:— 'Canon, you are but recently returned from the west; how does your patron, who is, it is said, an influential member of the nobility, although often preferring to act quietly, but not without effect, in the background, how does he assess the shadow of things to come?'

'My learned friend, your question is far reaching and savours of political probing. My Lord Berkeley largely keeps his own counsel on such matters, and when, on rare occasion, he seeks discussion about, for example, high matters of state, it is, almost, if not always, undertaken in an atmosphere of the confessional — or nearly so. Thus my lips are sealed.'

'Canon, you are too conceited, and blown up by the fact that your noble patron, according to current gossip that is, leans heavily upon you for advice. Have a care. Your very reluctance to reveal your mind in open conversation could lead to a suspicion that your thoughts, words and wishes may not be exactly what they seem, even a cover for a disloyal and subversive heart. Many a man has gone to the Tower for less. Have a care, my bumptious friend.'

Silence followed, a silence somewhat charged with fear, fear that a situation engendered by, maybe, if not exacerbated by, over-liberal libations, was getting out of hand, and could so easily lead on to an ugly finale.

Thomas ap John, a fellow of Merton, put his hand on the truculent's shoulder and said:— 'Henry, my friend, go back to College while still you can. You are baiting Canon Trevisa, and are not your normal good-humoured self. He has been tolerant with you, and not clubbed you as well he might have done — and who would have blamed him? — and as I probably would have done had I been in his shoes.'

'You bloody Welshman, keep your hands off me, or I'll slit your throat or prick you through. Are you disloyal too?' With that he drew a sword hidden beneath his cloak; but before it was fully freed from the folds he was overpowered, bound and thrown down in the corner to cool off. His sword was taken back to Oriel and Provost informed of the misconduct of his colleague.

Early in June the discussions on a possible power struggle between the King and the nobles took on a new slant, for rumours began to circulate that King Richard, widower of less than a year, was making tentative approaches at the French Court for the hand in marriage of Isabelle, daughter of King Charles VI. The princess was a child of six. In July the negotiations came into the open. This move by Richard was activated, so many felt, more by immediate considerations, i.e., to strengthen his present position and to make him less dependant upon the Lords and Commons, than by the longer-termed policy of obtaining an heir to the throne.

Once again Trevisa was troubled by this practice, pernicious custom he termed it, of child marriages for the sake of aggrandisement or dynastic expansion. Much though he loathed the idea, he was prepared to concede that it was a very powerful weapon, and one which current events, or the prospect of future possibilities, rendered expedient and often vitally necessary for survival.

(f) *A Fall from Grace*

The summer of 1395 passed into winter with Trevisa trying valiantly both at Berkeley and in Queen's to concentrate on his translation. He found, however, that during much of the time in the former location parochial demands built up in volume to such an extent that the manuscript of the *De Proprietatibus Rerum* lay virtually untouched for weeks on end. These instructions, at first, had been concerned only with matters of major importance; but soon, all too soon, in the eyes of most folk the locum seemed to have lost public favour. It might be more realistic to say not that he had been discredited, but that as far as his flock were concerned he had ceased to exist. Trevisa, on the other hand, despite constant pleas for peace and privacy, was being sought out as the one and only counsellor, confidant and sacramentalist. This feeling had increased rapidly during the spring and reached the point of finality as the result of an incident on the Severn shore.

Father Peter had gone down to Severn House to watch the building of fishing weirs for both putchers and kypes, by the salmon fishermen. This was, in effect, an attempt to make real contact with a very united, but dour, group of parishioners. After a while, and perhaps because he was obtaining little response, the priest wandered away from the main centre of activity. Time was forgotten in the examining of rock pools and the scenery generally. Suddenly he became aware that the water around him was rising swiftly. Then it was that he remembered that warning about the making tide. He raced for the shore, but the causeway over the rocks was now covered, and in his haste he floundered and fell. He struggled to his feet, fell again and finally slipped into a deep runnel and was swept upstream by the swirling current. Fortunately a break away kype came spinning past. This, by the Grace of God and because he was a fair swimmer, he was able to grab. These two factors literally saved his life, for by the time his plight had been noticed he was a hundred yards from the fishermen. Shouts echoed up the river bank and were passed on from body to body. Half a mile up river, at the Avon's mouth, a boat was manned and thrust out into the turbulent waters of the Severn. For several minutes the boat's crew struggled to gain a measure of manoeuvrability — and at last, after a hard battle, succeeded. They fought grimly to hold their vessel bow-on to the tide and, at the same time, to check somewhat the speed with which they were being swept up river. Their efforts were rewarded, for they saw the struggling partly kype-supported figure being, as it were, drawn towards them. Finally, as they neared the Ness, both boat and man were thrust into a stretch of somewhat calmer water near the rocky bank. The crew, summoning their last reserve of strength, edged their craft nearer and nearer to the exhausted priest until, at last, a boat hook made the vital contact. A quarter of an hour later the now unconscious swimmer was dragged up the bank, and his rescuers began attempts to revive him. Their methods, crude and rough maybe, were effective, and by the time a litter arrived the priest had regained consciousness.

The following day the locum, far from well, left his bed to thank those who had saved his life. He realized how foolish and careless, indeed culpably careless, he had been to forget the first instruction for those engaged upon Severn-side work. The advice given more than once, had been:— 'Watch for the running tide, and make certain of your line of retreat.' His neglect of this cardinal rule had endangered his life, indeed it had almost been forfeit. More serious still, it had gravely imperilled the lives of those four brave men who had thrust out into the river under conditions which were extremely dangerous. He felt ashamed, but thanked God that the others had, apparently, suffered no harm, whereas he felt extremely ill.

Two days later Lord Berkeley sent for the locum, and in a terse speech — it could be termed no other, for the 'prisoner-at-the-bar' was given no opportunity to explain his actions nor to make a defence — explained the frightening potential of his conduct at Severn House, and that, but for God's good Grace three widows and their families and a fourth mother would today have been mourning their breadwinners. His Lordship ended by forbidding the priest, as long as he remained a local employee, to take part in, or even attend, any such activities along the river.

The interview bit deeply into the heart of the locum. There was, in addition, the feeling of complete isolation. Trevisa, on his return from Queen's, sensed the situation, and in an attempt to ease the mind of the dejected man suggested, but in vain, that this idea was a figment of his imagination. This thought of parochial alienation became a fixation, and before Pentecost there seemed but one way out of the situation — he must resign. To this end he sought and obtained an interview with his Superior, to whom he explained the grim experience on the Severn, expressing his conviction that he no longer held the confidence and affection of his flock:— 'Father, the people of Berkeley, I am sure, hold me fully responsible, as indeed I was, for placing their fellows in dire peril. They feel — rightly — that it was only the Grace of God which prevented a ghastly tragedy. For this thoughtless and careless act they will give no forgiveness to me, and I have become completely discredited, and can no longer expect, or hope, to achieve much in that corner of the Master's vineyard.'

Two weeks later the locum left.

Trevisa viewed the departure of the locum with mixed feelings. The parish was, literally, being tossed back into his lap, and the prospect was, in some ways, pleasing. On the other hand a realistic appraisal made it clear that, for the moment at least, a return to Oxford, even for short periods such as a month, would hardly be possible. He was relieved that the *De Proprietatibus Rerum* manuscript could be brought down to Berkeley, but he feared that full time parochial demands would hinder very considerably his translation.

He discussed the situation with his patron and they decided that, for the time being at least, his rooms at Queen's would have to be given up and his work on the translation temporarily suspended. Before the end of June Trevisa returned to Oxford to hand back the manuscript and to settle his college dues. It was agreed by the Provost that the manuscript might again be borrowed by Trevisa should the situation at Berkeley enable the project to be resumed.

The only really discordant note was the revival once more of the demand that he,

Trevisa, should repay the debt incurred by the treasurer in 1369 and which had been passed on to Trevisa when he succeeded to that office. He, Trevisa, had indeed made some effort to clear the slate — not too seriously, of course, because at heart he had always repudiated the claim. He supposed, never-the-less, that ultimately he would have to settle the account — that day, however, was not yet!

(g) *A Cloud as Large as a Man's Hand*

The summer and early autumn gave Trevisa little time for extra-parochial duties. He was happy amongst his flock, but there was a nagging feeling that he really must find time to complete the *De Proprietatibus Rerum* — and the amount of work remaining was, in fact, quite small. He also considered the vague possibility of other less ambitious translations — some books of Holy Writ maybe?

During the winter and spring he found time to read through, check and revise his almost completed manuscript, and felt that with the arrival of yet another chantry priest at St. Mary's he might well find time for one or two very short visits to Queen's. This he was enabled to do, and by August the great project was virtually completed in draft form.

Once again national and parochial events impinged upon his time to an unexpected degree.

King Richard had, for sometime, been building up his personal position and his livery, tantamount to a private army, and his massed demonstration of armed strength at Kingston prior to the opening of Parliament in September constituted a warning to those opposing him amongst the nobility and commons who had survived the July purge, when Warwick, Woodstock, Arundel and others had been arrested. The King, they were made to see, would brook no active oppostion. Richard, in addition to those sporting the White Hart, which included the four hundred Cheshire Archers, had, they knew full well, effective control over the seventy-three cannon earlier cast for him by William Woodward.[5] These were indeed the most sophisticated weapons in the country and included a fearsome gun weighing almost seven hundred pounds which had eleven barrels firing lead shot and one hurling stone ball.

Trevisa had attended Lord Berkeley at the September Parliament, and also when his Lordship had gone to London late in November for the arrival of Isabelle in the city.

The severe winter caused many deaths in Berkeley — as elsewhere — and, parochially, Trevisa's time was fully occupied. Outwardly peace prevailed, but both Lord Berkeley and Trevisa felt uneasy. The latter commented:—

'Please God that this present quiet is not the Halcyonides dies of which Pliny wrote. Days when the winds dropped and the seas were calm and the brightly coloured kingfisher floated safely on its nest upon the smooth surface of the waters. A peace which was followed by furious winds and tempestuous seas. I like it not, my Lord.'

'Certes! I too like not this calm, but I like less the word-picture of Pliny! Let us hope that Richard, having established his position, will not allow himself to use that power for selfish ends, and to pay off old scores. May he handle Henry Bolingbroke carefully, friend though he is, I know that the latter has a swift temper. This coupled with the vast Lancastrian estates which will one day — and perhaps before long — be his, could create a dangerous situation. In the meanwhile I think it would be prudent to see to our defences. You, my friend, would do well to complete your work at Oxford while movement is easy. You may have, if real trouble comes, plenty of time, shut up in Berkeley Castle, to make the final fair copy of the *De Proprietatibus Rerum.*'

'What is it, Steward?'

'A messenger from Raglan has arrived, my Lord.'

'Take him to the Hall. I will come shortly.'

The recent grant of a dukedom — that of Hereford — to Henry Bolingbroke pleased Lord Berkeley who had a high regard for this able son of Gaunt. He felt, however, that to create Mowbray, Earl of Nottingham, Duke of Norfolk was cheapening the title — and unjustified.

Suddenly the fortunes of these Dukes fell. A quarrel between them was referred to a Committee of Parliament. It ruled that the issue must be settled by personal combat at Coventry on 16 September. The King forbad the contest and exiled both in November. Richard, however, did not confiscate Hereford's estates, and in fact, promised that even future properties, i.e. those of Lancaster, would be sacrosanct.

These events followed the general pattern of many royal dictatorships, and the phrase, 'regal despotism' was occasionally heard in private. Lord Berkeley was worried, feeling, as did many others, that civil war was, now, more than a possibility.

(h) *An End in Sight*

Once again Nativity-tide and the twelve days passed in the traditional way. There was, however, so Trevisa felt, a sense of strain, even anxiety. Many, although a hundred miles from London, were worried that mounting tension in the more important centres of population could spread to the rural districts. Civil war was a distinct possibility, and its effects in wintertime would, or at least could be, even more unpleasant. One could sleep rough in the summer without too much worry — except, of course, during the season of thunderstorms.

Events in the January Parliament at Shrewsbury did little to lift the feeling of apprehension. Richard, it seemed clear, was resolved to free himself from Parliament itself and to establish himself as the supreme, indeed sole, ruler.

Lord Berkeley took no part in the discussion, wishing no involvement. His chaplain, too, was concerned with the final phase of the *De Proprietatibus Rerum* project, and for the time being made little or no comment on the deterioration of the situation. The translation upon which he had worked intermittently for many years and had been his principal preoccupation for nearly three was almost completed, so nearly so that given health — and continued peace — he could expect to write 'Finis' before Ash Wednesday, perhaps even by the Purification.

Day after day the priest toiled on, taking off little time for meals and almost grudging that set aside for the saying of the daily offices and the mass. So hard — and late — he worked that on the Feast of the Epiphany his patron warned him that such pressure could not be maintained without damaging his health and, perhaps, imparing the quality of the project itself. The canon, fully aware of the self-imposed physical as well as the mental strain, agreed to set aside everything to do with the translation for three whole days and to limit his work on it thereafter to six hours each day, the Sabbath excepted.

The season of Epiphany, short that year because of the early date of Easter, was, for once, quiet from the parochial point of view. Hard was the weather, but not really severe, which accounted, so said the hoary heads, for the comparative health of the parish. The frosty nights and the bright days, even if there was little warmth in the sun, had helped to keep the bodies, even of the older folk, from falling victim to illness and disease.

Trevisa thanked God on behalf of his flock for this mercy. He added his own gratitude, because the sick visits were few in number — and what a relief this was when the days were short! This enabled him to press on with writing, very carefully, that which he hoped would be the final or fair copy of the *De Proprietatibus Rerum*. No difficulty had been experienced over obtaining membranes, as had happened when completing the *Polychronicon*, and by the feast of the Purification, his target date, the work, though not finished, was almost so.

Before mid-day on the sixth of February, Trevisa laid down his pen, got up from his chair, and walked quietly to St. John's Chapel, and in prayer thanked God that the Project had at last, after many a delay, been completed.

Later that evening, when Lord Berkeley returned from visiting his cousin, Sir John, at Beverston, Trevisa knelt before his patron, and, with pride barely held in check, handed the translation to his Lordship with the words:— 'I, your bedeman, present to you Bartholomew's *De Proprietatibus Rerum*, translated, by your request, into your native tongue. May it give your Lordship and all who read it great pleasure, and may the knowledge contained within this cyclopaedia benefit many people.'

Lord Berkeley was delighted and said:— 'Bedeman and vicar you may be, but friend, counsellor and teacher too, you are. I cannot fully express the extent of my gratitude for your erudite and devoted labour. This calls for a celebration. Steward! Bring in a flagon of that wine shipped from Bordeaux a year ago. It is a good wine, and it is fitting that this latest brain-child of the Canon, which has been safely delivered after much labour, shall be suitably Baptized!'

Later. 'Sir Priest! Your health and my gratitude.'

Shortly after the completion of the *De Proprietatibus Rerum* the news reached Berkeley that 'Old Gaunt' had died. This was followed quickly by the announcement that the ten years exile of Henry Bolingbroke, Duke of Hereford, had been extended to banishment for life, and that the vast Lancastrian estates had been sequestrated by the Crown.

Lord Berkeley was, at first, incredulous, for here was perfidy of the darkest dye in the very head of state. Had not Richard, less than a year ago, pledged his solemn word that the period of exile imposed was the outside limit, and that Henry's patrimony on the ultimate death of his father, Lancaster (and all realized that that event could not be long delayed), would be reserved for the Duke of Hereford? When the truth of these events was confirmed Lord Berkeley sat back and reviewed the national situation and its potentials; and what he saw in his mind's eye was disturbing, especially to one who, though a military leader, was at heart a peace-loving man.

'Trevisa, my friend, once more we see the truth of the Psalmists's warning; words which have deep relevance today. Richard is forsworn, and again risks the title "despot", or worse. The King has, basically, many good qualities, but his inner circle of boon companions have undermined the same, and have used flattery to such a degree that he has become blind to those fundamentals of kingship, honour, truth and equity, relying instead upon expediency and force. I am deeply shocked — and hurt too — by this volte-face, for I had, at one time, a deep regard for Richard, both as a sovereign and a man. I have, as you know, affection for Duke Henry, and I expect that many in England will resent bitterly the cruelty and injustice of this two-fold move against the house of Lancaster. It has, indeed, within itself vigorous seeds of dissension which could germinate and produce a bloody harvest. What say you, Sir Priest?'

'My Lord, I, too, was shocked, and agree that the repercussions could be considerable. I counsel you, however, to gang warily, and at this time to keep out of high circles and make no comment. King Richard, is clearly, in vengeful mood and seems ruthless and not too scrupulous in his actions. He may remember that your Lordship counselled moderation during his visit to Berkeley some years since.'

'Thank you, John, I will heed your warning. And now I must leave at once to see my brother and advise him too, friend as he is of Duke Henry, to watch his step and tongue. He is by nature impetuous and his associations with the Welsh have increased this tendency. Thank you again John, my old friend.'

The obvious tension building up in the country and the whole attitude of Richard towards kingship shown during the last two years worried exceedingly many thoughtful people, not least Lord Berkeley and his chaplain. Once again the baron and priest turned to the *De Regimine Principum* of Aegidius Romanus, and studied its statements and counsels, feeling that therein was contained much that was of relevance to the national situation as they viewed it. Both hoped, and prayed, that a trial of strength — civil war no less — could be avoided, but neither felt optimistic.

'My Lord, I like not this latest move of the King. The Lancastrian party, their friends, which must include Hereford's relations, my Lords Percy and Neville,[6] and much of the north, will surely be in a ferment because of the confiscation. They will reason that no one's property is safe from an avaricious and despotic ruler. Lancaster today, Northumberland and Westmorland tomorrow, may well be in their thoughts. It will need but little more to cause the smouldering fire of anger to burst into flame.'

'You forget sour old York. He still has influence in the north, or so it is said. He is the King's uncle and senior statesman, and he has no axe to grind. His presence may, and I hope will, impose restraint upon the younger and more quick-tempered members of the northern nobility.'

'Please God you are right, my Lord. The bell rings for vespers; I must leave. Farewell, and God grant our country peace in the days ahead.'

Weeks passed and news trickled through of growing discontent and murmuring against King Richard, but there appeared no sign of overt action — Trevisa likened the situation to that in Aesop's fable of the mice and the cat, with no subject wishing to make the first move!

Suddenly came the news that the King was preparing an expedition against a rebel chieftain in Ireland. In May it was confirmed that Richard was soon to sail, leaving the Duke of York as regent in his absence. He landed at Waterford on 1st June.

'Canon, have you heard of Richard's departure for Ireland? This is an act of crass stupidity. Now anything can happen, for York's retinue is not over large, while the main of the King's powerful supporters and the royal bodyguard — the only certain and, at this time, trustworthy troops — are overseas with the King.'

'Yes, my Lord, I have heard, and feel as you do that this move could be the precursor of real trouble for our country. Did not the ancients say:— "Quem Jupiter vult perdere dementat prius". 7 Richard's departure to Ireland could well mark for him the beginning of the end, for the Commons, as well as the Lords, are far from happy.'

'I agree. We, my friend, must, during this summer, remain in rustication, if we value our freedom, health and property! It is to be hoped that Lord James will do the same. In the meanwhile we must strengthen, even more, the castle's defences and lay in victuals so that we can, if necessary, withstand a considerable siege. Tell one of the servants to seek out the Captain of the Guard, and ask him to report to me at once. Prudent preparations must not be delayed. Good night, Canon.'

'Good night, my Lord.'

(1398/9) (i) *An Abbatial Interlude*

The news that his Holiness, Pope Boniface IX, had conferred upon the head of St. Augustine's the rights and dignities of a mitred Abbot was received with some astonishment in the southern half of the diocese of Worcester, where the antics and capers — which passed for ceremonial — of the abbot and certain members of his familia had aroused considerable caustic comment. Many now feared that the capricious and prideful ostentation of six years ago, which had incurred the displeasure of his Holiness and evoked severe papal condemnation, would be as nothing compared with the extravaganza and fopdoodlery that might be expected now that this new, and ultimate, dignity had been bestowed. It was the licence, or so it seemed to them, for future fooleries and vainglorious displays, the like of which they had never previously witnessed.

Abbot: 'Well Father Prior, I understand that there have been rumours of further meetings between Canon Trevisa and Master Purvey. These two have been working together for some years on further biblical translations. With Purvey, when in Bristol, I can deal, and I may be able to apply considerable pressure when he returns to London. This can be done because we have my Lord Bishop of Worcester and certain other senior members of the hierarchy on our side. With the Canon, however, I am powerless, for behind him stands my Lord of Berkeley with his powerful connections, secular may be, but too influential in ecclesiastical circles to risk offending by an open confrontation. Trevisa is ageing, and the time will come, sooner, may be, than we now expect, when the cure of Berkeley will be vacant. It is for that moment we must now begin to prepare.

'I have given considerable thought to the problem, and have consulted — unofficially of course — the Archdeacon and, privately, have touched upon the matter with the Bishop himself. Of course the questions were of a hypothetical nature, but I suspect that his Lordship, shrewd man that he is, had more than an inkling of what lay behind my questions. His reply was direct, very, and almost unguarded. He said, "My Lord Abbot, if I was the head of a community possessing the advowson of an important parish whereof the Lord of the Manor had influenced an appointment, and if I felt that a vacancy might occur in the not very distant future, and that secular pressure might again be applied, I would take strong but stealthy action. The Pope in Rome, in spite of his schismatic brother at Avignon, is still head of the Catholic Church, yes, even of the sometimes independant and wayward church in this country. Why not obtain a bull from his Holiness, bestowing upon you and your successors the right of appointment at the next vacancy, and possibly subsequent voidencies? Insist, too, that you have the further right of arbitrary removal if the chosen candidate should prove unco-operative, obstructive or even heretical. The bull will not be cheap, but if this appointment is of major importance to you and the community you must be prepared to pay the price. Let it be quite clearly understood that I have not given you advice, I have only told you what I might do if I was Abbot and faced with a similar situation!" Prior, what do you think of that piece of advice, for advice it clearly was?'.

Prior: 'Father, my Lord Bishop, to my mind, has given a clear directive, which for the future well-being of our community we must follow. A petition must be drawn up and forwarded to the Papal Office in London, and I believe this should be done without undue delay. Lord Berkeley will know, perhaps even better than we do, the state of his chaplain's — and vicar's — health. If he believes that Trevisa is in decline, and the signs are that this is so, his Lordship may forestall us and obtain, once again, a bull or bulls giving him the right of nominating a successor to the aged canon, both as vicar and chaplain. The former appointment, because of the considerable financial implications we must safeguard to ourselves.'

Abbot: 'Agreed. I will draft the letter tomorrow and it can be carried by the courier who leaves on the next day.'

Two days later the letter left for the Holy See, but it was full six months before the reply arrived at St. Augustine's and was delivered to the anxious Abbot.

As the weeks and months had slipped by the Abbot had become increasingly worried, because it was reported that the vicar of Berkeley was failing rapidly, and that the speed of the deterioration was being accentuated by the refusal of the Canon to curtail parochial activities or his scholarly labours. The Abbot felt certain that Lord Berkeley, when his chaplain and vicar had died, would wish to repeat the ruse of full twenty years ago by obtaining leave to make his own selection for both offices, before the Bishop and Abbot of the day had made a move. Conditions, of course, were then different, for my Lord had a chaplain, and was at variance with the vicar. Furthermore the selected candidate was at hand, in the person of Trevisa, who had long enjoyed Berkeley patronage. The present situation differed considerably, for Trevisa, so highly rated and respected by his Lordship, although ailing, was still functioning. This trusted cleric would not be cast aside like a worn out cloak, of this the abbot was confident, and in addition his spies reported no mention, nor even a suggestion, of a successor. Perhaps Lord Berkeley's delicacy of feelings and love for his aged priest made his Lordship reluctant to apply to the Holy Father for a licence to nominate, when the time came, a fresh vicar and chaplain. The Abbot, a hard and calculating man beneath his prideful exterior, hoped that fidelity to an old friend and confessor would wreck Lord Berkeley's cause.

The Abbot when the Papal Bull arrived could hardly credit his good fortune.[8]

Later he sent for the Prior, and together they began preparing their plans and policies for the permanent — they hoped — appropriation of the wealth inalienably attached — or almost so — to the vicarage of Berkeley. Both men sighed with relief, for victory was theirs and the prize rich, and nature, they knew from recent reports, would not long deny them the fruits of their scheming.

They felt, too, that they had to hand a suitable successor to Trevisa in young John Bonejohn, a man who could be trusted to further the interests of the Abbey, and who would carry out abbatical wishes without hesitation. The only fear they felt was that their Father-in-God, the Bishop of Worcester, who had oft cast avaricious eyes on Berkeley, and although he would not openly oppose the Bull, might well, in spite of his earlier advice, attempt to delay the implementation of the appointment on some technicality. The episcopal lawyers were adept, for a consideration of course, in such matters. The Abbot and Prior feared that some stratagem might be employed with the result that the diocese of Worcester, and that meant the Bishop himself, might well enjoy the revenue of the Berkeley vicarage to their loss. Time alone would tell.

Chapter 12
A Momentous Meeting

(a) Introduction

On Sunday July 27th (Trinity IX) 1399 there took place in Berkeley Church and in the Castle a series of what might be termed informal meetings of persons who, after the King, Richard, were about the most important figures in England at that time.[1] To understand even partially the reason for this small gathering of illustrious men, and to comprehend the rather extraordinary behaviour of several of the participants, it is necessary to re-examine very briefly the course of English history during the preceding twenty-two years.

Edward III died in 1377 and was succeeded by Richard, son of the Black Prince, the eldest son of King Edward. Richard, a lad of eleven, was, naturally, but a figure-head, with the real power resting in the hands of his royal uncles, the Dukes of Gloucester, York and Lancaster. The last, more generally known as John of Gaunt, was the effective regent[2] except during his periods abroad, as in Castile in the later 1380's.

Richard at the age of sixteen married Anne of Bohemia and began to gather round him a party of friends through whom he hoped ultimately to rule. Some of these he raised to high office; Michael de la Pole, for example, he appointed Chancellor — and this without reference to the Council.

In 1388 the Council appealed to Parliament for judgement on the favourites. The latter were condemned as traitors, some were executed and others were exiled for life. The King for the next eight years accepted the advice of his Council in ruling his kingdom, but in 1396 Queen Anne died and a powerful restraining influence had gone.

1397 began quietly. This, however, was but the calm before the storm. Richard, affable and apparently accepting the guiding hands of his Council, had been biding his time, gradually, so he thought, lulling his uncles and their fellow-nobles into a sense of false security. All these eight years Richard had never lost sight of his objective of absolute — in practice — rule, and when, as he believed, he was strong enough he acted swiftly, and many of the leading men in the Council were accused of treason and promptly neutralised. The King invited his uncle, Thomas, Duke of Gloucester, to dine with him. The Duke excused himself on the score of illness and at once the King marched to his castle and arrested his uncle. Arundel and Warwick were also taken. The King arraigned them before Parliament on a charge of treason. The members of that august gathering, conscious of the presence of a body of Cheshire archers in the yard of Wesminster Palace, bowed to the royal demand. Arundel was executed and Gloucester imprisoned in Calais. Shortly afterwards the Duke died in prison and ugly tales began to circulate suggesting that the causes of his demise were far from natural.

The Earl of Warwick, whose son married Elizabeth, Lord Berkeley's only child, was exiled for life. Nottingham and Henry Bolingbroke, son of Lancaster, however, appeared at first to have been spared, indeed they were both created Dukes (Norfolk and Hereford respectively). Later they too were exiled, the former for life and Henry for ten years, but with the clear understanding that the Lancastrian estates would not be forfeited on the death of Lancaster. In February 1399 Gaunt died, and at once Bolingbroke's exile was extended to life and the vast Lancastrian estates were confiscated by the King.

Richard, in spite of the alienation of so many noble houses, left on a punitive expedition to Ireland later that summer. His conception of kingship was one totally unacceptable to his people and, metaphorically, tore up the Magna Carta, for he declared that he, the King, was above all laws, for they emanated from him. These then were the relevant facts behind the momentous meetings in Berkeley Church and Castle on July 27th, 1399, recorded by Holinshed.

With the departure of King Richard to Ireland in May, to put down rebellion and secure the English 'pale', events moved quickly. Henry Bolingbroke, Duke of Hereford, landed at Ravenspur in Yorkshire [3] to claim, he maintained, merely the Lancastrian estates wrongly confiscated by the Crown. The Earl of Northumberland and many of the nobility flocked to his standard. Hereford was soon 'persuaded' that the king had forfeited his right to rule and that despotism must be crushed. The next heir was the Earl of March; but could the country hope to unite under one who was still almost a babe? Furthermore, even if Richard was defeated and deposed, was it in the interests of the nation that there should be another regency, whether individual or oligarchial, for a long period of years?

So Henry enlarged the claim to his dukedom and patrimony into one for the throne itself — a change of policy prompted, some said, by ambition, others by a deep sense of duty. The news travelled fast and so did the forces of Duke Henry. Marching southward, they followed almost exactly to Bristol the route taken by Queen Isabella and her lover, Mortimer, when in revolt against King Edward II in 1327.

The Duke of York, Keeper of the Realm in the King's absence, transferred the seat of Government from London to St. Albans, then mobilizing he moved westward.[4]

Richard, apprised of the situation, hastened to return but was held up in Ireland by contrary winds and did not land in Wales until July 27th, by which time his cause had been lost — if indeed it had ever had a chance of success.

(b) *Storm Clouds Gather*

Lord Berkeley was perturbed by the many rumours. Hitherto he had avoided carefully any overt action which might have been construed as an indication of taking sides with the Sovereign or with the discontented nobility who felt that the King's highhanded, indeed despotic, administration must be checked. If York really was moving westward he would probably make either for Bristol, Gloucester or Worcester to tap the Royalist reserve of manpower in South and North Wales, and also to attempt a speedy contact with Richard on his return from Ireland. Thus reasoned his Lordship, who prayed that the Berkeley luck would hold and that York would make for Worcester, Shrewsbury and North Wales, and that Lancaster would follow him. Lord Berkeley realized, however, that this could well not happen, and that he might be forced to a choice of sides. He had been a supporter of the Crown all his life, had been employed often on foreign service, [5] had, as the King's representative in Gloucestershire, taken musters in the west and raised forces to repel the French should they invade. [6] Richard had stayed at Berkeley and been royally entertained in the dubious days of 1388. Was all this training and background to stand for nothing?

On the other hand, the Earl of Warwick, father-in-law of Lord Berkeley's daughter, Elizabeth, had been exiled on a trumped-up charge (or so it was said) of treason. Furthermore, during the last two years Richard had acted unconstitutionally and had, with some justification, been labelled tyrant and despot.

Finally there were Berkeley's own friendship with Duke Henry. Could this be set aside?

What should he, Berkeley, do? To which side did honour and justice direct him? In this soul-searching dilemma his Lordship turned to his now ageing chaplain and confessor.

Trevisa was not surprised that his patron should seek his advice. Had they not often during the last ten years, and more especially in the last two, discussed theoretical situations somewhat similar to the present one, with always the ultimate question, 'Is it ever morally right to rebel and depose a lawful sovereign who had received the sacring?' In hypothetical cases it had been easy to give an answer, but now that the testing time had come, the choice was not so simple. One's future, material as well as spiritual, rested in the balance. One also staked one's family and fortune upon the wheel of choice. Trevisa for days had prayed hard for guidance in this tense situation. He had read and re-read the Gospels with the Master's teaching, and pondered deeply upon the arguments in the *De Regimine Principum*. But still the answer to this agonising problem was not clear.

Early on the 25th July a tenant reported that according to rumour the forces of York had divided. The Earl of Wiltshire, Bushey and Green and the main body of troops — few in number — were advancing on Bristol, while the Duke of York, the remainder of the Council and the Duke's personal entourage were making for Berkeley.[7] Here was ill luck indeed. At once the walls were manned and messengers sent to Bradston, Wanswell, Wotton and to John Poleyne to mobilize the tenantry, but not to advance on the Castle until explicit orders had been issued.

On the following morning, when further preparations had been completed, priest and patron walked over to St. Mary's Church, where they knelt at the altar rail and asked for guidance. Barely had the opening Pater Noster been said when a servant rushed up to his Lordship and whispered 'My Lord! A small number of horsemen approach from Stone. The captain thinks they may be the Duke of York and his party.'

The Baron rose to his feet, crossed himself and spoke quickly to the retainer. 'Tell the captain to man fully the walls and prepare the drawbridge and portcullis so that they can be positioned directly Father Trevisa and I return. Father, an Ava Maria, and a Pater Noster, and we must both be within our walls.'

The portcullis was dropped and the drawbridge raised, shutting out several members of the garrison who had gone earlier into the town. There remained, however, sufficient men-at-arms and archers to hold the outer perimeter walls against anything short of a major assult, and the advancing party obviously represented no such threat.

Lord Berkeley, even before the horsemen reined in beneath the walls, recognized the tall but ageing figure of the Duke of York, and, knowing his truculent nature was not surprised at the peremptory challenge 'Open in the King's name.'

Berkeley: 'Your Grace, it is understood that his Majesty is still in Ireland. Is this not so?'

York: 'My Lord of Berkeley is well informed as to the King's movements. Is he not aware that I speak for his liege Lord in his absence? Coming as I do on urgent royal business I demand entrance and hospitality in the King's name, that the matter may be discussed in private.'

Those within, feeling that the small party constituted no danger or threat, ordered that the drawbridge should be lowered and the portcullis raised. The personal greetings between Berkeley and York were distinctly cool, indeed my Lord Berkeley, patently embarrassed and displeased, was lacking somewhat in the civilities normally expected on such an occasion.

Hardly had the visitors entered the inner courtyard than the Duke turned to his host and said 'Let us apart. The matter is urgent and the time short. My Lord Egerton, come with us. Lead the way, my Lord.'

Berkeley: 'This way, your Grace. Canon, you will come with us.'

York: 'My Lord Berkeley! This is king's business and for your ears alone.'

Berkeley: 'Your Grace, the venerable Canon Trevisa is my confidant as well as confessor. You will speak to me in his presence or not at all.'

York: 'NO!'

Berkeley: 'Very well, the subject is closed. Shall we quench our thirsts?'

York: 'My Lord! My Lord! This is King's business! You cannot dismiss it thus! I have orders for you on the King's behalf.'

Berkeley: 'Then they must be delivered when my confessor is present.'

York: 'Very well then, but King Richard will not be pleased when this matter is reported.'

Berkeley: 'This way, your Grace. We will go to St. John's Chapel in the Keep. There we will not be disturbed, neither can we be overheard.'

'Will you be seated your Grace?' 'Father, a short prayer for guidance in these weighty matters that are to be considered.'

By this time York's irritation was obvious, and it was with great difficulty that he controlled himself.

'My Lord Berkeley, you will be aware that Henry Bolingbroke has feloniously landed in England, has gathered around him certain rebellious members of the nobility, claiming the restoration of the Lancastrian estates and, it is said, the crown itself! In the unfortunate absence of his Majesty I am mobilizing forces to oppose this traitor. You are known to have given loyal service to King Richard and his father, the late king, and you are his Lieutenant here in Gloucestershire for raising forces in time of danger. This is such a time. In the King's name I order you to muster men at once to oppose Henry, and to be ready to join your Liege Lord on his return from Ireland.'

A silence of perceptible duration followed before Lord Berkeley spoke:—

'Your Grace, I fully understand your position and the moral obligation upon you to raise an army on the King's behalf. Have you, however, appreciated the effect of his Majesty's actions during the last two years, beginning with the murder of his uncle, the venerable Duke of Gloucester, and the exile of such loyal noblemen as

Henry Bolingbroke, the Earl of Warwick and others?'

York: 'Berkeley! This is treason! You will pay for such defamation of his Majesty's character.'

Berkeley: 'Your Grace, you must hear me out. The King, upon the death of the Duke of Lancaster, broke his royal word by confiscating those estates, and without justification extended Bolingbroke's ten year exile to one for life. These are but a few of the matters which have disturbed many — nobility and the common folk. A number of the former declare that they, loyal though they are and wish to be, cannot support a King whose word can not be trusted and by whose orders many loyal subjects have been ill-treated or done to death. Should I now attempt a muster here in Gloucestershire the result would be a failure. The local discontent is considerable. The same applies over Severn, so I am told. John, do you, as one who moves freely in the west, agree?'

York: 'Speak not, old priest! Your master's words are treasonable. He will, ere long, be adjudged a traitor and executed, unless the King is merciful. Do not thus implicate yourself and suffer in his fall.'

Berkeley: 'Your Grace, moderate your words! My hostly obligations prevent me uttering any threat, but recall that you are within this castle whose walls are fully manned. Give Canon Trevisa a hearing. Perhaps his words and logic will succeed where mine have failed. John speak on.'

Trevisa: 'Your Grace, my patron has not overstressed the local feeling. I travel widely in the west and hear much gossip. Sorrow fills many hearts that the laws of this country and of God have, so they believe, been disregarded and replaced by a reign of fear and personal power. The Master who said that we should forgive our slanderers and advised the turning of the other cheek to those maltreating us, said also that one's neighbours should be loved and treated as one's self. St. Paul, too, reminded Christians that though the King should be honoured, God should be feared, and by implication obeyed, and the brethren loved. It is my belief that if Lord Berkeley, speaking in the King's name, should attempt to raise the local levies, there would be no real response and that many would go into hiding. They will not risk their lives for a King they have ceased to trust. Neither would they wish to kill their fellows to impose a rule which they consider takes away man's basic liberty and freedom, and is contrary to the will of God and to the country's laws. Your Grace! I beg of you ...' At that point shouts were heard without. A moment later the chapel door was beaten hard and the Captain of the Garrison dashed in and cried, 'My Lord! My Lord! An armed column is reported. Will Trotman of Nibley saw them on Stinchcombe Hill, and rode hard to warn us. Me thinks from what he says that the Lancastrian standard leads the van, and that of Percy, too, is there. A horseman rides ahead having, no doubt, a message for your Lordship.'

Berkeley: 'I will come at once. Raise the drawbridge and lower the portcullis. Your Grace, you must stay within the keep. We can discuss our future actions at a later hour. John, see that our guests have all they need, and then join me on the battlements.'

Within the hour from the ramparts Lord Berkeley, his captain and his chaplain heard distinctly the jingle-jangle of the trappings of the horses from the direction of Lorwing, and then, after a while, they saw the head of a marching column coming down the Heath. Almost at once a trumpet sounded at the Castle gate and the herald spoke:— 'I have a message for my Lord of Berkeley.'

Berkeley: 'Speak on, Sir Herald'.
Herald: 'My Master, his Grace, the Duke of Lancaster, prays audience with your Lordship and begs hospitality for himself, the Earl of Northumberland and six other noble lords. The rest will camp in the meadows below the castle.'
Berkeley: 'Prepare to lower the drawbridge and raise the portcullis, Captain. Sir Herald, bear my felicitations to his Grace. Tell him I feel deeply honoured and await his arrival with the greatest pleasure, provided that he comes in peace.'

The steward was then bidden to make all necessary preparations — and with haste. With that the Lord of Berkeley turned to his chaplain and said, 'You will accompany me to the gates, John. We will need cool heads tonight if we are not to lose them! The cleric answered:— 'Be not hasty in your speech, my Lord. Welcome and feast them all, but let them do the talking. In reply, if possible, be non-commital and plead that you have not heard much news since it was said that his Grace of Lancaster had returned from exile to justly claim — and mind you use the word justly — his patrimony.' Hardly had the chaplain finished speaking than the vanguard turned left handed up the Castle bank.

Duke Henry rode ahead and at the moat drew rein. 'My friend and comrade, well met! You, most graciously, have extended your hospitality to Lord Percy, these Lords and myself, if we come in peace. We come indeed in peace. His Grace, the Duke of York, is your guest, as we will be. He and I may not at this moment be in full accord, but when we have met face to face and talked, our mutual doubts and differences may be resolved. I trust you as a man of honour to respect our persons, as I respect those of York and your noble self.' Thus spake the shrewdest soldier and politician of his day, and one with charm enough, should need arise, to win a conflict with word and not with sword. Lord Berkeley was in a quandary. Should he take his Grace's word and show of friendship without demur, or should he seek to parley further from the castle walls? The Lancastrian forces were considerable, and perchance could take the castle by assault, though the conflict would be long and bloody. Common sense prevailed, and he replied 'Your Grace and your nobility are truly welcome. The trust is mutual, and the local truce twixt York and Lancaster will, pray God, be inviolable and advantage all. The drawbridge shall be lowered at this instant and we can pledge ourselves in a cup of best French wine.'

In the courtyard Lord Berkeley, the chaplain and two squires bowed low as the mighty Duke of Lancaster reined in his mount. 'Welcome your Grace! and welcome, too, my noble peers! You do us great honour, and one we fully appreciate. Pray enter and wash after your many miles of dusty travel. A meal will soon be ready. And may your stay bring mutual joy.' With that my Lord Percy glanced quickly at the Duke, but no word was spoken, and following my Lord of Berkeley and the Duke came noblemen enough, and pages, squires and full fifty men-at-arms. A goodly host indeed and one which ensured the person of the Duke, and would strain, at this short notice, the resources and ingenuity of the kitchen staff.

Through the outer bailey the party passed, and it did not escape Trevisa's notice that a dozen men-at-arms remained at the outer gatehouse, and another party halted at the inner courtyard gate. All this was done with the minimum of display, which spoke clearly of procedure ordered and rehearsed. No chances were being taken, and a silent warning was being issued to the men of Berkeley that one false move would lead to their deaths and to the sacking of the town.

The steward and all under him hustled as they had never hustled before, and by the time the senior guests had quenched their thirsts and performed the perfunctory ablutions courtesy demanded, the High Table was laid with the best that the castle possessed, and the many candles and torches in their sconces gave the Great Hall a festive air.

It became clear before the dinner was half way through that York was not relaxed nor appreciating the culinary efforts of the kitchen staff. Voice and gesture indicated a considerable measure of strain. Finally his irritation overcame him and he burst out 'My Lord Berkeley, how do you stand at this time? You are known to have shown loyalty and enterprise in the King's service in the past. Do you still place your hands between his in loyalty as of old? Tell me, how stand you?'

Berkeley: 'Your Grace, the question which you pose is, I most humbly suggest, not one to be discussed in public. Moreover we are far from London and the Kingdom's heart, we are not fully conversant with the current affairs of state. Your Graces and the noble Lords, our guests, know more, much more, than we do here. And what you tell us will no doubt have considerable bearing upon the reply to your question. The hour is late — it is already passed midnight — so I suggest we meet, Your Graces, Lordships and ourselves, when we have rested and our minds as well as bodies have been refreshed, for they are matters of high moment which must be settled. Because we deal with sacred matters as well as common, and because the need for privacy is great, I suggest to your Graces and my Lords that we meet within the parish church which lies beside these walls. Your men can guard the doors and give us peace to listen and to talk.' The Duke of Lancaster, a shrewder man than many present thought, rose at once, before the Duke of York could lift his ageing frame, and said 'My Lord of Berkeley is correct. Now is not the time, nor this the place, for solemn argument, for great decisions must soon be made. Are you agreed, my Uncle? and you, my Lords? If so, I am for bed, and I thank you, my Lord, for your gracious hospitality.'

Berkeley acknowledged Lancaster's generous intervention and his sudden closure of discussion with a bow, and spoke. 'Thank you, Your Grace, but before we retire may we fix the hour — ten perhaps? — and may I bring my learned chaplain, Canon Trevisa, and two of my household knights, upon whose honour and discretion we can all rely? Your rooms have been prepared. Sleep well, and may God guide us at our morrow's meeting.'

As the party rose the Canon spoke: 'Your Grace! My Lords! The issue before us is momentous. Mass will be celebrated at 7 a.m., with intention for a right decision and a happy issue out of our present difficulties. The chapel can be entered through this hall — in that corner. There will also be prayers for guidance when we meet at ten o'clock. God give you sound sleep, and may we through His Grace do that which is well pleasing in His sight. Good night! God Bless you all.'

Lord Berkeley, when the guests had gone, sought out his chaplain. 'John, I will need your help and support over and above your prayers — at ten — and desperately too. My Lord of York is anxious to involve us in the royal cause. The Duke of Lancaster, though contender for the crown, may hold out the olive branch within a velvet glove — even though it hides a mailed fist! Talk to them as you talked to me about the royal duties and the fate of those who abuse their rank and privilege. Pray for me, Father, and for yourself, for in this matter we sink or swim together!'

'My Lord, never fear! The terrors of the night-watches dissolve with the dawn of the day, and the Master has promised that He will speak through us — do you remember? "Take no thought how or what ye shall speak; for it shall be given you in the same hour what ye shall speak. For it is not you that speak, but the spirit of your Father which speaketh in you".'

(c) *The Day of Decision*

The sun appeared over the Cotswold edge into a clear sky as Trevisa came back from the parish church where he had early begun his preparations for the meeting of the nobility. There had been some difficulty with the Lancastrian guard at the outer gate. Their orders had been to let no one out before dawn, and they were reluctant to allow even the parish priest to leave. In the end a threat to rouse the Duke himself was made and at once permission was forthcoming.

To Trevisa's surprise almost the entire party of Dukes, Earls, Barons and several Esquires, came to mass, and the chapel of St. Mary was full. This, thought the canon, augured well, for it suggested that the vital matters which occupied all their thoughts weighed heavily upon mind, heart and conscience. The meeting, unless he had misread the signs, was to be a discussion, and not a cut and dried programme to be driven through at speed and by force of arms if needs be; unless — and this, thought he, was just possible with an unfathomable exterior like that possessed by Lancaster — Henry and his nobles were putting on this show of openmindedness to persuade Lord Berkeley to side with them. Perhaps they feared the Welsh, and with his Lordship's heir, Lord James of Raglan, across the Severn it was doubly important that Berkeley, and through him much of Gloucestershire, should not side with Richard. Yes, this was a very valid point, and gave his Lordship an importance hitherto unsuspected. He, Trevisa, must speak with his patron before the meeting began. The hoped for opportunity did not come, for one or other of the noble Lords seemed always to be with Lord Berkeley. Was this deliberate surveillance, a conspiracy to separate his Lordship from all who might bring a pro-king influence to bear upon him?

Well before ten o'clock Sir John Berkeley of Beverston arrived, having been warned in the early hours of his Lordship's command; and before the set hour all were assembled within the church, while a heavy guard was mounted at each door — Trevisa felt that this might serve a two-fold purpose, parishioners would be kept out, while the Berkeley and the Yorkist delegations could be silently arrested if the discussions were not to the liking of the Duke of Lancaster.

In the prayers which followed, the Holy Spirit was asked to guide and direct all their consultations and open their hearts and minds so that the decisions might be those most pleasing to God and those which would best benefit the realm at large. The Sovereign, too, was prayed for, that his life might not be put in peril on the high seas and that he might be brought safely home. This last prayer, so carefully phrased, was deliberately inserted that reactions might be observed — and they were! York started and looked up when the prayer began, but on perceiving Lancaster deep in devotion — or so it seemed — he dropped his eyes.

The Duke of Lancaster, the prayers ended, addressed the assembled members:— 'My Uncle, his Grace, the Duke of York, is Regent and the senior statesman present; as such it is his right and privilege to speak first.'

For a moment no one stirred, then York stood up:— 'Nephew and noble peers, I came here yesterday to solicit aid and arms for King Richard from my Lord of Berkeley and this neighbourhood, and to oppose all who were in revolt against the Crown. Fealty, and that alone, drove me on — against my will and better judgement it is true. To me had fallen the heavy burden of regency with its added bonds of loyalty. Like you, my Lords, for months a secret conflict has been waging deep down within my soul. Reports were rife of innocent victims of a cruel King being dragged to Tyburn, Tower and block. My youngest brother, Gloucester, was, as you well know, foully murdered in Calais Castle, and my noble nephew, who sits here, was exiled on a baseless charge for ten years, a sentence which later was extended to one for life, and all his patrimony stolen from him. Last night I thought long upon these deeds — and others just as vile — and my doubts began to grow. Despite these doubts, can I, as Regent and uncle of the King, withdraw support when he is far away? Can you renounce your oaths of fealty to the figurehead of government? These problems must be faced. I feel that for the country's sake our present difficulties should be solved by peaceful settlement, and not by force of arms, and so prevent a bloodbath in our land. Myself, I will not — come what may — draw sword against my King.'

Most looked to Lancaster to reply, but Berkeley forestalled his Grace — or was it by his leave? Lord Berkeley walked to the altar rails and turning, said:— "Will some one present please enlighten my colleagues and myself on the more recent national events, for we, here in the far west, are often days, indeed weeks, behind London and the more important centres of the Kingdom.' York jumped up to reply but was motioned down by Lancaster who said:— 'Your Grace! You have already spoken, perhaps I should speak next, and account for my presence here, if not in England. Northumberland will then narrate the feelings of the north and how he himself reacts today, and explain the agonies through which he and others have passed during the last year or more.' Trevisa listened with interest. This interjection and the tenor of the words showed clearly that whatever plot, policy or purpose lay behind this visit, here in the person of Henry, Duke of Lancaster, was the brain, the agent, may be the evil genius of the whole affair. Here was the man to watch and fear, not old York, vile-tempered and militant though he might be; and were not Henry's men encamped outside the castle's walls? — and were not fifty Lancastrian men-at-arms within those walls? Lancaster began, 'My Lord of Berkeley, you cannot be so isolated as you suggest. Bristol is a mighty port and so a centre of news and gossip, though much of the latter could often be without foundation. I will, however, take you at your word, and tell you how I stand. The news of the forfeiture of the Lancastrian estates, after the most solemn oaths to my aged father, reached me in France, and at once I planned to return - although in exile - to demand from the forsworn King [8] the restoration of my patrimony. On landing in Yorkshire I found the King had gone to Ireland and the north was in ferment. I had heard when overseas something of the reason for this discontent and fear, but as with the Queen of Sheba the half had not been told. Now, Percy, you had better take up the tale.' The Earl arose at once:— 'My Lord of Berkeley, you, a loyal supporter of the throne and a friend of Kings, must have been a worried man these last few years when the whole character of his majesty has so changed. Now, instead of a father to his people, we have a despot, cruel, selfish and determined. Justice is mocked, the laws are disregarded and the church is powerless to protest.

My noble Lords and I have pondered long and deep, hours have we spent in prayer' - a gross and flagrant exaggeration Trevisa felt! 'and we can conceive no solution save the deposing of the king. To this conclusion we had come when his Grace of Lancaster landed in our midst. God in his mercy for the country had answered our prayer, unworthy though we be. Here was the man, God's saviour for this nation in its loyalty and dire need. His Grace in his humility still hesitates to take up arms against his late liege Lord, although we tell him that it clearly is God's will. Come my Lord, are you happy now that you know the facts as they seem to us? And do you feel as we that as Judas was removed from his discipleship to which another, named Matthias, was appointed, so, too, Richard should be deposed?'

Slowly Lord Berkeley stood up to reply:— 'My Lord Percy is right. For many months indeed for several years, the learned canon and myself have discussed the abuse of power within this realm' — a dangerous phase thought Trevisa — 'and we have wondered what the answer was. Is it ever lawful in God's sight to remove a King who is not fit to reign? We searched the Scriptures and the writings of wise men from the past, such works as the *De Regimine Principum* of Aegidius Romanus. Like you, my Lords, we prayed for guidance. My chaplain will now address the meeting and will put before us the thoughts, nay the conclusions of Romanus, that most learned monk. This summing-up will also answer clearly the question of his Grace, the Duke of York, as to how we now stand in relation to the King.' His Lordship then sat down.

Trevisa walked to the sanctuary entrance and faced the whole assembly — how close a parallel it seemed to him between himself, and Lord Berkeley for all that, and some poor wretch arraigned before a Judge and Jury on some capital charge. His statements, like those of the prisoner at the bar, could win him safety or a felon's death:— 'Your Grace, your Lordships and Gentlemen, we are here to state clearly how we stand in relation to our oaths of fealty which each of us has taken. We all, at heart, are honest and loyal servants to the Crown, but of late our faith in kingship has been shaken, undermined may be, by the metamorphosis which has taken place in our liege lord, King Richard. Slowly the thoughts, furtive at first, entered our minds, "If this continues something must be done. The country cannot endure, must not be allowed to suffer, such cruel despotism". The obvious course — logical it seemed — was that the tyrant should be removed. It was at this point, I trow, that conscience began to trouble each of us. As time passed, and conditions became worse, so the need for remedial action grew more urgent. My lords, what *can* we do? We, your Lordships, as Council Members, and I, as a priest, have sworn to nurture and support the Crown — and so we do, but when the wearer of that emblem has proved himself unfaithful to his high calling, to the oaths made at his sacring, is it then lawful to remove the symbol from the head and the wearer from the throne? That, my conscience-ridden fellow subjects, is the frightening dilemma which faces us today. Full long and deep Lord Berkeley and I have pondered over this, have prayed for guidance and have searched the Scriptures, and after much labour and heartsearching we think, but only think, a mad or evil sovereign may be deposed. The Master who said "render unto Caesar the things that are Caesar's", said also "and unto God the things that be of God". It cannot be God's will that His people should be treated as the subjects of this realm have suffered these two years and more. Holy Writ reminds us, too, that we must not have fellowship with those whose works are evil. "Suffering for conscience sake" does not come within this context, and if St. Paul's directive to "Honour the King" suggests we stay our hands, the thrusting forth by the Master Himself of those who desecrated the Temple with their evil ways gives hope that deposing might receive God's Blessing. I believe, however, that this action, if taken, must be carried through with Christian charity and sympathy. Force and bloodshed must be avoided, and the patient — for the king is mentally ill and so a patient — must be well treated, even if placed under some kindly restraint. How this may or can be done is not for me, a priest, to say. My task is but to point to a course of action which will save this country from further tyranny and fear, and to warn you, one and all, that this must be done without brutality, and that the activating motive must be the public weal, and not selfish ends. And remember, one day we all will stand before our Maker to render account of our stewardship in His Vineyard here below.' With that the aged priest sat down.

Silence followed, a silence which could be felt. Finally the Duke of Lancaster got up and turning to Trevisa said:— 'We thank you, Father, for your guidance and advice, given as we would expect from a man of God, with clarity, wisdom and doctrinal backing. We will heed your warnings as to motives and desires, and will know ourselves the custodians of the people of this realm. Come, my peers, we have our brief and our directives from the learned Canon. Let us to the castle to work out how best our task may be accomplished. But before we leave let us kneel and ask the Canon, in God's name, to bless us in our planning and our enterprise.'

'Thank you, Father, we leave you to your meditation.' Thus the Duke's facade of dedication to a cause, if facade it was, continued to the end, and as a final gesture he remarked, 'If you, Father, have the time you are welcome to our deliberations, indeed we would be honoured with your presence.' With that the nobility of England, with Lord Berkeley in their midst, left the Church.

As the party passed through the courtyard the garrison commander drew aside his master and whispered:— 'An urgent message for his Grace of York from my Lord of Salisbury.'
Berkeley: 'Your Grace, a moment please. Tidings from Wales have just arrived.'
Messenger: 'My Lord Duke, a message from my noble master, the Earl of Salisbury. The news I bear is bad. The Welsh forces under Prince Owen Glendwr, nigh 40,000 of them, [9] are drifting away in large numbers from their camp beneath the walls of Conway Castle. They are disheartened by the King's long delay, and with nature's abnormalities and portents in the sky, backed by baleful prophecy of the fall of kings, have, by now, largely dispersed, believing the King already dead.' [10]
York: 'No word of this must pass your lips till my host and I have viewed these facts.' (Aside to Berkeley): 'My Lord, this news is dire, and when well known will squeeze the spirit from our men, and stifle all hope of reinforcements from Wales and the West. My nephew's delay is indeed fatal to his cause. Our hope, our only real hope, lies now in terms between King Richard and his Grace of Lancaster. For this we must work speedily before Lord Salisbury's plight is known. Let us negotiate, as though from strength, without delay. Come, let us hurry before his Grace marks our absence.'

The discussion continued in the castle all day, but by the end a definite course of action had been evolved. The Duke of Lancaster was now confident that, with Lord Berkeley throwing in his influence with them, Gloucestershire, Monmouth and Herefordshire could largely be relied upon not to oppose their scheme. Their plan was simple in concept, and the influence of Trevisa's warnings could be detected in the final draft.

The King would be invited to abdicate — and when he landed in England and found how small was his support, this he might well do. Richard would be required to declare publicly his abdication, and, if he could be persuaded, to name the Duke of Lancaster as the successor to the throne. No harm must come to the person of Richard, but it might be necessary for a short while to keep him as an 'honoured guest' in some castle, yet to be named.

The formula settled, the members rose wearily from their seats, but before they left the chamber York, silencing the conversation, spoke again. It was as though he wished to make a personal apologia, and force once more upon his peers their obligations to maintain the King as head — though titular may be — of state.

York: 'Well that is settled! Our Sovereign Lord retains his crown and dignity, but his powers will be restrained. No harm shall come to him, and his voice shall still be heard in council. We leave at morrow's dawn for Bristol to persuade, if persuade we can, the Earl of Wiltshire, Sir Henry Green and Sir John Bushey to accept our advice. But, nephew, mark well! I, myself, will raise no hand to their hurt, and in any future conflict, if this should come, which God forbid, I will take no part.'

Lancaster: 'Your Grace, I fully understand, and respect you as our senior statesman and our country's Regent for the time that is. God grant peace and affection twixt us and ours now and in the days to come.

You, my Lord Berkeley, will mobilize all archers and some extra lances, and therewith, in the King's name, defend the Severn passage and your castle against all comers. Good night, your Grace, and you my Lord, and God Save England!'

Thus ended a day of meetings the like of which have had no known parallel in Berkeley's long, historic and at times turbulent past.

Canon Trevisa, the next morning, was at mass when the Lancastrian forces left the castle and the Avon meadows.

The spirit of bonhomie at the time of the Duke's departure seemed a little forced, or so observers reported to the cleric, who knew the tension which lay beneath the surface. He recalled those first few nerve-racking hours, and those the following day within the church. A breaking down of negotiations at either time could well have resulted in deprivations, and executions within the castle, and fire, rapine and sword throughout the town.

Before nightfall a messenger rode in with the news that Bristol Castle was besieged. An embassage from the Duke of York had entered with orders from his Grace, but at the messenger's departure had not returned.

The following afternoon came word that the Earl of Wiltshire, Sir Henry Green and Sir John Bushey had surrendered, been tried, condemned and executed within a few hours. This left the garrison chilled, and doubly grateful that Providence had preserved them from a similar fate. It had all turned upon the acceptance by the Duke of York that Lancaster had no aspirations beyond the restoration of his patrimony — a very understandable demand in view of the method of deprivation — and the establishment once more of law and order within the Magna Carta context. Thus was confirmed Trevisa's convictions that in Lancaster one saw a man of many moods, controlled withal, but ruthless if thwarted or if need arose. The chaplain warned his patron against over-optimism and too great a reliance upon his Lordship's long established friendship with Duke Henry. He suggested, too, that a trusted messenger be sent with haste to Lord James Berkeley of Raglan counselling him to avoid, if possible, any involvement in the struggle between Duke Henry and the King.

Chapter 13
Towards Deposition

Later that evening, 29th July, a messenger arrived from Duke Henry bearing a seemingly courteous greeting which, however, caused both Lord Berkeley and his chaplain considerable concern. His Lordship was informed that his Grace would be returning to Berkeley with his entire force, less the Duke of York and his entourage, on the next day. The Duke, furthermore, 'invited' Lord Berkeley to accompany him on campaign in North Wales — a request that my Lord of Berkeley realized was in the nature of a command, an order to be disregarded at personal peril. This was disturbing enough, but the concluding paragraph caused additional dismay — the instructions given on July 27th that Lord Berkeley should mobilize a force of archers and men-at-arms to defend the castle and deny the Severn passage to all comers were still to be implemented, even at the expense of Lord Berkeley's personal train on the Welsh expedition.

Berkeley riders left soon after dawn on the following morning for Beverston, Bradston and Wotton. Sir John Berkeley was requested to attend a briefing conference in Berkeley Castle by noon that day, and all outlying normal campaign contingents were ordered to assemble five hours later. Within the garrison, too, on that Wednesday morning all was bustle. The castle had to be placed, virtually, on a siege footing, while Lord Berkeley's campaign party had the additional tasks of fitting themselves out for a period of service of an unspecified duration. Sir John arrived early, and formally took over effective command of the castle and the defence force, which, it had to be admitted, had not yet been fully formed.

Lord Berkeley wished Trevisa to accompany him, at least for the first few weeks, feeling that his shrewd advice might well be an important factor in his struggle for survival in the complexities of the political intrigue which lay behind this military expedition into which my Lord of Berkeley was, reluctantly, being drawn. Indeed the future could, he said, be likened unto a swamp traversed by a track that was both tortuous and ill-defined. If the expedition became long-drawn-out and a winter campaign, even in a modified form, kept the Duke's forces in the field, then Trevisa, with his chest weakness, would need to return to Berkeley.

The outcome of these deliberations, as far as the Canon was concerned, was soon settled. The chantry priests of St. Mary's Church, Father Matthew and Father Paul, would temporarily take over the vicar's duties and also act as chaplain to the castle and its garrison. Lord Berkeley, possibly to ease the first stage of the Duke's march for his chaplain, asked him to ride over to Upton St. Leonard that afternoon to confirm the orders sent earlier in the day. Thus Trevisa would have the whole of Thursday before joining Duke Henry's column when, presumably on the Friday morning, they would leave Gloucester either northward to Worcester or westward to Hereford.

An hour later the Canon cantered over the drawbridge, down the wordies and rode by way of the Heath to Stanley St. Leonard. After a meal with the brethren he continued to Upton St. Leonard where he found the mounted party completing their preparations. The tired cleric retired to bed early and spent Thursday morning — after mass — resting in anticipation of several long days in the saddle.

Back in Berkeley preparations for both enterprises continued and by the time the advance guard of the Duke's forces arrived order — of a kind — had been established. Lord Berkeley learned that Duke Henry had received news the previous day that the King had landed, as had been anticipated, in west Wales and was proceeding at speed to join Lord Salisbury, whom he had sent ahead from Ireland to raise forces in North Wales and Cheshire, where support for Richard was known to be strong. Henry had learned, too, that Richard's attempted recruitment in southwest Wales had, largely, failed.

Shortly after noon a Berkeley rider arrived at Upton St. Leonard with instruction for the six-strong campaign party to escort the Canon to St. Peter's Abbey before they themselves joined the main body on the Oxleaze, where camp would be established for the night. Trevisa on the leisurely ride down into the town of Gloucester thought over the possibilities of the future. The immediate prospect was attractive. He would, it must be assumed, be able to observe for himself the exiled Archbishop, the great Thomas Arundel. This could, indeed should be, an interesting experience. To many clerics it would have seemed a golden opportunity to jockey for position and to promote self-advancement. No such thoughts, however, entered Trevisa's mind. At heart a scholar and a countryman, Trevisa viewed high office in the Church as a hindrance to the satisfaction of his personal inclination, and something to be avoided. This was not to say, however, that he did not enjoy the experience of close association with the members of the ecclesiastical hierarchy and the nobility. The truth was the very opposite. It had been this two-fold attachment to scholarship and social and intellectual intercourse which had influenced him for many years to divide his life between the university, mainly Oxford, and Berkeley parish and castle. The presence of a fellow historian, Adam of Usk, in the Duke's train was a pleasing thought, and the news that the intended route lay through Hereford suggested the possibility of a brief re-union with Nicholas Hereford — indeed the next few days could be very enjoyable, especially so if the fine weather continued.

Trevisa, on arrival at St. Peter's found that the main party, including the Duke, Lord Berkeley and Adam of Usk, had ridden in an hour earlier and that their Lordships had taken fresh horses and ridden out to the Oxleaze to inspect the camp and to confer with the commanders. Adam, however, was saying his office. Later when both clerics had fulfilled their devotional obligations they met to discuss the future. Trevisa was soon confirmed in his opinion — formed during the brief moments that they had had together in Berkeley a few days earlier — that Adam was a staunch supporter of the Duke and was extreme in his views regarding the King. Richard must, at all costs, be removed from office and rendered incapable of causing further trouble, even if this entailed imprisonment or death itself — quoting, perhaps rather ineptly thought Trevisa, the statement made by Caiaphas that it was 'expedient that one man should die for the people'.

Masses were said soon after first light and by eight o'clock the head of the column had crossed the far branch of the Severn and was passing through Over on the Ross road.

The forces camped for the night in the flat meadows on both banks of the Wye between the town of Ross and Wilton Castle. Many leaders remained with their men, but the Duke, the Archbishop and certain of the nobility enjoyed the hospitality of the de Greys of Wilton Castle, while Trevisa, Adam and other clergy were accommodated at the Bishop of Hereford's manor house next to Ross Church. Trevisa was grateful that the building stood high above the river meadows where the night and morning mists might have affected his chest.

Duke Henry was a little surprised, even put out, that so few of the local gentry, except their hosts, had come forward with offers of help, friendship and fealty. The Talbots of Goodrich Castle might be excused, maybe, as Lord Gilbert Talbot was barely fifteen years old. Perhaps Lord Berkeley's warning to his nephew, my Lord of Raglan, had been passed on?

The Duke decided on an early start for the morrow so that Hereford could be reached before noon. A messenger was sent at once to that city acquainting the Bishop and the civil dignitaries of the proposed plans. Lord John Trevenant, Bishop of Hereford, an outspoken critic of the King's behaviour, would be co-operative — after his enthronement had he not brought considerable pressure in Council upon those who were attending the King and influencing him (as far as had been practicable)? The Duke that evening despatched Adam of Usk with a gift to the Prior and community of the Hospital of St. John of Jerusalem in Garway Church. John offered to accompany Adam, but Lord Berkeley strongly advised against the additional strain involved. The Knights of St. John formed a military order which found favour with Duke Henry.

The first troops moved off before six o'clock, but the baggage wagons were not under way until nine. Trevisa rode ahead of the main mounted party to enable him to visit Garway, and Adam received permission to act as his guide.

To the Duke's pleasure they found a large and enthusiastic reception committee awaiting them at the Wye bridge close to the gate of the city. An address of welcome was read by the Mayor, who then presented his councillors as men who stood firmly on the policy of freedom for the individual and who opposed strongly the despotic acts of the Sovereign. The Bishop was represented by his Archdeacon who conveyed his Lordship's greetings and assurances of support. Amongst the assembly Trevisa saw Canon Nicholas Hereford, but it was a full hour before he was able to greet his old friend, now no longer a Lollard but a firm upholder of the Establishment [1] — and flourishing as a result.

Later that afternoon, while the Duke conferred with my Lord Bishop and the other members of the nobility had come in to offer fealty and aid, the two canons met again. Trevisa was surprised to see how well, remarkably well, Nicholas looked. John, the younger by ten years, realized that he appeared ten or fifteen years older — he certainly felt it! Perhaps it was the long years spent in the Severn Vale which bred so much rheumatics and chest trouble. Both clerics believed that the King was mentally disturbed and that the situation of the last year or more could not be allowed to continue. At this point they parted company on policy. John was of the opinion that Richard should remain as the figure-head, but that power, the effective power, should be vested in a Council of State. Nicholas considered that Richard should be removed from office and another placed upon the throne — but who? The nominated heir, Lord Edmund Mortimer, was a child. York was old, perhaps too old, and he certainly had neither the mental calibre nor the moral fibre to rule at a time when force and forethought were needed. Duke Henry seemed the obvious choice, but his ambition, ruthlessness and suspect integrity made many — including Nicholas, — fearful of the consequences of such an elevation. If rumour was correct Richard's forces were evaporating, and so it seemed to the canons that there was little or no alternative to Duke Henry either as the head of a council or King itself. Time alone would give the answer. At that moment, Oxford and literary work seemed a thing of the past and as they discussed the old days they wondered how scholars such as William Middleworth and others reacted to the present national crisis. William, they felt, must be an extremely worried man for he was known to be a strong supporter of the present King and often employed by him in cases of conscience or doctrinal dispute. They hoped that if this civil war, for it was nothing less, ended soon and without too great and widespread bloodshed, further opportunities for study — perhaps some co-operative effort, such as the biblical project of the 70's — might again be possible. With that hopeful note (or was it nostalgic, wishful thinking?) they parted.

That night Lord Berkeley told his chaplain that the Duke was confident, so confident indeed that he had decided not to push on at such speed. Support for his cause he believed was substantial. Furthermore it was being commonly reported that Lord Salisbury's forces were dwindling, and that Richard had almost no effective army. If this was so in Wales and Cheshire, where the King's cause was supposed to flourish, how could he expect to muster an adequate body in England where, it was said, most major castles from Carlisle to Corfe were being held by pro-Henry supporters?

The following morning, Sunday, 3rd August, mass was celebrated in camp and the main forces moved off towards Leominster, while the Duke and his principal advisors conferred again with the Bishop and other influential supporters directly High Mass, with the Bishop as celebrant, had ended. His Grace and his party of conferrers were later entertained by the Bishop before setting out, escorted by a mixed force of some hundred mounted archers and men-at-arms. The following morning the entire force left Leominster (where further Herefordshire contingents had arrived) for Ludlow. There the nobility and escorts remained, while the footsoldiers and some mounted troops pushed on to Stokesay, so that the Tuesday's march could be reduced from twenty-eight to twenty-one miles — Henry certainly thought of his men and strove to maintain them in good physical condition and in high spirits.

Monday afternoon and evening at Ludlow Castle was, again, a morale booster. The welcome from the townsfolk was genuine and vocal, and a number of the lesser nobility sent reinforcements for the Duke.

That night a heavy thunderstorm turned the route into a muddy track, and although the sun shone the following morning the going remained heavy all day, and it was a leg- and saddle-weary force that entered Shrewsbury shortly after seven o'clock. Their fatigue had been increased when, three miles outside Stokesay, a message was received that a Welsh force under Owen ap Llewellyn was shadowing the advanced contingent. The strength of Owen's party was put at 'several hundred', not large it was true, but sufficient to cause trouble for the main body of the Duke's column and a major threat to his Grace's entourage and its escort. A halt was called and at once defensive positions were taken up. Sir John Till, taking with him a small force of archers and lances, hastened back along the route to warn and augment the Duke's party. At the same time two small recce groups, each with a local guide, set off to seek out and report on the shadowing Welsh.

By the time the Duke rejoined the main force one recce party had returned, bringing a reassuring report. The earlier news had grossly exaggerated the Welshmen's numbers; they were probably no more than fifty to eighty, at most, and appeared to be a motley contingent whose probable purpose was easy loot, the sudden attack on small parties of stragglers, and an equally quick get-away.

It was, indeed, a tired column which marched into Shrewsbury that evening. The scene that met their eyes was, however, heartening, a duplication, almost, of their welcome at Hereford.

At Shrewsbury many influential people, including Sir Robert and Sir John Leigh, Lord Scales and Lord Berdolfe, came to Duke Henry. In addition representatives of the city and county of Chester sought audience and offered the corporated submission of their bodies. It was a clear indication that the royal cause was at a low ebb. The Duke decided, in view of the obvious state of affairs and to rest his forces, to remain in Shrewsbury for a day or two — a decision welcomed by the troops, but not in the same degree by the townsfolk.

Trevisa was bored and tired. He hardly saw his patron these days, for Lord Berkeley was constantly in attendance upon the Duke, who had a full programme of talks and discussions with his council and other bodies. It seemed clear to the Canon that Lord Berkeley had been won over completely to the Duke's cause. It was as though the friendly relationship which had exited before the exile of the latter, and which had not been incompatible with the royal favour enjoyed previously by Lord Berkeley, had been reborn. His master's future seemed bright, but Trevisa was not happy. He did not object to his patron opposing the King, the latter fully merited deposition. It was rather that he feared for Lord Berkeley's future. He, Trevisa, had seen a very different facet of the Duke since the latter had left Berkeley on 28th July. He was still, at times, the suave and charming personality of yesteryear, but now the hard and ruthless side of his character was much in evidence. Maybe events had wrought this change. Those who had defected from King Richard could as easily defect from 'King' Henry — if so be the latter achieved the throne. Lord Berkeley might well find himself (as friends of King Richard, such as the Earl of Wiltshire, had found themselves) led to the executioner's block though innocent of real crime, save that of opposing a possible unsurper. Trevisa had pointed this out to his Lordship at Hereford, but his argument had been swept on one side. The chaplain consoled himself with the thought that the traditional luck of the Berkeleys — or was it a shrewdness greater than was generally appreciated? — would probably bring his patron out on the winning side, as had happened to Berkeleys in past generations.

On 8th August the Duke's forces left Shrewsbury. They camped for the night outside Whitchurch and by four o'clock on the afternoon of the 9th had entered Chester. Here came final confirmation that the support for Richard was negligible and that Duke Henry's tide of fortune was running at flood. This could be seen in the increased number of defectors from the ranks of the higher nobility who were arriving almost daily. These included the Dukes of Aumerle and Surrey and the Lords Lovell, Stanley and Worcester. The last, Thomas Percy and brother to the Earl of Northumberland, had been the King's chamberlain and had publicly broken his staff of office, signifying his defection.

At Chester the Duke, obviously to impress the waverers, made a 'Jollie muster of his armie in the sight of the citie'. ² Holt Castle soon surrendered to the Duke and thus, so said Holinshed, jewels to the value of 200,000 marks and 100,000 in coin fell into Henry's hands.

Trevisa enjoyed the leisure time at Chester and fully recovered from the fatigue of the many days in the saddle. He, however, was nauseated by the spectacle of numerous clergy, led by members of the hierarchy, shuffling (it could not be termed marching) in procession to make what was tantamount to an act of homage to the Duke. Adam of Usk approved of this obvious ceremonial submission, but then Adam was Henry's man.

On August 18th news arrived that the King had been ambushed by the Earl of Northumberland with his 400 lances and 1000 archers,. and escorted to Flint Castle. The Duke at once rode to Flint taking with him, amongst others, Archbishop Arundel and Lord Berkeley. Trevisa, to his amazement, was bidden to accompany his patron. The Canon was convinced that the King now fully realized that he was completely in the Duke's power and that the best he could hope for was life. The Archbishop assured Richard on this score, stating that the Duke and his followers would in no circumstance allow the King's person to suffer harm or loss.

Thus, said Holinshed, the Archbishop 'prophesised not as a prelate but as a Pilate '. ³ . Richard, nevertheless, offered to resign his throne — a final gesture that was witnessed by Lord Berkeley. ⁴

Later the King, under close escort, left Flint. The party, headed by Duke Henry, rode via Chester and Nantwich to Newcastle where the Earl of Warwick, having been released from prison on the Isle of Man, joined the cavalcade. The freedom and health of his daughter's father-in-law gave Lord Berkeley great pleasure, while the fact that the Earl enjoyed the Duke's favour constituted an added assurance of Elizabeth's future prosperity. The journey continued via Stafford, Lichfield and St. Albans to London, where the King was 'safely' lodged in the Tower.

Trevisa left Flint on 21st August for Berkeley bearing with him instructions to Sir John Berkeley that the precautions ordered by the Duke could be relaxed, and the forces stood down and allowed to return to their normal occupations.

Harvest was in progress when the Canon arrived, a harvest which promised a goodly yield if the fine weather continued for a week or two.

The vicar was happy once more, happier indeed than he had been since the Duke of York had ridden over the Berkeley Castle drawbridge nearly six weeks earlier — and what momentous weeks they had been, bringing civil war, fratricide and, it seemed likely, an end to the Plantagenet dynasty. He had thought much about his country's future during his long but leisurely ride back to Berkeley. At the same time he had attempted to analyse his feelings towards the main contestants in the struggle for the crown, and also his reaction to the personality of Archbishop Arundel.

Trevisa had been surprised at his own vacillation of feelings towards King Richard and Duke Henry. During the meeting between the latter and the Duke of York in Berkeley Church he had clearly stated that Richard should be deposed and the Duke of Lancaster raised to the throne. The savage and brutal handling of events in Bristol had compelled him to see the Duke in a new and cruel light. Richard, he now felt, should retain his throne and dignity, but that power, ruling power, should be vested in a council of state, difficult and disadvantageous though such a body might be in some respects. He had become increasingly sorry for the King and saw in him a man, who, though he had largely brought on the ugly situation, was to be pitied in that every man's hand was against him, and that many were bent on degrading before destroying him. The Archbishop, in Trevisa's eyes, had shrunk in stature. The prelate seems a scheming politician more than a man of God, and so basically unfit to lead the Church in England. Yes, it was good to be back at Berkeley in the quiet of the Severn Vale.

The September days were warm and still — too close some said. The vicar rode and walked throughout his cure and it appeared to him that his chest had not been affected by the arduous campaign, indeed that he was fitter than he had been for some time.

The tiny community at Bradston College had taken on a new vigour, no doubt due to the recent appointment of Father Ambrose as its head. The brethren worked freely in the vicinity, helping the elderly parish priest at Slimbridge and visiting the sick at Halmore, Hinton and the Ness — a practice that Father Bernard had latterly not encouraged.

The Canon's chief ecclesiastical worry was St. Mary's, the parish church. The roof had been repaired and repaired and half the nave had been re-leaded. This patching policy might suffice for a few years, but with much of the timberwork underneath in poor condition the time must come — and within thirty to fifty years at latest — when a complete re-roofing would become necessary. That could well be a moment of danger. Of late the point of union between the two halves of the nave was showing strain. The tying property of the roof timbers, the master mason had said, was an important factor and held everything in position. The extending of the dry moat to the north and northwest of the castle more than two hundred years ago had been fatal as far as the church was concerned. The taking down of the chancel and eastward part of the nave and re-erecting them at an angle to the westward half had been decided upon, so the records stated, with some trepidation. It had been successfully accomplished in spite of the extensive foundations of earlier buildings interfering with the erection of the north wall of the chancel and compelling the east end to be raised two feet and the whole upward slope of the eastward end to be increased considerably. The greater height of the new pillar bases had been but one of the alterations necessitated.

The organ loft, approached by the rood stairway on the north side, was also in need of extensive repairs, but these, too, could be postponed for a while. Trevisa consoled himself with the thought that probably the problem of the re-roofing and of the organ loft would not become desparate during his incumbency, which, clearly, was drawing to its close.

The new glass for the wheel or rose window at the westend of the nave had been completed. This, the most recent memorial to the late Lady Berkeley, was, he considered, not of the quality that had been expected. The colours were too garish, while the designs themselves, the Resurrection scenes (1) the three Marys at the tomb (2) Jesus appearing to Mary of Magdala (3) Jesus appearing to St. Peter, as recored in 1 Corinthians, Ch. 15, V.5, all lacked 'life'. Lord Berkeley would be disappointed.

On 20th September a messenger from his Lordship arrived. Parliament was in session and events were moving inexorably to the climax of deposition. His patron suggested, in view of the Canon's part in the meeting of July 27th, that the latter might wish to witness the final implementation of the policy first formulated in St.

Mary's Church. Arrangements had been made for the vicar to stay at the Abbey of Westminster — most convenient for the present parliamentary sittings.

It was with mixed feelings that Trevisa set out on Thursday the 22nd September and moved in easy stages via Oxford — where he stayed the night of the 24th at Queen's — to the city of Westminster where he arrived on the 27th. Two days later, as a guest of Lord Berkeley, the Canon sat through the proceedings which were concerned entirely with the King's condemnation and deposition. The final draft of the deposition read as follows:—

'Witnesseth, that where by the authoritie of the lords spirituall and temporall of this present parlement, and commons of the same, the right honorable and discreet persons heere under named, were by the said authoritie assigned to go to the Tower of London, there to heare and testifie such questions and answers as then and there should be by the said honourable and discreet persons heard. Know all men, to whome these present letters shall come, that we, Sir Richard Scroope archbishop of Yorke, Iohn bishop of Hereford, Henrie earle of Northumberland, Rafe earle of Westmerland, Thomas lord Berkelie, William abbat of Westminster, Iohn prior of Canturburie, William Thirning and High Burnell knights, Iohn Markham justice, Thomas Stow and Iohn Burbadge doctors of the ciuill law, Thomas Erpingham and Thomas Grey knights, Thomas Ferebie and Denis Lopeham notaries publike, the daie and yeere aboue said, betweene the houres of eight and nine of the clocke before noone, were present in the cheefe chamber of the kings lodging, within the said place of the Tower, where was rehearsed unto the king by the mouth of the foresaid earle of Northumberland, that before time at Conwaie in Northwales, the king being there at his pleasure and libertie, promised unto the archbishop of Canturburie then Thomas Arundell, and unto the said earle of Northumberland, that he for insufficiencie which he knew himselfe to be guilty of, to occupie so great a charge, as to gouerne the realme of England, he would gladlie leaue of and renounce his right and title, as well of that as of his title to the crowne of France, and his maiestie roiall, vnto Henrie duke of Hereford, and that to doo in such conuenient wise as by the learned men of this land it should most sufficientlie be duised & ordeined. To the which rehearsall, the king in our said presences answered benignlie and said, that such promise he made, and so to do the same he was at that houre in full purpose to performe and fulfill'.[5]

Later the sentence of deposition was borne to King Richard at the Tower:— 'In the name of God Amen. We Iohn Bishop of S Asaph, Iohn abbat of Glastenburie, Thomas earle of Gloucester, Thomas lord Berkeleie, William Thirning justice, Thomas Erpingham & Thomas Graie knights, chosen and deputed speciall commissaries by the three states of this present parlement, representing the whole bodie of the realme, for all such matters by the said estates to vs committed: we vnerstanding and considering the manifold crimes, hurts, and harmes doone by Richard king of England, and misgouernance of the same by a long time, to the great decaie of the said land, and vtter ruine of the same shortlie to haue beene ... And for the same causes we depriue him of all kinglie dignitie and worship, and of any kinglie worship in himselfe. And we depose him by our sentence definitiue, forbidding expresselie to all archbishops, and bishops, and all other priests, dukes, marquesses, erles, barons and knights, and all other men of the foresaid knigdome and lordships, subjects, and lieges whatsoeuer may be, that none of them from this daie forward, to the foresaid Richard as king and lord of the foresaid realmes and lordships, be neither obedient nor attendant.'⁶

That same evening Trevisa met Adam of Usk, who had a gloomy tale to tell. He had been, so he said, in the Tower, and had, by chance overheard the King in conversation. The royal mood was melancholy and ruministic, uttering words of woe and deep despair, calling to mind that reported outburst in Wales before Aumerle, Salisbury and Scroope, when his army and final hopes were fading fast:—

'For God's sake, let us sit upon the ground
And tell sad stories of the death of Kings;
How some have been deposed; some slain in war;
Some haunted by the ghosts they have deposed;
Some poisoned by their wives; some sleeping killed;
All murdered.'⁷

All hope had, clearly, been abandoned by the unhappy King, and the aged cleric's heart was sad. Was Richard, too, amongst the prophets? His kingly ancestor, Edward, suffered in the Berkeley's care. Would it now be Richard's fate also to perish in the dark?

The following day Trevisa, still fearful for Richard, took leave of his patron and returned via Oxford to Berkeley.

Chapter 14
Eventide

Eventide

The sudden death in mid-September, 1399, of Robert Poyntz, son of the late Richard Poyntz who had nobly supported Trevisa in the controversy with the late Dean of Westbury, greatly saddened the cleric. This second fatality within a year left the Poyntz family without an heir-male. Their estate consequently reverted to Lord Berkeley, who bestowed them, with undue haste Trevisa considered, upon Phillip Waterton and his wife, Cicely, for services rendered [1] — a poor choice indeed. Waterton had, it is true, accompanied his master on the campaign to North Wales and played his cards with great care. Cicely, too, had ably supported her husband's cause — some evil-minded gossips hinted that the services she performed were too personal, failing even to qualify as works of supererogation. Trevisa, knowing his master, discounted this, but felt that others, such as John and Elizabeth Winter or Robert and Alice Herblinge, deserved more, but had received less. [2]

Trevisa was worried, for a time, by the lack of friendliness now being shown by the Prior of Longbridge Hospital in Canonbury. Jealousy, perhaps, was partly responsible, as maybe were the Prior's leanings towards Richard Plantagenet. Lord Berkeley's insistence upon manorial dues of doubtful legality was, however, the most important contributory factor. How different was the relationship with the Infirmarians of the Hospitallers in the town, but then, that was a military order [3] and, presumably, more disciplined — and far-sighted too — than that outside the castle's gate. Trevisa, at times, felt that his worry over the Longbridge Priory might, perhaps, be generated by a mental condition within himself, brought on by his own fatigue, rather than a factual reality.

Trevisa was, indeed, tired, hence perhaps the contemplative mood. He reviewed the last twenty-five years, looking mainly, it is true, at the progress which the English language had made, especially in the written word, both in literature and legal usage, during that period. He felt, with the translations of the *Polychronicon,* the *De Proprietatibus Rerum,* the *De Regimine Principum* and other lesser works finished, with *Piers the Plowman* revised and with his not inconsiderable part in Wyclif's biblical project while at Oxford in the 1370's completed, that a great deal had been accomplished personally — more, indeed, than he, even in his wildest and most ambitious early days, had contemplated. Was the *De Proprietatibus Rerum* to be his final contribution towards the ultimate victory of the English tongue?

The Canon was nearing sixty and, at times, none too well. Little did he realize that the events of the last year and more had imposed great strains, mental and physical, upon him, and had taken a heavy toll. His Lordship's vacillation in the field of reality towards the Houses of York and Lancaster had not helped matters, indeed they had placed a tremendous burden upon his chaplain. Trevisa, since the Bull of Pope Urban VI [4] had virtually appointed him His Lordship's confessor, had striven hard (a) to guide him spiritually and (b) to prevent him, in his folly and ambition, from committing acts which would have led to disaster and death. Trevisa, occasionally, had had to smother his own conscience to protect his master. Walking on a knife-edge, as he had done since that fateful day in July, when Henry, Duke of Lancaster, the king that now is, and Edmund of York had faced each other in the chancel of Berkeley Church, had fatigued his aging body, and drained his very considerable physical reserves much more than he cared to admit.

He would try to rest awhile, confining his activities once more to the affairs of the parish and castle, if, that is, his Lordship's ambitions allowed. Perhaps next year, with vigour returned, he could embark upon another major work of translation? Perhaps William Middleworth, if not too involved in duties of state,[5] would collaborate? He would invite him to Berkeley. His Lordship had several times recently expressed a wish to meet Middleworth again, especially now that, in addition to him being vicar of Wrington, he was receiving royal recognition and moving in high circles.

Trevisa enjoyed the next two months, with the fine and comparatively warm weather persisting until mid-December when, quite suddenly, winter really set in. Much of his time had been spent in walking and riding round his extensive cure. Everywhere he went people greeted him with affection and shy pride. This reception puzzled the cleric, and never did he know the reason for the warmth of this feeling. He did not realize that to him had been attributed the saving of the town and parish from fire and sword, when the violent Duke of Lancaster and his host had entered Berkeley. Soldiers and servants, disregarded by their betters, had later reported that it had been the man of God and letters who had calmed tempers and guided deliberations, and so kept two thousand swords and spears from spilling Berkeley blood during those fateful hours.

Christmas brought many problems. The Chantry priests of St. Andrew and St. Maurice in Berkeley Church were ill and unable to help in the numerous masses of the festival — even the soul masses which constituted their own cures and obligations. The deep snow, very early this year, made it difficult to visit the outlying tithings and hamlets, and more than one poor soul crossed the great divide without the cleansing and comfort of the Viaticum. To Trevisa the one consoling thought was that the brethren of Bradston College were parochially-minded and, unofficially, looked upon the scattered houses in their area as 'the parish'. Finally, the most cruel of fates, the two upper chambers of the dumpy tower over the north porch of St. Mary's collapsed into the westend of the north aisle during the gale — the worst within living memory — which accompanied the heavy snowstorm. Another casualty of the same storm was the chancel roof of the chapel of 'Our Saviour and His Saints'.[6] Trevisa thanked God that this at least was not officially his problem and responsibility. He doubted whether the structure would ever be rebuilt. The community was now so few in numbers that they could easily be accommodated in one of the chapels in St. Mary's. This would, indeed, be the most sensible thing to do.

On the feast of the Circumcision came news that certain of the nobility, mainly from the eastern counties, had risen, seeking to restore ex-King Richard to the throne. A few days later it was reported that they were marching westward from London, and that a force, loyal to King Henry, was in pursuit. Was this to be a repeat of last July? The Canon, frankly, was worried. The strain of those few hours six months ago could not, he felt, be calmly faced a second time, especially so soon after that momentous meeting. Lord Berkeley, too, said that another combined visit from the protagonists of the Houses of York and Lancaster was unthinkable. He immediately mobilized his tenantry and prepared the castle for a siege. My Lord was indeed worried. He knew that Richard still had a considerable body of sympathizers, and strange things could happen in party warfare. He, Berkeley, having received considerable royal favours from Henry, could not really change sides again. It consoled him, however, that, as far as he knew, Richard was still safely in Pontefract and that Henry, cruel, cunning Henry, appeared firmly seated upon the throne. No! with Percies and Nevilles backing Henry, he, Berkeley, could not see any future in Richard's cause — his star (or rayed sun to be heraldically pedantic) had really fallen, and no Berkeley had yet backed a loser.

On the following day they heard that Richard's supporters had reached Cirencester on the 7th, and had suffered a setback at the hands of John Cosyns, the local bailiff. It was with obvious relief that Lord Berkeley heard that the westward march of the rebels had been halted. He was horrified, however, to learn a little later that, despite the terms of surrender, the leaders, the Earls of Kent and Salisbury, had been executed in the market square. [7]

Trevisa, too, while shocked at the treachery of King Henry's local lieutenants, was not sorry that the strain of July would not again have to be faced.

January was drawing to a close before the snow had finally melted, and by that time much of the rubble of the fallen tower and the aisle roof of St. Mary's and of the chancel of the smaller church had been cleared away. William, the master mason currently employed at St. Augustine's Abbey, came up from Bristol on Wednesday the 28th to survey the damage. His comment at the end of the inspection shook the vicar. 'Well, Father', he said, 'it is an ill wind that brings no good. I never liked that tower, for it was unworthy of your church. Keep the bottom stage as your porch, and, maybe, build a room above it as a school room. And if you could persuade the community to use one of the chapels in the parish church permanently — not temporarily as you have suggested — the nave which is none too safe now as well as the chancel of the community church could be demolished. The tower, still sound in every way, could have the archway into the nave filled in, and used as a bell-tower for both communities. You may find opposition to this scheme at first, but do not be deterred. It will be accepted as beneficial in the end. In the meanwhile we can rebuild the west end of your north aisle, and shore up the lowest stage of the fallen tower for safety's sake.' Lord Berkeley and John Daubeny, the Abbot of St. Augustine's, were staggered when they received William's report, more shaken, indeed, than had been Trevisa.

Lord James Berkeley of Raglan came over to Berkeley in February bringing with him a fork-tailed kite, fully trained it was said, to pit him with the geese that wintered from November to March in the Severn estuary between Hill and Elmore. The parish priest, interested as he was in the chase in its varied forms, was anxious to witness the experiment. Lord Thomas Berkeley agreed that the trial should be viewed, at a distance, by any of the local tenantry and guests. Trevisa saw no reason why the kite, having been trained — so it was alleged — on the Neath and Tregarron marshes, should not be successful at Berkeley. There was, however, so it seemed to him, one real danger. It was conceivable that the kite would select and stoop at a goose over the river and, plummeting down with its victim into the tide, become waterlogged and drown. Robert Gwynnell, Lord Berkeley's falconer, was sceptical about the whole affair and, privately, opined that this particular sporting contest should be called off. It was unfair, he hinted, leaving out the water hazard, to ask the kite to tackle a bird of the size of a goose. 'Him might a kill an odd goos or two on they Welsh marshes, but they aint a got thurr our numbers. If un strikes in a fair gagelen [8] they wing beats may 'arm or perchance kill un, cos a goos wing be powerful strong.' He feared, too, that with high stakes involved, as clearly, there would be, pride and tempers — unless kept well in hand, and that was not always easy — might cause personal rifts and even bloodshed.

The first phase of the falconry trial was very successful. The kite made its kill, a single bird flying past, cleanly and overland. Later a gagelen was located on the Dumbles. The pre-arranged dispositions were made and put into operation. A beater crept close to the geese and waited. The falconer slipped his charge who, seeing the feeding birds, circled overhead, but seemed a little uncertain. Suddenly, apparently reassured by the fact that the geese had ceased to talk and were clearly nervous, the kite stooped. At that moment, at that very second, the beater stood up and waved his flag. With a thunderous roar of wing beats and cries of alarm the birds lifted. The kite checked and swung away from the skein, much to the surprise — and annoyance — of Lord James and his falconer. Soon afterwards a similar opportunity occurred near Frampton'Pill. This time a beater was not employed. The kite was to be allowed to plan his own campaign. Once more he circled overhead, but for far longer. The grazing geese again fell silent and drew together. This time the strike was made, but only just. At the moment of impact the whole gagelen jumped. The next that the party saw of the kite he was circling very high overhead, while his intended victim was slowly rejoining the skein, shaken no doubt, but apparently little harmed. It was a full hour before the kite could be lured to hand, and in consequence further flights were abandoned. Lord James and his falconer were angry, mortified, and, above all, perplexed by the behaviour of their trainee.

During the time of waiting Gwynnell was smug:— 'Did I not tell ee', he said, 'it'ud be too much on it? Thic bird be a ruined afor many a day. Un'l take a long time to forget they goosen a liften'

Both wagering parties, those backing the kite, and those waging against him, believed they had scored a partial victory — had he not made a kill, yet had he not refused subsequent opportunity? Trevisa, called in as arbiter, declared that the contest was a draw, and any wagers null and void. This verdict was accepted by all.

During the evening, back at the castle, the contest was discussed at length, and it was clear to all that Robert's observations, both before and after, were shrewd, and probably very near the truth. The kite had been trained on the Neath and Tregarron marshes where the geese were far fewer than on the Berkeley estate. Secondly the bird had almost always been flown at passing geese or at singletons or very small parties, which normally had been put up ahead and before slipping. The thunderous roar of hundreds of wings, and the volume of the raucous alarm calls of the geese had clearly unnerved the kite.

During the week preceding Lent [9] Lord Berkeley sent for his chaplain on the pretext of a discussion on lenten penance and practice. It became clear to Trevisa within a few minutes that there was more behind the summons than seasonal observances. The priest, finally, took the bull by the horns and said, 'My Lord, there is something more on your mind than the Church's teaching on devotion and discipline. Can I, as your chaplain, vicar and confessor, help? Speak plainly, my Lord.'

Lord Berkeley, with slight initial reluctance, replied, 'Father, I confess that I have an ulterior motive for our meeting. I have read and re-read your translation of the Gospels of Nicodemus and St. John, as well as the book of the Revelation. I have seen, too, as you know, certain of the works that you, Hereford and Middleworth undertook at Oxford under the guidance of my old tutor, Wyclif, for such he almost was for a time. May God rest his soul. Would you be prepared to translate further books of the New Testament into English for me, Canon? I will willingly install a temporary chaplain and locum here at the castle, if you feel it desirable, perhaps necessary, to undertake this work at Queen's. I would also approach my Lord Bishop and my Lord Abbot to give you leave of absence for a period. If, on the other hand, you are prepared to work at the task here in Berkeley no doubt the Chapters of St. Peter's Abbey in Gloucester and of Llanthony Secunda could be persuaded to allow you to use their libraries, and, with a little episcopal pressure, would probably permit you to borrow certain books. You will recall that the Llanthony Community, with its fine library, were most generous when you laboured on the Education of Princes . [10] I was told years ago by the great Doctor, that Llanthony has at least five Latin copies of the Bible , [11] as well as a considerable number of separate books of the New Testament — the Old Testament does not appeal to me to the same degree. Even the new community of the Black Friars has several Bibles and a fine copy of the Acts of the Apostles. This, following the Gospel of Luke, I would like placed high on your programme for the translation. St. Luke, even in the Latin tongue, is so sympathetic that I beg you to begin your labours with that book. If you wish to invite any of your colleagues in the earlier projects, such as Hereford or Middleworth, to assist or advise, please do so, and I will make it worth their while. Parchment and other material must be ordered.'

This sudden turn of events surprised and pleased the Canon, who was feeling increasingly the strain of parochial work in the widely scattered area of his responsibility. He was unwell, had been indeed for some time, but did his best to hide it. To his worries and prayers this could be the answer, God's answer. It would at least give opportunity for some measure of recuperation — a necessary requisite to any further major work. It was without hesitation, but without unseemly haste, that Trevisa, in consequence, agreed in principle to His Lordship's request, and promised to produce suggested plans soon after Easter.

Chapter 15
A Glorious Sunset

(a) *New Possibilities*

Trevisa spent considerable thought on Lord Berkeley's request. The prospect of possible further translations excited him — had he not played with the idea last October? Then the time factor had loomed large, too large for a serious undertaking of this nature. The whole situation had now changed. It was his Lordship who was now making the request. Furthermore he had promised considerable support with higher authorities for leave of absence to study. The scholar, as he pondered over the proposition, gradually became conscious of a fundamental change in his own attitude towards Oxford. He found, to his surprise, that the university no longer possessed the attraction for him that once it held. Trevisa, upon analysis, decided that this was understandable. He was now nearing sixty, and no longer had the vigour of body that once had been his; furthermore none of his former colleagues and friends would be in residence. He would be lonely, and would still have to conform to Provost Carlisle's whims and regulations without, now, friends to support him — not too pleasant a prospect. No! Oxford was, in this year of Grace 1400, an unattractive proposition, and would not be accepted unless the unavailability of necessary library facilities made it essential.

A three-day visit to Gloucester was arranged and a careful inspection of the book situation undertaken. This proved heartening. Material there was in plenty, and the librarians and chapters of St. Peter's Abbey and Llanthony Priory were very co-operative.

The librarian of the latter community was as generous as had been his predecessor in the earlier days, indeed even more so. He promised that where there were three (or even only two in certain circumstances) copies of required books in the library they could be borrowed. He made it clear, however, that the loan was dependent upon an assurance from Lord Berkeley that the project had his blessing — and 'perhaps His Lordship might care to make a donation to the Priory funds?'

The following week Trevisa, having ascertained that Middleworth was now at home at Wrington, rode down to stay for two days with his old Oxford colleague.

Middleworth made it clear, at the start, that with his parochial and extra-parochial duties he would not be able to co-operate fully in the scheme of translation. He said, however, that he would come up to Berkeley in the near future for further discussions. He would endeavour also to make other visits as time allowed, and would be very happy to try and help in any way that Trevisa wished.

The Wrington discussions were wide-ranging, and produced some definite ideas, which could be submitted for the approval of Lord Berkeley.

First. A Locum. A full time chaplain (a young one if possible) would have to be obtained to enable the canon to concentrate on his Lordship's project. The latter would, of course, have to negotiate, as he had already promised, with the necessary authorities.

Secondly. St. Luke's Gospel. This could be, as had been requested by Lord

Berkeley, first on the translation programme. The Acts would have to wait, however, until all four canonical Gospels had been completed. They believed that his Lordship would see the logic of this order.

Thirdly. They pointed out that the whole scheme would depend upon the availability of books on loan, so that much of the work might be undertaken at Berkeley. His Lordship's influence could well be vital in also persuading St. Augustine's Abbey, in Bristol, to allow any necessary material to be borrowed for lengthy periods.

Middleworth promised that he would make time to stay at Berkeley for a few days when it was known that his Lordship had accepted points 1 and 3 of their recommendations, and had implemented his previous promise to negotiate with the various authorities.

Lord Berkeley at once approved the suggestions. All these arrangements, however, took time, and it was early May before Trevisa and Middleworth were ready for their final discussions. By this date the locum, one Henry Wilce, had been appointed and had taken up temporary residence at the chantry cottage of St. Andrew. He had been granted permission by the Lord Bishop of Worcester to relieve Trevisa of most of his duties, in the parish and at the castle. Abbot Daubeny of St. Augustine's, had, subject to certain safeguards, also given his blessing to the appointment. Both Trevisa and Middleworth were pleased with the locum, considering him a man of scholarship, and one who might well be of some help in the task of translation.

Lord Berkeley suggested that since Trevisa would be working mainly at Berkeley he might consider using the now redundant St. John's Chapel in the Keep as his study and library. This proposal had the added advantage that the precious books on loan would at all times be, literally, under close guard.

On May 10th Trevisa and Middleworth rode to Llanthony to examine the possible material, which Trevisa had seen previously, in that Library. They planned also to ride on to St. Peter's Abbey in Gloucester, where other books might be available. St. Luke's Gospel would be their first priority. They would, however, consider the Marcan material in both libraries. St. Mark's Gospel would have been their first choice for the translation programme had it not been for Lord Berkeley's request. This latter Gospel was generally recognised to be that of Holy Peter, the Apostolic leader, who in prison at Rome dictated it to John Mark, his amanuensis, hence the place of importance which that Gospel held in the Church.

The librarian at Llanthony, true to his word, agreed to the loan of a copy of St. Luke and gave Trevisa his choice. Furthermore, he offered a copy of St. Mark's Gospel. The authorities at St. Peter's were equally co-operative. It was, consequently, a well satisfied pair of clerics who returned to Berkeley on the evening of the 12th.

Trevisa and Middleworth the next morning talked carefully over the policies to be followed in the new translations, and especially in the controversial matter of a literal rendering of the Latin text, or a freer, and slightly colloquial method, letting the sense of the sentence be the deciding factor. Both felt that the second would be by far the better scheme, and believed that it would also win the approval of the vast majority of people. The purists within the Church, and at the universities too, would, no doubt, oppose with tooth and claw what they would term this new-fangled and sacrilegious treatment of the Scriptures. Lord Berkeley agreed with their suggestion, and so the less stilted style, to the relief of Trevisa, became the working mode.

Wilce quickly settled down to life in Berkeley. His youthful vigour and obvious enthusiasm both endeared him to the local people and took much of the burden of parochial administration and pastoral care off the shoulders of the vicar. The latter thus was enabled to devote much of his time to the task imposed upon him by Lord Berkeley. Before the end of June the translation of St. Luke, with substantial glossary notes, had been completed. Middleworth, coming up early in the month, had read the first seventeen chapters of Trevisa's work and fully approved of the freer and more colloquial style, which was in marked contrast with the translation made earlier at Oxford by himself, and, indeed, with the whole of their own translations completed under the direction and guidance of Dr. Wyclif at Queen's some twenty years ago. The great Doctor had always been idiomatic in his own personal translations of short passages of scripture for sermons and other works, but had not allowed Hereford or any of them a very loose rein in their biblical undertakings. Purvey, more recently, had come down firmly on the side of lucidity, with sense and not slavish literality as his guiding principle.

Middleworth opined that Trevisa's new translation, if continued in a like style, would be as acceptable to most people as would the revised edition of the Bible recently completed by John Purvey. This work was generally acknowledged, so said Middleworth, by scholars who had seen various portions of it, as infinitely superior to the earlier translation in smoothness, accuracy and in intelligibility.

Trevisa wished to submit the work, when two or three Gospels had been finished, to Hereford, their former colleague, now Chancellor of Hereford Cathedral, for his comments. Middleworth counselled that if another opinion was necessary, Purvey was the better choice. A decision on this matter was deferred sine die.

Lord Berkeley was enthusiastic when he read the first draft of St. Luke, and suggested that a professional scribe should be obtained to make a fair copy of the translation, enriching it with illuminated initials from time to time, and, may be, a fair picture or two. His Lordship suggested St. Augustine's or St. Peter's Abbeys might, for a consideration, provide such a man, adding that the copying must be done at the castle so that the Canon might check each page before the more delicate touches were undertaken. Thus precious time would be saved, enabling the main work of translation to progress with as little delay as possible. This insistence upon speed, and the time factor emphasis, disconcerted Trevisa. Was his Lordship possessed suddenly of foresight? Was he, Trevisa, to be found struggling to complete the New Testament as Bede had fought for breath enough to finish the Gospel of St. John? No! he would not be hurried. The task must be carried through with great, very great care and not rushed as had been the latter part of their work at Oxford. In any case, observed Trevisa, the translations must be seen and approved either by Hereford or Purvey, concluding 'and I would like to discuss the matter of method and style being followed with my critic or colleague — and in person and not by letter.' Lord Berkeley agreed.

By the end of September the first draft of the translation of St. Luke's Gospel and that of St. Mark had been completed. They had been fully checked by Middleworth, and most of the suggested amendments had been incorporated. The next logical step was to obtain, if possible, the criticism of Hereford and, perhaps even Purvey, preferably with a personal discussion on some of the problems.

In the meanwhile it seemed sensible to begin on St. Matthew's Gospel, provided that a suitable copy or copies could be borrowed. There were several such at St. Peter's and Llanthony in Gloucester and in St. Augustine's in Bristol, but for some reason these were less numerous than the other Gospels. Furthermore, the librarians appeared more reluctant to lend these books now that it was generally known that the purpose was the making of a translation. The hierarchy of the monastic bodies were showing increased opposition to the possession of English copies of the Scriptures — even by those, such as Lord Berkeley, licenced to own and read these works. No doubt, however, with the considerable influence which his Lordship could bring to bear upon St. Augustine's; and with the added incentive of a suggested benefaction towards the extensive building and rebuilding programmes which were draining their resources, that community, at least, would co-operate. They might even loan, if the inducement was sufficiently attractive, the recently acquired modern copy with amplitude of glosses. Its legibility too, was much in advance of the other copies at Bristol. St. Augustine's might also be persuaded to lend another book, presented to them but a short while ago. This, a copy of St. John's Gospel, newly translated from a Greek manuscript, differed somewhat in phraseology from the books which he, Trevisa, had used in the past.

Lord Berkeley, when consulted, readily agreed to approach Abbot Daubeney, of St. Augustine's, on the desired loans, and also promised to send, with suitable escort, the English translations of St. Luke and St. Mark either to Purvey in London or Hereford at Hereford. To Trevisa was left the task of making the detailed arrangements with whichever was prepared to undertake the desired scrutiny.

As the winter approached the Canon found himself more involved in parochial affairs than he had been during the summer. Henry Wilce, the locum, fell sick in November — he had not been fully well for several weeks previously — and after a partial recovery over Christmas he went into a steep decline and died on January 29th 1400/1. The funeral took place on the 31st, and at once the school, previously held in the room above the church porch, demanded the Vicar's presence.

Trevisa was impressed with the progress made by the pupils during the period in which they had been under the care of Wilce. They had had the handicap of moving to and settling into fresh accommodation following the collapse of the northside tower. This they had taken in their stride, and both pupils and staff agreed that the chantry chapel of St. Andrew was preferable to the bleakness of the church of Our Saviour and His Saints nave in the northern half of the churchyard.

Once again January and February proved the most trying of all months from the point of view of health. Physically resistance is at its lowest, and in spite of mildish weather sickness built up until by mid-February it had reached epidemic proportions. Then, suddenly, a crew member of Lord Berkeley's ship, The Margaret, trading with Bordeaux and other French ports, developed one of man's most deadly eneimies, smallpox. This spread with great rapidity, and before the end of the month forty-one people were infected, many of whom died. Trevisa, remembering the example set by Bishop Grandisson during the great plague outbreaks, devoted much of his time to the comforting of the sick, dying and bereaved. Mercifully, the epidemic, though violent, was short-lived, and by mid-March was almost at an end.

During the early days of March the Canon and Lord Berkeley had also been concerned for the welfare, indeed the life, of John Purvey. They knew him to be a stubborn man who maintained that martyrdom was fully justified, indeed often essential for the health and vigour of a particular cause. My Lord and his bedeman recalled their earlier discussions with Purvey on this subject, and prayed that he would not sacrifice himself upon the altar of misplaced — as they held — principle, but would recant, as had Nicholas Hereford, thus preserving his considerable academic ability for the benefit of the English race through the opening up of the Scriptures and literature generally in a tongue understood of all. What a waste of a good and Godly life had been witnessed when William Sawtrey (whom Trevisa had met, and of whom he had approved, while at Oxford) had recently been burnt at the stake. An excellent brain had been lost — and to what purpose?

Time and time again at Oxford, in discussions with Wyclif and his closer associates, Trevisa had advocated an outward acceptance of the word transubstantiation, while, if needs be, maintaining mentally that the change was a spiritual, an ethereal one. What was the point in paying too much attention to exactitude of phraseology when dealing with deep theological mysteries, which frankly, were far beyond man's intellectual comprehension — the finite vainly struggling to define the Infinite? The essence, the fact that really mattered, was the same, whatever man might say. Christ was uniquely present at the eucharist. Why bother one's head, let alone risk one's life, in the unprofitable exercise of attempting to describe the method adopted by Christ to effect that presence?

The rumour that Master Purvey had been arrested and thrust into the Archbishop's prison at Saltwood Castle, in Kent, caused great anxiety to the Canon. Had not Hereford and others told of the harsh treatment meted out to many victims in that ecclesiastical house of correction?

Trevisa, while sympathizing with the Lollards in their condemnation of the all-too-prevalent corruption and arrogance in high places, and the smugness and bigotry of many regular clergy, could not support them in certain of their fundamental dogmas. He felt, however, that Purvey with his more balanced and impartial outlook on life — so different from the vigorous and impetuous Nicholas — would conform to the required minimum, so that he could continue to further, even if only surreptitiously, the cause of general biblical knowledge.

A travelling pardoner brought the news on Passion Sunday that John Purvey had recanted at St. Paul's Cross during sermon time on March 6th. This came as a relief to chaplain and Lord, who had remained fearful that Purvey might continue his refusal to abjure lollardism. Confirmation of Purvey's change of heart was received two days later when Father Prior of St. Augustines came to inspect the proposed repairs to the chancel arch in St. Mary's, and to discuss plans with his masons. Neither his Lordship nor the Vicar made any expression of opinion concerning Purvey's abjuration, knowing that the Prior was strongly opposed to lollardy, and had disapproved of the latter's visits to Berkeley in the past. Yes, even in the early 1380s, and before Trevisa had become vicar, Father Prior had suggested that it was not wise to associate too closely with one who had worked openly with Wyclif, even after the latter had left Oxford and retired to Lutterworth. Lord Berkeley had resented this veiled threat, while Trevisa had been annoyed that his interest in Purvey's revision of the English translation of the Bible, made under Wyclif's supervision at Oxford, had been frowned upon, and that he, Trevisa, had been suspected of leanings towards the Lollards.

It had been encouraging to Trevisa, with so major a task of biblical translation imposed upon him, to feel that he had Middleworth so close at hand, and even Hereford within a short two days' journey. It had to be admitted, however, that the latter seemed no longer to possess the same zest for translation that once he had shown. This, may be, resulted from the newly bestowed honours with their demanding duties, although it is possible that the fear of once more being labelled a Lollard may well have played some part in this attitude.

The return of Purvey to Bristol, following his recantation and subsequent release from prison, had been an added joy; for here was yet another experienced translator, with whom he could discuss problems as they arose, and one, furthermore, who, as an ex-amanuensis of Wyclif and a one time visitor to Berkeley Castle, was a persona grata with Lord Berkeley. The news which reached Berkeley in June that Purvey would shortly be leaving the West of England and moving to Kent came as a bitter blow to Trevisa. [1]

(b) *Bright Portents for Lord Berkeley*

During the summer Lord Berkeley had received several messages from King Henry — for King he now was, whatever certain individuals or factions might feel or do, so tight was his hold and so powerful his arm. It seemed to Trevisa that his patron, now that there was but one central and effective authority, and consequently no conflict of allegiance, might well be entering in upon a fresh period of prosperity and perhaps, royal employ. [2] Well, if his Lordship should once more take part in martial exercises, be it by land or sea, he would have to engage a younger chaplain to serve his portable altar, for he, Trevisa, could not even contemplate becoming, once again, a peripatetic priest and camp follower.

(c) *The Setting Sun*

Autumn wore on into winter, and the cold and stormy winds swept up the Severn valley as November gave way to December. It was then that Trevisa began to feel the strain of the task. In spite of warm clothing and the fire in the great Hall — he had found that he could no longer work in the chill of St. John's Chapel in the Keep — his fingers failed to control the pen as once they had. His brain, too, seemed to become numbed, while bending over the book and parchments brought on violent coughing spasms, the like of which he had, hitherto, not experienced. The more he struggled to complete each chapter the more evident it became that death was beckoning him on. He realised then, for the first time, that the planned translation of the canon of the New Testament was, for him, a physical improbability. This fact faced, Trevisa redoubled his efforts, determined that the Gospels at least, and perhaps, if God gave him the strength, the Acts and the Revelation too, should be finished before the progressive weakness compelled the abandonment of his work.

Christmas came with a temporary return of fine and mild weather. The Canon celebrated the Midnight Mass at St. Mary's, and to his amazement the hugh church was full. The rush lights flickered and cast strange shadows in chancel and nave. The

Gloria in Excelsis Deo was chanted with, so it seemed to the ailing cleric, special significance. To him it spoke of the fulfilment not only of ancient prophecy, of God made flesh, but of a life of service to God and man drawing to a close, of an approaching meeting, face to face, of a man and his Maker.

The next morning brought reaction, the inevitable fatigue of that long and exacting service had taken its toll. It was the feast of the Circumcision before the Canon could leave his bed and stagger, and stagger indeed he did, to the chapel of St. Mary in the castle to celebrate low mass.

Later that day he bade his servant bring table, parchment, ink and St. John's Gospel to the Great Hall; and so began a new assult upon the translation.

Chapter fourteen was an exhilarating experience. The Master seemed to be speaking to him in particular, saying 'Let not your Heart be troubled, put your faith in me, for I go to prepare a place for you'. Was this, Trevisa wondered, his Celtic imagination running riot, an hallucination born of weakness, or was Christ speaking through the written word, telling him not to grieve, that another must complete his task? Happier still was the cleric when he translated verse sixteen:— 'And I will pray the Father, and he will give you another Comforter, that he may abide with you for ever'; followed by verse eighteen:— 'I will not leave you comfortless; I will come to you.' At this point the Canon leaned back and recited the Veni Creator Spiritus, and thanked God for guidance and sustaining strength throughout his sixty years and more. Then with confidence and a light heart he continued his work.

St. John's Gospel was completed that same week, such was Trevisa's frenzied energy. Time, he knew, was short, desperately short. No longer could he contemplate revisions by William or advice from Purvey in distant Kent. He was on his own now, with still much to do, even if the very limited objective of the Gospels, Acts and Revelation was to be achieved. The Canon wished to embark upon the Revelation, but with the time factor much in mind, and remembering that his Lordship already possessed a Norman-French translation of that book, he decided The Acts should receive priority.

Trevisa spent Monday, January 9th, at Bradston College, and discussed with the members of that tiny community, first the welfare of his people in the cluster of houses close to the chapel, and secondly the position at Halmore and Purton. The Canon feared, with some justification, that his new curate, John Tetbury, was failing in his pastoral care for these last two outlying hamlets. Brother Thomas assured him that the brethren would, for the time being, take over, officially, full pastoral responsibility for all three places if he, the vicar, so desired — they had, as Trevisa well knew, been visiting in those areas before the advent of the latest curate. The Canon was relieved as he rode slowly back to the castle late in the afternoon. That evening — physically worn out — he could not work.

The next day Trevisa began translating the Acts of the Apostles. By the eve of the Conversion of St. Paul, the first eight chapters had been completed. The Canon might well have begun chapter nine that night, but emotion welled up, suggesting a deferment; and what could be more appropriate than that the translation of the account of conversion should be undertaken on the anniversary of that most momentous event in Paul's whole life?

On the morrow when Trevisa was penning the words, 'Then had the churches rest throughout all Judaea and Galilee and Samaria', he paused and prayed that the bitter conflict now constantly troubling the Church, might cease, and brotherhood, true Christian brotherhood, might be established. Minutes later a servant noticed that the vicar had slumped forward over His work.

In bed during the following day the cleric realized that, in all probability, he had translated his last chapter of the Bible. During the evening Trevisa reminded his patron that John Purvey had made a translation of the whole New Testament, and had, no doubt, retained a copy of that work. A lay clerk, the canon suggested, should be dispatched to West Hythe, where Purvey was rector, with a request that he might be allowed to transcribe those portions of the New Testament which he, Trevisa, had not had time to translate. Lord Berkeley, after some hesitation, agreed.

(d) *Nunc Dimittis*

Canon Trevisa became increasingly weak, while the cough suddenly worsened and racked his whole body. When, in mid February, his sputum was flecked with froth and blood, those around him realized that the cleric's life was drawing rapidly to its close. March came in like a roaring lion and the patient barely had strength to sit up in bed. The pale horse was, indeed, approaching with speed.

On the fifth of the month Trevisa, when Lord Berkeley was sitting by his bedside, thrust out his hand and grasped his patron's sleeve and whispered, 'My Lord, the end draws near. I have a favour to ask. Might a messenger ride with haste to Wrington and bid Father William Middleworth come at once. He was always a fine horseman and still rides around his scattered parish, I'm told. I wish to make my confession and receive the Sacrament from him who is my oldest and dearest friend and colleague.'

Half an hour later Henry Tracy clattered across the courtyard and within a further two hours thrust a letter into the Abbot's hand at St. Augustine's. Henry's lathered horse was led away, and within the hour the Berkeley rider could see the tower of Wrington Church in the distance. 'Please God the priest will be at home', he muttered to himself, and perhaps to his Master also, as he galloped down the hillside track to the village. His prayer, if so intended, was answered.

Father William called to John, his servant, and bade him saddle the roan gelding and bring him to the door. He, himself, went to the church and collected the pyx from the tabernacle, and a quarter of an hour later the pair left Wrington. They walked their horses up the steep track to the downs and discussed their route. Henry, obviously, would have to call at St. Augustine's to change horses, but what of Father William? Should he press on, by-passing the Abbey? or should he, too, take the slightly longer route and beg a change of mounts from my Lord Abbot? With but three hours or less of daylight speed was essential, as indeed it was equally so for the mission's sake. They decided finally to stay together. This would ensure that Father William would not lose his way when leaving Westbury by the forest track, a shorter route and quicker than that which ran along the valley's edge, where streams in winter were often swollen and in flood, making the going heavy.

The exchange at St. Augustine's was quickly made, but gave the travellers time to take a bite and down a draught of ale. The sun had sunk below the hills of Dean before the horsemen, wet and weary, cantered into the castle yard. Willing hands helped them to dismount and Father William was led straight to the chaplain's room in the keep. The dying Canon momentarily flung off, or so it seemed, the weakness which had borne him down, and in a voice clear and distinct greeted his confessor. 'Welcome old friend! Fifty years and more ago at Glasney you championed me in my first real fight. Do you remember the altar candle with which you smote the foe? And now you come to aid me once again. This time I face man's final enemy, but with you at hand I am quite content.'

Silence fell upon the room, and the watchers withdrew on tip-toe from the bed and knelt upon the rushes near the door. Priest and penitent spoke in low whispers and the Viaticum was administered and received. Almost at once Trevisa fell asleep — a sleep from which there would be no earthly awakening, or so those present felt.

The minutes passed, and suddenly the watchers heard a whispered cry, 'Ann, My Darling,' and, softer still, 'My Lord and My God', and saw the scarlet stain upon the bed. Then in their imagination they heard trumpets sounding upon a distant shore.

Postcriptum

In the year of Trevisa's death, 1402, one of the Bristol Thorpes mentioned in this text, John, a burgess of that city, married Isabel, heiress of the Sanigers of Wanswell Court, and so established the Thorpe line which lived there for 270 years. They advanced their fortunes until by the early 17th century they were related to many of the leading Gloucestershire families, e.g. the Berkeleys, the Porters, the Throckmortons and the Tracys. The most distinguished member of the family, George Thorpe, is today accepted by many in America as one of the outstanding men in their early colonial history.

EXETER
Causes of Vacancies

	Induc.	Death	Exch.	Resign	Not Stated
1345 Oct 15 to Dec. 24	6	2	—	2	2
1346	30	7	13	5	5
1347	40	14	5	6	15
1348					
Jan-June	17	6	2	5	4
July	8	1	3	1	3 (1 NF)
Aug	3	2	—	—	1
Sept	7	4	—	1	2
Oct	2	—	—	1	1
Nov	10	4	1	2	3
Dec	6	3	—	1	2
1349					
Jan	32	4	—	1	27
Feb	35	1	1	—	33
March	61	9	2	2	48
April	54	2	—	3	49
May	48	2	—	2	44
June	46	3	1	—	42
July	37	1	—	—	36
Aug	16	—	—	—	16
Sept	23	1	—	—	22

Oct	15	1	—	2	12
Nov	17	—	—	1	16
Dec	14	—	—	—	14

1350

Jan	7	—	—	—	7
Feb	9	—	—	—	9
March	9	—	—	1	8
April	12	—	—	3	9
May	5	—	1	1	3
June	9	—	1	—	8
July	6	—	—	—	6
Aug	1	—	—	—	1
Sept	12	—	—	2	10

HEREFORD

Causes of Vacancies

	Induc.	Death	Exch.	Resign	Not Stated
1345					
Oct 15 to Dec 24	5	1	2	—	2
1346	6	—	1	2	3
1347	7	1	1	2	3
1348					
Jan-June	1	—	—	—	1
July	3	1	2	—	—
Aug	—	—	—	—	—
Sept	—	—	—	—	—
Oct	1	1	—	—	—
Nov	1	—	—	—	1
Dec	4	2	2	—	—
1349					
Jan	1	1	—	—	—
Feb	4	3	—	1	—
March	8	5	1	—	2
April	10	8	—	1	1
May	11	6	—	—	5
June	15	9	—	1	5
July	40	18	2	5	15
Aug	25	2	—	—	23
Sept	19	—	—	—	19
Oct	11	—	—	—	11

Nov	11	–	1	1	9
Dec	4	1	–	3	–
1350					
Jan	7	1	1	2	3
Feb	2	–	–	–	2
March	5	1	–	3	1
April	9	1	1	3	4
May	5	–	1	–	4
June	4	–	–	–	–
July	–	–	–	–	–
Aug	–	–	–	–	–
Sept	1	–	–	–	1

WORCESTER
Causes of Vacancies

	Induc.	Death	Exch.	Resign.	Not Stated
1345 Oct 15 to Dec 24					
1346					
1347					
1348					
Jan-June	12				
July	1				
Aug	1				
Sept					
Oct					
Nov					
Dec					
1349					
Jan	13				
Feb	12				
March	14				
April	14	13	—	—	1
May	39	30	2	4	3
June	45	36	1	3	5
July	67	52 (1 Preb)	5	10	0
Aug	1st-6th 13	8	—	4	1 (New Creation)

References

Chapter 1

1   Now known as Normansland.

2   Now moved to Blacklands and, much restored and altered, is used as a storage shed.

3   He and his elder brother, Otho, came from Castle Grandson (modern spelling) on the shores of Lake Neuchatel. Chaucer referred to the last de Grandisson owner of the Castle, Otho, the poet-warrier, at the end of his Compleynt of Venus — Skeat's Chaucer, Vol. 1, p.404.

4   John Smith, *Lives of the Berkeleys,* Mss in Berkeley Castle. Published in three volumes by the Bristol Gloucestershire Archaeological Society, 1883-5, Vol. 1, fol 258, comments that 'The Pope very angry herewithall, did foe revile the Archbishop as hee dyed for greefe and anger fooneafter'. Archbishop Walter Reynolds certainly died later that same year!

5   According to H-Randolph, Vol. III, p. vi. Smyth, I, fols 257 and 258, gives 28 June as date of death..

6   Appendix 1, for comparative figures in other West of England dioceses.

Chapter 2

1   Sir Peter was Canon at Glasney in 1331-4.

Chapter 3

1   In 1947, when in Pembrokeshire on holiday, a fledgling buzzard was induced to follow me around. Young rabbits had been the initial lure. In 1948 'Buster' — my name for him — was still in the area, and on the second evening again followed me home. In 1949 he was no longer there. Probably he had mated and moved to fresh territory.

2   I heard these nightingales' choruses, by day and night, in the Reims area during the late spring of 1940, and I recall many single birds singing during daytime in western Gloucestershire when I was living there between 1915 to 1967. For quotation see T.A. Coward, The Birds of the British Isles and their Eggs, Vol. I, 2nd Impression March 1920, p.218.

3   For the taking of the Bachelor's degree in 18 months at Paris, where it was not uncommon, see Rashdall Vol. I, p. 454 and Vol. II part II, pp. 677/8.

Chapter 4

1   The Mariners Arms stands today at this spot, and two 13th/14th c ecclesiastical-type windows recently discovered in an inner wall of the hostelry, would appear to support the belief in its religious foundation — Knights Hospitallers have been suggested.

2   J.R. Magrath, *The Queen's College,* Oxford 1921, Vol. 1, p.105.

3   J.T. Rogers, *History of Agriculture and Prices,* (1866), Vol. 1, pp. 136-7.

4   The Queen's College Long Rolls states that delays en route had been caused by 'intemperies et pericula'.

5   Domus Nostra.

6   Rogers, Ibid., pp. 136-7, for further details of journey, etc.

7   Rogers, Ibid.

Chapter 5

1   See MS. Veel p. 385.

2   Smyth I, fol. 427.

3   Sometimes called Isabel.

4   James, the second son of Lord Berkeley, married Elizabeth and lived at Raglan Castle. He was known as Sir James, the Welshman. Their son, James, in 1417 succeeded his uncle as James 1, the eleventh Lord of Berkeley.

5   Emden in his biography of Oxford graduates to 1500 holds that Nicholas Hereford, the Lollard, cannot be indentified with the Hereford family of Sufton at Mordiford near Hereford. Dr. Linton Smith, Bishop of Hereford, 1920-30, in his articles in the Transactions of the Woolhope F.N.C. on (1) *Nicholas Hereford* (1927 pp. 11-19) and (2) *Herefordshire Lollards* (1930, pp.1-6) has made out a good case for identification. I believe the Bishop was correct in his assumption. See also J.E. Gethyn-Jones, *John Trevisa An Associated of Nicholas Hereford,* Woolhope F.N.C. Transactions, 1971, pp. 241-244. H.R. Hodgkin records that Hereford, Trevisa and Middleworth had all been in residence together at Stapledon Hall (Exeter College) in the early 1360's - p.37.

6   Bailiffs for the Abbey of Flaxley to whom the Grange had been given on its foundation in 1148. See J.E. Gethyn-Jones, *Dymock Down the Ages,* revised Ed., 1966, pp. 69-74.

7   Now belived to have been Macatonium, Gethyn-Jones, Ibid, pp. 1 and 8-13.

8   The following is a verbatim quotation from a letter received at the chantry in May 1973 from a total stranger. This is not the only occasion on which this monkish figure has been seen in Berkeley Church, J.E.G.-J. 'I went to the church, spent a few moments in prayer and meditation, the following is an account of what happened. It appeared to be early evening, dusk had fallen. A monk dressed in a dark brown habit, carrying a Missal and candle, came from the far right corner. He stopped about halfway up the aisle to the side Memorial alter, to light a candle set into the wall. He proceeded on through the doorway just past the side altar, giving me his name, Brother Bernard, as he passed. This doorway, it would seem, led to their living quarters, but I would say it was many, many centuries ago'. A Brother Bernard is mentioned in the Berkeley section of Domesday.

9   Edward the Confessor (1042-1066)

10   The account of the ghastly events connected with the death and re-awakening of the witch is recorded by several medieval chroniclers, e.g. William of Malmesbury and Higden of Chester. The former stated that he had received his information from one 'of such character, who swore he had seen it, that I should blush to disbelieve' (B.2.C.13). The date of the death was said (by William of Malmesbury) to have been 1065 or thereabouts. Trevisa would undoubtedly have known of the

Berkeley witch legend through Higden's *Polychronicon* which later, he, Trevisa, translated.

11 Smyth, II, fol. 448, Smyth's spelling of Wengrave is followed throughout.

12 Smyth, II fol. 449.

13 Smyth, II fol. 449.

14 Smyth, II, fol. 449.

15 Died in 1337.

16 Wyclif and Middleworth and two other secular fellows were expelled from Canterbury Hall in March 1367 (Emden, p.2103). Their appeal to the Roman Curia was finally rejected in May 1370, by which time Middleworth had entered Queen's Hall with Trevisa and Hereford.

17 J. Wills, *Queen's College,* Little Guide Series, 13th ed., p.106.

18 Ibid, p.108.

19 Smyth, I and II.

20 Hodgkin, Ibid, p.37f.
See also D.C. Fowler, *John Trevisa and the English Bible,* Modern Philology, November 1960, pp. 95-96.

Chapter 6

1 Hodgkin, p.33.

2 Ibid, p.33.

3 Registers of Bishop of London.

4 Ibid, 3 March 1370.

5 Fowler, *Traditio,* Fordham University Press, New York, Vol. 18, 1962, pp. 305-306.

6 e.g., Three successive parliaments (1362-4) were opened by speeches in English from the Chancellor. (G. Sampson, *The Concise Cambridge History of English Literature,* C.U.P., 1941, p.68).

7 Newbold Pacey, Co. Warwick — Perry, Ibid., LXII, Historical MSS. Commission, *Report II (Queen's College, Oxford)*, 1870, p.140.

8 Professor Fowler in his *Piers the Plowman, Literary Relations of the A and B Texts,* University of Washington Press, Seattle, 1961, makes out a strong case for Trevisa's authorship for the B text of that work.

9 A.B. Emden, p. 801, now Lambeth Palace MS. No. 104.

10 There is some confusion in the *Close Rolls,* in J.R. McGrath's *History of Queen's College* (2 vols) and in R.H. Hodgkin's (*Six Centuries of an Oxford College*), concerning the expulsion of certain fellows from Queen's during the period 1376-79. In various Close Rolls, Whitfield, Middleworth, Trevisa, Thorpe, Frank and Lydford are directly mentioned as excluded for unworthiness. It is not, however, clear whether these expulsions took place at one and the same time. In the cause of simplication I have assumed that all were expelled during the same troubles. It must be remembered, too, that there are considerable gaps in the College Rolls — especially for September 1375 to June

1378, and in the Indentures of Recepts up until October 1380. Thus vital evidence on these matters is missing. I have also substituted Hereford for Middleworth, believing that the latter's punishment may have stemmed from another cause — hence maybe his speedy reinstatement. His long association with Wyclif, both at Canterbury Hall and at Queen's, may also have had some bearing upon the switch.

11 Trevisa, in his dialogue between a nobleman and a cleric upon translation, included within a MS. copy of his translation of Higden's *Polychronicon* (B.M. MS. Harleian 1900, ff 42-43b) presents a similar discourse between a Lord (Berkeley?) and a priest (Trevisa?) on the ethics of biblical and other translations. This may well be taken as Trevisa's defence of his own translations. In the dialogue it is the nobleman who supports, indeed advocates, the policy — and practice — of translation. Trevisa undoubtedly felt that it would create a deeper — and more favourable — impression upon his readers if the argument was put forward by a member of the nobility, and especially one of Berkeley's standing. I have reversed the roles, believing that this may well represent the true position. I have also expanded, somewhat, the discussion. The same theme is contained in Trevisa's epistle to Thomas, Lord Berkeley, which follows the above dialogue on 43b of the Harleian MS.

Chapter 7

1 Bishop James Berkeley, Bishop of Exeter, 1327.

2 'Thomas, Lord Berkeley, reputed to have been a disciple of Wyclife [who] held a non-resident canonry of the collegiate church of Westbury-on-Trym'. Trevisa also held a similar canonry. *Cambridge History of English Literature,* C.U.P. 1908, vol. 2, p.74.

3 Bulls of Pope Urban VI, both dated, 'Non Julii (7th) Pontificus Nostri anno secundo.' These bulls are in the muniments room at Berkeley Castle, and figure on p.175 of Jeayes, who incorrectly dates them as 1379.

Chapter 8

1 G.A. Holmes, the *Later Middle Ages,* Edinburgh, 1962, p.198.

2 Smyth, 1. fol. 439.

3 Ibid ii, fol. 452.

4 Ibid, ii. fol. 459 and 460.

5 Ibid.

6 This manuscript was left by the Bishop in his will to Exeter Cathedral Library. It is now in Lambeth Palace, MS. 104 — Emden p.801.

7 Smyth, 1, fol. 390.

8 Ibid, fol. 404.

9 Exeter diocese. Granted dispensation, as a son of a priest, to be promoted to all orders. Granted L.D. Oct 1383 for all orders. He was licenced to study at Oxford for 2 years, 27 Aug 1385, and again 2 Sept 1385. Have assumed that he was the son of Master John Cornwall who was a grammar master at Oxford in the 1340 and was described as married — see Emden. Trevisa in his *Polychronicon* translation wrote of John Cornwall and Richard Pencriche as early champions of the English language in the scholastic world.

10 *A Calender of the Register of Henry Wakefield, Bishop of Worcester,* Worcestershire Historical Society, New Series, Vol. 7, p.57.

11 M. Deanesly, *The Lollard Bible,* C.U.P. Reprinted 1966, pp. 8-11, 130, 238, 254, 258-9.

12 Wyclif's remains were disinterred later and thrown into the river Swift, a tributary of the Avon — hence the prophecy
'The Avon to the Severn runs
The Severn to the sea,
And Wycliffe's dust shall spread abroad
Wide as the waters be.'
Oxford Campanion to English Literature, 2nd ed. April 1940. p. 858.

13 B. Smith & E. Ralph, *A History of Bristol and Gloucestershire,* 1972, p.49.

14 Wakefield, p.xxi.

15 Wakefield, p.xxi.

16 Smyth, ii.fol. 455

17 The last Medieval Summons of the English Feudal Levy, 13 June 1385, *The English Historical Review,* Vol. LXXiii, Jan 1958, pp. 1.ff.

18 See, *'On the Ancient Inscriptions in the chapel at Berkeley Castle.,* J.H. Cooke, B. & G. Trans, Vol. I, 1876, pp. 138-146, and illustrations.

19 Slightly 'modernized version of that on 280a of St. John's College, Camb. MS. H1.

20 Wakefield, Ibid, p.150

21 The death of Trevisa and the institution of his successor on 22nd May 1402 are fully documented in the register of the Bishop of Worcester. No trace, however, has yet been found on any entry recording his institution. Perhaps its omission was the result of events such as those narrated above.

Chapter 9

1 See *Polychronicon* comment, book II, p.61.

2 Dr. M.C. Seymore, in the Introduction to Vol.1. of the *D.P.R.*, O.U.P. in 1975 wrote, under the heading, 'The Manuscripts of Trevisa's Translation of the *De Proprietatibus Rerum*', 'In 1372 Simon Bredon bequeathed a copy of De Proprietatibus Rerum to the College (Queen's) and it is highly probable that Trevisa used this manuscript (now lost) for his translation. As Bredon left all his other books elsewhere, this bequest may have been made in response to some desire expressed by Trevisa while fellow of the College'. For Bredon's will — see F.M. Powicke, *The Medieval books of Merton College,* 1931, pp. 82-6.

3 Modernization of Trevisa's translation made by Professor D.C. Folwer for the Trevisa exhibit in the Historical Fesitval with Flowers held in Berkeley Church May 1-3 1970 — the seventh centenary of John Trevisa's ordination.

4 Perhaps a reference to the deposition of King Edward II in 1327 in records (now lost) of the proceedings in the parliament of that date.

5 The court scene is based on a copy (c.1700) of a 14th century episcopal decree. The copy is preserved in Stone Church, and the text used here is that in Professor Fowler's article on Trevisa in *Traditio,*

Vo. 18 (1962) pp. 303-311. Some licence has, of course, been exercised.

6   Ibid, p.310

7   25 May 1388

8   12 February 1388/9

9   P.R.O., Ancient Petition no. 7355.

10 Smyth I, f. 437, Lady Elizabeth died on 13th July.

Chapter 10

1   Possibly 'John' the Chaplain of Berkeley Chantry who took part in the Bradston Chantry enquiry on 2 August 1392 (Wakefield, 96, Sec. 607) and the John Dyer who in 1398 was given a messuage in Berkeley and other property (for services rendered) for his life time, and that of his wife and daughter —Smyth, II, f.469.

2   Based on the 1398 return — see Maynard Smith, *Pre-Reformation England,* Macmillan, London, 1938, pp. 45-50.

3   The five shilling fine for the birth of a child to a priest.

4   C.C.R. Rich II, Vol. III, 1385-89, p.665.

5   I.H. Jeayes, *Descriptive Catalogue of the Charters and Muniments ... at Berkeley Castle,* 1892, pp. vii/viii.

6   Smyth, iii, pp. 77-8.

7   Ibid, ii, f.459 — see Comp. de Berkeley, 12. (13 Rii)

8   Ibid, iii, f.77/78.

9   Emden, p.666.

10 Ibid, p.940

11 Treaty roll. no. 75, Public Record Office. This modernized version is from Professor Fowler's article:— *'New Light on John Trevisa'* in Traditio, Vol. xviii (1962) p.313.

12 Smyth, ii, f.477.

13 Ibid, ii, f.477.

14 Fosbrook, *Gloucestershire,* Vol. 1, p.457, states that the Earl was buried at Stone 16 R ii.

Chapter 11

1   H.P.R. Finberg, *An Early Refernece to the Welsh Cattle Trade, The Agriculturcl History Review,* 1954, Vol. 2. pp. 12-14.

2   Opposite the West end of Church (a) Fisher, 1864 Edition, p.8, (b) 1543 Street Map of Berkeley.

3   K. Edwards, *The English Secular Cathedrals in the Middle Ages,* Revised Edition, 1967, pp. 83-90.

4   Rhys-ap-Gethin.

5   T.F. Tont, *Chapters in Medieval Administrative History,* Vol. 4, p.473.

6   Hereford's wife was a Neville, and he was cousin to the Percies.

7   [He] whom Jupiter wishes to destroy he first makes mad.'

8   This Bull, of Boniface IX, dated 26 Apl. 1399, 'granted to the Abbot and Convent of St. Augustine appropriation motu proprio of the perpetual vicarage, value not exceeding 43 marks, of the parish church, long held to their use, of Berkeley, that of the monastery not exceeding 800. Upon the resignation or death of the vicar they may have the vicarage served by one of their canons regular or by a secular priest, appointed and removed at the pleasure of the Abbot'. Cal., Pap., Reg., letters 5, L.191.

Chapter 12

1   Smyth, II, fols. 455-6, R. Holinshead, *Chronicles of England, Scotland and Ireland,* London, 1807 Edition, Vol. II. p. 853.

2   John of Gaunt had also governed during the senility of King Edward.

3   Henry landed first at Pevensey — unopposed. Later he re-embarked and sailed up the east coast to be nearer the main Lancastrian areas of influence. M. McKisack, *Oxford History of England,* Vol. 5, (14c) p. 492.

4   Ibid, p. 492.

5   Smyth, II, fols. 454-455.

6   Ibid, fol. 455, stated that Lord Berkeley 'too much favoured' Henry, Duke of Lancaster.

7   McKisack, p. 492. Where it stated that 'York and the remainder of the Council took refuge in Berkeley Castle, Gloucestershire.'

8   *Cambridge Medieval History,* C.U.P. 1932, Vol. vii, p.479. 'Richard .. falsified the Rolls of Parliament ... [and] ... took possession of the Lancastrian estates.'

9   Holinshed, Ibid, p.854.

10 *Richard II*, Act II, Scene IV, Lines 7-16.

Chapter 13

1   W.N.F.C. Trans. 1927, pp. 11-19, Hoskins, Ibid. p.36.

2   Holinshed, Ibid, pp.856.

3   Ibid, p.857.

4   Smyth, Vol. II, fol. 456.

5   Holinshed, Ibid, p.862.

6 Ibid, p.864.

7 Shakespeare's version of Adam's account, Richard II, Act 3, Scene 2.

Chapter 14

1 Smyth, II. fol. 469.

2 Ibid

3 Knights of St. John of Jerusalem — Smyth III, fol. 92.

4 Jeayes, Ibid, p.175, Bull is dated 9 July 1379 — 2nd year of the Pope. Smyth II fol. 466, has miscalculated and calls it 1380.

5 Emden, p.1280

6 The tower of this church was pulled down in 1753, and the present tower built upon the same site. The date of the destruction of the main body of the church is not known. Bodleian MS. RAWL. B. 323, Berkeley and Sharpness Gazette, 23 Oct., 1971.

7 T.A. Ryder, *Gloucestershire Through the Ages,* p.59. See also C. Baddarley, *History of Cirencester,* pp.188.

8 A 'gaggle' is, normally, used if a party of geese is on the ground, a 'skein' when in flight.

9 Ash Wednesday was on 3rd March.

10 The *De Regimine Principum* of Aegidius Romanus. At least two copies of this work (one 13c, one 14c) from Llanthony Library have survived. Both are now in the Library of Lambeth Palace — Nos. 111 and 150.

11 Two of these, both 13c, are today in (a) British Museum, Earley 613, and (b) Corpus Christi College, Cambridge, 485.

Chapter 15

1 Admitted as Rector of West Hythe 11th August 1401 — Emden, p.1526.

2 A shrewd forescast indeed, or was it prophetic perception? Smyth, II, fols. 456 ff, records that:
    a. In July 1402 Lord Berkeley joined King Henry at Hereford to take part in an expedition against Owen Glendwr, and a year later was made a guardian of the Marches of Wales.

    b. In March 1403/4 Lord Berkeley was appointed Admiral of the King's ships from the mouth of the Thames to Lands End, and also a Privy Counsellor. Admiral Berkeley was instructed to be afloat that year for three months. He had in his own retinue 5 Bannerets, 11 Knights, 285 Esquires and 600 Archers. His 21 ships, it was ordered, must be double manned with mariners. The King was to receive ¼ and Lord Berkeley and his men ¾ 'of all gaine got at sea from the enemies." This sounds suspiciously like a privateer expedition, but Smyth tells us that off Milford Haven (in the next year it is true) they attacked 140 'tall ships' sent by France to aid Glendwr. Admiral Berkeley's fleet burned 15 ships, 'tooke 14 others stuffed with men, armour and victuals. And so returned with honour and profit.' This certainly, was a naval engagement of importance to the country, as well as being lucrative to Admiral Berkeley and his men.